SEASON OF LIGHT

1788. Asa Ardleigh, the impressionable daughter of a country squire, has travelled to Paris with her newly wedded sister, Philippa, it is the heady days before the Revolution. In Paris Asa first falls in love with dashing revolutionary Didier Paulin. But as the storm clouds gather over France, Asa must return home. Meanwhile in England, no one knows of Asa's liaison. A fortuitous marriage to Harry Shackleford beckons for Asa, as well as the solution to the family woes. But then disturbing news reaches Asa from a France now seething with violence, and Asa must decide whether to follow her head or her heart...

SEASON OF LIGHT

SEASON OF LIGHT

by

Katharine McMahon

Magna Large Print Books
Long Preston, North Yorkshire,
BD23 4ND, England.

British Library Cataloguing in Publication Data.

McMahon, Katharine
    Season of light.

    A catalogue record of this book is
    available from the British Library

    ISBN   978-0-7505-3641-7

First published in Great Britain in 2011 by Weidenfeld & Nicolson
An imprint of the Orion Publishing Group Ltd.

Copyright © Katharine McMahon 2011

Cover illustration © Collaboration JS by arrangement with
Arcangel Images

The right of Katharine McMahon to be identified as the author of this
work has been asserted in accordance with the Copyright, Designs
and Patents Act, 1988

Published in Large Print 2012 by arrangement with
Orion Publishing Group

Magna Large Print is an imprint of Library Magna Books Ltd.

Printed and bound in Great Britain by
T.J. (International) Ltd., Cornwall, PL28 8RW

Apart from the historical figures,
all the characters in this book are fictitious
and any resemblance to actual persons
living or dead is purely coincidental.

It was the best of times, it was the worst of times, it was the age of wisdom, it was the age of foolishness, it was the epoch of belief, it was the epoch of incredulity, it was the season of Light, it was the season of Darkness, it was the spring of hope, it was the winter of despair, we had everything before us, we had nothing before us, we were all going direct to Heaven, we were all going direct the other way – in short, the period was so far like the present period, that some of its noisiest authorities insisted on its being received, for good or for evil, in the superlative degree of comparison only.

From *A Tale of Two Cities* by Charles Dickens

For Martin

Part One

Paris, 1788

Chapter One

On the arm of John Morton she floated from the carriage and crossed a courtyard where fountains played amid cravat-sized strips of lawn. A pair of footmen in blue and gold livery bowed them into a marble-floored entrance hall, glossy under the thin soles of her slippers. Double doors were flung wide open, admitting them to a chamber filled with light; suddenly, sensationally, Asa realised that her entire life had been a preparation for the Paris of May 1788.

Sunshine flooded through a dozen windows draped with silk of palest eau de Nil, sparked off the crystal droplet of a chandelier, a gilt-framed mirror, a woman's earring. Music trickled from a spinet, swagged skirts swayed and merged, and laughter trilled amid a scent of lilies and almond biscuits. Asa's hand dropped from Morton's wrist as other conversations faded and there was just one voice, over there by the window; one speaker, to whom all faces turned.

'Has everyone heard about the events in Grenoble?' His voice was low but emphatic and the gaze of his sky-blue eyes flashed from one face to another. 'The people have risen in defence of their magistrates. They have refused to let the *parlement* be disbanded. The king has been foolish in attempting to force through his reforms without the *parlement*'s consent.'

'Your support of the reforms does you credit, Didier,' called a woman's voice. 'As such a fine lawyer, you are bound to be elected to the *parlement* one day. The old constitution would serve you well.'

'What do I care about my own future, Madame de Genlis, if I could be rid of this old constitution? I would give everything I have – wouldn't we all – to serve a new France?'

'And in Grenoble? What was the outcome?'

'The outcome was bloodshed, martyrs among the common people, some of whom could scarcely have known what they were fighting for, and casualties among the soldiers brought out to keep the peace. But just think, Grenoble hardly has a reputation as a seat of rebellion – what has happened there could happen anywhere.'

Asa, who had crept to the very edge of the group, was transfixed. Yes, this was it. This was being alive; to be amid people who were actually at the heart of tumult and change. She might have been a million miles from her home in Sussex, where even in the most heated debate at the Abolitionist Society nobody spoke with half such passion. This man, Didier, was vigorous and clean cut. A single slanting gesture from his hand opened a future of infinite possibility. And yet, as he ran his fingers through his unruly dark hair and clapped a friend on the shoulder, he also revealed himself to be boyish, perhaps scarcely older than Asa herself.

'That's my brother Didier. I told you about him, remember?' A touch on Asa's elbow; Beatrice Paulin, daughter of a professor at Caen university

16

and Asa's sole connection in Paris. 'Look at the state of his clothes. He's a disgrace. If he didn't spend so much time at the Palais de Justice representing penniless clients who do nothing for his pocket or his career, he might be able to afford a new shirt.'

The sleeves and high collar of Paulin's coat were indeed shiny with too much wear, his necktie askew as he tugged at it in the heat of the moment, his shoes worn down.

'What does it matter?' Asa whispered. 'What do clothes matter? Surely he puts the rest of us to shame for caring about them at all.'

Meanwhile a young poet had unfurled a scroll with mock solemnity and was reciting a poem entitled 'Liberty', lamenting the fact that although the French people had helped to free America from the tyranny of British rule, they still found themselves under the heel of an absolute monarch at home, bankrupting themselves into the bargain. Asa could not help glancing back to the window, where Didier Paulin stood amid a knot of young men deep in conversation. He was at the centre of the group, talking very fast and gesticulating with scholarly fingers, favouring one listener then another with a glance from those astonishing blue eyes. Next time she glanced at him, Asa drew breath sharply, because he had caught sight of her and seemed to pause. She turned her head away abruptly so that a lock of burnished gold hair, in a shaft of sunlight, fell across her breast.

'Come and meet Madame de Genlis,' said Beatrice, leading Asa towards their hostess, who was holding court from a sofa near the hearth.

17

Her corsage was of peach and white roses and her frivolous retroussé nose seemed at odds with the brilliance of her wide-set eyes.

'So this is the little English scholar my dear friend Beatrice has been telling me about. You are most welcome, Mademoiselle Ardleigh. What do you think of our Paris?'

'I think it is a city of extremes, madame.'

'Indeed it is. But don't be deceived by appearances. You might think it would suit some of us very well to rattle through the streets in our great carriages, oblivious to the suffering of those crushed beneath our wheels, but every right-thinking person in Paris longs for change.'

The ladies around her eyed Asa's narrow waist and vivid complexion as they fluttered their fans in agreement. 'Take my dear friend the Duc d'Orléans,' added Madame de Genlis. 'He may sometimes seem intent only on pleasure, and may not always find the appropriate words, but one shouldn't be deceived. His was the lone voice that dared tell his wretched cousin, the king, that he could not force edicts on the *parlement*.'

'Though she would say that,' whispered Beatrice as she and Asa moved away, 'since everyone knows the pair are lovers.'

Goodness, wait until I tell Caroline Lambert about all this, thought Asa, and she glanced nervously at John Morton, who had bustled over to them and might have overheard. Thankfully he had other matters on his mind.

'You will not believe who's just arrived; a relative of yours, Harry Shackleford. I met him earlier in the week and he said he might be here today. He wished to be introduced to you. If only your sister had been well enough to accompany us.'

'What kind of a Shackleford is he?' demanded Asa. 'I hope he is not from the branch of the family who will inherit Ardleigh.'

'That's it, the Shacklefords of Compton Wyatt in Somerset. This is the younger brother, more's the pity, but then the older is already married, I believe.'

'Then I would rather not meet him, Mr Morton, if you don't mind. Perhaps when Philippa is better...'

Too late; the young man, resplendent in coral-pink satin and looking very hot in his high boots and tight cravat, was weaving through the throng towards them.

'My dear sister-in-law,' said Morton, 'may I introduce a young man who is very anxious to make your acquaintance: your cousin, Mr Shackleford.'

'*Distant* cousin,' Shackleford corrected, gazing at Asa admiringly. 'Miss Ardleigh, I can scarcely believe my good fortune in meeting you here in Paris.'

As he bowed over her hand Asa was treated to a glimpse of elaborately dressed hair and a whiff of citrus perfume. Meanwhile Beatrice had faded into the crowd. Oh dear God, prayed Asa, please let her introduce me to her brother before he leaves. 'Mr Shackleford,' she said coldly.

He spoke with the drawl of one educated at Eton and Oxford. 'Delighted to make your acquaintance, Miss Ardleigh. I'm so sorry to hear that your sister is unwell. I had hoped to meet you both here and congratulate her on her marriage.'

Asa made a cursory bow. What right had he, a stranger – no, worse, a usurper – to pretend concern for Philippa?

'Will you give her my kindest regards?' he urged, still gripping her hand.

'If you wish.'

'How d'you find Paris?'

'I am fortunate to be here.' Asa withdrew her hand. Out of the corner of her eye she spotted Beatrice's sea-green gown and beyond, still by the window, the brother, Didier. Had he noticed that she had been cornered by the most foppish man in the room?

'And Paris shares your sense of good fortune, Miss Ardleigh. Even had I not met your brother-in-law I would still have known you were in town. Everyone is talking about you.'

Asa lifted her chin. The name Shackleford was anathema to her at the best of times but here, in Madame de Genlis's radical salon, she felt tainted even talking to him. Everyone must know that the Shackleford wealth came from slavery and this man exuded ill-gotten gains.

'Mr Shackleford intends to be in Paris for several weeks,' said Morton, 'so we shall see a good deal of him, I hope. And then perhaps we shall meet up with him again in Rome. He is travelling. Mostly for pleasure, he says, and the culture. And some business.'

'Business, Mr Shackleford?' Asa said. 'What kind of business might that be?'

'My father's business really. He expects me to be the family's ambassador whilst I'm in Europe.'

'And what might you be an ambassador for, exactly?'

Shackleford was watching her cautiously, as if he sensed she was waiting to pounce. 'Trade. You know. Of various kinds.'

'Various *kinds?*'

'What I've found very disappointing, Shackleford,' said Morton hastily, 'is that so few people in Paris speak English. I have much advice to offer – I should so like to enlighten these fellows as to the merits of a well-run parliament – but I can't make myself understood. I have to rely on my dear sister-in-law here.'

'Mr Morton tells me you are quite the linguist, Miss Ardleigh,' said Shackleford, still with a dewy-eyed look of fascination. 'Now that I admire. My own French is stilted, my German and Italian worse.'

'I am lucky to have had an excellent teacher since I was eight years old.'

'Do you read in French?'

'I do.'

Both Shackleford and Morton were regarding her as one might a performing dog. 'And which is your favourite novel, Miss Ardleigh?' said Shackleford.

'At the moment, Goethe's *Werther*, of course. Isn't that the answer you'd expect of any young woman at present, Mr Shackleford? But I am also reading the Abbé Raynal.'

His brow lifted. Good, her comment had hit its mark. He could not be quite so foolish as he looked if he recognised her allusion to a writer who had made a scathing attack on the practice

21

of slavery.

And then all other thoughts were driven from her head because Beatrice approached, gripping her brother's hand. 'Here is Mademoiselle Ardleigh, Didier. Her teacher in England is our father's dear friend Mr Lambert. Do you remember, he stayed at our house in Caen when we were children?'

Paulin's unpowdered hair was held back by a crumpled ribbon and his blue gaze concentrated on Asa as if the rest of the room were an irrelevance. 'You need no further recommendation, mademoiselle, if you are a friend of Monsieur Lambert.' His lips had a distinctive upward tilt at either end so that he seemed on the verge of laughter. Minutes earlier, as she had watched him talk about Grenoble, Asa had thought him impassioned and serious, but now there was a lightness to his voice and smile that was somehow heart-rending by contrast.

She had no choice but to introduce Morton and Shackleford. 'Delighted to make your acquaintance, Paulin,' said Morton a little stiffly – he had learned to be circumspect in the presence of carelessly dressed Parisian radicals.

'I hear that you are a lawyer, Paulin,' Shackleford said. 'Thought of taking up the law myself but decided it would require far too much study. Curse of the younger son, to be without direction.'

Paulin raised his fine brows and replied in fluent English. 'But there is so much to be done. How can anyone lack direction in times such as these? And if your family happens to have money,

22

that always helps.'

'Then we must dine together, and you can tell me what's needed.'

Paulin shrugged. 'We'll dine, yes, if you like. But really, you don't need instruction from me. Look about you, Shackleford. You'll soon see that France is on its knees.'

The clock was striking six, which in England would have signalled the end of dinner, but in Madame de Genlis's salon was the impetus for women to pick up their skirts and gentlemen to lead their ladies towards the door, as if some invisible force were funnelling them towards other important assemblies.

Morton was deferential in his leave-taking of Shackleford: 'We will meet again on Friday next, at *Figaro*. And do call at our hotel, the Montmorency, where my wife' – the word *wife* was spoken by Morton with a self-conscious smile that never ceased to infuriate Asa – 'will be delighted to receive you.'

A lock of Shackleford's powdered hair had lost its curl and hung over his cheek as he kissed Asa's hand once more. By the time he'd backed away, with obvious reluctance, Didier Paulin was standing beside Madame de Genlis, arms folded, absolutely at ease as he inclined his head to offer her a confidence.

'Didier is an affectionate soul,' said Beatrice. 'Some men would forget their family at times like this, but not Didier. That turquoise handkerchief he carries in his pocket used to be my mother's. She died three years ago and he wears it in remembrance of her because she came from generations of silk weavers.'

'Beatrice, we have so much in common,' said Asa. 'Except in my case it was different – it was my fault. My mother died giving birth to me.'

'Then you have suffered the most,' said Beatrice gravely. 'I at least was brought up by my mother.'

The room was emptying. Any moment now Morton would offer to escort Asa back to the hotel. Paulin abruptly crossed the room and slipped his arm around his sister's waist so that Asa, while rejoicing in his nearness, felt a pang that she did not have such a brother and that no male arm except her father's had ever held her close.

'Didier, I've not seen you for days,' cried Beatrice, resting her head on his shoulder. 'You must come to visit Father and me tomorrow, and eat a proper meal.'

'What's a proper meal?' He pinched her cheek and kissed her. 'You and Father would like to fill me up with foie gras, I suppose.'

Asa noticed Didier's ink-stained fingers as they rested on the folds of Beatrice's skirt. 'How long have you been in Paris, mademoiselle?' he asked her.

'Over a month.'

'And how much longer will you stay?'

'I cannot be sure. I am here as a companion to my oldest sister on her wedding journey and our plans depend on my new brother-in-law, Mr Morton.' Asa nodded towards Morton, who was still mercifully engaged in elaborate farewells.

'Then I must hope to see you again soon.' These

24

words, like soft, momentous blows to Asa's heart, were followed by a short pause. 'I suppose you have visited Versailles, Mademoiselle Anglaise, like every other visitor to our city.'

'Indeed I have.'

'And?'

'It filled me with dismay. So much money squandered on so few.'

'Did you view the state rooms?'

'We did, although my brother-in-law was more interested in the gardens since he is designing his own. I had no wish to glimpse the queen in a state of undress. They say her son is very sick and that makes me feel sorry for her. But is it true she orders a new gown every other day?'

Had she said the right thing? Was compassionate contempt for the monarchy an acceptable attitude? Apparently so.

'Mademoiselle, I'm sure my father would like to meet a friend of Monsieur Lambert's. I heard Monsieur Morton say you will go to *Figaro* this Friday. We shall also be there.' Releasing Beatrice, he darted forward and took Asa's hand.

'Ronsard,' he murmured, 'do you know his work?'

She shook her head.

'You should. I feel as if I recognise you because you are in every word he writes.'

On the brief journey back to the hotel, Morton talked exclusively about Shackleford: 'Such a pity he's only the younger son. He seemed very taken with you. Couldn't keep his eyes off you, in fact, begged me to introduce you. Your dear sister will be sorry to have missed him. He has many acquaintances in Paris and says...'

Meanwhile Asa was reliving her conversation with Didier. Her blood surged with the recollection of every word, the slight pressure of his thumb on her palm. *Ronsard.* Why had Mr Lambert never introduced her to the poetry of Ronsard? How ignorant she must have seemed. Well, by the time she met Didier at the theatre next week she would have educated herself

At the Montmorency they found Philippa collapsed against the pillows, nauseous and clammy skinned, insisting weakly that the source of her troubles must be last night's veal. Morton wanted to call a doctor at once but was urged by his wife to wait until morning. So Asa, having bathed her sister's face and combed her hair, spent an anxious, emotional evening in her own room. To her middle sister, Georgina, she wrote a long letter about her meeting with the notorious Shackleford. To her friend, Caroline Lambert, she described in glowing terms her meeting with sensitive Beatrice Paulin and her radical brother.

Chapter Two

Next morning the doctor made the astonishing diagnosis that Philippa might be expecting a child.

'It can't be true,' cried John Morton, crimson with embarrassment and gratification. 'We have been married barely six weeks.'

'Nonetheless,' said the doctor, 'I believe it to be so. Thirty-two years old is, if you'll excuse me, an advanced age to bear a first child. You must take great care of your wife.'

'We shall go home at once.'

'Certainly not. A journey at this time, particularly for a woman so afflicted by sickness, might be fatal to both mother and child. During these early, critical months I prescribe bed rest and no excitement.'

Asa, who had served as interpreter throughout this fateful conversation, therefore received a temporary reprieve from the dreadful prospect of an early return to England. For the time being, however, all sightseeing trips were at an end, so she devoted herself to nursing her sister, sitting at the window and supplying vignettes of the street scene below, reading aloud from *The Vicar of Wakefield* or writing letters home to Philippa's dictation. The disturbing news from England was that Georgina had persuaded their father to take rooms in London for the summer: *so that neither of us will miss you both quite as badly.*

Philippa, in her weakened state, was fretful. 'There's no telling what will become of Georgina in London. Father won't keep his eye on her. He hates London, she knows he does. I'd have brought her with me if I'd thought this would happen.'

'For her sake I wish you had; for mine, I'm glad you didn't,' said Asa as she dabbed her sister's pale temples with lavender water.

'The point is, what use would she have been to

me here? She'd have spent the entire time prancing about in front of the mirror or looking at fashions. Perhaps in London she'll meet someone like my Mr Morton.'

'Does such another being exist?'

Philippa opened one eye, revealing a faint gleam of humour, then turned her head wearily on the pillow. 'I do hope she doesn't do something rash.'

Morton spent his days bustling to meetings and salerooms. After a dinner with his Freemason friends he returned pop-eyed with news. Apparently the whole of Paris was talking about the possibility that the king would have to call an Estates General, the nearest equivalent to the English Parliament, in order to squeeze money out of his reluctant people by raising taxes.

'I've told them,' said Morton, 'they must follow our English model and introduce an elected parliament. And there must be a fair system of taxation. In England we all expect to pay our way.'

'Mr Lambert says that our system has a far greater impact on the poor than it does on the rich,' objected Asa. 'Everyone has to use salt and soap but the rich pay the same for these goods as the poor.'

'That's a very simplistic attitude, if I may say so,' said Morton.

'He says a tax on income or assets would be much fairer and more productive.'

'And extremely intrusive. As if one could tolerate investigations into how much one was worth.'

'Asa knows nothing about it really,' said

28

Philippa. 'Mr Lambert hasn't a penny to spare so perhaps he doesn't know any better, but I really wish he wouldn't bother the girls with such ideas.'

Since Morton did not expect women to have ideas of any kind, let alone financial or political, his daily walks with Asa, taken at Philippa's insistence in the Jardin du Luxembourg, were tense occasions, especially as Asa was ever on the alert for a glimpse of Didier. Her hopes were dashed time after time, though a few days after Madame de Genlis's salon a maid knocked on Philippa's door and announced the arrival of Mademoiselle Paulin.

So excited was Asa at the prospect of seeing Beatrice again, and so full of hope that she might, after all, be accompanied by her brother, that she flew down the stairs with her hair unbrushed and her skirts flying. Beatrice, wearing a plain straw bonnet over her smooth hair, greeted her calmly and the pair took a turn or two among the potted plants in the hotel's atrium. 'I came to tell you that I shall definitely be at the theatre on Friday,' said Beatrice. 'Didier will accompany me if he's free. Otherwise Father, who normally hates comedy, has promised to go with me because he says it would be a good opportunity to meet you.'

'We may have to go home soon. My sister is very sick. I don't even know if she'll be well enough to go to the theatre.'

'Perhaps if she isn't Didier and I could collect you? In the meantime he sent you these books. Strange boy. Diderot I can understand, but Ronsard is quite out of fashion.'

The instant Beatrice left Asa raced up to her own room and closed the door. The volume of Ronsard had tissue-thin pages and was bound in faded blue calfskin. Within the front cover were inked a number of signatures, including that of *D. Paulin* in a flowing hand. Lying on her bed, Asa feverishly translated poem after poem. '*Donc, si vous me croyez, mignonne, Tandis que votre âge fleuronne... My darling, give me the flower of your youth...*'

Her reading was interrupted after a short while by the announcement of another visitor: Shackleford. Again without bothering to smooth her hair, she went reluctantly down, the little volume of Ronsard tucked deep into the pocket of her skirts. Her visitor, in ice-blue satin, his hair immaculate, was watching ardently as she descended the stairs.

She did not spare his blushes as she relayed the news about Philippa. His response was a stuttered confusion of pleasure and concern. 'If there's anything I can do for your sister's comfort, please tell me. Fruit? Wine? Flowers?'

'Thank you. As you can imagine, her husband supplies all her needs. Besides, she and I have very simple tastes, Mr Shackleford. We were brought up in the country.'

'Of course. I could tell at once ... unspoiled, unaffected... But my dear Miss Ardleigh, you look a little pale yourself Might I perhaps take you for a turn in the carriage?'

'That is kind of you, Mr Shackleford, but I must stay here with my sister.' Asa had conducted the entire conversation from the bottom step, as if to imply that every second away from the sickroom might constitute a threat to Philippa's health. Shackleford gave a wistful smile and bowed himself out, turning one last time as he reached the door. Asa, feeling guilty at using Philippa as an excuse, spent the rest of the afternoon at her sister's bedside, silently translating Ronsard while she slept.

The following day Shackleford called again, decked out this time in matching waistcoat and breeches of embossed gold satin, and a many-buttoned mid-blue coat. As Morton was absent from the hotel, Asa was again forced to spend a short interval with him.

'I do wish you would come out and about with me, Miss Ardleigh. I'm quite at a loose end.'

'It surprises me that anyone could be at a loose end in Paris.'

'I've visited often before, and for long periods at a time. There's much I could show you, Miss Ardleigh. It seems all wrong for you to be so confined on your first trip to the city. We could go to the races. Shopping. I could take you to the Louvre Palace...'

'I am quite content here. How could I enjoy myself knowing that Philippa was suffering alone?'

'Your devotion does you credit, Miss Ardleigh.'

'You wouldn't say that if you knew how much I owed my sister. When my mother died Philippa was barely thirteen, yet she dedicated herself – all her young womanhood – to my care. Can you be surprised that I wish to look after her now?'

Shackleford had an odd way of listening, with

his head down, so that he glanced at her from beneath his eyebrows. 'I should have liked a sister like that. I have one brother, Tom, and we were packed off to school very young. He was several years older than me and refused to acknowledge a cub of a brother so we're scarcely acquainted.'

Surely he was not expecting her to pity him?

'Perhaps soon your sister will be stronger and you'll be able to ride out again,' he said. 'Paris is restless. It's a remarkable place. Even I am fired by the atmosphere here.'

'Even you, Mr Shackleford?'

'I tend not to engage myself much with politics, but I am meeting people who talk about the subject all the time. There's no avoiding it. Your friend Paulin, for instance, never talks about anything else.'

She paused. 'He's scarcely my friend.'

'Really? I had assumed you were family friends. He speaks highly of you.'

'Goodness, I'm surprised he even noticed me.'

'Indeed he did. Praised what he called your astuteness.' He twisted a leaf from an unfortunate miniature orange tree. 'I saw him in action yesterday at the Palais de Justice. Afterwards we dined together. He believes the system is about to crack. The country is bankrupt, the peasants are squeezed for every penny while their landlords allow flocks of ornamental doves to strip bare a year's crop.'

'It seems to me that English landowners,' said Asa, recovering her composure, 'including my father in Sussex, are just as careless of their tenants' crops when in pursuit of a fox. I should im-

32

agine that your Somerset huntsmen are scarcely more considerate.'

'I can't comment on that, Miss Ardleigh. Haven't been home in months. Avoid the place, truth be told. And my father would rather be at a desk than on a horse. The Somerset hunt despairs of him, I'm sure.'

Asa was irked by his flippant attitude to his father's business. Observing his polished boots and oversized buttons, she could not think how he held up his head, given that to allow him to buy his finery some tragic soul had been betrayed, whipped and enslaved. Abruptly she brought the conversation to an end.

However burdensome Shackleford's presence in Paris might be, Asa consoled herself with the knowledge that because Morton had invited him to share their box at the Odeon, the outing to *Figaro* was less likely to be cancelled. Philippa was eager to meet Shackleford and was therefore determined to force herself out of bed for the occasion.

'What a shame it would be,' she said stoically, as a hairdresser attached ivory ribbons to her headdress, 'if I'd not been able to wear my new pink bodice after all the trouble Georgina took with the ruffles. Which reminds me, Asa, I've been meaning to give you this.' She took a little box from the dressing table. 'Georgina has Mother's wedding band. You shall have her engagement ring, now that I have my own.'

The ring, which was composed of three sapphires, each circled with small diamonds, had been much admired by Asa ever since she was deemed old enough to look at it. It fitted the third finger of her right hand perfectly, and when she felt its cool weight on her skin she had no words, could only kiss her sister's hand.

'There,' said Philippa, dabbing the corner of her eye, 'I think Mother would have been proud to see you now, Asa. You're beginning to look a little like her, particularly when you take the time to dress your hair properly.'

With Morton and Asa's support, Philippa descended successfully to the carriage. The short drive along the rue de Vaugirard was remarkably smooth with no sudden turns or jolts, and it seemed to Asa that the ring, as she stretched and twisted her finger to admire it, lent the evening even greater significance. Philippa was delighted by the theatre's buttercup interior, the froth and flounce of the ladies' gowns, and the roaring crimson and gold of the auditorium.

Shackleford, who was waiting for them in the box, bowed as he took Philippa's hand and told her how delighted he was to meet her. 'All these years I have been starved of relations and now I have found two. And how glorious you look in white, Miss Ardleigh,' he said, turning to Asa. 'Everyone will want to be introduced to you.'

She scarcely managed a smile. Didier would not be coming, she thought. It was absurd to think he would have time to view a frivolous comedy. The high-piled curls of the ladies, spiked with jewels and feathers, were distressingly garish; likewise Shackleford, whose shoes were adorned with monstrous steel buckles. Seated to her left, he kept turning to look at her face, as if to satisfy himself that she was enjoying the play.

During the second interval there was a knock on the door of their box, however, and Beatrice Paulin was ushered in, followed by her brother. Asa embraced her, then stood back as Didier greeted the Mortons. He gave her only a little bow of acknowledgement but she sensed from a touch of awkwardness that he was painfully aware of her. The play, the theatre, the company now seemed enchanting. How foolish Asa had been to think Didier would not come; he fitted in here as he would in the law court, salon or street because he was absolutely himself And she could not help noticing that his eyes, when they at last met hers, were as full of anticipation as her own must have been.

Beatrice, as dark haired and clear skinned as her brother but with a smooth brow and dainty hands, linked an arm through Asa's. 'You know that *Figaro* was not performed in Paris for years? The censor lifted his ban only at the insistence of the queen. Even she had the sense to realise a play is more subversive when it is forbidden.'

'The trouble is,' said Didier, 'that we all identify with the cheeky barber who outwits the corrupt nobleman.'

At that moment Philippa swayed, seized a chair-back, and began to fall. Asa and Morton sprang forward just in time and guided her to a seat. Paulin rushed away to fetch a glass of water. After she'd recovered a little it was decided that Philippa must of course return to the hotel escorted by Morton, if Shackleford would assist them down to the carriage. He might then come

35

back and accompany Asa until the end of the play: it would be such a shame for her to miss it and the tickets had been so expensive. 'But perhaps it would not be right for you to be alone in the box with Asa. Oh, it's so difficult...' murmured Philippa.

'I am here,' cried Beatrice, 'and if you would prefer, Madame Morton, my brother and I will take your sister home in our carriage.'

Thus Asa was seated between brother and sister, with Shackleford, when he returned from helping the Mortons, banished to the far side of Beatrice.

For Asa the play was simply a gaudy backdrop to the man beside her, whose elbow at one stage brushed her arm so that she sat absolutely still lest he move away, and whose whole being pulsed with energy and pent-up excitement. Beatrice, tranquil and laughing, responded patiently to Shackleford, who occasionally leaned back for a glimpse of Asa, who in turn ignored him.

During the next interval Didier's talk was sensational. 'You watch, Mademoiselle Ardleigh. A hundred thousand Figaros are ready in France to stand up to the forces of oppression. The Estates General will be called and then we will seize our opportunity.'

'That's it,' said Shackleford, who had drawn his chair closer. 'There doesn't seem to be a man in Paris at the moment who doesn't wish to be involved in political change. Except for me, of course. I'm all for taking the long view. Plan carefully before you lift the lid, that's what I say.'

'The king's ministers, Brienne and Lamoignon,

are floundering,' said Didier. 'But it's not yet known how delegates to the Estates General will be selected. There are three estates, Mademoiselle Ardleigh, the nobles and clergy, about half a million in all, and everybody else. At the moment this vast majority, twenty-five million people, has no voice at all. But even if the Estates General were to be called, the nobles and clergy would carry more weight.'

'What about the women of France? Will they also prove themselves a force to be reckoned with, like Suzanne in the play?' asked Asa.

'I am surrounded by women even more radical than myself. You should hear my sister and her friends in her little salon in Caen. You would be very at home among them, mademoiselle.'

'In England my friend Caroline and I attend political meetings with her father, Mr Lambert. We are abolitionists.'

Didier leaned closer to her. 'I knew, when I met you, that our flame burned in you also. But then you are a friend of Monsieur Lambert.' His breath fanned her neck as he whispered: 'What did you think of Ronsard?'

'Thank you for lending the book to me. I thought some of his poetry very beautiful.'

'And the rest?'

Could she risk it? She turned her head and looked into his face, which was inches from her own. 'Some of the poems were insipid. Others unreadable.'

He grinned. 'Don't be too harsh on him, mademoiselle. He was stone deaf, you know, but above all a pioneer. He and his little group

37

changed the course of French poetry. The book I lent you was my mother's. It is very old. Take good care of it.'

'Forgive me, Monsieur Paulin, I didn't mean to sound ungrateful.'

He touched her arm. 'I like your honesty. And it might be that our French poetry loses a little in translation. *Mignonelette. Doucelette...* How to convey the feeling in English?' The tip of his thumb performed a tiny circle so that every sense was concentrated in that point on her arm.

At the end of the play Shackleford accompanied them downstairs. By now awash with happiness Asa regretted that she had not been kinder to him. His eyes were so warm and his manner so diffident that when he asked permission to call at the Montmorency the next day and enquire after Philippa's health her smile was unguarded. As she took Paulin's arm, she sensed that Shackleford was longing for one more glance.

In the carriage Beatrice talked about their childhood in Caen and explained that she and their father, the professor, had come to Paris for a holiday and in order to visit Didier, whom they'd not seen for nearly a year. Didier's rented apartment, not far from the Montmorency, was too small to accommodate them, so Beatrice and her father stayed in rooms off the rue St Honoré.

Didier sat opposite, occasionally looking out of the window, often gazing at Asa. In the half-light of the carriage, as the beam of a street lamp swung between them, she caught his eye and smiled shyly. In return his sober gaze held hers as if he were committing her face to memory.

At the hotel he alighted, watched as Asa managed her gauzy skirts, then kissed her hand and drew her close by locking her forearm within his own. 'When do you leave Paris, Mademoiselle Ardleigh?'

'I don't know. When my sister is better.'

'Will you attend Madame de Genlis's salon next week?'

'If my brother-in-law chooses to accompany me.'

'Otherwise Beatrice will come for you. I'll see to it.'

He kissed her hand again, this time on the joint of her middle finger. When their eyes met she read him with absolute clarity and knew, even then, that he would demand everything from her.

She sat up late that night, describing the trip to the theatre in a letter home to Georgina; *Figaro*, Philippa's sickness, Shackleford – the implication being that notwithstanding the trip to the play, it was somehow rather dull in Paris with Philippa so confined. To Caroline she began by writing that the king was bound to agree to the calling of the Estates General.

I am so grateful to your father for giving us an introduction to the Paulin family. Were it not for them, we would see only the Paris displayed for wealthy visitors. Thanks to the Paulins, I gain more than a glimpse of what is happening beneath the surface. The truth is, the state is bankrupt; the king must have more money but cannot get it without reform. At the moment, there is stalemate, but just you wait.

Beatrice Paulin is perhaps twenty-three or twenty-four, she adores her brother and is very gentle and considerate. She reminds me a little of you, perhaps because she too is learned and thoughtful, and has a slight otherworldliness about her. Her brother, younger by a year or so, although thinking a little too much of himself, shares all our passions. Oh Caroline you would feel so at home here amid the talk of equality and liberty, whereas my poor brother-in-law hardly knows how to respond when Didier Paulin shakes him by the hand. Didier is the new France, and Morton fears him as he fears the pamphlets that drift like snow at our feet whenever we visit the Palais Royal. But to be with Didier Paulin – and his sister – is to believe that everything could change.

Chapter Three

Philippa's pregnancy was confirmed by a second doctor, who said that in a few weeks, when the most dangerous and distressing phase had passed, they should leave Paris and travel to Switzerland as originally planned. He said the mountain air would help to rebuild her strength.

'I beg to differ,' said Morton. 'I shall not put my wife through the ordeal of yet another journey, particularly in these times of unrest. As soon as she is well, home we will go.'

With this brief exchange, Asa's fate was sealed. The prospect of a prolonged trip was snatched away and a few weeks were all that remained. She certainly could not complain, had no voice in the matter, but it did seem harsh indeed that this, the greatest adventure of her life, should be curtailed, even by such joyous news. On top of that, she had to endure another five days before she would see Didier Paulin again. In the meantime, Morton took her to the gardens of the Tuileries Palace, to the dusty galleries of the Louvre, and shopping at the Palais Royal. On every excursion, Shackleford appeared as if by chance.

In the Palais Royal, Morton remembered that he had to run an important errand on behalf of his wife and suggested that Shackleford keep Asa company until he came back. At first she didn't mind too much. The day was breezy and warm and it was pleasant to pause by the fountain, to walk along the avenues from shade to sunshine and to make a mental note, for Georgina's sake, of the dozen ways a fashionable lady might arrange a strip of muslin – purportedly to cover, but actually to draw attention to, her bosom. Asa could not fail to notice admiring glances at her own new straw hat and the soft billows of her skirts. The borders of the gardens were planted with scented flowers and there was a hum of voices along the shadowy arcades. And because the Palais Royal belonged to the king's obstreperous cousin, the Duc d'Orléans – the one member of the royal family who proclaimed himself for the people – and this same Orléans was intimate with Madame de Genlis, Asa felt herself a little nearer Thursday and the salon, when she would meet Paulin once more.

She expected the usual asinine conversation

41

with Shackleford, but on this occasion he startled her.

'Your brother-in-law happened to mention that you are an abolitionist, Miss Ardleigh.'

'So I am. I'm surprised Mr Morton told you since he does not approve.'

'I suspect he thought it best that I should know the worst.' He gave her a quick, sideways glance. 'I wonder; how did you come to be so radical?'

'My closest friend is a woman named Caroline Lambert. Since a young age, we have spent many hours in each other's company. Her father is a brilliant teacher and a minister. She and I have been guided by him.'

'And the rest of your family, are they sympathetic?'

She was irritated by the hint of irony in his smile. 'The rest of my family are glad that I have received, through Mr Lambert, an exceptional education, considering I am merely a girl. My father, as you may know, is a widower and was too preoccupied to see to my education beyond what my sisters could teach me. In any case, he has no money to spare. Neither has Mr Lambert, for that matter, but most of what he earns is devoted either to providing us with books or to charitable causes.'

'Such as abolition.'

'Not just abolition. Mr Lambert encourages us to confront injustice of all kinds. I have seen things, Mr Shackleford, that have made me unable to sleep at night. But you call abolition a charitable cause. To define it as such is to diminish it. I believe it is absolutely wrong for one human being

42

to own another, and therefore an absolute necessity that slaving should be abolished.'

'I admire your clarity, Miss Ardleigh, especially as I assume you haven't encountered the iniquity of slavery yourself.'

She stopped walking. 'You mean it's much more comfortable not even to try to imagine the source of our tea and coffee. Mr Lambert would never allow such evasion.'

Shackleford's enthralled gaze was fixed on her face. 'Some evils, I fear, are easier to correct than others. I used to know a chap called Brissot in London. Met up with him again here, last week. He's very hot on the idea of abolition. But he won't find it easy, I suspect, to convince his fellow radicals at this point in time.'

'Of course it won't be easy.'

'So I told Brissot. Nonetheless, he has persisted in setting up a society called Les Amis des Noirs, which happens to meet a stone's throw from this very spot. It seems to me, most people will think abolition is a step too far. They'll say that the French should concentrate on arranging some kind of elected parliament, then feed themselves, then free their slaves.'

'Perhaps if you were a slave, Mr Shackleford, you would not be quite so eager for everyone to take their time.'

'That's certainly true. But I struggle, Miss Ardleigh, with how it might be done sooner. If we can't achieve abolition in England, where the situation is relatively stable and most of the population isn't starving, how can Brissot, in France? Fact is I've never seen so many hungry people.'

43

'Then both evils must be cured, don't you think? The starving in France and the enslaved abroad?'

'You ask me what I think. I don't have any answers. All too tricky.'

Asa bit back a scathing comment and walked on. He remained close to her shoulder.

'We've been beating about the bush, you and I, Miss Ardleigh, but I'm sure you know my family wealth is built on slavery. I can't help it, I'm afraid. My father and brother run the family business, I run myself, that's how it goes.'

Asa gazed at him fiercely, her heart beating a little faster. 'But don't you see, now you're in Paris and have listened to all the arguments, that you must act?'

He cocked his head and smiled at her devotedly. 'Miss Ardleigh, it's true, I've felt more purposeful of late. But the question remains, what should I do?'

'Anything can be done, where there is a will,' she replied sharply.

'It's all so straightforward to you, Miss Ardleigh.'

'And is it so difficult for you, Mr Shackleford?'

'It is, if you did but know it. Much simpler to stay on the move, turn a blind eye and get on with spending my father's money.'

'Yes, that's certainly the easiest choice.'

'But I've begun to feel that my ambition, or lack of it, has been transformed during the last few weeks. Oh, it's not just Brissot and your friend Paulin. It's you, Miss Ardleigh.' He raised his hand as if to take hers. 'I never imagined that I would meet a relative – even a distant one –

44

such as you.'

'Whereas I,' she said, 'would rather not be reminded of a connection that will one day leave me destitute, thanks to the entail on my father's estates.'

'Oh, my brother would never allow that to happen, I'm sure. And it need not be so. Miss Ardleigh, there is a way forward that is advantageous to us all. I have dared to think that with you at my side I could achieve anything.'

Appalled to realise that this was almost a declaration and that some kind of deal must have been struck between Morton and Shackleford, Asa said slowly and distinctly: 'I will ask my friend Mr Lambert to send you pamphlets on your return to England. You could join the Society for Effecting the Abolition of the Slave Trade if you wish. But I wonder if you're serious? It seems to me that, for the last half-hour, you have simply been using the subject to form a bond between us.' She looked about for Morton and, there being no sign of him, sat at the end of a bench and turned her face away.

'Miss Ardleigh, if you would just hear me out. Left to my own devices I'm a fool, rather weak, I admit it. I don't know which way to turn. With you...'

He had dared to sit beside her, was craning forward to see her face, but she held up a hand. 'Don't you see, even so much as an acquaintance with you is a betrayal of all the values I hold dear. I cannot believe in the integrity of anything you say when every stitch you wear is bought by slavery. In my view you are irredeemable. I beg

45

you, never attempt to raise this matter again.'

She was actually shaking as she registered the shock in his eyes. He got up and stood a little distance away, turning his modish, flat-brimmed hat in his hands and looking up at the sky until Morton came back.

Chapter Four

It was arranged that Professor Paulin and Beatrice would escort Asa to Madame de Genlis's next salon. Having spent an hour dressing for the occasion, Asa presented herself to Philippa for inspection.

'Well,' her sister pronounced, 'at least Paris has achieved what I never could: a well-turned-out young lady.'

This was a rare compliment and perhaps, Asa thought hopefully, something of an understatement. Georgina, by far the best needlewoman of the three sisters, though bitterly frustrated by Philippa's marriage to Morton, had not allowed pique to get in the way of her love of fashion as she prepared her sisters' travelling clothes. Asa's gown was of dainty light blue muslin, the perfect backdrop to her mother's sapphire ring.

'Are you sure you're not well enough to come with me?' Asa pleaded. 'I should so love you to meet Beatrice.'

'Good Lord, Asa, she'd terrify me if she's anything like your Caroline Lambert. I've been confined to these four walls for so long I'd have nothing to say.'

'You always have something appropriate to say. You taught me all I know about how to behave in company.'

'Nonsense. I don't think any of us had enough practice at being in society, which is precisely why I'm so worried about what Georgina might be getting up to in London. Asa, you must make the most of every opportunity here in Paris. Perhaps Mr Shackleford will attend this salon and introduce you to his friends.'

'I've never wanted any company other than that of you and Georgina, and Caroline,' Asa protested, kneeling by her sister's bed and burying her face in the quilt. 'I feel so sad for you now; you are never able to go out even though all of Paris is waiting to be explored. How do you bear it?'

'Asa, why these tears? I'm confined here for the best of reasons. Can't you see how the prospect of becoming a mother means more to me than a few trips to a Parisian salon? Dry your eyes or you'll have me weeping too, and what would Mr Morton say to that? It's your job to have a marvellous time on behalf of both of us, and to tell me about it afterwards.'

Professor Paulin, who wore an old-fashioned black frock coat and whose eyes were a more faded blue than his children's, smiled kindly at Asa. 'My daughter has spoken highly of you,' he said, 'and I, of course, am delighted to meet any friend of Charles Lambert. Tell me how you came

47

to meet him.'

In the presence of Didier's father, Asa could scarcely utter a coherent sentence. 'The Lambert family used to live in London but Mrs Lambert, as I expect you know, died of typhus and since Caroline, the only child, had also been dangerously ill, Mr Lambert brought her to Littlehampton, a seaside town within a few miles of my village. It's typical of him that his first concern was to enquire about finding a suitable friend for her. He and Caroline simply called at our house – I was seven at the time and I remember these pale, sad strangers being received by my sister Philippa with great kindness. I had no idea then that they would come to mean so much to me.'

'You were fortunate indeed if Lambert became your teacher. I spent time with him in Geneva and England as well as France and believe him to be a first-rate scholar.'

'And yet so patient, even though we were only girls. He taught us Latin and Greek, as well as French.'

'And, I don't doubt, you learnt a fair degree of strong-mindedness, which is a common trait among young women these days, I find. If Beatrice is with her school fellows, the likes of Charlotte and Estelle, I hardly dare go near them for fear of being dubbed reactionary.'

When they arrived at the salon on the rue de Belle Chasse they were drawn at once into the clever, seditious talk.

'We are in the absurd situation,' said Madame de Genlis, 'of being up in arms against the king because he wishes to reform our legal system –

48

which is, of course, corrupt. We all know the *parlements*, our highest courts, are full of the richest and most privileged men instead of the most able. The *parlements* must be reformed. Unfortunately the king cannot see that, because *he* hates them, we find ourselves forced, through our antagonism to him, to love them.'

'Madame speaks well.' A voice by Asa's ear, so close that her cheek was warmed by his breath. Didier. She had steeled herself for a long wait but here he was already. He drew her aside; his eyes were bright with joy. 'You are here, Mademoiselle Ardleigh. That is all I ask. But there are wheels within wheels here. Madame de Genlis is on the side of her lover, the Duc d'Orléans, and he, gambler and womaniser that he is, makes a strange champion of the poor.'

'Why strange?' Asa was amazed that she could conduct a lucid conversation when it was as if a soft, thick cloak had been thrown over her.

'The Duc d'Orléans is a philanderer. He loves the good life and possesses a fortune of seven and a half million *livres*. Yet he claims to be on the side of the people and has even been living in exile for the last year because of his radical views. Can one trust such a man not to be acting for the sake of expedience? It's no secret that he thinks he would make a better job of ruling France than his cousin.'

'And yet, if he were on the side of the king, you wouldn't trust him either. What is the poor man to do?'

Didier smiled. 'You're right. In my eyes, he can't win. Besides, we need all the friends we can

49

get. But mademoiselle,' again he lowered his voice, 'later, if we can find a little privacy, may I have a moment of your time? I must speak with you.'

He was called away and for another half-hour they were apart, though not for a second was Asa unaware of him as he circulated through the crowded salon; his dark unruly hair, that mischievous smile, the sudden shout of laughter.

Eventually she came to rest by a window, ostensibly to watch the spinet player. Partially obscured by ornate drapery, she pretended to herself that she was not waiting for Didier. But soon he had worked his way across the room and was beside her, sitting shoulder to shoulder, so that both appeared to be intent on the music. The scent of him, an indefinable blend of soap and the musk of his skin, drew her closer.

'My sister tells me you will be here in Paris only a short while longer,' he said. 'What are we to do?'

'About what, monsieur?'

'You are far too honest to pretend you don't understand.'

She remained silent.

'What are we to do? Even at the most unexpected moments, in the midst of a court case, my thoughts stray to you. There, I have said it.'

She ached with the wonder of his words but lifted her chin higher, staring blindly at the musician.

'Will you meet me?'

Astonished, Asa turned her head and saw that he was very pale.

'Please. If you don't understand me,' he said, 'move away from me now. But when you look at me in that way... All I ask is that you will walk with me; that we should have time to talk to each other properly.'

'A walk? Why, yes. That should be possible.'

'Tomorrow, then. Four o'clock. I'll come for you.' His gaze dropped to her mouth.

This time he did not kiss her hand as he bowed abruptly and left her side, and it was that lack of a kiss, even more than the prospect of being alone with him, which ensnared her.

That night Asa was tormented by doubt. If she asked Philippa's permission to go for a walk alone with Didier Paulin it would certainly be refused. If he simply visited her, they might perhaps sit together in the hotel parlour – that, surely, would be allowed. But it was impossible to imagine meeting Didier in that public space, choked by all they would be unable to say. And to walk with him on the Parisian streets, to see Paris through his eyes; how could she resist?

If only Caroline were available. Caroline, un-equivocally radical in her politics, was equally clear in her principles.

Rousseau, Goethe, Shakespeare, all urge us to follow the dictates of our heart. Have we not always argued, Caroline, that we must love? cried Asa inwardly.

Not at the cost of duty, said the absent Caroline. You may meet Didier, of course, but why be so secretive?

Because we're not like other people. We have no

51

time for a slow declaration of our feelings. Already, I am sure that I love him.

Then tell Philippa.

She won't understand. There's no time. We'll be leaving soon.

What is the alternative, Asa?

There was no dilemma after all, Asa decided. She would meet Paulin in the hotel atrium and take tea with him. Where was the difficulty in that?

Next day the weather was fine and Philippa sighed because Asa was indoors again. 'If only Morton would come back and take you for a drive. Is there no chance that your friend Beatrice will call?'

'If she did ... perhaps she and I might take a walk together.'

'Of course. That's the solution. Why don't you write her a note?'

So in the end there was no need for subterfuge. One Paulin was practically the same as the other. Philippa had given permission. If Didier happened to come, and there was always the dreadful possibility he might not, there could surely be no harm in walking a little way with him? At four Asa put on her bonnet and went downstairs. She saw him from the landing, pacing about by the desk, and her heart lurched with fear and longing. How astonishing that nobody else had remarked on his beauty; the turquoise handkerchief tucked carelessly into a pocket, the glossy tangle of his hair. He at once took her hand and placed it on his arm as if there was no question that it belonged there. 'Shall we go out? Are you free? Should I perhaps go up and see your sister?'

'My sister is resting...'

Outside, in the city, everything was sharply defined: a half-clothed beggar on the street corner too weak to raise a hand for money; a vendor of milk up from the country; the shadows of a man and woman linked together – Asa's bonneted head close to Paulin's shoulder. And where her ungloved hand, with its sapphire ring, rested on his arm, she felt a steady pulse.

'In London,' said Didier, 'is it like this?'

'I've been to London only once, though of course there are beggars everywhere, even in our little village. But in England few face actual starvation because the land is well managed. Here in Paris everything is so extreme. Even the heat of the sun feels cruel.'

At a crossroads they turned on to a road bordered on one side by a row of narrow houses, on the other by a high stone wall. 'The Carmelite house of St Joseph,' said Didier. 'And there, number forty-seven, is my house. I have to collect some papers. Do you mind?'

His usually bright eyes were tentative and she trembled as she understood what he was asking, yet she could hardly wait on the street, so she followed him up a narrow staircase, by now almost blinded by terror and desire. At one point he paused until she was abreast of him and they stood only inches apart, catching their breath.

His apartment was shabby but airy and light with a long window overlooking the street. It smelt of coffee and of sun baking on to ink and parchment. And of Didier. In the monastery garden on

53

the other side of the wall Asa could see a path fringed by beech hedges, beds of low-growing shrubs and a small stone building with no windows. The fact that Didier's apartment stood opposite a religious establishment was reassuring; Asa grew calmer as she watched him search through a pile of files, apparently oblivious to her. His desk had a single drawer that was so crammed with papers it wouldn't close. There were stacks of books and, partially hiding the bed, a varnished screen on which were folded various items of clothing, including the coat he had worn to the Odeon.

After he'd sorted his papers Didier cleared a chair for her and poured tepid coffee from an earthenware jug. Asa pretended that her attention was on the jug, which she thought the loveliest object she had ever seen, roughly glazed with a pattern of blue leaves on a translucent white background. In reality she was so aware of Didier that even his smallest action opened a seam of nerves along her skin. He drew up the only other chair and sat opposite, his knees nearly touching hers, elbows resting on his thighs. Though they rarely glanced at each other at first, gradually it became impossible to look away.

'Tell me what you have been doing today,' he said.

Asa's lips felt thick and strange. 'My sister is still unwell so I have been reading to her. But she was strong enough to sit in a chair by the window. I think we'll be leaving in a couple of weeks.'

'So soon?'

'My brother-in-law is torn between fear of the

54

journey and a longing to get her back to England.'

'And when you are in England, will you stay with Monsieur and Madame Morton?'

'No. I'll go home to Sussex, where I live with my father and other sister, Georgina. She is ten years older than me. Georgina wanted very much to come to Paris, but she and Philippa don't always see eye to eye and someone had to stay with Father.'

'I must be grateful to your sister, then, that she chose you,' and Didier's knee, perhaps inadvertently, touched hers.

'You see, Philippa had almost given up hope of marriage, but then she went to stay with an aunt in Guildford – it was Georgina's turn to go but she hates looking after anyone and had a cold so Philippa went instead. John Morton happened to be in the area looking for a plot of land. Georgina feels she missed her chance. So now she has gone to London with Father, who will be miserable, I expect. He hates staying in a town.'

'Three sisters. Your family is like a fairy story, mademoiselle. And your mother is dead, like mine?'

'She is.'

'But no wicked stepmother.'

'None.'

'Perhaps that is why we are so drawn to each other – we are alike. That, and our acquaintance with Mr Lambert.'

'Do you remember him, then?'

'But of course. He and my father met long before I was born, when they were students in

Geneva. They shared a preoccupation with the meaning of freedom, not to mention a love of the French philosophers and an admiration for Rousseau, who, as you may know, your friend Monsieur Lambert was privileged to meet when Rousseau was in England. I was a very young boy when Monsieur Lambert came to our house, and yet he spoke to me as if my opinion mattered. He encouraged me in my studies and wrote me a letter of congratulation when I was granted a scholarship to study in Paris.'

'That is exactly Mr Lambert. The quality of a person's ideas is all that matters to him, not whether they are rich or poor; man, woman or child. It never troubled him, for instance, that while he and Caroline are Dissenters, I am Church of England.'

'And we are Roman Catholics, at least in name. I could hardly have studied at the College Louis le Grand otherwise. But I share with you, I'm sure, a belief in tolerance.'

Sipping Paulin's coffee, watching the detail of him – a curl of dark hair on his forehead, the frayed corner of his cravat, the deep arch of the half-moon on his thumbnail – and listening to the words spilling from his eloquent mouth, Asa was conscious that an entirely different conversation was taking place; one so urgent that the words died on their lips.

At the end of half an hour a nearby clock struck five and Paulin reached for her cloak. 'I am writing an article for an *affiche* – newssheet, that is – on the imbalance within the Estates General. I must deliver it to the printer's tonight.'

56

No need, then, for Asa to have felt so anxious. How foolish she had been not to trust him. But as she put on her cloak he reached over her shoulders and held the two edges together against her throat so that the length of his body was pressed to her back and his forehead to her hair. They stood thus joined as he whispered: 'I have never spoken your name. Tell me your name.'

'My name is Thomasina, though my sisters have always called me Asa.'

'What shall I call you?'

'Whatever you want. Anything.'

'Thomasina. Thom-as-ina.' Each syllable was like a kiss, and Asa thought his lips might touch her throat or cheek. But he broke away, took her by the elbow and ushered her from the room. In the street he said nothing at all and she almost had to run to keep up with him.

Outside the Montmorency he bowed and his thumb brushed her palm: 'If I write, will you come to me again?'

Chapter Five

All that night and the next morning Asa was determined not to see Didier again. She was furious with herself for deceiving Philippa and betraying her upbringing, especially her friendship with Caroline, whose father she and Didier had used as a conversational hook and to whom she could no longer write with honesty. If Didier planned to marry her, he should court her by conventional means. Why not? In a few years' time, when he was established as a lawyer, he would be able to support her. Never mind what her family would say if she told them she intended to marry a Roman Catholic French radical. Of course, there was no question of him coming to England and living at Ardleigh. He was needed in Paris. Well then, she must wait, she thought, like every other respectable girl.

But the blue and white jug had been so beautiful, as had standing at his window and seeing sunlight in the leaves above the monastery wall. It reminded her of lying in the shade of the beech tree at Ardleigh. This was the confusion – with Didier everything seemed familiar yet utterly strange. It had felt exquisitely significant to the point of physical pain to have sat in his little room holding a coffee cup between her palms, yet it also seemed as right as reading a book in the Lamberts' parlour, as right as walking on the Downs with her father to inspect the sheep. So how could it be wrong?

For two tormented days she heard nothing more from Paulin. Why should he remember me, she thought, when he's busy making plans to change France for ever? And in the meantime Asa was restricted to the Montmorency or the interminable walks in the Luxembourg Gardens with her brother-in-law, who had become more aloof since Shackleford's withdrawal. Once or twice Philippa, who felt less nauseous by the day, said she might join them. Time was running out.

Didier's note, when it came, said: *Demain. À*

quatre heures. Chez moi.

Once again Asa's feelings veered from ecstasy to an agony of indecision. The next day Morton had an engagement and Philippa said she would rest but perhaps get up later. All afternoon Asa walked about the hotel or sat in her room attempting to read while outside the window the city teased with its racket and energy. As the clock chimed three thirty and Asa was pacing her room thinking, Shall I go? I cannot, a maid knocked and announced that a gentleman was awaiting her in the parlour below.

Didier must have come to fetch her.

But it was Shackleford who stood amid the stunted orange trees, apparently fascinated by the little fruits and dressed in a mist-coloured riding coat with three collars.

'Miss Ardleigh, forgive the intrusion. I wanted to enquire after your sister, and to say goodbye.'

He was infuriatingly hesitant. Time was passing yet Asa had no choice but to offer him tea. After dithering for a moment he said he would drink a glass of lemonade. Now that her chance of seeing Didier was under threat, she knew that the only thing that mattered was that she should run to meet him in the rue du Vieux Colombier.

'I am going to Italy, Miss Ardleigh, and then farther afield, so I doubt you will see me again.' Shackleford stood with folded arms, tapping the brim of his hat against his elbow.

Go, go, go, she thought.

'I know you think very little of me, Miss Ardleigh. I cannot regret what I feel for you, but I regret what was said between us in the Palais

59

Royal. It was far too soon. I hardly know what came over me that I should have pressed you so early in our acquaintance ... that I could ever have expected...'

Asa took a sip from her glass and stared at her lap. Just *go*.

'I wanted to say that I hope one day you and I shall meet on better terms. After all, we are cousins, of sorts.'

In her frustration Asa glanced at him suddenly, as if the directness of her gaze might force him to leave. He smiled wryly, and his features became more defined; a crease between jaw and cheek-bone, and rather deep, complicated furrows in his forehead for a man said to be under thirty. 'That's why I came. That's all; to ask you not to judge me too hastily.'

The clock on the mantel struck the quarter. 'I wish you a very pleasant trip in Europe, Mr Shackleford.'

'I shall probably not stay in Europe. Who knows? My father has all kinds of plans for me. Africa. The Americas.' He paused, expecting her no doubt to ask further questions or even to berate him once more for his family trade. Again those unsettling eyes scanned her face. 'I'll be on my way, then. Give my kindest regards to your sister, Miss Ardleigh.'

If she didn't say another word he would be forced to leave immediately. Sure enough he sighed, bowed and with only one backward glance, was gone.

In a flash Asa was up the stairs, had seized her cloak and bonnet and glanced in the mirror. She noticed that her cheeks were pink and her eyes burning. But as she crossed the Cherche-Midi, weaving between a couple of wagons, it occurred to her to look back – she thought she'd seen a man wearing a grey coat standing at the street corner as she emerged from the hotel. Yes, it was Shackleford, who had now clapped on his hat and was striding away. Surely he hadn't caught sight of her. A horse obscured her vision and when she looked again he was gone.

She was nearly a quarter of an hour late. Didier was waiting for her at the street door and dashed forward to meet her, holding up his hand as if her excuses were an irrelevance. Again they climbed the stairs in silence, but this time, when they reached the middle landing, he took her hand and did not let go until they reached the apart-ment, where he again poured coffee from the leaf-patterned jug and sat a little closer, so that her knees were actually enclosed by his as they drank.

'What have you been doing, Mademoiselle Ard-leigh, since I last saw you?'

'Very little. I am late because, just as I was leaving, my cousin Mr Shackleford came to call.'

'Ah yes. I know him.'

'His family wealth comes from slavery. I want nothing to do with him.'

'You are a harsh judge, mademoiselle. Must a man be criticised for what his father has done? I have seen Mr Shackleford time and again in Paris. To his credit he has friends everywhere, among all types of people, and he admires you

61

very much.'

'When my father dies,' said Asa, 'Shackleford's older brother will inherit Ardleigh. You see, our English laws are as unjust as the French. Because the property is entailed through the male line we three girls will have nothing and Georgina and I will be homeless. So not only is Shackleford the son of a slave trader, he will also be a cuckoo in our nest. Can you blame me for turning him down?'

'You turned him down? In what way did you turn him down?'

His arms were folded and she had to look away from his blue gaze to the plain knot of fabric at his throat. 'There was ... a type of proposal.'

'And would you turn down every other man in Paris?'

A gardener was clipping the monastery hedge. Asa could imagine the snip of metal through leaf and twig, the smell of the cut leaves. When Didier got up she thought for a moment that he would pick up her cloak; instead he stood behind her chair, brought his mouth close to her ear and let his hand fall softly on her shoulder.

'Had you not come, I would have died,' he whispered.

He placed a kiss on the side of her neck over the cloth of her little muslin scarf but immediately afterwards, as if to distance himself from his words and the momentous kiss, he stepped aside. 'We should leave this room or at least talk of other things.'

She looked out at the monk in the garden. 'Yes. We'll talk. Then I'll go.'

'And yet you and I have nothing more to say. We understand each other completely, having both drunk from the same cup. You and I, we want the same things.' As if unable to help himself he drew closer, brushed the back of his fingers against her neck and smoothed her hair from her forehead. The gardener on the other side of the monastery wall made a little heap of cut leaves with the side of his foot. Didier raised her chin with the edge of his thumb. The expression in his eyes melted her bones. His kiss cracked her open.

Nobody had taught her this. She had not understood, as a witness to the decorous embraces of Philippa and Morton, that a kiss might be this extraordinary exchange of lip and tongue. She stood in his arms, broken by the dark hot place he had opened inside her. He said, caressing her cheek, stroking her hair: 'I have nothing for you, Thomasina, except my love. The last thing I anticipated when I came to Paris was you. I am amazed at myself. I had thought, if ever I married, it would probably be to a girl from my home town and in the meantime anything to do with love would have to wait. But now there is you. I can't make you promises, I don't know where I will be next week or even tomorrow. It is your choice whether you go now or stay. If you want, I will take you back this minute to your sister.'

His face, with the upward quirk of his lips, was too beautiful and she was too stunned by his kisses. She put her mouth to the corner of his lip and this time he locked her in his arms and drew her so close that her breasts and stomach, through the soft layers of muslin, shaped themselves to him. His body was hard and unfamiliar and the scent of his skin tangled her thoughts. His tongue made quick, soft strikes against her teeth and his hand shifted from her waist to her buttock, pressing her closer still so that his fingertips produced shocking flames in her flesh. As he kissed her ear and throat she opened her eyes and saw the blue sky and the green, blowing tops of trees.

Again and again the voices in her head tried to speak but were answered by just one phrase: There is so little time. She stroked the top of his head as he kissed her neck and breast where the fabric of her under-shift was loosely gathered. When he looked at her again his eyes were blurred by desire. 'I have felt, until this moment, that in France we might as well be slaves, we are so stifled,' he said. 'Your love has liberated me. You make no conditions, you give yourself freely.'

'I can't help myself.'

'I want you to choose, every time.'

'I do. I choose you.'

His hand slipped from her breast to the small of her back. She was sure his touch, even through her dress, left a trace on her skin. 'You must think very carefully. Perhaps I ask too much. I'm going to take you back to the hotel, before it is too late.'

The sudden pulling away felt like rejection. They straightened their hair and clothes, but as he gathered a sheaf of papers, he seized her elbow and kissed her again, clasping the back of her head so there was no escaping the astonishing demands of his mouth. He said: 'Think. Choose. Remember, there is only this. I can't even be sure, from one day to the next, whether it will be the last time I walk free or if I shall be clapped in irons.'

'Are you in such great danger?'

He laughed. 'Ah, don't look like that or how can I bear to part from you even for a moment? But listen. You should know the truth. At the moment the government is treading carefully because it is nearly bankrupt and therefore desperate to see a rise in taxes. It has to make concessions to the people. But we all know, those of us who write in radical newspapers and make our voices heard, the likes of me and Brissot and Danton, that at any moment we are likely to be arrested and slammed into the Bastille. And who knows if we would emerge from that place alive and whole? That's why I can't make you any promises.'

Asa kissed the beautiful, intact face of her living, bold lover, then he led her back down the dark staircase, this time pausing to embrace her so that her head was pushed against the rough plaster wall and her mouth ached. They parted at the crossroads and she hurried back to the hotel, sprayed with dirt thrown up by horses, battered by collision with other bodies and the press of traffic that forced her into the gaps between buildings. In her room she curled up on her bed, touched her bruised lips and held her arms tight across her breast as she thought of Didier, by now on his way to court, where he was to represent a woman at risk of being imprisoned for debt. She knew that when he pleaded his case, the taste of her mouth would be on his tongue.

That night she wrote a brief note to Georgina about the improving state of Philippa's health. A letter to Caroline was composed out of a confused desire to conceal and confide.

In Paris, the rules that we are used to do not apply. Some beautiful new order is struggling to emerge. I can feel the city rattle its chains. And something else is happening. I cannot give you details. I cannot even tell you his name. But Caroline, I have fallen in love.

And oh, Caroline, love is not as we always thought it would be. In my head, I thought I understood what Shakespeare meant, and Rousseau. I didn't know it would be body and soul, night and day. I didn't know I would look at myself in the mirror and wonder how I could ever deserve him. I didn't know that my sense of self would dissolve, and that instead, all I would want is him. But don't be alarmed. I'll come to my senses at any moment. And then I'll tell you his name. When plans are made, when Philippa knows, then I'll tell you...

Chapter Six

The Mortons were annoyed to discover they had missed Shackleford. 'Had I known he was in the hotel of course I would have made an effort to come down,' said Philippa. 'What did he say, Asa?'

'Only that he did not expect to see us again because he was going to Italy, then farther afield.'

66

'I had such high hopes. Mr Morton said he was very taken with you.'

Having attended to his wife's pre-dinner needs – Was she warm enough? Did she require an extra cushion? Should he fetch another shawl? – Morton could at last give his full attention to Asa.

'Imagine what joy it would have given your sister if she'd been able to write to your father to tell him you were engaged to Mr Shackleford. He suggested that he might propose to you, informally, of course, until your father's permission had been sought. I presume nothing of that nature took place?'

'I could not bear to be in a room with him, let alone marry him. I'm sure I made that clear.'

Philippa glanced anxiously at her husband. 'There is no need to be so extreme, Asa. You talk such nonsense. It would have been a great opportunity for you.'

'You know why any such match would be impossible, Philippa. His wealth comes from slavery.'

'I'm sorry that you have allowed your prejudices to blind you to the advantages of such a connection and to the very great honour it was for Mr Shackleford to have taken an interest in you,' said Morton, who had never spoken so sharply in the presence of his wife. 'His family is extremely wealthy and influential and he is a man with whom I should like to have done business. Only this afternoon I was talking to an acquaintance of his who plans to deepen the links between French and British interests abroad.'

'What do you mean, *abroad?*' cried Asa. 'Mr Morton, surely you don't wish to involve yourself in the West Indies?'

'I export cotton. Indirectly, I'm already involved. And I'm concerned that my trading interests should be protected. Had you been prepared to pursue your acquaintance with Mr Shackleford, you would have done me a great favour, Thomasina.'

Philippa, who was looking quite healthy that evening, glowered at Asa. 'I'm sure Thomasina did not mean to offend you in any way, my dear Mr Morton, and would do everything in her power to please you. I will speak to her later. If only I had been in full health, I might have...'

'Dear Philippa, I'm not blaming you. Never. Please don't upset yourself.' He patted Philippa's hand and cast another reproachful glance at Asa. 'We shall speak of other things. Tell your sister about your letter from Georgina.'

'Ah yes,' said Philippa, dabbing her eyes and giving Asa a look which said, Be grateful I have saved you from my husband's wrath. 'Georgina writes that she has met a gentleman called Mr Warren who has very good prospects indeed, and whom she is sure may propose at any moment. I do hope Father will pay attention and look into this Mr Warren. But at least Georgina is excited and cheerful. And thank God I shall soon be well enough to go home – perhaps in time, if necessary, to prevent lasting damage.'

Five days later, Asa again fled the hotel to meet Didier, although she stood for some minutes in the shadow of the wall opposite his apartment before she dared go in. It is the time, she thought,

68

the time leaves me no choice. Morality, in Paris, was turned on its head. To be a patriot was to despise the king. To be a peacemaker was to accept the status quo and force years more suffering on the poor. To be pure in heart was to long for tumult. Besides, it seemed to Asa that she had been committed to this moment long before she first set eyes on Didier; in fact ever since she had been chosen, rather than Georgina, to come on this wedding trip.

Staring up at Didier's window, she thought of the screen which divided his room. Her own body, in the dappled shade of the beech tree, felt young and intact. Nineteen years old. What was she thinking of? There was only one possible way forward: the right thing to do was to wait.

So she climbed the stairs slowly, heart in mouth, telling herself that she was here simply to drink a cup of coffee; that was all. And perhaps Didier had come to the same conclusion, for he sat at a distance while they talked of Philippa's improved health and the wrangling that was still going on about how delegates to the Estates General might be elected. Asa had not seen him as self-contained and remote. After a while she thought miserably: perhaps he doesn't desire me at all. There he sat in his shirtsleeves, one arm hooked over the back of his chair, so beautiful with his bare throat and dishevelled hair, a faint sheen of perspiration on his upper lip.

As the conversation died between them, she got up abruptly. 'I'll go, then. My sister might be missing me.'

'As you wish.'

69

Struggling to hold back tears, she walked to the door, but at last he reached out and caught her hand. 'Why did you come?'

'You wrote to me. I thought you wanted to see me.'

'And you. What did you want?'

'I wanted to be with you.'

'Here you are.'

'Why are you being so cold, Didier? I don't understand. We have so little time.'

'Yes, we have little time, as you keep telling me. But what am I to do about it? There is nowhere for us to go. It seems to me that we have reached the end. I don't have anything to offer you. Not a penny. Certainly not a roof over your head or any kind of future. I wish I had never met you.'

'Don't say that, Didier.'

'For God's sake, Thomasina, I am flesh and blood. To be with you in this room is torture. Yes, I invited you, but the truth of you, your beauty, the way you are looking at me ... can't you see what you are doing to me?'

'Didier. Why do you think I'm here? I'm perhaps not as foolish or naive as you think.'

'You are unprotected. I have been totally in the wrong. It's madness. If I had met you some other time, last summer or next, everything would have been much clearer. We must wait...'

'I can't wait.' She kissed the back of his hand. 'I love you, I love you. That's all. What does anything else matter?'

She clung to him, wrapping her arms about his waist so that she felt his hot body under the fabric of his shirt, burying her face in his neck

70

and inhaling the lovely scent of him. Soon he was caressing her waist and breast, kissing her throat, drawing her towards the bed. 'Is this what you want?'

'Don't ask. How can you ask?'

They fell amid the crumpled sheets and thin blankets and she shuddered as he kissed her breast and began to unhook her gown, kissing the newly exposed skin between each fastening, working at the billows of her skirts with his knee. Didier's touch on her naked breasts was reverential. Asa's bare toes traced a vertical bar on his bedstead and her skin contracted beneath his hand. He smelt delectable; of hot damp flesh, coffee, of Paris. How astonishing that this great brave soul should be, at this moment, absorbed completely in Asa Ardleigh, so that as he kissed her, as his hand made soft, long strokes along her stomach, she felt almost sacrificial. This moment, this country, this body, all were Didier's, and she made no resistance but gladly embraced the sharp pain of union, the shocking motion of flesh. His face was glistening with sweat, his eyes closed, and he was absorbed in some passionate, unstoppable race that was both animal, as he groaned and seized a handful of her hair, and spiritual, for when he opened his eyes he studied her with such mystified love that she curled her legs and arms round him and reached up to be kissed.

For a while afterwards she lay beneath him, smiling, astonished at herself, grieving at his slow withdrawal. But then, as he lay with his mouth pressed to her throat, and she looked again at the cracked ceiling and the edge of the screen, and

71

heard the clatter of the street, she felt corrosive flickers of guilt. What had she done? What would she say to Caroline? Philippa trusted her. She turned her face into Didier's arm.

'Don't be afraid,' he said, kissing her cheek. 'We will marry. I'll find a way.'

'Is that a proposal?'

He laughed. 'Of course. Mademoiselle Ardleigh, my wanton English girl, will you marry me?'

'I will. Today.'

'Today I am called to a meeting. Besides, I have not a penny to my name.'

'I don't mind. I could live here with you.'

'Do you think I would allow that? This plain little room is not what I want for my wife. No. I wish to meet your father proudly and tell him I am a man of means and status. We'll only have to wait a few months. That is all.'

'What shall I tell my sister?'

'Don't tell her anything.' He kissed her breast as his hand slid between her thighs and his beautiful fingers, so expressive and emphatic when he spoke, concentrated all their delicacy on her. 'It would hardly be appropriate to tell her about this, I think.'

All would be well: they would marry. No one need know about this lovemaking. He had tossed his creased shirt over the screen, which was painted green on the side facing the bed, brown on the other; there was a tarnished barley-twist candlestick on the table beside his pillow; the walls were lined with tottering heaps of books, many with pages uncut. His hands, his mouth, were caressing her body, so that at last she stopped listening to other clamorous voices in her head and followed his touch. As the blood began pounding in her veins she smelt, through the open window, the faint, herbal whiff of the monastery garden.

'I can't believe that you love me,' she whispered, 'of all the women in Paris. I'm not French, I'm not beautiful, I'm not Catholic.'

They lay nose to nose, lip to lip. 'Perhaps I love you because you are foreign, you are Protestant and your face is full of surprises.'

'What kind of surprises?'

'I look at you one moment, for instance now, and I think: no, she is not truly beautiful. Her hair is just an ordinary brown, her chin is too pronounced and her nose too small. And then I look again and I think: but she is the most beautiful woman I have ever seen because of what I read in her eyes and because, when the light changes, when she turns her head, she is suddenly so lovely that my heart misses a beat. You are a distraction, Mademoiselle Ardleigh, you take up too much of my time and thoughts, and yes, I am obsessed by you.'

'You should be warned that although my family is poor, it is very old. You would probably call me an aristocrat and hate me for my name, if I were French.'

He kissed her shoulder and ear. 'I care nothing for your family name. I care only for you, the way you are now. At home the question of love was so complicated. The women of Caen are hungry for change, but there's a ravenous quality to their hunger, even when it comes to love.'

'Don't you admire them for that?'

'I do, yes, but I see a more subtle version of that fire burning in you. It's there in the way you make love to me. Very shocking, mademoiselle, I might add. But otherwise you are uncomplicated. You make no other demands on me. You ask for nothing except this. That is what I love.'

Chapter Seven

On the second Saturday afternoon in July Philippa insisted on walking in the Jardin des Tuileries, although the weather had turned oppressively hot. While rejoicing in her sister's recovered health, Asa could not help feeling dismayed, because later that day she had planned to meet Didier. What if they were not back at the Montmorency in time for her to plead the need for a rest in her room, thence to escape? What if Philippa enjoyed herself so much in the open air that she chose to travel farther, to view the construction of the Magdelaine Church, for instance, or the ancient St-Eustache? But there was no dissuading Philippa, whom weeks of sickness had inclined to tears when contradicted. So they helped her into protective scarves and gloves and a deep-brimmed hat to shade her from the sun – later they realised that the exceptional heat had been a portent of the hailstorm that was to follow – and drove to the Tuileries, where Philippa progressed at snail's pace, leaning on both Morton and Asa.

A palace clock chimed two. Morton said they should stay only an hour so as not to overtire his wife, but Philippa was enjoying herself, for the first time relishing her pregnancy and delighting in the toffee-apple shadows cast by trees planted in regimentally straight rows and the bustle of Parisians who paraded through the gardens with their infants and their flowered hats and their miniature dogs. She loved the rainbow colours of the women's gowns, the new fashion for airy skirts unsupported by hoops, the mix of flower seller and aristocrat, maidservant and artisan's wife. She did not choose to see the prostitutes lurking in the shadows or the beggars who crouched in crowded squares, scratching in the dirt for any scrap or coin.

Strolling along broad or narrow avenues, the Mortons made unfavourable comparisons with London parks, which they said were designed to resemble nature at its most random and lovely, none of this French obsession with symmetry. They sank on to a stone bench and rested, progressed down broad flights of steps, leaned on parapets, paused in a patch of deep shade then, as they moved forward again, encountered a crowd of young people who were hurrying towards them in a babble of talk and laughter: at the forefront, the leader, Didier Paulin.

For once Asa had been too preoccupied to look out for him. In any case, she had thought that he would be working in the Palais de Justice. So it was as if in a dream that she spotted him in the midst of that group of young people; a very public version of Didier, dressed in work clothes but apparently in holiday mood as he flung his arm about a friend's neck and gave him a playful punch.

Would he even notice Asa, let alone acknowledge her? And what was it about him that delighted her each time she saw him? He was such a boy – the grin, the tousled hair – so beautiful as he made a characteristic movement with his hand, thrusting the palm forward, oblivious to her at that moment, yet intimate even with the place on her instep which, when touched, caused her to yelp with laughter.

The momentum of the group was interrupted as Didier's companion glanced across, caught Asa's eye, swept off his hat and bowed with exaggerated gallantry. Philippa paused. The young man nudged Didier, who, noticing Asa, stopped mid-sentence. Recovering quickly, he came over, took Philippa's hand and said: 'My dear Madame Morton. Do you remember me? We met at the Odeon, *Figaro*. I have since met your husband and sister again at Madame de Genlis's salon.'

He then kissed Asa's hand, very correctly. The group of young people had settled like a flock of birds, the girls in cotton gowns and straw hats or high lace caps, the young men in colourful jackets and plain breeches.

'These are my English friends,' Didier told them. 'Monsieur and Madame Morton and Mademoiselle...'

'Ardleigh,' said Asa.

'And these,' he explained, 'are my very dear friends from my home town of Caen. We have just met my father and sister. These people have

76

travelled all the way to Paris with a deputation of nobles to inform the king that Normandy is calling for a regional equivalent of an Estates General, as well as one for the whole country.'

The young people surrounding him shared the same light in their eyes as the Lamberts and Paulins. Asa yearned for their freedom, to be walking arm in arm with Didier through the Tuileries. On the other hand only she knew his first-floor room with the blue and white coffee jug; only she would lie with him a few hours later, grip his hard body and feel his flesh in hers.

'I very much hope your delegation will be successful,' said Morton, ill at ease in so public a place with a group of young people.

'I doubt it. We are as likely to be clapped in irons as to be granted a hearing. But we have to try. The king may arrest us, he may imprison our leaders, though all we are asking for is a voice – you mark my words, by the end of tomorrow some of us will be in the Bastille. But the tide of history has turned. Not even a king can stop it. It will happen soon: reform or revolution. Either way we will be allowed to speak and then, who knows, the old order in France will be dismantled for good.'

Morton, red in the face with alarm, claimed that his wife was tired and must be escorted back to the Montmorency. But as the two groups walked away from each other Asa hung back, partly to compose herself, partly in hope.

'Thomasina.'

Didier had run along a parallel avenue and now emerged between the trees. The Mortons continued along their own path as Didier seized her hand and pulled her into a different avenue. For a moment there was no one watching; just as well, because he held her face in his hands and kissed her. 'I love to see you out here in the sunshine, so funny in your English bonnet, so beautiful with your rosy cheeks and smiling mouth. But I know a different Thomasina and I shall be waiting at six when I shall kiss her again, like this.'

He was ablaze. Asa sensed a new pulse in him that tightened his arms and made him hold her ever closer. 'What is it?' she said. 'What has happened?'

'It is because of you that I feel like this. You are my talisman. It is our time. Everything will be swept away. The whole of France is astir.'

He gave her another kiss; next moment they had both returned to the main avenue and were once more walking away from each other. Glancing back, Asa saw that he had made a little run, and that one of the girls, slight with curling dark hair, had broken loose from the group, waited for him, and had taken his arm as he drew close.

Asa was soon at Philippa's side, covering her mouth with her hand and aching with desire. As they reached a crossing of paths she glanced round one last time. Didier and the girl were still walking arm in arm. Both turned suddenly and glanced back as if they had been talking about her.

That night Didier did not wait at the street door but stood at the window and called for her to come up. He was barefoot, his shirt open at the throat, and he filled her pottery cup with red wine. Though he pulled the threadbare curtains across the window to shut out the sunlight, the room was very hot. He told her they had very little time that night because he and Beatrice had arranged to meet up again with the party from Caen.

'Can't I come too?' Asa asked.

'I thought of that, but it would not be appropriate. Too many explanations would be required. And you distract me.'

'Perhaps you don't want me to stay now, then.'

'How could you suggest such a thing? If you knew how much I have been wanting you...' He took the cup from her hand, sipped a mouthful of wine, then tipped back her head and kissed her so that the cool liquid trickled from his mouth into hers. His hand worked on the pins in her hair until the soft weight of it fell against her neck. There was no time to undress; instead they clawed at each other's clothes until he had uncovered her and could press kisses into her stomach and thighs. She was moaning, reaching for him, clasping his face as he made love to her, his eyes tight shut, his body taut and urgent.

Afterwards he whispered again and again: 'My English love. Mademoiselle Anglaise. My love.'

Nevertheless, he was in a hurry to help her dress and escort her home. Their parting at the corner of the Cherche-Midi was perfunctory; the faintest of bows, a dashing away and the raising of a hand. *'À mardi,'* he called.

79

The next day, Philippa was well enough to break-fast in the hotel dining room.

'So,' said Morton, smiling at her fondly, 'I shall arrange for us to leave tomorrow morning.'

Asa stared at him. 'We can't possibly. My sister...'

Morton clasped his wife's hand. 'Your sister says she is quite well enough, as long as we take the journey in easy stages. Besides, I am convinced that the dangers of staying far outweigh those of leaving.'

'What dangers? We have been very comfortable here.'

'Yesterday, those people we met, the professor's son; what he said about the turning of the tide was the final straw. We have been here barely three months yet I fear that in even so short a time France has reached a tipping point. I'm all for reform, yes, but give the people too much headway and who knows where it may end. It is my duty to see you both home safely.'

'But what Didi ... Monsieur Paulin said was just talk. There's no need to be alarmed. I'm sure that Philippa would love to stay a little longer, now that she is better. She's hardly seen Paris.'

'Really, Asa, to tell the truth, I should very much like to be back in England, and to become acquainted with my new home,' said Philippa. 'Besides, I am very anxious about Georgina. I know you will be disappointed to have our journey cut short but we are in dear John's hands. If you would help with my packing, when you have finished your own, I'm sure I shall be quite rested and ready to depart by tomorrow.'

'But what about the friends I've made? It would be rude not to say goodbye.'

'A note will be sufficient.' Philippa's warning glance quelled further argument. Immediately the meal was over Morton went out to make preparations for the journey while Asa hurled clothes into her trunk. By this time tomorrow she would be miles from Paris. She and Didier had not arranged to meet again until Tuesday. He was spending today with his father and Beatrice. How could she get word to him?

In her distraction she failed to notice that a storm was gathering. A prolonged rumble of thunder took to her to the window, where she saw that the sky was ink black and people were scurrying, head down, intent on getting inside before the rain came. She must act at once, in case the weather became too severe for her to leave the hotel. She scribbled a note – *I must see you. We leave in the morning. I cannot bear to think we may not even say goodbye ... here is my address in England, in case the worst should happen...* – put on her bonnet and cloak, and ran downstairs.

In the lobby she could scarcely make her way through the crowd of people who had pressed in from the street, seeking shelter. It was not rain falling, but hail. Lamps were lit as if it were midnight. Asa went to the door but was pushed back by more people stumbling in, shaking hailstones the size of conkers from their collars and hats. There was nothing to be seen of the opposite side of the street, only a curtain of ice, the hailstones so large that a horse bowed its head to the ground and a mother shoved her little boy under

81

a barrow for protection. People clutched each other as the lobby blazed white then was shaken by an extraordinary clap of thunder.

Surely it must abate soon. But the storm went on and on until at last Asa ran up to Philippa's room, thinking: I'll see her first, reassure her, then I'll deliver the note, whatever the weather. Philippa was sitting on the bed, eyes fixed on the window. 'Oh, Asa. What shall we do if we can't get away tomorrow?'

'There's no hurry,' Asa replied. 'A day or two won't matter.'

'It's foolish, I know, but I feel as if I will not be fully well until I leave here. Stay with me and help with the last of my things. At least then I shall be ready, whatever happens.'

Never had it been more difficult for Asa to be patient with Philippa, to fold and refold her clothes and then to unpack the entire trunk because a fringed shawl which would be needed on the journey had been placed at the bottom. Each time the thunder clattered above their heads Philippa patted her stomach, as if to comfort the unborn child. Finally, after the hail turned to torrential rain and then to drizzle, Asa said she must see to her own packing. Instead she ran downstairs and outside, where rainwater gushed over her feet, drenching her skirt. The air was cold and the streets almost empty except for a woman standing at her door in tears: 'The pots in the courtyard. There is not a plant left standing.'

At one point Asa had to run through to the rue de Sèvres, parallel to her usual route, to avoid the rivers of filth rushing along the cobbles. By the time she reached Paulin's apartment she was exhausted and soaked through. His landlady, flustered by the damage done to her roof by the storm, was impatient and disapproving as she took Asa's sodden note, saying she had no idea when Monsieur Paulin would be back. For an hour Asa walked up and down the street, marched round the Carrefour de la Croix Rouge under dripping trees, stared up at his window. He did not come. It was now nearly three in the afternoon, but still she paced to and fro, then at last went back to the Montmorency and hastily changed her clothes.

Morton returned at five and said the storm had done irreparable damage. It was rumoured that the crops had been devastated, and the harvest in most of France would be ruined. 'Well then, we cannot possibly leave tomorrow,' said Asa. 'The roads will be in chaos.'

'On the contrary, I am all the more determined to make an early start. There may be riots, when people realise the damage that has been done. The country has no stores, and no money to import crops. In my view the king and his ministers have made a grave miscalculation. We shall leave in the morning.'

Asa returned to her room, pushed up the window and leaned into the street. He must come. But still there was no sign of Didier, and she had to endure an interminable dinner during which the talk was of nothing but the storm and what might have been the cause – natural or otherwise – of such unseasonable weather. Afterwards Morton insisted that his wife have an early night in preparation for the morning, so Asa spent half an hour helping Philippa to undress. As her hair was brushed with long, hypnotic strokes, Philippa confided that she was a little homesick and could not help being grateful to the French for their unrest, which provided the perfect excuse for departure.

'I feel that John will be more settled in his own home. And the thought of another hotel, even in Italy or Switzerland, of being confined to a room as I have been here, fills me with dread. I know you must be disappointed, Asa, at having to go back to Ardleigh, when you might have spent the summer abroad...'

Asa squeezed her shoulder. 'Your health is my first concern. There will be other opportunities. And I shall be glad to see Caroline.'

Afterwards she stood again by the window in her room. Didier did not come.

Just after eight o'clock she raced along the passage, down the stairs and into the lobby, barging into a portly fellow guest who fell back against the wall in astonishment. Outside, the air was clear, as if scourged by the hail. She crossed the rue du Cherche-Midi and stood deep in the entrance to a courtyard so she could watch the street. Surely Didier would have returned to his apartment by now and received her note? After quarter of an hour she began to walk, oblivious to the fact she was wearing unsuitable shoes and her head was bare. Nobody noticed. All of Paris was stunned by the storm. But she sensed as soon as she reached his street that he had not come back. Summoning all her courage, she again knocked on the door, and this time received only a curt: 'I've told you, he's not here.'

She waited until it was almost dark and the lamps were lit. By the time she made her way back to the hotel her skirts were heavy with mud. Surely, this time, by some miracle, he would be in the lobby. But there was no sign of Didier, and no message. Hour after hour she sat at her bedroom window, though she knew there could be no question of him coming now. If only wretched John Morton had made up his mind earlier, then she could have warned Didier last night that they were leaving. If only they'd never met Didier and his friends in the Tuileries.

In the morning she sat heavy eyed and sick with suspense as Philippa sipped a tisane and ate a mouthful of brioche. He will come, Asa thought, as she watched the trunks being stowed on the roof of the carriage. Morton gave her his arm to lead her on to the wet street and in the seconds it took to cross the carpet of clean sacking between the hotel and the carriage steps, she strained for a glimpse of Didier, convinced he would still come and snatch her away. She even imagined Philippa's astonishment when she and Didier announced their determination to marry at once, the hurried explanations, the untying of Asa's trunk.

As the carriage made its tortuous way through Paris, Asa pressed her face to the glass, sure that he would follow. In half an hour they halted at the gates to show their papers. Now, now he would race up and claim her. But soon the horses were picking up speed on the open road, spattering the carriage with mud.

Three days later, in Calais, her face a mask of calm, she finally admitted to herself that he would not come; that there would be no pounding of hooves, no shouting of her name. Soon she was walking the breezy gangplank, the ropes were uncoiled, a strip of sea was widening between ship and harbour and she, Asa Ardleigh was being carried relentlessly to England while her lover, her Didier, was left behind in Paris.

Part Two

England, 1792–93

Chapter One

By the time the Morton party had returned to England in July 1788, Georgina was engaged. Within another month she was married. Her new spouse, Mr Geoffrey Warren, who had been introduced through a hunting acquaintance of her father's, described himself as a financier and had impressed Georgina with his natty dressing and talk of prospects. Too late it transpired that none of his elderly relatives was about to die after all, let alone leave him their fortune, if they ever had any, and almost all his business ventures – including, incidentally, his marriage to Georgina Ardleigh – were to prove ruinously ill advised. But one of Georgina's most endearing traits was her belief that at any moment her luck would change, and although it took nearly four years, in August 1792, it suddenly did.

The Warrens' lack of funds was in part due to their love of gambling. Georgina preferred cards, Warren the dice. Normally the establishments they patronised were more Billingsgate than Pall Mall, but that summer they had an unexpected invitation – issued as part of a gambling debt to Warren – to a party in St James's Place, and it was there that Georgina first noticed a fair-haired gentleman dressed in black, who was drinking heavily and placing ever more extravagant bets.

89

The talk, as usual, was of the scandalous events in France: London was still reeling from the news that a mob of low-lifes had invaded the Palace of the Tuileries, threatened the lives of the king and queen, and forced the Revolutionary Assembly, France's new but ramshackle equivalent to the exemplary British Parliament, to declare an end to the monarchy. The French royal family was now interred in some dreadful prison and twelve hundred people were dead, mostly the king's Swiss guards but also a considerable number of the Parisians who had invaded the palace.

'So death, at least,' said the fair-haired gentleman, 'is proving egalitarian in France.'

'A state of affairs in which the future of our nearest neighbour is decided by mob rule cannot be countenanced,' replied Warren. 'Soon we'll have no choice but to declare war on the French or vice versa.'

'You seem rather excited by the prospect of war,' said the stranger, scooping up a heap of chips.

'That,' whispered one of Georgina's gossipy friends, 'is young Harry Shackleford. I say young, but actually he must be well over thirty by now. What I meant is, he's the *younger* Shackleford. If I were you I wouldn't let your husband play him at dice much longer – he'll be bankrupt within half an hour.'

Georgina, decked out in a gown copied from the style known as *chemise à la reine*, after a dress worn by Queen Marie Antoinette in her pre-revolutionary attempts to emulate a shepherdess, put her hand to her throat. '*Shackleford.* Tell me more. My distant cousins are called Shackleford. When my father dies it's a Shackleford who stands to inherit everything.'

'But surely you must have heard? It seems to me that nobody's talked about anything else for weeks. Harry Shackleford has recently inherited several hundred thousand pounds and vast estates in Somerset.'

'*Somerset*. Our relatives are from Somerset.'

'Then claim kinship quick. You see, until a couple of months ago Harry Shackleford was worth virtually nothing. Then the news came that both his father and his brother had died at sea, in very odd circumstances.'

'What can you mean?'

'Who knows? The thing is, they were on a voyage to Jamaica but never arrived. Nobody's sure what happened. Some say disease, others mutiny or revolt. But one way or another Harry has inherited the lot.'

The minute there was a pause in play Georgina gathered her skirts, glided over and dropped a deep curtsy so that Shackleford was confronted by her magnificent bosom and a froth of silver-sprigged muslin. 'Mr Shackleford, forgive me, but I felt I must come and offer my condolences since we're related. In fact, I believe that I too should have been wearing black, or perhaps purple, if only I'd known.' Shackleford, bewildered, stood up and bowed. 'My name is Georgina Warren. You've been dicing with my husband for the last half-hour and neither of you realised you were relatives. I'm a daughter of Squire Ardleigh of Sussex. Do you see the connection?'

After her bosom, Georgina's smile was by far her best feature. Her nose was broad and her face rather square but her smile, which revealed a full set of white teeth, was delectable, and the accompanying toss of curls had certainly been the downfall of Geoffrey Warren. But it was her words, on this occasion, which had a bizarre effect on Shackleford, who drew breath sharply and even seemed a little flustered.

'Mrs Warren, I'm delighted to meet you. How very kind of you to make yourself known to me. Is your family well?'

'Goodness, they're all extremely well, I'm sure. Unlike your own. Oh, it's so sad. You lost both your father and your brother at the same time, I believe.' Her eyes filled with tears.

Shackleford shrugged. As Georgina later commented to Warren, who had been a somewhat drunken witness to the encounter, the man couldn't have seemed less concerned about his dead relatives.

'It was a blow to find myself suddenly head of the family,' he said.

'Good Lord, it must have been an *appalling* shock. How long ago did it happen?'

'Late last year. I was abroad, in Sierra Leone, and was called back to take up the reins.' For a moment he looked distracted, then said with much more animation: 'I met your sister – sisters – in Paris, you know, a few years back. Since then I've scarcely set foot in this country.'

'Oh, I remember, yes, they wrote to me about you and said how *thrilled* they'd been to make your acquaintance. My sister Philippa has three children now. Can you imagine? All boys, and thriving. John, Edward and something... My brother-in-law, Morton, is doing extremely well. Fingers in many... Warren and I are always being invited to their beautiful new house in Surrey.'

'And your younger sister ... Thomasina?'

'Oh, Asa. You met her too. Of course. Asa is Asa. Much as ever.'

All this while Georgina was conscious that the rest of the room was agog; Shackleford was possibly the most eligible gentleman in London that season and yet his entire attention was on Mrs Georgina Warren. His light brown gaze was fixed on her face and he had placed his hand high on the wall beside her, effectively cutting off the rest of the party, including her husband. The thought even crossed Georgina's mind that if Shackleford really admired her and wanted to embark on a clandestine liaison, Warren would just have to turn a blind eye.

'Does she...? Is she...?' Shackleford said. 'I believe Miss Ardleigh was living with her father in Sussex.'

'That's right. Still the same. There are never any changes at Ardleigh, but fortunately Asa never grows bored. In any case, she spends half her time these days at Morton Hall during Philippa's confinements, so that keeps her amused.'

Such was Shackleford's intense interest that Georgina had to make a mental readjustment. Good Lord, why had Philippa, when recounting events in Paris, not mentioned Shackleford's interest in Asa?

'Is she still as dedicated as ever to the cause of

93

the French Revolution?' he asked. 'Or have recent events dampened her enthusiasm? I rather think she's the type to have joined a correspondence society.'

Several hundred thousand a year, thought Georgina. Shackleford father and son had died on their way to the West Indies, and she was fairly sure she'd heard that the Shackleford wealth came from sugar. Obviously, then, she would have to conceal the fact that Asa included abolitionist activities in her list of causes. 'I admire Asa very much,' she said, watching him carefully, 'because she's so principled. She was already mad on the French before she visited Paris, and of course being there turned her head completely. I believe she must have read every news article that's ever been written on the subject of the Revolution. We're always arguing about it. I'm afraid as a result of her strong opinions – they *are* only opinions, mind, and she's always open to persuasion – she has never married. It's such a tragedy. I've always thought she was the prettiest of us three Ardleigh girls.'

His sudden smile was enough to make Georgina flick open her fan and cover her eyes for a moment.

He said obligingly: 'I've never met such a striking trio of sisters.'

Georgina gave a trill of laughter and shook her curls. So Shackleford, believe it or not, really did have a tenderness for Asa. Well, Asa must be worked on – with such a fortune at stake, even she would have to see sense. 'Are you staying long in London, Mr Shackleford?'

94

'Possibly. I have a mountain of business, as you can imagine. My father's lawyers and I are ploughing through a mass of deeds and contracts. But Compton Wyatt, our estate near Bristol, has also been much neglected since Father's death so I should go home.'

Georgina rested her hand on his. 'Please remember that we are here, ready to help in any way you like. We are your family. My husband, I'm sure, would be delighted to offer his services.'

Shackleford's smile was touchingly diffident. 'Next time you write to your sisters, mention that I was asking after them. And wish them well.'

Chapter Two

Georgina might have felt less optimistic about the chances of a match between her younger sister and Harry Shackleford had she been present at a meeting, that September of 1792, of the Littlehampton Abolition Society. The double doors of the assembly rooms had been flung back to accommodate fifteen people, including two lady friends of the rector's daughter – the Misses Champion and Hillhouse. They were visiting from Bristol and had been invited to speak about their acquaintance with Mr Thomas Clarkson, the tireless reformer who had visited slaving ports up down the country compiling evidence on the abuses of the trade, particularly in relation to the high mortality rate of British sailors.

At the end of the meeting Miss Thomasina Ardleigh gave her usual report on the Revolution in France. Since her visit to Paris in the summer of 1788, she had become the established expert on how Littlehampton abolitionists might best support their brothers and sisters across the Channel. Fortunately she was a compelling speaker because her words had to compete with the clink of cups and a faint scent of fruit cake as tea was prepared in the lobby. Furthermore, her sisters would have winced had they seen the outfit in which she'd chosen to make this public appearance. From some closet at home she had extracted an outmoded jacket and matching skirt in faded green that had once belonged to Philippa. However, her hair, which had been bundled into combs under her best straw hat, curled disarmingly, and her eyes shone as she gripped the back of a chair and spoke without notes.

'We must write again and again to our friends in France – Monsieur Brissot and other members of Les Amis des Noirs – so they never doubt for a moment that they have influential friends here. We must support them in their battle to have the cause of abolition heard above all the other urgent demands which are being made on the Revolutionary Assembly. We must ensure that the cry of Equality Liberty and Fraternity applies as much to slaves toiling under the burning skies of the West Indies as to the French people struggling to emerge from beneath the heel of tyranny.

'I read this morning that the issue of abolition has been fudged yet again by the new Assembly and that there are factions who insist that the cause must wait until France is on a more secure economic footing. The slaves who have staged a successful uprising in the French colony of Sainte-Domingue need our support as never before. The French government is preoccupied with its own affairs. The country's enemies are assembling on its borders, there has been unrest in Paris, including more violent deaths, and it is being said that peace must be achieved at home before such an ambitious reform as the end of the slave trade can be attempted abroad. But we know that for one human being to own another is absolutely wrong, and that abolition must take priority over everything else. We must not let the fate of hundreds of thousands of slaves be obscured by this moment of history.'

Over tea Asa was besieged by ladies seeking the address of Les Amis des Noirs. 'I am fifty years old,' said one of the visitors from Bristol, 'and it has taken me years to realise the extent to which the fortunes of my own family, as well as my city, are bound up in this iniquitous trade.'

'Few of us are unaffected, Miss Champion. I'm ashamed to say that I have distant relatives of my own living near Bristol who have made a fortune from slaving. Their name is Shackleford. Perhaps you've heard of them.'

'Well, of course. The Shacklefords of Compton Wyatt are one of the foremost families in the county. What a tragedy – father and son travelling on the same ship, neither returned. Mr Clarkson will be interested to hear of the circumstances of the accident, if such it was, when they become clear. He is determined to prove, once and for all, that slave ships are in fact a graveyard rather than an excellent training ground for our British sailors, never mind the slaves.'

'I had heard of the accident,' said Asa. 'It is the older Shackleford boy, I believe, who died.'

'That's it. Thomas. Nobody knows much about the younger son except that he's been abroad for years and has something of a reputation for extravagant living. I'm afraid we aren't pinning our hopes on the new heir being either a reformer or an example to his fellow traders.'

'As I have met the younger Mr Shackleford – years ago, in Paris – I fear you are right.'

'But Miss Ardleigh, despite your unfortunate connection with the Shacklefords, your words this afternoon were an inspiration. If ever you're in Bristol – perhaps visiting your grand relations,' said Miss Hillhouse mischievously, 'do please come and address our society.'

After tea Mr Lambert, who was completing an article on the comparative conditions of slave ships and prison hulks, walked home by the most direct route. Asa and Caroline watched him head off along the lane, trim and short in his brown coat, a little stiff legged, hands clasped behind his back as he composed his thoughts but ever on the alert for an unusual bird or flower. They chose to take a long detour along the West Beach. Because it was late September, the sun was already sinking and the sky full of rushing clouds.

Caroline never wore enough clothes – there was always a bit of neck, wrist or ankle exposed – yet she halted, arms gripped against her chest to protect her from the wind, as Asa took out Georgina's latest letter and thrust it into her hand.

'The Shacklefords I was talking about to Miss Champion – the cousin who is to inherit Ardleigh – you may remember I met him in Paris? Well, now he's turned up in a London gaming house.'

Caroline's narrow face was full of amusement as she read the letter. 'He's certainly won Georgina's heart. What a shame she's not free to marry him herself.'

'Their meeting is a thorough nuisance. I shall never hear the last of it.'

'Georgina seems to think that you're a few short steps from being wed to him. You must admit it would be convenient. He's rich, not much above thirty, and one day he will oust you from your family home if nothing is done about it.'

Asa chased her along the beach, batting her with the letter. 'Don't suggest it even in jest. Every penny of Shackleford money comes from slaving. And I loathed him in Paris. He was shallow and clingy, a dandy with no ideas of his own. I hardly think it possible that he could have retained an interest in me all this time, given my harsh words to him then. In any case, marriage, as you well know, does not appeal. You and I are going to set up a school together and be a couple of old maids.'

They linked arms and stood so close to the breaking waves that their toes were threatened and they had to dash backwards. Caroline picked up a grey pebble and tossed it far out; then another and another. 'You've surely not ceased to hope?'

'That I'll marry my Frenchman? Caroline, it has been more than six months since I last heard from him.'

'But you've kept faith for so long. How could you give up now?'

'You, I know, would never give up. But I don't even know for sure whether he's alive or dead. You've read the newspapers. There are rumours of a massacre in Paris prisons. What if he was there? What if he'd offended someone? After all, in his last letter he told me he was about to be appointed to high office. Nobody is safe in Paris at the moment.'

'As you say, in France everything is at odds, which is precisely why you haven't heard from him. I thought he told you it was too dangerous for him to be sending or receiving mail from England.'

'That's what I tell myself, but he could have found a way. He must know of people travelling to London who could carry letters for us. Oh, Caroline, sometimes these days I worry I might even forget what he looked like. I have read his letters so often they are disintegrating.'

'It's not like you to despair.'

'Four years, and each year the letters come a little farther apart. Is it reasonable to expect any man to wait so long?'

'This one, you said, would wait for ever.'

'That's what he told me. But we thought the

Revolution would be swift and clean and that it would be only a matter of months before argument and opposition were over. We never imagined all this pain. Can you blame me for thinking I'll never hear from him again?'

Even as Asa spoke these words and watched the curl of a breaking wave, she felt the sharp pang of loss, not just of Didier, but of the love affair which had defined her for so long. Without Didier there would be a howling sense of purposelessness; the death of expectation. Her idea of her own significance, of who she was, was founded in him, and the oblique discussions with Caroline about the undying nature of true love.

'Well, if I can't marry him,' she said briskly, 'I shan't marry anyone, because I'd rather a million times live with you than with anyone else.'

'Except your French rebel.'

'If he's alive. If he's still as he was then. If he still wants me.'

They walked on, holding their hats in the wind, a couple of scarecrow women in old-fashioned skirts. Caroline squeezed Asa's arm. 'It's good to know I only come second best to a nameless revolutionary. I shall take heart from that.'

Chapter Three

Georgina was filled with a missionary zeal. First she asked for a loan of twenty pounds from Philippa. *I rarely ask for much*, she wrote untruthfully, *and this is for a* vital *cause*. When the money arrived she ordered a gown of shell-pink muslin with a double frill at the neck and purple silk ribbons wound round the sleeves and forming a sash at the waist. Her husband she kitted out in a navy blue frock coat, the most sober item of clothing he'd worn in years, then told him to have his hair cut.

The Warrens subsequently went out and about in London society, especially to any event that was free, in order to play the Shackleford hand. They attended church services and sales of work for fashionable causes such as the poor French émigrés who'd fled the Revolution; they walked in Regent's Park and occasionally splashed out on a concert; they emphatically did not swear, or even gamble much. Gradually they clawed themselves up a rung or two on the social ladder.

'As we share a great-great-grandfather, do you think I should be in deeper mourning?' Georgina would ask when enquiries were made about her relationship with Shackleford. 'We shall, of course, be visiting dear Mrs Shackleford at Compton Wyatt as soon as she is well enough, to pay our respects.'

In return Georgina learnt from her new female acquaintances that Harry Shackleford had been abroad for more than three years, that Compton Wyatt was a boundless estate consisting of numerous farms and villages, that the family owned glassworks, a bottling factory and shipbuilding concerns in Bristol as well as plantations in Jamaica. By dint of determined investigation and shameless name-dropping, the Warrens soon managed to crop up wherever Shackleford happened to be, though Georgina never thrust herself upon him, nor did she allow Warren to raise the question of business investment except *en passant*.

Obviously, however, he was allowed to share his disquiet about the detrimental effect of the Dolben Act on slave-related profits: 'For goodness' sake, the law insists on allowing every slave sixteen inches rather than twelve down in the hold, as well as endless hours of refreshing exercise on deck. How can we compete with the French if we have to sail our ships half empty?' But it might be as well if Warren didn't mention to Shackleford the reason why he'd lost a considerable sum of money following the Revolution in France; at least until they were better acquainted.

If Shackleford entered a room there was always a discreet shuffle of people edging towards him, wanting to issue invitations, tell him about their latest charitable cause or bring a daughter to his attention. It was said that his father had died so suddenly that the family affairs were in some disarray and that, at his house in Eaton Square, Shackleford was besieged by a stream of lawyers, petitioners and business associates hoping to influence him. For recreation, whispered the rumour-mongers, he gambled heavily and drank to excess. Georgina thoroughly approved of his taste; he tended to wear black or dark grey, of course, but his coats were of silk, his linen immaculate and his hair gleamed golden in candlelight. At such assemblies, he never stayed in one place but moved from group to group as he sought out Georgina. 'Delighted to see you, Mrs Warren.'

'And I you, Mr Shackleford.'

'You are looking very well.'

'As indeed I am.'

He half turned away and then asked, as if in afterthought: 'And your family ...?'

'Quite well, thank you. My older sister Philippa is expecting another child, next year. She hopes for a girl. Asa ... Thomasina...'

'Thomasina?'

'Just the usual. Busy with village affairs. Father has bought a new hunter, she tells me.'

'I suppose your sister has no time to visit London?'

'Or inclination,' said Georgina. 'That's the thing. She's devoted to my father and her life in the country.'

Shackleford smiled and raised an eyebrow. Apparently this bucolic image of Asa didn't quite match his memory of her in Paris. 'Send her my kindest regards,' he said, and there was no doubting the sincerity in his somewhat bloodshot eyes.

Despite his obvious interest in her sister, there were two serious flaws in Georgina's plan. The first was Shackleford himself, whose air of world-weariness grew markedly more pronounced if his family or home were mentioned and who showed no desire to issue invitations to or even talk about Compton Wyatt. The other snag was that when Georgina had last seen Asa almost a year ago – the Warrens had to be desperately short of funds to resort to a stay at Ardleigh – her sister had given no sign whatever of altering her resolve never to marry. The thought of Asa behaving well in a London drawing room or adorning some elegant house in the country was a stretch even for Georgina's fertile imagination. Painstaking steps would therefore have to be taken before Asa was put in the way of Harry Shackleford again.

And here Georgina had her second stroke of luck. A flood of high-born French émigrés, prominent for their aristocratic brows, aquiline noses and air of bewildered refinement, was now frequenting London soirées, having fled their homes in France. Through their attendance at church in Bloomsbury, Georgina and her husband were introduced to a Mrs Silburn, who was famous for offering accommodation to refugees of the Revolution and knew everyone. Some of these people, she said, though too noble ever to have lifted a finger, were now being forced to earn a living by teaching piano or sewing. When she reflected upon the conversation afterwards, Georgina could not remember whether it was thanks to her own inspiration, or Warren's, or in response to Mrs Silburn's enquiry whether they knew of anyone in need of a genteel French companion, that she had the brilliant idea of employing such a French woman herself and sending her down to Ardleigh.

Asa was mad about the French. Why not provide her with a companion who would not only tame her and teach her a spot of etiquette, but also knock some sense into her about the iniquitous state of affairs in France? The stories told by the refugees were hair-raising and Asa ought to hear them.

At Christmas, therefore, Georgina was introduced to a Madame de Rusigneux. 'She says she's *Madame* but we believe she's a marquise,' whispered Mrs Silburn.

Madame de Rusigneux proved to be every bit as intimidating as Georgina had hoped; rather short, admittedly, very thin, about thirty-two years old, with dark hair pulled back firmly from her brow, enormous tragic eyes and exquisite hands. She spoke in a very low, heavily accented voice, and when asked what accomplishments she possessed, looked so affronted that Georgina was crushed. 'I can do everything required of a lady,' stated Madame de Rusigneux. And then, as if to assure Georgina that she certainly had not taken offence, she added with a smile: 'A French lady, that is.'

'Well, my sister was born and bred a lady, but she doesn't behave like one. Do you think you could show her how to be like you? Could you tell her the truth about your country? She needs to be shown that domesticity and decorum are what's needed rather than revolution and bad manners.'

That evening Georgina wrote an excited,

scarcely comprehensible letter to Philippa, setting out her plans for taming Asa and demanding her sister's support in approaching their father.

Chapter Four

Squire Ardleigh invited his youngest daughter to walk with him on the Downs, ostensibly to inspect the ewes that were close to lambing. They found the flock in good shape, grazing with their rear ends full-square to the wind. Father and daughter were so well used to each other's company that they generally had little need for words, but on this occasion Ardleigh thrust his hands behind his back and looked at his feet. 'So, Asa, it seems that your sisters have plans for you. They have found you a husband.'

'What nonsense is this?'

'Georgina says it's practically in the bag that you will marry my heir, Mr Harry Shackleford. She says he remembers you from Paris and she's convinced he'll take one look at you and offer for your hand.'

'But Father, I've not seen Mr Shackleford in years. Anyway, when I met him in Paris I didn't like him at all.'

'Georgina says every girl in London is running after him. How could you resist such a scheme, Asa?' Although he was smiling, her father wouldn't meet her eye. 'Your sisters are adamant that you should marry someone and Shackleford seems to me as good as any – indeed, better than most, given that he's to have Ardleigh.'

'I'm happy as I am. Besides, you need me.'

Her father thrust his hands deep into his pockets. 'Give it some consideration, my Asa, if not this Shackleford, then someone else. I've provided very badly for you. I would hope that Philippa might take you in after I'm gone but one can never be sure. I'd rather see you settled with a husband of your own. And if the man in question happened to be my heir, so much the better. Wouldn't you love to keep Ardleigh?'

From their vantage point they had an excellent view of their manor house nestling in the plain, its missing tiles and broken chimneys disguised by distance; the village clustered round the church with its blunt tower and graveyard speckled with tottering stones, including that of Asa's mother.

'You're nowhere near death, Father. Look at you, in the pink of health. This conversation is absurd. We'll carry on as always. And I'm certainly not marrying Shackleford.'

'I'm afraid it's too late for objecting to at least part of the plan. Money has been spent, or rather committed. John Morton's money, that is.' He took out Georgina's most recent letter, smoothing it against the stiff sleeve of his coat. 'Your sister says you need female influence, that you've gone wild what with your meetings and your lectures and your books. She's hired you a companion.'

'A *what?*'

'Seems that the Warrens were at church of all places. Got a recommendation. Interviewed the woman. She's to arrive on Friday eighth of February, by the stage. All I know is she's a French countess or such, down on her luck.'

'*French.*'

'Georgina says London is littered with French gentlewomen looking for an income.'

The wind was playing havoc with Asa's cloak and hair. 'But Father, you hate the French.'

'This woman is a refugee, calls herself Madame de something or other. I shall make her welcome if she turns out to be good for my Asa.'

'What about Philippa? What does she think of all this?'

'Philippa has persuaded Mr Morton to pay the first month's salary. I'm to find the rest.'

'But she's expecting her new child in a couple of months. She'll need me at Morton Hall.'

'You can take the French woman with you.'

'My brother-in-law wouldn't let her pass through his gates. Everyone knows he's lost all sympathy with the French. Philippa says he's disappointed in them and believes every French person to be a potential revolutionary or spy. Father, please. Put a stop to all this before it's too late.'

For a moment her father held her tightly and kissed her forehead. Then he pushed her away, took off his hat and thrust it back on his head, crooked. The wind struck him a slanting blow as if in punishment. His eyes were watering.

They walked on until they were high on the ridge and could see, on the other side, the long decline through yet more woodland, smallholdings and hamlets to Littlehampton, where Caroline lived, and then the sea and beyond, where water and cloud merged, the invisible France.

'We'll try the companion for a month, Asa. You might like a bit of female conversation. No obligation to marry anyone, eh?'

Half an hour later they were back at the manor house, where they were met at the door by their housekeeper, Mrs Dean, who'd heard from the butcher, who'd got it from his brother ridden over from Chichester, that yesterday France had opened hostilities with Great Britain and the Netherlands. The countries were now officially at war.

Chapter Five

Madame de Rusigneux, the new companion, did not arrive in auspicious circumstances. The second Friday in February 1793 happened to be the day when the village chose to put on a charivari, or rough music as it was called by the lads responsible, on account of a tailor and his wife who had moved into Key Cottage a year ago and who kept their neighbours awake with their arguments and the hurling of pans. Both parties were to blame; the tailor because he was too weak to keep his wife quiet; she for being a foul-mouthed hoyden.

Tailor Dacre, improbably tall and thin, took absurdly short steps for his long legs when delivering work to the rectory, the farm or farther afield in Littlehampton. He was always in a hurry and had exchanged at most half a dozen words with Asa when summoned to the manor by Mrs Dean to be handed the squire's breeches for mending or copying. His wife, a white-skinned, jutting-jawed woman with a fuzz of red hair, never acknowledged Asa when they met in the village. Straw effigies of both, the tailor clad in a petticoat and with an obscenely prominent horn tied to his forehead, his wife in trousers, were perched on a cart and paraded through the village to Key Cottage, where half a dozen or so youths clashed saucepan lids, clattered broomsticks and built a pyre on which to burn the figures. The tailor and his wife did not emerge.

Squire Ardleigh was a dozen miles away, slaughtering a deer. Asa, who had been preparing for her new companion by emptying a chest in the spare room, ran to a window overlooking the street to see what all the fuss was about.

Some of the village women were attempting to rein back the boys, but the mob went on creating a racket, kicking the door with their dogged feet and yelling insults. It seemed to Asa as she seized her best hat (with some vague idea of impressing as lady of the manor) that there was rebellion in the air, wafted across the Channel or whipped up by the prospect of war, and that it was her duty to stop this persecution, if only to prove that revolutionaries need not resort to violence but should instead use reason.

The wind that had blown all week still tormented the shrubs in the garden and worried the faulty latch on the gate. It was only a few paces to

111

the tailor's cottage, where the din was an assault to the ears. The boys were brawny and overbearing with loud voices and calloused hands. One of them repeatedly slammed an old cauldron against the stone step of the cottage, another kicked at the door.

'Stop that,' Asa shouted, but her voice was a reed compared to the clang of metal on stone, so she dashed forward and stood among the boys. They were such an odd mix of familiar and foreign: boys wearing the very same breeches, passed down from father to son, that had been part of Asa's daily window-scape since birth; boys whom she had envied as they played outside in the dirt when Philippa used to take her visiting; boys who had sat scrubbed and resentful, Christmas and Easter, in the back pews of the church.

'That's enough now,' Asa said, hands on hips, addressing Davie Woodcock, the blacksmith's son, who was shorter than the rest but more vocal. 'What are you thinking of?'

Davie picked up the cauldron, held it inches from Asa's head and beat it with a chunk of metal lifted from his father's forge. She saw both insolence and fear in his eyes. Standing between him and the door, she put her hands over her ears and shook her head. When the boys laughed reluctantly and stopped their noise she thought she had won, but in the silence she heard an ominous crackle behind her; the pyre had been lit and in a moment flames were licking obscenely round the splayed legs of the effigies. 'Put that out at once,' she cried. 'Good God, we're not pagans.' By now help had arrived, in the form of the vicar's gardener, a labourer or two and the blacksmith. In moments the flames had been doused, Davie clouted by his father, and the crowd dispersed, leaving Asa standing outside Key Cottage with her servants clustered a short distance away.

She hammered on the door. 'Mr Dacre. Are you there? This is Thomasina Ardleigh. It's quite safe to come out now.'

Not a word.

'No need to be alarmed. Mrs Dacre, can you hear me? The boys have all gone away. Very well, you stay inside and we shall send you a dish of supper from the manor.' She glanced round for approval but Mrs Dean was expressionless. 'Father or I will call again in the morning.'

As she turned towards home she noticed, beyond the thinning of the smoke above the pyre, a stranger. The woman's head was thrown back and she was staring at Asa with shocking concentration. Short and slight, she wore a dark cloak almost covering a skirt of greyish blue, and a neat straw hat fastened on abundant hair. Two travelling bags had been set down at her feet. Her cheeks were sunken, her complexion olive-tinged. It dawned on Asa that this must be her new companion, due to arrive that afternoon by stage-coach.

Asa composed herself by adjusting her hat and smoothing her skirts, then crossed the green, giving the smoking pyre a wide berth. At nearly a head taller than the stranger she felt gawky, as if her limbs had been poorly fitted to her body. 'You are just arrived in Ardleigh?' she said, too loud.

'I am Madame de Rusigneux.' The stranger's voice was unusually low for a woman. She put out her hand, delicate as a bird's claw.

'My name is Thomasina Ardleigh.' Through the softness of the woman's glove Asa felt the shock of French blood pulsing against her fingertips; this was the first foreigner she had touched in more than four years. After her hand was released she realised that the French woman was also trembling, and who could blame her? Whatever must she think of a village – not to mention a squire's daughter – that allowed such barbarity?

The blacksmith was ordered to carry Madame's bags and they processed back to the house. In Ardleigh's snug parlour Asa and the French companion faced each other, one on either side of the hearth. The subdued chatter of the servants in the hall faded; there was now just one actuality, Madame. Of her many objections to a companion, Asa had not considered the most significant of all: that Madame de Rusigneux's arrival would tear open the wound of Asa's separation from Didier so that it seemed like only yesterday she had left the Hotel de Montmorency, sniffed the wet-straw stench of the sacking beneath her feet and looked frantically about in case he should come.

Madame smelt of woodsmoke, the confinement of a long journey, and the profoundly foreign musk of France. But when she smiled it was as if an entirely different person had entered the room; her eyes warmed, a dimple played beside her lip and the severe line of her cheek softened. 'You showed much courage, mademoiselle.'

The blood juddered in Asa's veins. That accent. In a clipped voice she replied: 'Those boys would not have hurt me. The tailor and his wife were simply the butt of a high-spirited prank.'

The parlour seemed to shrink away as, in the firelight, Madame became more sharply defined; the exquisitely narrow nose, a little reddened at the tip owing to the wind, brows which rose and fell at an angle above those obsidian eyes. Her figure was so slight it was a wonder she hadn't been blown away. Asa, by contrast, felt as formless as dough in her housekeeping dress, its woollen skirts kilted up, and the absurdity of her best bonnet.

Since the talk with her father on the Downs she had planned this first encounter in considerable detail. She would extend the welcome due all strangers, of course, but she would resist the companion's attempts to groom her into marriage material. She would instead seize the opportunity to practise her French and to hear first hand about the events taking place in France. Meanwhile she would set about finding Madame de Rusigneux a new position with another family.

What Asa had not anticipated was that behind Madame's trim little figure would hang a ghostly green and brown screen, crumpled sheets, the scent and touch of a man. Nor had she expected that the new French companion would show no sign of aristocratic snobbery or indeed make any attempt to impose but would instead wait, like a servant, to see what would happen next.

Having offered tea, which was refused, Asa showed Madame to her bedchamber. In allocating

115

her the lesser of two spare rooms, she had decided to show this new companion, an exiled noble-woman, that at Ardleigh everyone was equal. Now she regretted her choice; the room was mean and dark with its narrow bed and view of the stable-yard. Madame looked about her without comment but received the news that dinner would be eaten unfashionably early, at five, with an incredulous raising of her eyebrows.

Feeling herself dismissed, Asa stumbled to her own room, stripped to her shift and searched in the closet for something more presentable to wear. It was as if Madame, being French, was a chink through which Didier might enter.

Madame appeared a few seconds after the gong, as fresh as if she'd taken a scented bath. Her gown proved on closer inspection not to be plain at all, but of some thick, silky fabric, softened with age and embossed with darker swirls. She wore an airy muslin fichu crossed at the bosom and tied in a bow behind her. Candlelight complemented her loose dark hair and naked throat so fetchingly that the squire, who as usual came late to the table, though sporting his best wig, stopped dead and ran his finger under his cravat. In his heavy features Asa read first belligerence – this was a *French* woman, after all – then a glint of appreciation. When Madame de Rusigneux extended her arm a frill fell away from her wrist and the squire hesi-tated only an instant before enclosing her hand in his great fist and carrying it to his lips.

Since the older sisters had left home, behaviour at Ardleigh mealtimes had become very slack.

116

The squire sat at one end of the long oak table in the dining room, Asa to his right facing the hearth. The dishes were so old that the pattern had worn away in places, the silver was tarnished, the glassware clouded. Father and daughter were used to speaking with their mouths full, if they spoke at all. Madame, by contrast, attended to every mouthful as if it was the most delicious she had ever tasted, laying down her knife as she chewed and taking it up again only when her mouth was empty. The squire, who had finished his meal in a few minutes, glanced at her from time to time, taking in the fall of her hair, the exposed flesh above her scarf, the dainty workings of her jaw.

After a few minutes of growing consciousness that as the only gentleman present he ought to open the conversation, he asked in the coaxing tones he might employ with an unbroken horse: 'Where have you been living in London, madame?'

The French woman set down her fork, laid her hands on either side of her plate and looked him in the eye so directly that he took a hasty swig of wine. 'Monsieur, I have lived some weeks with a very kind family in Chelsea.'

'Aha, then you'll be well acquainted with our River Thames. What do you think of it? How does it compare to your French rivers?' He twinkled at her, a trick he used to win over the prettiest maid when he asked her to pull off his boots.

'I have had no time to look at the river,' said Madame. 'Since coming to England, my one aim has been to find work so as not to be a burden to my friends.'

'No doubt you left France in a bit of a state. Forced to get away, were you?'

Madame quivered like a bird dislocated from its nest. Before Asa could rescue her she said: 'I lost everything. All of it. There was a fire.'

'Husband? Children.'

'No children, thank God.'

The squire stared at her and wiped his mouth – first on his cuff, then his napkin. 'We heard of the burnings and persecutions. I expect you were punished for being from an old family. Had Ardleigh been in France, we'd have gone up in smoke too, I'm sure, given our family name. And now your king is dead. Terrible thing to kill a monarch. In England we gave up that kind of thing more than a century ago. What do you make of it, madame?'

Her shoulder lifted, affording him a tantalising glimpse of a smooth, full bosom before it was concealed again by the fichu. 'In my country I have grown afraid of speaking my mind.'

'You're quite safe here, madame. No one will repeat a thing beyond this room.'

'Forgive me, Monsieur Ardleigh.' Madame gripped her lower lip between her teeth and averted her face as a tear hung at the corner of her eye. The squire watched, fascinated, as it swelled and was dashed away by a dainty hand. 'I am sure I can trust you, monsieur. You have already shown great kindness in inviting me to live under your roof as companion to your daughter.'

'Ah, now, my daughter, you'll have your hands full with her. The poor gel was brought up by her sisters. They did their best with her, it's true, but they were no substitute for a mother. My wife was a beautiful woman, that's her portrait over the hearth – delicate in build, not unlike you, madame, and of very fine birth. The Ardleigh name goes back to the Domesday Book but my wife's family was probably more ancient than that; she was a Dinsford, of Kent.' Madame twisted her head to admire the portrait, thereby displaying her long neck. Ardleigh swallowed as his gaze shifted from his wife, whose hair was drawn back under a little cap and whose dainty chin was framed by ruffles, to Madame's naked throat. 'Of course, whatever else you teach Asa, you won't have to bother with French. She's already fluent, ain't you, Asa? Asa was in France for a couple of months with her sister. Came back every inch the French woman.'

Madame's great eyes now concentrated upon Asa. 'When were you in France, mademoiselle?'

'Nearly five years ago. I accompanied my sister Philippa on her wedding trip.'

'And did you like my country?'

'I found it extraordinary.' Asa's heart was beating violently. Madame nodded, as if satisfied with the description.

'She came back with her head full of revolutionary nonsense, didn't you, Asa?' said her father. 'We heard nothing from you for months except tirades about equality and justice. She won't even condemn the brutes for executing King Louis. And I should warn you, madame, that my daughter is rarely in the house; always trotting about the countryside on some cause or another. And she's

119

an abolitionist, doesn't allow a grain of sugar or a spoonful of coffee in the house in case they're the products of slave labour.'

Madame's smile was like the play of firelight on the skin. 'I knew already that your daughter was a force to be reckoned with. It seems to me she dealt very well with the disturbance that occurred today in your village.'

'Disturbance, eh? I heard there'd been some kind of nonsense.'

'You must speak to those boys, Father,' said Asa. 'I dread to think what might have happened if the tailor had shown his face.'

'They meant no harm,' said the squire, splashing more wine into his glass.

'What business is it of theirs if Mrs Dacre shouts at her husband sometimes?'

'Let me be the judge of when to interfere with my own tenants.'

'Father, this can't be ignored. The Dacres must have been very frightened.'

'As I've said, Asa, leave it to me.'

Madame's glance flashed between father and daughter. 'I have not tasted the pears cooked in honey before. The effect is delicious. Is the fruit perhaps from your own orchard?'

Harmony was restored. The squire smiled at Madame, a flash of the old gallant who had swept the high-born, gentle-eyed Miss Dinsford off her feet, as he extolled the virtues of the Ardleigh orchard. Soon Madame said that she was exhausted and would retire, if nobody minded. After she'd gone, the squire pushed back his chair and splayed his legs, a signal that Asa was no longer required. She retreated to the parlour fire and her mother's nursing chair. Boards in the ceiling shifted as Madame walked about upstairs. It was as if her little figure had such density that the ancient timbers of the manor might not withstand her.

Within reach of Asa's hand was a locked bureau; the key hung on a chain round her neck. There she kept her housekeeping notebooks, her newspaper clippings about the Revolution in France, her diaries and her letters from Didier. His last, discussed exhaustively with Caroline, dated August 1792 after a gap of six months, had forbidden further correspondence. Mail was being intercepted and read, he said, and letters to and from England might lead to his arrest. France had declared itself in a state of danger. Enemies were hovering on the borders waiting to march through the provinces, scoop up counter-revolutionary support and enter Paris in order to liberate the king and overthrow the Revolution.

My dearest Thomasina, he concluded, *it breaks my heart to write thus to you. I shall never forget you, and perhaps some day, in our brave new future, we will be together again. Mais pour le moment, silence entre nous. Je pense à toi.*

Silence entre nous. His words had seemed like a shrug: I can do no more. But with Madame in the house, this elfin emissary from France, Asa found renewed hope. Surely Didier would never give up. She took out his first letter, dated 14 July 1788. It had been waiting for her at Ardleigh, at the end of the ponderous journey home from France with the Mortons. The handwriting on the envelope, a reckless scrawl, had stopped her heart:

Good God, Thomasina, where are you? I stand outside your hotel. I wait in my room thinking you are bound to come. I pace the streets. I tear my hair. I cannot sleep. I cannot bear the sight of my own pillow because your head used to lie on it...

And on the 17th:

You are more present to me in your absence than when you were here. God, when I think of the lost opportunities. I should have snatched you from your hotel room and married you there and then. Write to me. Tell me all your thoughts...

After another week, in reply to hers:

Yes. I said we would be married. We will be married. You must be my wife. You are my darling, my exquisite English mademoiselle. If I could, if I had the means, I would turn up at your door and go down on my knees...

A cruel letter, this last, because for months afterwards, whenever a horseman passed through the village or there was a knock on the door, Asa had expected him. How could he exist without her, when she found it well nigh impossible to draw breath without him?

And now, Madame de Rusigneux. The bedsprings above Asa's head creaked. Madame would be lying between unfamiliar sheets, watching a moonbeam float across the rafters. What filled her head? What dreadful memories or yearning for home?

Chapter Six

Next day Madame arranged herself at a table in the parlour, feet pressed together, back straight, hair tucked demurely beneath a plain cap as she drew a piece of paper from a hidden pocket. It was a list in Georgina's dashing hand and included the following: *Posteure and diportment, table manners, etiquette, conversation, entering a room, fine sewing, dance, all tipes, dress, music. And don't forget painting.*

'So,' said Madame de Rusigneux, 'I have compiled a programme of study for the first week. After that we shall see.' Another slip of paper appeared, this time in a flowing, continental script: *Day the First. 1. Posture. From standing to sitting. 2. The hair. The Dress. 3. The portrait in miniature. 4. The use of the fan. 5. The dance.*

It felt to Asa as if the jaws of a trap had opened. At the end of this road lay Shackleford. And yet Madame was so poignant in her smallness, her determination to perform her role, that she could not easily be rebuffed. 'It's unlikely I shall have time for this, today or any day,' said Asa, touching Madame's hand apologetically. The French

123

woman's fingers contracted and for a moment she closed her eyes.

'Madame, you and I must reach an understanding. My sisters have one idea of my future, I another. They believe there is some urgency for me to marry because if Father were to die I would have to leave Ardleigh and become dependent on them. My own plans for the future don't include marriage.'

Madame received this news as if it was a considerable blow. 'Could you tell me, what are these plans?'

'I hope to earn a living by teaching, once Father no longer needs me. My friend, Miss Lambert, and I are going to run a school.'

Everything about the French woman was precise; the fringe of her eyelashes, the neat ears, the cut of her fingernails. 'Well then, I think we might reach a compromise which would suit us both. Don't you see, mademoiselle, there's much I could teach you that would be of use in the future you describe.'

By midday they had arrived at a truce. Asa had spent the intervening hours pretending business to prove her point; rarely had the servants been chivvied into such a flurry of activity, from window cleaning to the sorting and slicing of apples. Meanwhile Madame had set up a work station by the window in the parlour. She brought down a battered leather portmanteau which Asa would later come to regard as having magical properties, so many and varied were the items that emerged from it. On this occasion out came a roll of cloth containing all the materials needed for the painting of a miniature: a set of brushes so fine they were composed of only a few hairs, a fragment of parchment, a couple of charcoals and a magnifying glass.

On being made aware that Madame de Rusigneux had a rare skill with the paintbrush, Georgina had suggested that she take Asa's likeness so that it could be shown off in London, to Shackleford or other suitable young men. It seemed to Asa that she might as well read while Madame made sketches for the miniature – that way both would be occupied without actually having to comply with Georgina's programme of education – so she pretended to be absorbed by an edition of the *Analytical Review*. Madame attended so fiercely to her drawing, however, that Asa's thoughts scattered like feathers.

'When did you learn to draw, madame?'

A long pause while Madame performed a number of tiny strokes. 'When I was a child.'

'Is it normal for a lady to paint miniatures in France?'

A similarly prolonged silence, during which Asa's question, in all its unintended impertinence, ricocheted from wall to wall. 'Why, do ladies not paint in England?'

'Some have lessons, yes. But few ladies, myself included, can paint with any degree of success.'

At this Madame smiled; a flash of sunshine. It occurred to Asa that Madame de Rusigneux was unlikely to have had much cause to smile in recent years and that the precision with which her clothes, limbs and hair were arranged, far from reflecting some inner calm, might be an effort at self-control.

'The last few years must have been turbulent for you, madame,' Asa said softly, in French.

'Turbulent.' Intense concentration on tiny strokes. 'Ah, if you only knew.'

'Can you bear to speak of it?'

Although Madame said nothing her entire upper body inclined towards the drawing so that Asa could no longer see her face, only the white cap and mass of dark hair. 'My family is scattered. My parents are in Switzerland. My brother is dead.'

'And your husband?'

'I have no husband. You must understand. My name... I am so afraid.'

'Forgive me, madame, that was very clumsy of me.'

They were now interrupted by a hammering at the door; Mrs Woodcock, the blacksmith's wife, begged to see Asa at once. 'You'd best come to Key Cottage.'

Half the village was hurrying towards the tailor's house. The wind had dropped but there was a flurry of sleet as the small crowd at the cottage gate stood aside to let Asa pass. The door, which yesterday had been shut fast, swung wide open. In the days of previous tenants there'd been a row of decorated plates along the hearth and a blazing fire fed, no doubt, by logs pilfered from woods belonging to the manor. Now the hearth was empty except for a few desolate cooking implements. Under the window sat the tailor's work table, although there was no sign of scissors or pins. Otherwise the cottage was bare.

'They're cutting him down, I expect,' said Mrs Woodcock. They went through to the yard in which the tailor had hanged himself using a makeshift rope constructed of fabric odds and ends knotted together and slung over the branch of the beech tree that thrust over the wall from the manor house garden. The blacksmith had climbed up on a stool, probably the same as that employed by the tailor to reach the noose, and was attempting to encircle the body in his arms. He recoiled as it swung round suddenly and Asa glimpsed Dacre's dead face.

'What do we do now?' asked Mrs Woodcock, as her husband laid the corpse on a plank.

Sleet spattered against the man's cheeks. His dull eyes were wide open, as if in surprise.

'We must lay him out,' said Asa.

They all squeezed back inside, first the men with the makeshift bier, then Judith Woodcock and Asa. Clustered in the main doorway, thereby rendering the interior darker than ever, were Mrs Dean and other servants from the manor. Asa directed that the tailor be laid on his rickety work table and his body covered with a strip of cambric taken from a roll they found underneath. When she attempted to close his eyes her little finger skimmed the globe of his eyeball. Springing back, she noticed for the first time that Madame de Rusigneux was standing just inside the door leading to the bedchamber, her cloak wrapped about her so closely that only the pale shape of her face was visible. She was staring not at the dead man, whose feet in their large, misshapen shoes pro-

127

truded so lamentably, but at Asa. In other circumstances her alien presence might have drawn considerably more hostility; certainly it explained why the manor-house servants had not allowed themselves to be pressed inside.

'How was the tailor found?' Asa asked.

'I was passing and saw the cottage door was open,' said Mrs Woodcock, 'and no smoke from the chimney.'

'Where is Mrs Dacre?'

'No idea.' Judith Woodcock's voice had gone small and brittle. Mrs Dacre, then, had been cast as the villain who had caused this death. But what had been the timing of the tragic events in this cottage? Was the tailor hanging even as the boys burnt his effigy on the pyre or had he waited until dead of night? And was it before or after the departure of his wife? Could any woman be so heartless as to leave the house knowing that her husband was swinging from the branch of a beech tree?

'Surely the charivari wouldn't be enough to cause a man to hang himself,' said Asa. 'Was there anything else, do you suppose?'

'They was poor.'

'Many people are poor.'

Judith's face closed up. 'The poor gets themselves into all kinds of difficulties, Miss Ardleigh. Such that *you* could not imagine.'

'What now?' said the blacksmith, wiping his hands on his leather apron.

'A man must be sent to fetch my father,' said Asa, shaken by what Judith had said. 'I believe he's trying a new horse on the Downs. And I will

128

send to Pulborough for Dr Clegg. In the meantime we must shut up the cottage and two men must watch the door.'

With Madame at her shoulder Asa walked swiftly home, issuing orders that more men should be sent to find Mrs Dacre. When everyone had gone she crouched by the parlour fire and warmed her icy hands. I must wash them, she thought, remembering the dry convexity of the tailor's eyeball.

Madame de Rusigneux had resettled by the window and picked up her charcoal. Neither spoke. Only as Asa left the room did she notice that Madame must have been violently affected by what they had seen because her hand had jolted, causing an ugly black line to scrawl across the sketch of Asa's face.

'Madame?'

The French woman's eyes were shot with pain. 'I was so sure, I had prayed, that I had left such terrible events behind.'

Chapter Seven

Thirty miles away another crisis was unfolding. Philippa Morton had been brought to bed nearly a month early with her fourth child, so that even as tailor Dacre was cut down from the beech tree, coachmen were driving towards Ardleigh posthaste in order to carry Asa back to Morton Hall. They arrived at seven in the evening just as the squire was returning from Key Cottage, where, as local magistrate, he'd inspected the scene and spoken with the vicar about an appropriate spot outside the churchyard for the burial of the corpse.

'There's never any peace,' he muttered as one boot after the other went flying along the hall. 'And now you're telling me you have to be off, Asa. Does no one think of me?' He covered his eyes with the back of his hand.

Or me? Asa thought, marching upstairs to pack a bag. Does anyone ever consider the disruption to my life? First, in went books – Diderot, Rousseau, Ronsard – but her heart ached as she covered them with slippers and petticoats. Already she anticipated the constraint of limbs and mind that would come upon her tomorrow as she arrived at Morton Hall and from which there'd be no release until she was home again. Next she knocked on Madame de Rusigneux's door and told her that she would have to remain at Ardleigh because these days Mr Morton, a former visitor to France and whose house was filled with French objets d'art, could not bring himself to mention that nation without a whitening of the lips.

Madame listened in silence but at five the next morning was in the hall, portmanteau packed.

'Madame,' said Asa, 'I told you last night, there's no question of you coming with me. The children will need all my attention. And then, as I said ... you would not be welcome ... you are French. My father, I'm sure, would enjoy your company here.'

Madame gave Asa such a look of wounded confusion that the idea of leaving her at Ardleigh now seemed preposterous. Cursing Georgina first for sending Madame, then for rendering herself unavailable for sisterly duties at Morton Hall by the fact that she was always far too busy, and anyway (as Georgina herself exclaimed with a burst of girlish laughter), what *use* would she be either to Philippa or her brood, Asa hammered on her father's door. 'We're leaving. Madame de Rusigneux will come with me after all.'

He grunted and appeared with his shirt half stuffed into his breeches. 'Send my best to Phil.'

'Perhaps you'll ride over for a visit once the baby is born. And Father, promise me you'll pursue those village lads over the charivari. And that you'll keep looking for Mrs Dacre.'

'I'll do what's right.'

'Father, it must be done today. Don't put it off.'

'Mind your own business, Asa.' He ran his palm across his bleary face, then relented and held out his arm. 'You're a good girl, one of the best, but you carry the weight of the world on these little shoulders of yours. Now run along to Morton and have some fun.'

During the drive Asa was at first too preoccupied to take much notice of Madame. The coach was travelling in entirely the wrong direction. Today Caroline was expecting her in Littlehampton but there'd been no time for more than a brief note to explain her absence. She had been looking forward to discussing the French woman's arrival and the disturbing events at Key Cottage. Particularly haunting was the fact that the tailor had ended his life only a few feet away from the philanthropic Miss Ardleigh's parlour.

But after a while Asa was ashamed to realise that Madame, who was pressed into a corner, was watching her intently, as a whipped puppy might. 'You must have a very low opinion of Ardleigh, madame. You've been here only two days yet so many distressing things have happened.'

'It's true. But when I met your sister in London she gave me to understand that you needed to be shown how to behave like a lady. Mademoiselle Ardleigh, I think many ladies would have a great deal to learn from you.'

'Thank you, madame, but I do regret that you have witnessed such violence in our village given that you must have endured so much already in your own country.'

'Mademoiselle Ardleigh, I have seen things in France that make your banging of pans and tormenting of a poor man hardly of significance at all.'

'The world, at the moment, seems out of sorts,' said Asa. 'How has it happened when in the Paris of 1788 we were all so full of hope? I remember the day an edict was issued suspending laws of censorship on pamphlets and books. Afterwards we were forever trampling on papers which had been written in a rush of excitement, begging for change. And now we hear that censorship is to be reimposed.'

'Ah yes. Those were good times.'

'What were you were doing in the summer of '88, madame?'

'I was at home with my family.'

'And where is your home?'

Pause. 'My home is in the south of France.'

'In a village or a town?'

'A small town. Frenelle.'

'What sort of house did you live in, madame?'

'The sort of house that in France we call a chateau.'

'And what is Frenelle like, since the Revolution?'

'Frenelle is a home no more. What we never understood is that change is a monster. A people that had no voice seized a voice for itself and then, when all its demands were not met, resorted to pike and stone and flame.' Another silence. 'The Revolution has discovered that the only way to prolong its life is to crush those who oppose it.'

'There must be another way, madame. I still believe that good will prevail. The people I met in Paris were so fine.'

'People change. Power, politics, money, those things make people change. Sometimes small hatreds such as we saw yesterday can determine the fate of thousands.'

Madame, swathed in her dark cloak, took up scarcely any space at all, yet it seemed to Asa that the vastness of her experience filled the carriage. 'You are an exile,' she said softly. 'Were you in such danger that you were forced to leave the country?'

Madame closed her tortured eyes and shrank deeper into the cushions. 'Memory. The memory was too much for me.'

'Memory, madame?'

'They murdered my brother.'

Madame said no more. Her fingers gripped the handle of her portmanteau, as if it gave her strength, as the carriage swung between the imposing gateposts of Morton Hall and clattered along the avenue of sapling poplars.

There could have been few houses of medium size that provided a greater contrast, one with another, than Ardleigh Manor and Morton Hall. Although Ardleigh had retained the name *Manor* it was in fact a small-windowed rabbit warren of an ancient place, with narrow staircases, crooked passageways and rooms far too low ceilinged ever to be fashionable. John Morton, on the other hand, had built a mansion in the classical style: airy, warm, long-windowed and with a gracious entrance hall from which rose a swirl of staircase. The furniture was mahogany and newly bought, including a modern type of piano with eight octaves which nobody at Morton Hall could play, the hangings were of delicate pastels, and the ornaments judiciously selected during the fateful honeymoon in France.

The two older boys, John and Edward, came hurtling down to greet Asa but stopped short at the sight of Madame de Rusigneux, who, suddenly roguish, knelt, opened her portmanteau and tilted her head to indicate that the children should come closer. 'I have little presents for you,' she whispered, producing a paper of sugared almonds for the younger, a little fan for the older. 'Look.' She demonstrated how the rosebud painted on its creases unfurled into a full-blown flower as the fan was opened. 'You must take great care

134

of it,' she said, placing it in John's palm, 'but then you seem to me a very careful boy.'

Morton threw open the door of his library, hands outstretched: five years of marriage had thickened his paunch and given him an air of a man who had entirely moulded the world to his purpose. 'Our Thomasina is here so all will be well.'

'May I present my new companion, Madame de Rusigneux,' said Asa.

Morton halted, stared and managed a formal bow while Madame extinguished herself so that she was a blue shadow beside her bag. A footman was ordered to escort her to the housekeeper's parlour. 'You and I, Thomasina,' said Morton, 'will take our tea in the library.'

Books at Morton Hall had been bought by the yard. Some of the leather-bound volumes were unreadable, others incomprehensible, being in languages nobody understood. Asa was instructed to sit in front of the desk while Morton lowered his voice, as if surrounded by spies. 'I should have made it crystal clear – I won't countenance a French woman in this house. I was opposed to her employment in the first place but my dear wife convinced me that I would never have to meet her.'

'Then Madame de Rusigneux and I shall have to go home. I didn't want her either, Mr Morton, but here she is.'

'She's French.'

'Not all French are violent revolutionaries, sir.'

'You are quite wrong. We were all deceived. In Paris I thought they were capable of greatness.'

Their eyes met briefly as they recalled the potency of that Parisian summer; the flutter of gowns at Versailles and the pamphleteers in the Palais Royal. 'But look at what they did to their king. I shall never trust the French again.'

'My companion is an aristocrat, surely the very reverse of our enemy since she came to England seeking refuge. Georgina believes she is a marsquise.'

Morton nodded and took an unhappy sip of tea. 'That, I suppose, is something.'

'How is Philippa?'

Irritation was replaced by anxiety. 'Very ill. I've never seen her like this, already more than a day in labour and no sign of the child. I hope when she sees you she'll be calmer.' He looked so much like a frightened boy that Asa could not help loving him. 'If the French woman must be here she shall have no contact with the children. We are at war. The maids are whispering that we may be invaded at any moment. I don't want her talking to my boys about France or anything at all. They wouldn't be able to sleep at night.'

As soon as John Morton had decreed that Madame should be given a room on the third floor and would eat her meals apart, Asa hurried upstairs to see her sister. Hitherto, Philippa had delivered her infants as efficiently as she managed everything else; this time it was different. The local midwife, fetched in haste at the start of labour, had detected an abnormality in the baby's position, and the London physician was shaking his head and applying poultices. Philippa had the strength only to squeeze Asa's hand and give her

136

a flicker of a grateful smile.

As she kissed her sister's forehead, Asa felt a flash of rage at John Morton for putting her through such an ordeal again. Three sons were surely enough to secure the Morton empire. Death in childbirth was a family weakness, after all. How terrified Philippa must be, each time, to remember the day of Asa's birth.

Asa supervised the children's bedtime and dined with Morton, who lived by the tenet that if one kept up the appearance of normality, normality would prevail. Later she climbed to the upper reaches of the house, looking for Madame de Rusigneux, but the narrow passageway, which still smelt faintly of new timber and was lined on both sides by closed doors, defeated her. There was no response when Asa called Madame's name.

Downstairs, in her own bedchamber, she strode from window to hearth, hung about outside Philippa's door and met her brother-in-law, also in his robe, pacing the hall. While his fears doubtless centred on the fate of his beloved wife, Asa was ashamed that her own were compounded by the knowledge that if Philippa died, care of the motherless boys would devolve to her. Bitterly she reflected that a couple of days ago the only threat to her liberty had been the arrival of an unknown French woman; furious with herself, she tried to suppress any thought but passionate prayer for her sister's survival. Life simply could not go on without Philippa, a woman who dealt with difficulties by attending to the small things, who used to bustle about Ardleigh, aged fifteen, with little Asa perched on her hip because there was no money for a nursemaid. Philippa, queen of detail, of little domestic comforts that transformed life from possible to pleasurable, and who had embraced marriage like a general who'd spent years kicking his heels at home and suddenly been sent on a triumphant campaign.

By five the next morning there had still been no birth. The maids and children woke and the household rolled on into the day. The housekeeper begged for an interview with Asa to discuss the menus and whether the seamstress should come as arranged to fit the oldest boy for a new coat. As it was raining the children couldn't go out and their squabbling penetrated the newly constructed walls of the house. Morton removed his wig and ran his hand through his few remaining hairs. The baby remained unborn. Philippa, glimpsed from the bedroom door, was unconscious, her breathing laboured and her face ashen. In desperation Asa ordered that the nursemaid should take the boys out, rain or no rain, visit every part of the gardens, and then give them hot baths; anything to remove them from underfoot. Afterwards she paced about wondering how she could call herself a modern woman when she was helpless in the face of such a simple matter as childbirth, and how, in this age of reason and revolution, they should all be incapable of saving her sister.

This time when she arrived at the narrow staircase leading to the attic she was more persistent and knocked on one door after another until she came to what must surely have been the smallest room in the house with its high round window and lack of fireplace. Perched on the edge of a narrow bed, wrapped in a shawl and a blanket, Madame de Rusigneux was absorbed in writing a letter.

'Madame.' So extreme was Madame's reaction – she started violently and dropped her pen – that Asa was shocked into tears. 'I thought you would want to know about my sister. The baby will not come. The doctor suggests the use of forceps but the midwife says there is an obstruction which means that such a delivery is out of the question.' Noticing belatedly that Madame's fingertips were blue she added: 'You should come down. I'll find you somewhere with a fire. Forgive me, I had no idea they'd given you this room.'

Madame put aside her letter, straightened her shoulders, as if having made a momentous decision, stood up and smoothed her skirts. 'Perhaps I could help. It is the custom sometimes in France for ladies to be present during each other's births.'

What on earth did Madame think she could do for Philippa when an experienced doctor and midwife had all but given up? 'I don't think Mr Morton will let you near his wife,' Asa said at last. 'He's suspicious because of the Revolution.' She smiled ruefully to show Madame that she did not share Morton's views.

Madame made no comment but the situation was so desperate it would surely be wrong to refuse any offer of help. 'I'll try to persuade him,' said Asa. The next moment they were in Morton's library and he was shouting, as predicted, that over his dead body would Madame lay hands on his wife. The French woman was unflinching, so that perhaps he felt, as Asa now did, that her foreignness might be their salvation and even providential. Besides, they all knew there was nothing to lose.

Morton took the stairs to Philippa's bedchamber three at a time and introduced Madame as a woman who 'might know something'. The room was broiling hot – a fire raged in the hearth, and the windows and curtains were shut. A maid cowered by the fireplace while the midwife bathed Philippa's neck and chest. After a few moments of hissed protest the doctor stamped downstairs shouting that he could not be responsible for the consequences, he had been ousted at the very moment when he was definitely going to intervene, and in heaven's name who was this foreigner, this witch, who had beguiled them all?

Madame threw open curtains and shutters so that a gust of wintry air fell on Philippa's face and her eyelids fluttered. The maid was ordered to reboil the water. The midwife, who had proved herself clean and capable during Philippa's other deliveries, was shaken by the hand. Madame de Rusigneux then turned to Asa, who was clutching the corner of Philippa's sheet as if it were a lifeline. 'Mademoiselle Ardleigh, perhaps you might accompany Monsieur Morton downstairs. This room is quite small and we are many.'

Asa got no farther than the top step, where she perched while Morton went down to pacify the doctor.

After two hours they were called back. Philippa had been delivered of a pallid creature, to be called Kate, who squirmed in the crook of her mother's arm, mouth agape like that of a fledgling. Asa knelt beside her sister so that they were cheek to cheek, as in the old days at Ardleigh. 'A daughter at last,' murmured Philippa. 'Your new companion is a remarkable woman. I cannot believe that it was Georgina who discovered her.'

Chapter Eight

A fortnight later the Warrens arrived to view their new niece. Warren, dressed in eye-wateringly tight breeches and high boots, took one cautious look at the baby and backed away, muttering that he'd best keep Morton company in the library. The three sisters were therefore left alone: Philippa reclined in bed, infant at her breast (Madame de Rusigneux, whose word on these matters was now law, advocated maternal breastfeeding for at least six months), Asa sat by the window and Georgina, decked out in unseasonable sky-blue muslin and with her hair gummed, padded and powdered to form a helmet of curls and ringlets, flitted between dressing table and mirror.

Little Kate was declared adorable but shouldn't she be eating gruel or some such, she was so pale and puny? Philippa looked as if she had been put through the wringer, Georgina added. 'And how is our French companion? I don't see much evidence that she has transformed you, Asa. Where is she?'

'Painting in the blue parlour, I expect.'

'We're not paying her five pounds a year to indulge her love of painting.'

'She saved my life,' murmured Philippa, stroking her daughter's head.

'She's not paid to be a midwife either.' Georgina, who professed herself relieved that she'd never had to endure childbirth, hadn't the stomach to hear more than the briefest account of how Philippa, even at the point of death, had been hauled from the bed by the French woman and the midwife, and marched up and down from hearth to window, though her legs buckled and she had to be supported. Doctors were an abomination, Madame de Rusigneux and the midwife had agreed during the course of these perambulations, what with their dirty hands and their sketchy knowledge of female anatomy. And then Philippa had been made to kneel on all fours, like a cow...

'Enough,' said Georgina, opening a little fan of their mother's depicting a pair of lovers cavorting under a tree, which she wore attached to her wrist so she wouldn't lose it. 'I just thank the Lord that all ended well. I can't understand why you require more babies, Phil. You have no idea what you put me through each time. I was there, remember, when our mother was in childbed with Asa.'

After a moment's silence Philippa said, 'We cannot arrange everything to save your nerves, Georgina. In any case all was well, thanks to Madame.'

142

'My point is that Madame de Rus ... Rusa... Rusigny is paid to educate Asa, not to footle about with her paintbrushes. She tells me you won't even sit still long enough for her to finish your portrait, Asa, so that's no good. And she's achieved nothing, I presume, in terms of improving your manners, not to mention your appearance. Look at you.' Her round eyes raked Asa's face as if she expected her sister's features to have become more regular since Madame de Rusigneux's advent.

'I've been occupied with the children,' Asa replied.

'Madame should be helping you. It would do those boys good to pick up a little French.'

The truth was that Madame was still kept apart from the children. Since her intervention in Kate's birth she had been allotted, at Morton's command, a guest room on the first floor and the use of Philippa's parlour. She also joined the family for meals, during which Morton took pains to involve her in conversation though he still could not bring himself to mention the enemy, France. But far from gaining the trust of the household, she was regarded by some with even more suspicion than at first. The doctor's cry, that she must be a witch, had done immeasurable damage, so that the maids were caught whispering in corners and the nursemaid pulled the children away. As Asa's duties allowed no time for deportment lessons, Madame spent hours alone in the parlour, where she might be glimpsed through the half-open door, head bent over her work. Whenever she could, Asa would look in to ensure the fire was burning well or to admire her companion's progress. Each day Madame painted a different vignette of the children – always an approximation, as she said, because of course they would not model for her. The resulting pictures were whimsical; cherubic little boys playing ball by the fountain, clustered in order of height on the stairs or slumbering, their heads pillowed on their hands.

Georgina sighed. 'I suppose I shall have to organise everything, as usual. The fact is,' dramatic pause, 'I have invited a surprise visitor to Morton Hall. We can expect him at Easter.'

Poor Kate was jolted from Philippa's breast. 'Easter is barely a month away. I shall scarcely be out of bed. Whoever can you mean?'

Georgina perched on a stool, leaned her elbows on the dressing table and gazed fondly at herself in the mirror. 'I met with Mr Shackleford again. Isn't that a coincidence? I said that you and Mr Morton would be bound to want him to call since we are all gathered together. What an opportunity for him to become acquainted with the Ardleigh side of his family all at once, I said. It's far better for him to meet Asa again here – you have nothing to be ashamed of at Morton.'

'There's no question of Mr Shackleford visiting at present. The household cannot stand any more disruption. If he does come, it must be when I am back on my feet. You have no right to treat this house as your own, Georgina.'

'Well, it's done now,' her sister replied, playing with her curls and turning her face from side to side to admire the effect, 'so we must all work hard to make the right impression. We have to

144

catch Mr Shackleford before he's had a chance to look about for a richer bride.'

'If he's as eligible as you seem to think I don't see why he would choose Asa at all,' said Philippa, patting her baby's back. 'I was not at my best in Paris, it's true, but I don't remember there being any firm signs of an attachment between them. After all, Ardleigh will be his whether he marries her or not.'

'Family name,' said Georgina triumphantly. 'The Shackleford fortune is built on trade – sugar, glass and the like. Our name is in the Domesday Book and Mr Shackleford could not have been friendlier to me. He seemed to be positively angling for an invitation. He will be staying with friends near Cobham before Easter, which is why I invited him to call on us here.'

'*Before* Easter? When exactly?'

'We made no firm engagement so we must be prepared for all eventualities. I'll attend to Asa's wardrobe and Madame will have to work on her manners.'

'You talk about Asa as if she were not in the room,' said Philippa, glancing belatedly at her younger sister. 'I have agreed with you all along that we must consider her future but we have no right to coerce her into marriage.'

'Thank you,' said Asa.

'Don't worry, my Asa,' said Philippa, 'nobody will force you to marry anyone you can't abide. As if they could.'

In the formal garden a dark-cloaked figure skimmed across the frosted lawn and slipped through a gap in the privet hedge; Madame de

145

Rusigneux on her daily walk.

'Philippa is quite right. You're wasting your time, Georgina,' Asa said without turning from the window. 'I refuse to marry this Shackleford.'

'How can you say that when you haven't seen him in years?'

'I am completely opposed to him. I will not, in any way, be associated with money made through slaving.'

'I wonder, then, that you consent to spend another minute in this house,' Georgina remarked triumphantly. 'With all due respect to your Mr Morton, I bet he has plenty of interests in the West Indies, Phil?'

Philippa patted her child's back and wouldn't reply, it being one of her oft-repeated maxims that a woman should never intervene in her husband's affairs. Exasperated, Georgina shook out the many frills on her skirt. 'If you marry Shackleford, you'll be able to influence him, Asa. Look at what I've done with my Geoffrey.'

There was a significant pause during which Philippa could not help catching Asa's eye.

Stifling a smile, she said, 'Our main consideration should be what is best for Asa.'

'Shackleford is the obvious choice,' insisted Georgina. 'And, as I said, it seemed to me that he was extraordinarily eager to come here.'

'I won't marry him,' Asa said, heading for the door. 'I refuse to be a sacrificial lamb. You need not worry about my future. If Father dies, I'll go and live with Caroline.'

Georgina laughed. 'Wonderful. The pair of you won't have a ha'p'orth to rub together.'

Morton Hall was full of discord – a distant wail in the nursery, Warren shouting in the library: '...I'm not asking you to commit yourself; for God's sake...' as Asa dashed along the passage to her own bedchamber, where she stood with her palms pressed to her forehead. She could hear the pounding of hoof-beats; Shackleford's horse on the drive, Shackleford bearing down on her.

After a moment she opened her writing case and sat, pen in hand. She must act to break this impasse which had her at the beck and call of her sisters. Now, surely, she should write to Didier and tell him she had run out of time. But still she hesitated over the page. What would be the consequences for Didier of receiving a letter from England?

Or perhaps, she thought, plunging her nib into the ink bottle, all this time I have been a coward; perhaps Didier has been waiting for me to make a move. He hasn't sent for me to go to France because he doesn't want to put me in danger. Of course he has been silent – out of love for me.

So she wrote:

I will come to you, before it is too late. I would rather a million times be with you in France, whatever the risks, than without you here in England. Please, send for me. The pain of being parted from you is sharper now even than on the day I left Paris. Then, I had hope. Now, all that is left is the shadow of a dream of you. I grieve, night and day, for what might have been...

She sealed the letter, addressed it to the rue du Vieux Colombier, flung on her cloak and hood, raced down the servants' stairs and let herself out of the house.

It was over a fortnight since she had stepped beyond the gates of Morton Hall. With Easter barely five weeks away, specks of new life had begun to appear in the hedgerows, a tinge of green on the blackthorn. For years, it seemed, she had been waiting for this moment, when love would take charge again. And now she was in the grip of the old madness it felt wonderful; the violent assault on the heart and nerves, the rush of desire.

When she reached the town she walked demurely, head down, aware that Guildford would be full of Philippa's acquaintances. As it was, the post office clerk scrutinised first the letter, then Asa. 'Do you know, I've gone months with nobody sending a letter more than thirty mile and now I have two ladies corresponding with France in one afternoon.'

The other lady in question, thought Asa, could well be Madame, posting or collecting a letter from home. If so, she might still be in the town. It would be good to have a little company, even perhaps to share confidences about Georgina's expectations. But there was no sign of Madame in the High Street and certainly Asa had not passed her in the lane. For a while she dawdled, going from one shop window to the next, sniffing woodsmoke and occasionally glimpsing the interior of a snug parlour. Perhaps her sudden melancholy was provoked by being on the outside of so many lives, but now she felt drained and hopeless. The letter would never reach Didier and even if it did he would not reply. She pictured a loveless future, locked in bitter struggle with her family.

It had grown much colder. Asa began the walk home along Quarry Street, past the church where her aunt, cause of the momentous meeting between Philippa and Morton, was buried. It would be remiss of her to go by without at least pausing by the small white cross marking her grave. But as she opened the lychgate she realised that she was not alone; a woman lingered just outside the church, perhaps trying to decide whether or not to enter. Asa was about to call out – there was no mistaking that trim figure in its dark hood – but then she noticed that Madame was actually standing with her face to the porch wall, forehead pressed to stone. Her fist, in which was clutched a paper of some kind, struck the wall twice and she gave a low sob.

Asa crept closer, put out her hand and softly touched her companion's shoulder. 'Dear Madame...'

Madame sprang aside, fist raised as if to beat Asa away. *'Vous.'*

'Madame, I just...'

'Laissez-moi. Vous m'avez suivi?'

Asa gabbled in French: *'Je suis désolée. Je ne voulais pas vous faire peur.* And no, of course I wasn't following you. I came to town to post a letter.'

'Aren't there enough servants in the house who would post a letter for you?'

'It was a private letter. I certainly wasn't following you. Believe me, I just happened to see you. Forgive me.'

Madame rose to her full height. 'There is nothing to forgive.' She took out a perfectly folded handkerchief and attempted to dry her eyes. 'I should never have come here, to a graveyard. I just wanted to be alone.'

'I understand that need well enough. I'll leave you in peace.'

'This letter forwarded to me from London,' Madame held out the scrunched envelope, 'which today I collected. My brother, my most dear brother... I thought it could not be worse. I thought they had given him a Christian burial at least. Now it seems I cannot be sure.'

'What do you mean, madame?'

'*Excusez-moi*.' Madame again turned her face to the wall and extended her hand as if to keep Asa at bay. '*Mon Dieu*... Already he has endured every possible indignity. And now this. I cannot bear it.' She clenched her arms about her waist and doubled up as she sobbed again. 'To allow him no decent burial – as if he were a common criminal or a traitor. *Mon frère*. Gabriel.'

'Who has done this to him? What happened?'

'All priests had to sign an oath of loyalty to the new constitution of France. My brother would not sign because he thought there might come a time when he would be compromised. And yet he loved the Revolution; he prayed for reform constantly. They killed him because he chose to put his service to God before his service to the Revolution.'

'Who is *they*? Who killed him?'

150

'Marat. Danton. Their followers. Those fanatics who believe that every person in France must think exactly the same.'

'Surely, madame, the whole point of the Revolution is that people should be free to live and think as they wish.'

'I wish I had never been born. It is my fault. I summoned my brother to Paris because I thought I could protect him. I told him that I had friends who would look after him. Instead, he walked into a trap. Therefore it is I who killed him.'

'But if it was a trap, how could you have known?'

'I thought I had influence. I behaved like a queen, urging my brother to come. And then I was betrayed by the very person I trusted to save him.'

'I'm sure you acted in the best possible interest of your brother.'

'You know nothing about it. But I tell you, I shall never forgive those evil people and I will not rest until justice has been done.'

'Not evil, surely. You mustn't think that.'

'Don't tell me what to think.'

'Of course not.' Asa tried to take Madame's hand but she shrank away. Her arm was rigid, palm facing Asa to ward her off so that she retreated along the path until she was level with her aunt's grave. When she turned back there was no sign of Madame.

The lane, after the lamplight of the town, was very dark and the cold bit at Asa's throat. From time to time she staggered on clods of frozen mud. Several times she looked behind her, even waited for a few minutes; still no Madame. It was a relief to reach Morton, where the lawns were silvered with moonlight and the pools in the water garden glazed with ice. In the house, Asa raced up three flights of stairs to the nursery, where the children were at tea so that the warm air was scented with jam and hot milk. Seizing the nearest nephew, she nuzzled her cold face in his neck until he squealed with glee and his brothers pestered to be given the same treatment.

Later that evening, at dinner, it was clear that the brothers-in-law must have been arguing about money, since they barely said a word to each other. Seated between them, Madame de Rusigneux was at her most demure, neck and bosom swathed in a white muslin scarf, hair parted and drawn into a plain knot. From time to time Asa attempted to meet her eye but Madame was too busy displaying her exquisite table manners or responding to Warren's gallantries.

Georgina, who had long since learned that the way to please Morton was to admire his wife's housekeeping, commented exhaustively on each dish, the sheen on the silverware, the starch in the napkins. 'Oh, by the way, Asa, where did you go gallivanting off to this afternoon? Little John saw you running down the drive and made a tremendous fuss because he wanted to go out too. You should have taken him.'

Not by a flicker did Madame de Rusigneux, who was eating a lemon cream, show any reaction. 'I had a headache and needed a walk,' Asa replied.

'So did the boys. It was thoughtless of you to be gone so long. Anyway, Madame de Rusigny, there must be no more racketing about the countryside for Asa. I shall take up the reins of the household so you can both concentrate on your lessons. Where will you begin?'

Madame gave one of her unforgettable smiles. 'We will begin,' she said, 'with the fan.'

When the ladies retired to the ivory drawing room Georgina ensconced herself in Philippa's high-backed armchair near the fire and, fiddling with a ribbon tied round the neck of her little dog, said she couldn't wait to watch the first lesson, she might learn something herself. Madame de Rusigneux and Asa occupied either end of a sofa which had been chosen by Morton for its elegant curves rather than its comfort; between them, on the cream and pink Aubusson rug, was the illimitable portmanteau.

A smile played at the corner of Madame de Rusigneux's mouth as she dipped forward and removed from her bag a rounded, elongated box about the length of a woman's forearm, of plain polished wood, wider at the top than the bottom. With expert fingertips, she flipped back the lid to reveal a velvet-lined interior containing a number of black silk fan cases from which she selected two. She then closed the lid and returned the case to her portmanteau.

Like an actress gathering herself for a climactic scene, she waited with the two fans in her lap, her hands resting lightly on the sofa at either side. Georgina held up the dog so that its legs dangled as she blew kisses. But when Madame's gaze met

Asa's the expression in her eyes was entirely at odds with her dainty gestures. It was a plea so passionate, so striking, that Asa's heart lurched: Say nothing about what occurred this afternoon.

Madame loosened the drawstring of a fan case and a fan whispered forth, and then, with an infinitesimal flick of the wrist, was half unfurled in a puff of pre-revolutionary French dust.

Like a proud mama exhibiting her precocious offspring, Madame said: 'Beautiful, is it not?'

With the merest twitch of finger and thumb, she spread out the full semicircle. No wonder she had fled to England, Asa thought; France's austere Revolutionary Assembly would never have tolerated a woman who treated a trinket, albeit a priceless one, with such reverence. Passing the tip of her index finger to and fro, Madame pointed out the glorious detail of piercing on the guard sticks, how the painted silk had been stiffened and varnished with a substance called *vernis Martin,* and how the scene, of an expedition in a balloon above a pre-revolutionary city street, had been contrived so that the red balloon expanded as the fan opened.

When Asa put out her hand Madame withdrew the fan and smiled almost flirtatiously, forcing Asa to move closer so that she could smell the disturbing perfume of Madame's skin; the frosty lane beyond Morton Hall, the churchyard's aroma of earth and stone.

'Let me see,' cried Georgina. 'Well, I must say I've never seen such a wonderful fan. The painting of these figures is as fine as any I've seen in pictures here at Morton.'

154

'Ah,' said Madame, 'but the fan is not to be admired as a painting. A fan's purpose is to enhance the beauty of its bearer. Displayed by itself, it is a dead thing.'

'And how appropriate that a fan should carry the picture of a balloon,' exclaimed Georgina. 'I'd adore to go up in a balloon. Can you imagine? Did you ever see one, madame?'

'I did.'

'Was it like this?

'The balloon I saw trailed ribbons of red, white and blue.'

'The tricolour. So even balloons are in patriotic colours. Is nothing free in France any more?'

'Madame Warren, the balloon itself is a symbol of freedom, or it purports to be so. Our king did not know what he was seeing when he watched the first balloon fly over Versailles.'

'What was he seeing?' whispered Georgina.

'Why, a breaking of boundaries. You see, this fan was painted before the king was deposed. Here ladies and gentlemen in old-fashioned finery parade along an elegant street. And here we have the red balloon, its basket full of sight-seers, floating overhead. In just the same way a balloon once flew over the great palace of Versailles. All that was private was now revealed. All the secrets of the royal household exposed. A king who was thought to have been, until that moment, more a god than a man was shown to require clean linen, stables for his horse and carts to carry away his waste, just like anyone else. How could the king know as he stood watching the balloon that he was looking at a harbinger of such change?'

It was time to begin the lesson. The ballooning fan was folded away and replaced by a much plainer specimen. 'In London,' Madame said, flicking it open to reveal a pattern of scrolls and blue flowers, 'there was once an academy dedicated to the language of the fan. In France, before the Revolution, we ladies used to be taught every nuance, to avoid misunderstandings. For example, if I open the fan and carry it in my left hand, I invite you, Mademoiselle Ardleigh, to come and talk to me.' She looked Asa full in the eye, fluttered the spread fan and smiled so that Asa had no choice but to move closer. 'Above all,' Madame whispered, 'we want there to be no misunderstandings, especially in affairs of the heart.'

'I very much doubt,' Asa murmured, 'that an English gentleman these days would know the subtleties of the fan.'

'Even if one does not know its language precisely, one can comprehend the messages of the fan.' Madame's free hand dropped on to Asa's thigh, where it rested lightly, above layers of petticoat. 'What, for instance, do you suppose a lady might mean when she does this?' With the open fan Madame covered her left ear, half closing her eyes.

'Oh, that's very expressive. I can guess that one,' Georgina chipped in. 'You've a secret.'

'That's exactly what it means. How very clever you are, Madame Warren. And this?' The fan was dropped on to the sofa beside Asa.

Asa picked it up. 'You are offering it to me.'

'I am telling you that we are friends.' Another

156

smile, sweetly apologetic for the bleak moments in the churchyard. 'And now, my dear mademoiselle, if you were to close the fan and hold it next to your heart, you would be telling me that you trust me, and that I have won your love.'

'And what must she do with the fan to attract a lover? That's what I'm most anxious to hear. Do tell,' said Georgina.

'Why, she must close her fan thus, and she must touch it with her other hand, and then he will know that she wants to be near him.' Playfully Madame tapped Asa's chin with the tip of the fan. Her eyelids were half closed, her head thrown back, and there was not a vestige of the weeping woman by the church porch. 'But she must be very careful, because if she holds the fan thus in her left hand, and twirls it round, she will be telling him that she loves not him but another. Thus, as I have said, Madame Warren, you must beware the language of the fan.'

Chapter Nine

Even Philippa, propped against soft pillows in her opulent bedchamber, could not be entirely protected from the tensions induced by the Warrens' continued presence at Morton Hall. Asa's lessons with Madame were constantly interrupted as Georgina rushed about giving needless instructions to the servants and failing to control the restless children. Warren spent his days striding from one room to the next in a sudden fit of purpose-fulness that led him only to a different window. Sometimes he hung about outside the library, hoping for another audience with Morton or to request the loan of a horse, which he rode – awk-wardly – into Guildford from whence he returned red in the face and reeking of alcohol.

Meanwhile the lessons proceeded: deportment, embroidery, French conversation and painting, but not music, as Madame said she could not play well enough to teach Asa anything new, because in her youth, she said, she had concentrated on her art. The lid of the wondrous piano in the music room therefore remained locked, though in the afternoons they danced, following Rameau's manual, with its diagrams of ladies and gentle-men in stiff-skirted coats and gowns posturing as they performed the minuet or the jig. Madame and Asa reverenced, paraded and twirled, hands clasping and unclasping, Madame's arm occa-sionally supporting Asa's waist as she counted out the steps.

Asa's feelings veered from irritation at the waste of time spent dancing, to nervous sympathy when she remembered the scene in the graveyard, to reluctant pleasure at learning new skills and being the subject of so much attention. Madame was an excellent teacher, a stickler for detail with hands so fine and features so expressive that she was fasci-nating to watch. Praise was rare, but if Asa did succeed in performing a complicated sequence of steps she found herself blushing with pleasure.

Though no letter came from France, Caroline Lambert was a regular correspondent. Her main

158

news was that Mrs Dacre, wife of the dead tailor, had been discovered working as a dairymaid some fifteen miles from Ardleigh. Identified by the bundle she kept under her pillow containing the tools of her husband's trade – scissors, pins, measure and needles – she'd been plucked from her pallet in the barn, bundled into a covered wagon and transported to Chichester Gaol, where she now languished on the charge of theft of her husband's property.

However, wrote Caroline, *there are rumours that she will eventually be tried for murder, given that she is supposed to have watched or even assisted her husband in hanging himself and not lifted a finger to save him. When I visited her she refused to speak to me. There is something very disturbing, even sly, about her silence. I said I would write to you, and that you might perhaps visit her, but she made no response at all. Perhaps she will confide in you. She must. You and I know only too well what they do to women who kill their husbands. Perhaps the law is less barbaric than in our youth, but still...*

I think you would agree, Thomasina, that visiting Chichester Gaol is one of the most arduous duties my father ever imposed on us. The sheer hopelessness lowers my spirits – and the dreariness. Today I was more than usually aware of these things because I foresee a time when the prison might become a home from home to me. Father has been warned that he may be arrested because he has refused to dissolve his Abolition Society and is suspected of inciting revolutionary behaviour. Of course, he won't curtail his activities so I doubt he'll be at liberty for long. All in all I very much wish you were home, Thomasina.

Asa had taken this letter outside to the wilderness. Samuel, aged eighteen months, was clasped to her hip while his older brothers picked daffodils for their mama in anticipation of her emergence from confinement the next day. John shouted: 'Look, a horse. Whose is it? I don't know him.' Pounding along the drive was a huge black creature carrying a rider dressed in a coat of forest green.

Shackleford. It must be. Asa seized Edward's hand and shouted to John: 'Let's run.' Headlong down the slope they raced, plunging into the woods, where they played hide and seek until the boys complained of hunger and cold. Fortunately only Asa had heard the servants shouting in the garden or seen Madame de Rusigneux appear at the top of the bank, swathed in a shawl. After staring into the trees for a few moments Madame had raised her hand and turned away.

By the time Asa and the children went back to the house the visitor had gone and Georgina was in a rage with Asa for missing him. Tomorrow, she exclaimed, there would be no escape. Tomorrow, Shackleford was invited to dinner.

The entire household was assembled in the hall to watch Philippa, decked out in a lavish bronze satin gown and supported by her beaming husband, descend the staircase and shake hands solemnly with her servants, many of whom had been up since dawn chopping, baking and roasting for Mistress's first dinner and the advent of an important visitor. Both Asa and the fowls slaughtered for the occasion were to be prettied up to impress Shackleford – Asa in a new gown, the fowls in a sauce of prune and redcurrant.

Asa's dress had been designed by Georgina, sewn by Philippa's seamstress and modified by Madame de Rusigneux. Never had she worn anything so insubstantial. Madame said that hoops and tight corsets were entirely out of fashion; instead the skirt must be supported by petticoats and adorned only with a deep sash beneath a low-cut, gathered bodice, like her own. The entire ensemble felt to Asa as if it might drift away. Even Madame had a new dress, Georgina's cast-off, which she'd painstakingly picked apart and resewn in her favoured style. Under scrutiny from Georgina, who praised the quality of her pin-tucks, Madame said that all French ladies were expert at fine sewing, though generally, she added with a wistful smile, they were not required to make seams.

When Shackleford was announced Asa shrank into the shadows of the ivory drawing room. Even from a distance she could tell that he was leaner than she remembered, his golden hair was un-powdered and he was decked out in a midnight-blue coat, intricately knotted cravat and a perfume that flooded Asa with desire – not for Shackleford, but for the afternoon of their first meeting in Paris, in Madame de Genlis's salon, the gathering of clever, light-hearted people and a hot, appreciative glance from Didier Paulin's blue eyes.

Georgina rushed towards Asa, the panniers of her striped skirt blowing back like sails. 'And this

161

is my dear little sister, Thomasina, who of course you remember.'

Asa would not meet his eye but curtsied low, as she had been taught. She then seated herself demurely and, opening her fan, held it perilously close to her left ear: I want to get rid of you. However, her intention to behave with reserve before Shackleford was forgotten when she saw Philippa enthroned in her habitual chair, fully recovered from the birth, and she could not resist jumping up to kiss her. Every movement, she sensed, was noticed by Shackleford. And he in turn was watched avidly by Georgina.

The shame of it, thought Asa, the shame of being on display like one of Morton's ornamental shepherdesses. The books that Asa had studied with Caroline, her work among the poor, the vigorous walks she had taken on the Downs, above all her precious love affair; all that made up Thomasina was reduced to this muslin-wrapped bag of flesh labelled *Miss Ardleigh, available to the highest bidder.*

At dinner Philippa was restored at last to her place at the far end of the table while Asa sat on Shackleford's right, opposite Georgina, Madame de Rusigneux and Warren. As he was being served, Shackleford said: 'I have been hoping to see you again, Miss Ardleigh, for a very long time.'

She wouldn't look at him.

'We were in Paris, you and I, at an astonishing moment in its history.'

'Indeed we were.'

He was such a powerful presence to her; the

162

scent of him, the glow of his hair filled her with anguish because he was so inextricably linked to the confusion of those last weeks in Paris. Did he remember the miniature orange trees in the atrium of the Montmorency or how he'd stood at the street corner and perhaps seen a cloaked figure dash from the hotel? It ought to have been unlikely – in the intervening five years he was said to have travelled the world. And yet, sitting a few inches from him, Asa sensed that he recalled every single thing about her.

She laid down her spoon, according to Madame's instructions, but did not raise her eyes from the two large buttons on his cuff. 'I understand that I must offer my condolences, Mr Shackleford.'

'You mean the deaths of my father and brother? It was indeed a shock.'

'At least now you will have something to occupy your time.' Asa resumed eating, angry that she had given Shackleford the dubious satisfaction of knowing that she remembered his indolence.

A side of beef was brought to the table and Morton embarked on a favourite subject: his eponymous estates. 'This is our own beef, of course. Famed for its succulence up to twenty miles away. Do you keep beef cattle at Compton Wyatt, Shackleford?'

'I suspect so,' said Shackleford.

Warren laughed sourly. 'It must be something to own so much land you don't even know what type of cattle you have.'

'Hush, Geoffrey, Mr Shackleford's only

163

teasing,' said Georgina, 'but then, Mr Shackleford, you've spent so many years abroad I expect you're scarcely acquainted with your own home. I've heard from my acquaintances in London that Compton Wyatt is one of the most distinguished houses in the West Country. The name itself always contrives to make me think of cascades and mazes and sunken gardens. Am I right?'

'D'you know, I haven't noticed a maze. I must have a look the next time I'm there.'

'Oh, I adore mazes,' cried Georgina, clasping her hands, 'you must plant one at once.'

'Of course, you and I, Shackleford, both chose to leave France before the whirlwind struck,' said Morton, and there was a reverential hush along the table; acknowledgement that a great concession was being made to the visitor by this mention of the enemy. 'I expect that you were introduced, as I was, to gentlemen who have since become significant figures in the new government, and whom you would have hoped might have benefited from the insights we offered into our British constitution.'

'You, Mr Morton, might have offered insights. I'm afraid I did very little but stand by in awe.'

'But then I'm considerably more advanced in years than you, my dear Shackleford. I can quite see how the young might have been seduced by all the excitement. Whereas I knew for sure that little good would come of the talk I heard in every salon.'

'Ah, I remember those salons, particularly that of Madame de Genlis. How could I forget, when

164

it was there that I first set eyes on Miss Thomasina Ardleigh?'

Miss Thomasina sat motionless at his side, unable to eat, filled with the most exquisite pain. Would Paulin be mentioned? Did Shackleford remember him?

'Just a small part of me regrets coming away when we did,' Morton continued. 'There were great business opportunities and I was on excellent terms with Brissot and Roland – and the brother of that friend of yours, Thomasina – Paulin, was it? – who was such a rising star. I tried to persuade them that they must insist on reform at the highest level right from the start. I said that much as we esteemed our own dear king, we would not dream of allowing him to veto the edicts of our parliament.'

'I wonder you don't go into politics, Morton, since you know so much about it,' said Warren, well into his fourth glass.

Morton glanced uneasily at his wife. 'I am considering it. Having experienced at first hand the consequences of bad government in France, I feel myself well placed to help steer our country away from such turbulence. Now that my dear wife is recovered, I shall join our Guildford Reeve Society. It seems to me that this country is in peril of sliding into insurrection just as our neighbours have done. Only last year a mob ripped up the new toll gate near Chorley. It is time for the right thinking among us to protect our fine system from both radicals and rebels.'

As the conversation drifted to more general matters, Shackleford again leaned towards Asa.

165

'Seeing you again, Miss Ardleigh, I can't help but be transported back to those days. It's astonishing to think that nearly five years have passed. I have often wondered about you: what you were doing, how you were. Did you stay long in Paris after I'd left?'

She regarded him properly for the first time; the rather heavy-featured face flushed with wine and determination to please, the sheen of his hair. 'A few weeks only. My sister was not well, as you may recall, and Mr Morton was anxious to bring her home.'

'And your friends in Paris – the Paulins – do you still write to them?'

The question, spoken in the act of lifting his glass, seemed guileless but the table was suddenly quiet. 'Goodness,' she said, laughing. 'I was there such a short time my friendship with Beatrice Paulin scarcely had time to blossom. But it's true I am in correspondence from time to time.'

'Her brother, the lawyer, has done very well, I believe. You've probably heard there are to be committees of surveillance all over the country, to keep an eye on strangers and suspicious types who might be engaged in counter-revolutionary activity. I believe he's been quite a leading figure in drawing up the plans.'

She took a sip of wine. 'I hadn't heard. We're very cut off here at Morton.'

'Of course. Whereas in London people love to talk about France. Everyone hopes that the French army will collapse. The revolutionary government must be very nervous at present. Seems

166

to me that in France it'll soon matter very much whose side one happens to be on.'

'Side? You mean for or against the Revolution? Surely it's a little too late for that.'

'I mean factions. Differences of opinion about what to do next. Old arguments about whether or not the king should have been killed and if France should have gone to war. There is rumour of counter-revolution.'

'I've heard the same,' said Warren. 'It's a mess. Normandy, Brittany and the Vendée all champing at the bit. Read in *The Times* that there's bound to be insurrection there. Civil war. Folks can't stand being hungry, can't stand conscription, so they're fighting back against the National Guard.' An array of dishes from creamed potatoes to game stew was now paraded down the room and arranged at the four corners of the table. 'D'you know what I'd do if I was Mr Pitt? Not waste another farthing on kitting out the navy or army to fight the French. I'd send funds to anyone who felt inclined to stage a rebellion, give them a bit of support by the back door. How would that be, Madame de Rusigny?'

The attention of the table now turned to Madame, who, with a most unusual lack of appetite, was gazing at her plate. She shot Warren such a look that even he laughed self-consciously.

Shackleford said: 'May I ask, Madame de Rusigneux, which part of France you are from?'

'From the south-west.'

'I have travelled widely in France. Perhaps I have visited your town?'

'It is a town called Frenelle.'

167

'Frenelle. Don't know it. Do you have family there?'

Asa, remembering events in the churchyard, was about to intervene, but Warren interrupted: 'Thing is, Shackleford, as I've been telling Morton, now is the time to invest. What do you say? Put money into sugar and coffee and pick up all the trade the French are losing with their wars and their shilly-shallying about the rights and wrongs of how to proceed with this abolition nonsense. The latest I've heard is that they're likely to forbid any trade in human traffic,' his pale, drunken eye stared at Asa defiantly, 'so we could slip in there and take over plantations the French will be forced to abandon.'

'At every stage,' said Morton hastily, glancing at his wife, 'what the British must do is set an example. The French have to make a mighty roar about their Declaration of the Rights of Men whereas we have a peacefully elected, democratic...'

Asa could bear it no longer. 'Oh, the French have certainly followed our example by excluding so many groups from their constitution, not least slaves and the poor and women. And you say we have a democratic parliament, Mr Morton? Is that really the case? Most of our cabinet is titled and therefore unelected.'

Morton flushed but smiled fraternally at Shackleford. 'You see, Shackleford, how I am ruled by women. Even my newest child is a girl, heaven help me.'

'Some would call you the happiest man alive,' said Shackleford.

Morton looked gratified and folded his hands across his belly. 'Indeed, I count my blessings, now my dear wife is restored to health. Whatever my spirited little sister-in-law says, there's much to be proud of in being English.'

'And yet,' said Asa, 'did you know that our friend Mr Lambert, who as you well know would not hurt a flea, is threatened with imprisonment because he happens to believe that men should not be slaves? Are you so proud of that, Mr Morton? Forgive me, Phil, but I won't remain silent. We are very quick to criticise the French, but when an old, frail man is bullied and threatened...'

'Good Lord, Asa,' cried Philippa, 'I'm sure you're exaggerating as usual. Nobody is going to arrest your Mr Lambert.'

'I had a letter from Caroline yesterday and she is truly fearful. So no, I don't believe we live in a land of the free. And Mr Shackleford, you asked me earlier what I have been doing since I left Paris. The answer is that I have never forgotten the marvellous people I met there, nor the hope I experienced then. I wish I could have stayed. Forgive me if this offends you, Madame de Rusigneux, but I would give everything I possess to have been among those women who brought the king and queen back to Paris when they were lurking in Versailles, banqueting while half of France starved. I would have gone to every meeting, joined every club, and one day I shall go back. I must. Certainly,' and here she looked deliberately across the table at Georgina, 'I could never marry a mere Englishman, or settle for any kind of half-life in England.'

There was a startled silence. Georgina, glancing in horror at Shackleford, said: 'Oh, I second that. We must all go to Paris, I say, whenever the Revolution is over. Whatever happens, I'm sure the French will never lose their sense of fashion. Look how smart we all are tonight. Madame de Rusigny has transformed us, haven't you, madame?'

Philippa moved that the ladies retire to the drawing room, where little Kate would be brought down to be kissed by her aunts. No sooner had Madame retreated to a dark alcove than Georgina hissed furiously at Asa: 'How could you talk such nonsense in front of Shackleford? After all the trouble I've been through to get him here. Well, I wash my hands, I really do.'

The gentlemen followed with almost indecent haste – presumably both Morton and Shackleford were eager to escape Warren's attempts to embroil them in a business opportunity. Shackleford would not be persuaded to stay the night and therefore had a long ride through dark lanes and intended to leave at once. Despite Asa's speech at dinner, he stood over her for some minutes as she caressed little Kate, until at last he pressed her free hand and begged that he might soon be allowed to call at Ardleigh, if he happened to be passing.

Chapter Ten

Asa was convinced that Didier's reply would be waiting for her at Ardleigh. When she and Madame de Rusigneux arrived home two days after Easter, on 10 April, the squire was away in Northamptonshire and the house smelled of beeswax and underuse. There was no letter from France, though Asa interrogated Mrs Dean and the maids about the post and searched every shelf and drawer. Instead she had to be content with leafing through Didier's volume of Ronsard's poetry and plundering the old store of his letters.

23 June 1789

...Dear God, Thomasina, if only you were here to see this. We have a National Assembly. I am a member of that assembly. I, Didier Paulin, am a lawyer, not a priest and not a noble, yet I have been given a voice. We are drawing up a new constitution. I rush from meeting to meeting. We draft a thousand proposals and articles a week. We dare to confront great ministers such as Mirabeau as if he were our equal – he is our equal – but when I come home, yes, to the same little room with that same varnished screen which you wrote of so fondly in your last letter, the same bed, all I want is you. Too late I understand that where there is no Thomasina, there can be no real joy, even in the midst of Revolution. Even to be part of all

171

this means nothing at all because it is not made real, discussed in the arms of my beautiful girl, my Mademoiselle Anglaise.

My bird. I feel the beat of you. My body aches for you...

The letters had to be locked hastily away because Madame de Rusigneux brought down her portmanteau and laid out paintbrushes, dancing manual and a selection of fans. 'Ah, no, madame,' said Asa, 'now we are home there is no time for lessons. Today I must deal with the accounts and tomorrow I have to visit Mrs Dacre, the tailor's wife, who is in prison.'

Madame shrugged her little shoulders. 'Then I shall go with you, of course.'

'I would prefer to speak to her alone.'

'You may leave me in the town and meet me again at the end of the day. Besides, mademoiselle, you should not be riding out in the trap on your own.'

'One of the grooms will be with me.'

'Nevertheless, I must accompany you. It is not a happy experience, I know, visiting a prisoner. You take a commendable interest in this tailor's wife.'

Asa added a column of figures in her notebook. 'Do you not think it is my duty? Would you not have done the same, if it were your tenant in Frenelle?'

Madame extracted a drawing book from her portmanteau and began to sketch a vase of catkins and the narcissi which the villagers called 'Cheerfulness', brought in by Mrs Dean to welcome Asa

172

home. At one point, when Asa glanced up from her accounts, they exchanged an absent-minded smile. A log stirred, the flames leapt, and Mrs Ardleigh's little clock, with its pair of floating cherubs above a china face, ticked softly. Perhaps, thought Asa, to have a companion was not such a bad thing after all. There was completion to the room which reminded her of the old days before her sisters' marriage.

Next day they parted company outside Chichester cathedral and Asa darted along first one side street then another into the teeth of a wind that wafted city smells; tar and fish, manure and soot. Prisons, said Mr Lambert, for too long had been places of sheer hopelessness, the disgraceful anteroom to trial, execution or transportation. Once, a decade or so ago, when he had taken the girls to visit an elderly chandler locked up for debt, a young woman, hearing that Lambert was in the prison, had begged to see him. Caroline and Asa, aged about fourteen, had stood at the door of her filthy cell while Mr Lambert held the prisoner, a stranger, in his thin arms. The previous day she had been found guilty of murdering her husband – afterwards Lambert told the girls that the wretch had beaten her every night for a year, often with a poker on her thighs and buttocks, until at last she turned on him and caught him a single blow with the same instrument. Her punishment was delayed because the judge had decreed death by burning and the place of execution had to be specially prepared. Since her husband owned her, according to the law, she had committed petty treason in killing him. The girl's face had been hidden in Lambert's shoulder but a mass of chestnut hair tumbled down her quivering back. Ever afterwards, in nightmares, Asa had seen that hair in flames.

Lambert, who attended the execution, had not eaten for a week.

Asa was to meet the tailor's wife in another part of the prison, but still she shrank from the memory of the girl. Mrs Dacre took charge, pulled back the rickety chair with her foot, then dropped into it and folded her arms. Her face was arresting with its square jaw and white complexion crowned by a mop of reddish hair. Her eyes were wild and staring between lashes matted with pus. 'Well?' she said.

'I've come to see what I can do for you. Mrs Dean has sent a jar of broth and a blanket in case you're cold.' The words of cheer rang false in the tomb of a prison. Mrs Dacre leaned back, deliberately revealing the convex curve of her belly. Asa felt a stab of dread. 'I see you are with child, Mrs Dacre.'

'Seems so.'

'Caroline – Miss Lambert – did not mention that to me.'

'I doubt she noticed. It would not occur to an innocent such as her.'

'It might go in your favour, the fact that you are expecting a baby.'

'How's that, then?' The woman's head was on one side and she watched Asa as a snake might a mouse.

'You only took what belonged to you and your

174

husband,' Asa said at last. 'All that's needed is an explanation. Could you tell me, perhaps, the circumstances of your husband's death? Was he dead when you...'

'What would you like me to say? That I tied my husband by the neck to a branch so that I could steal his scissors and whatnot? That I told him I was leaving so he hanged himself for sorrow?'

'The truth,' whispered Asa.

'Ah, the truth. When it's my word against nobody's, nobody is bound to win.'

'Mrs Dacre, you do know that you are likely to be accused of murdering your husband if you were a witness to his hanging. Are you aware how seriously such a crime is regarded? You have to prove that you had already left the house when he died.'

'What proof could I give of that?'

'Did anyone see you leave?'

'Not that I know of.'

'Why did you abandon him?'

'You tell me why I should have stayed. I left so that the dolt might have a life, not lose it. It was me they hated, not him. They can stand weakness in a man but they can't stand strength in a woman, or rather a woman who has been strong but who has overstepped the mark. Why were they beating their drums that day so that the cottage shook and a pan clattered off the hook above the hearth? Because of me. Who would give him work, the way he crept about the village with a cuckold's horn stuck to his brow? Ah no, we'd have had to up sticks, the pair of us, and start again in another village. By Christ, I swear I would have killed him

175

with my own bare hands if I'd stayed to watch his fingers shake as they fumbled with the packing, his bony feet stumbling in the lanes, those moping eyes begging for work.'

'Why did you marry him, Mrs Dacre, if you felt like that?'

'I liked the skill in him. I had been brought up among men who could crack open a turnip with an axe or pull lines of potatoes from a field but who had no skill to speak of. I saw Dacre in his window, when he came to our village and had a nice little room of his own rented off the rector. I saw his straight back and his crossed legs and the way his hand flew across his work. He would purse his lips like this. I wanted the neatness and niceness of him. I didn't know his hands would go limp when they weren't cutting cloth and his lips would be cold and wet when they weren't gripping pins. He drove me mad.'

'And the child?'

'You know. *You* know.' Of all things, Mrs Dacre's seeping eyes seemed to be filled with pity for Asa. Her face had a peculiar nakedness, stripped of the soft flesh that disguises thought. 'God help you, Miss Ardleigh. You came here today because your conscience wouldn't let you stay away. Who delivered the clothes up to the manor when my husband had finished them, and who did she happen to meet in the stable-yard one morning? What went on under the beech tree in the garden when you had ridden out of the village in your little trap? He looked upon me with those lonely eyes of his and laid down his coat like the gentleman he is, never caring that on the other side of the wall my willow-man was stooped over the placket on a pair of the rector's breeches. Ask your pa why he was so long coming home at nights, being as how he'd tie his horse to a post in the woods, and who he was with up there on the edge of the Downs.'

'Why did you let him?' Asa whispered.

This Mrs Dacre found so funny that she pushed her toes against the table legs, swung her chair on to its back legs and roared. 'I let him, did I? Well, I suppose I did. I'd never conceived a child so I thought I was safe. We was both a bit chill, a bit alone. I liked the energy in your pa. I didn't want money from him, if that's what you're thinking. I knew there'd be none of that.'

Asa thought of all the years at Ardleigh when she and her father had passed each other on the stairs with barely a word; the evenings she'd sat over her books and letters in the parlour, dreaming of Didier while her father lounged in the dining room with his port. If she'd been less preoccupied, might she have spared them all from this? 'Tell me what happened the night of the charivari, Mrs Dacre. It may save your life. I could speak up for you in court. My father, as you know, is a justice...'

'Nothing happened except that Dacre was huddled against the door with his arms round his knees. He couldn't understand why the village hated us so. His snivelling tormented me until I told him whose child I was carrying and how the village thought I had brought shame on it by what I had done. I told him it was punishing me – and him, my doltish husband – for letting it

177

happen. Then in the night, while he slept, I got up and packed a bag.'

'But you took his tools. How was he to make a living?'

'I had to have something, Miss Ardleigh, for the child. I was going to sell them.'

'And will you tell the court this at your trial?'

Mrs Dacre shrugged. Her hand was on the side of her belly and Asa thought of baby Kate at Morton Hall with her lace-trimmed nightgowns and gossamer-fine shawls. 'I will do my best for you, Mrs Dacre.'

'Will you, now? That I would like to see.' The woman stared, full of defiance and contempt as Asa left a heap of coins on the table.

Chapter Eleven

Madame was at the cathedral promptly at two, as arranged. They exchanged a word or two of greeting but otherwise Asa was too distracted to speak and Madame sat in the trap stiffly, her face hidden beneath the brim of her hat. The groom whistled and peered round from time to time to see what was wrong.

At last Madame de Rusigneux murmured: 'You seem very low in spirits, Mademoiselle Ardleigh.'

'As anyone would be, I'm sure, after visiting the tailor's wife.'

Madame sighed. 'To visit any prison causes grave distress. It is a reminder that even we who seem to be free are behind bars.'

'Madame?'

'In Chichester I heard news from France. Our General Dumouriez has defected to the Austrians. He has become an émigré, like me, and to be an émigré is to be a prisoner, since we will be killed if we return.'

'Dumouriez has defected? What a blow that must be to the French army. He was a great general, I believe.'

'Yet he has abandoned his men. The consequences will be very terrible. I fear for my country. Dumouriez's friends, the Gironde, will be tainted with his treason. The likes of Marat and those who killed my brother are without scruple. They will say that anybody who used to associate with Dumouriez is France's enemy; they will be blamed for all the ills that have befallen France. Blood will flow, mark my words. When things go wrong, everyone wants a scapegoat...'

The sun came out, scenting the air with spring growth. 'Will no one in this life ever face up to their responsibilities?' cried Asa as they drove through the village. 'Must we always find someone else to blame?'

Her father's horse was being rubbed down in the stable-yard. Fired up by her conversation with Madame, Asa leapt from the trap. In the kitchen, which was unusually crowded with a village girl at the sink, another at the spit, Mrs Dean called out: 'Miss Ardleigh, thank the Lord you're home, I need a word.'

Asa didn't pause. Without bothering to take off her hat she stood in the hall and yelled: 'Father.'

No reply, so she flung open the door of his business room, which was chaotic with guns, boots and papers, then the dining room.

She ran upstairs. 'I must speak to you. Where are you?' She pounded on his bedroom door until she heard his voice from below.

Madame de Rusigneux was outside the parlour, pulling off her gloves. Inside stood the squire, still in his boots, and a visitor, Mr Shackleford, who was wearing beneath his riding clothes a waistcoat of some ridiculous, feminine pink. His face was alight with pleasure as he greeted Asa with a sweeping bow.

She barely nodded. 'I must speak to you alone, Father.'

There was a startled hush: even the squire knew that his daughter had been monstrously rude. Madame swept forward full of smiles and offered Shackleford her hand. 'Mr Shackleford, what a very great joy it is to see you again. We are just back from Chichester.' Her pronunciation gave the name a quaint susurration – *Shishester.* 'We are very tired so you must excuse our appearance. I hope you have been made comfortable and offered tea.'

'The housekeeper very nobly assured me that she could even provide me with dinner. But perhaps you were not...'

'I've just this moment come in myself,' said the squire, rubbing his palms together and undoing the buttons of his riding coat. His hands, with their blunt fingertips and grimy nails, made Asa shudder.

'You received my letter, sir? Telling you that I

had business in Brighton with a former trading partner of my father's, and that I would call at Ardleigh on my way?' asked Shackleford.

'Letter?' The squire contorted his face into a blend of contrition and bafflement. He might have received a letter, was the implication, and omitted to mention it, but they were all to forgive a bumbling old man for his incompetence.

'If you had no notice that I would call,' said Shackleford, 'I shall not dream of imposing any further. Please excuse me.'

'But we insist,' said Madame. 'Miss Ardleigh and I would enjoy your company at dinner. Mrs Dean, I believe, already has the meal under way. Will you stay the night?'

'Ah no, as I said, I have friends on the coast.'

With Madame's arm linked firmly through her own, Asa had no choice but to be led up to the bedroom. 'What will you wear for the dinner?' Madame asked.

'I won't change my clothes. I never do,' Asa retorted.

'You have mud on your skirts. Your boots are dirty. You must brush your hair.'

'Madame...'

Madame's thin forefinger was raised. 'You will do exactly as I say. It is my duty to ensure that you treat this guest, as all others, with courtesy.'

Between them the housekeeper, the companion and the guest conspired to redeem the evening. The dining parlour was snug in the candlelight, Madame's dark eyes glittered, and Mrs Dean surpassed herself with her roast fowls and venison pie.

'So what do you think of our Ardleigh Manor, Mr Shackleford?' asked the squire. 'Or should I say *your* manor, since you stand to inherit.'

'It feels to me like a home. It has delightful touches, those tapestry cushions, lovely old rugs, flowers.'

'And there are three villages, a couple of hundred acres, seven farms. Pity you won't be here in the morning, I could have ridden about with you.'

'Another time, perhaps. I am still vexed that you had no idea I was coming, Miss Ardleigh. What must you think of me?'

For the first time she met his honey-brown eyes. 'We are only just back from Morton Hall,' she said, a little more kindly, 'otherwise we would have been better prepared.'

'How are your sister and her child?'

Asa could not help but speak fondly of her baby niece, and the squire, who had ridden over to Morton Hall on Easter Sunday, extolled the exceptional virtues of his grandsons. Madame said little but kept a watchful eye, smiling and nodding as if to prop up the conversation, and signalling to the maids when the dishes were to be cleared.

'You must be wondering about the purpose of my visit,' said Shackleford, 'although it goes without saying that having rediscovered my new relation I would wish to see her again. And Madame de Rusigneux, of course. Fact is, my mother and I wish to invite you to Compton Wyatt. Mr and Mrs Warren have agreed to visit at the beginning of May when the weather will be finer and we can perhaps explore the estate and picnic, and I thought you might come too, Miss Ardleigh, and Madame de Rusigneux, and you, sir. I wrote to the Mortons but they have replied that it is too early for Mrs Morton to stay away from the house, with the baby so young.'

Surely, thought Asa, my behaviour at Morton Hall should have been enough to crush his hopes. Has he no sensitivity at all, that he pursues me in such a fashion? Meanwhile her father, who never, under any circumstances, sat about with elderly ladies, looked appalled. Once more, Madame saved the day. 'May I accept the invitation on behalf of myself and Mademoiselle Ardleigh. Of course, I cannot speak for Monsieur...'

'Doubt I'd be free,' said the squire.

'Nor I,' Asa said.

'Ah, Mademoiselle Ardleigh,' interrupted Madame, 'you are thinking of your housekeeping. But there are two of us now, mademoiselle, to manage affairs, so I'm sure all will be restored to order by May.'

A honey and plum tart was brought and the meal continued. Asa thought: If Didier's reply comes quickly I shall be spared a visit to Compton Wyatt. When she again paid attention to the conversation, Madame, most uncharacteristically, had introduced the subject of France. 'You have been in London, Monsieur Shackleford. Perhaps you have heard, then, about our General Dumouriez?'

'Absolutely. Talk of the town. Everyone's very excited. Some say there'll be an end to the war because the French army won't hold together. I have my doubts. Rather suspect the revolutionary government will take an even harder line. They've already arrested Orléans.'

'Orléans?' exclaimed Asa. 'But he was a great supporter of the Revolution. Don't you remember, when we were in Paris...?'

She should not have referred to their shared time in France – Shackleford's eyes shone with affection. 'Orléans was a friend of Dumouriez. The whole lot will fall now, like a pack of cards.'

'The whole lot?'

'The Gironde. Those who oppose the Montagne, or hardliners, the likes of Marat, Danton, Robespierre and your old friend Paulin, Miss Ardleigh. These men are in the ascendant. The rest will be crushed.'

'I don't understand,' cried Asa, 'why are these terrible things happening in France? It should not have been like this. Why do people hate each other so much?'

Shackleford leaned a little closer. 'We always hate what we fear. The leaders of the Revolution are terrified that if there is weakness within, there'll be an attempt by foreign powers to intervene and restore the monarch.'

'That'll be tough even for the French,' said the squire, 'given that they've lopped off Louis's head.'

'Saw it myself,' continued Shackleford, watching Asa, 'the one time I visited my father's plantations. Abject fear. Not the blacks, no, though they had cause enough. It was us, the British. What we feared was rebellion. So we were brutal.'

'Same with animals, see,' said the squire.

'Vicious when they're afraid. Never find yourself cornered in a stable with a frightened horse.'

Fortunately Shackleford had the tact to depart immediately after the meal, although he was full of apologies for breaking up the party. As he drew on his gloves in the hall, he and Asa were alone for a moment. 'Miss Ardleigh, I am well aware of what you think of me but I'm not seeking to hound or torment you. All I ask is your understanding.'

'I understand you very well, Mr Shackleford.'

'Not entirely, perhaps. Please give my compliments to Mrs Dean, for the dinner. And never forget that my first wish, Miss Ardleigh, is that we might be friends.'

His horse had been brought to the gate and a couple of village women watched as he mounted and rode away. Madame stood at the bottom of the stairs, her face contorted into sharp angles and hollows as she pleaded a headache.

The squire was still at his place in the dining room. Asa went in and closed the door, sat beside him and drew the decanter close, as if to study the facets cut into the crystal.

'So that was Shackleford,' said her father. 'The one all the fuss was about. Seems amiable enough, I suppose, though I can't see him running an estate. Doesn't know the first thing about animals or land, I'd say. He's very taken with you, Asa. What d'you think of him, eh?'

'I visited Mrs Dacre in Chichester Gaol this morning,' she said.

He looked surly and took a deep swig of wine.

'She is with child but I expect you already knew

185

that. What are you going to do, Father?'

'I? What should *I* do?'

'Good God, it is your duty. Is that so difficult? I know that the child is yours.'

He pushed his glass so that it struck the decanter, scraped back his chair and made for the door, but Asa got there ahead of him and clung to the handle. 'If you do nothing that woman will hang. They'll be baying for her blood. You have to act on her behalf. Get her a lawyer.'

'What is all this? I will not be ordered about by women or held to ransom by a sluttish thief and I will not have my own daughter talking to me in this way.'

'We must face up to what has happened, Father. I don't understand why you are allowing her to be punished. I believe she was fond of you.'

Asa knew him so well that she could have numbered the moles on his hand but she had never pushed him so far. His bloodshot eyes were piteous. 'You will persist in probing what you cannot understand. We had an agreement, she and I. She promised me there was no danger of a child. Good God, Asa, you have no idea what passes between a man and a woman.'

Asa felt her self-control slip another notch as she recalled that narrow bed behind a painted screen, whispered avowals: *I have kept you safe ... we will be married...*

'You must claim the child. We must pay for its upkeep.'

'It will do the woman no good. The tailor's dead and she as good as killed him. She lied to me and told me Dacre would not care what she

186

did one way or another. Then he went and hanged himself.'

'You could get her released, I'm sure, if you tried.'

'It's the law, Asa. Even I can't go against the law. Where would we be if I could? Do you want us to become like the French, dammit? Besides I have no money to pay for bail or the child, let alone a lawyer. Now if you were to marry Shackleford...' He shot her a wily look.

'There's no point now in Georgina trying to marry me off to Shackleford, since our name is tarnished. You have fathered another infant – doubtless not the first since Mother died – oh, don't look at me like that, Father, I know it's true – and it won't even have a name. Its mother is in prison and its father is refusing to own it.'

Flinging himself into the nearest chair, he dragged off his wig, ran his fingers through his hair and looked at his daughter pleadingly. 'I've said I have no money.'

'Then sell things. Sell horses. Sell a saddle. Sell your land, any that isn't entailed. But don't sell me.' Seizing him by the lapels of his jacket she shouted: 'You love me too much for that. Surely you wouldn't want to sacrifice me?'

As he took her by the shoulders and tried to quieten her, he was weeping too. It was the most dreadful moment, to see tears seeping down his cheeks.

'Father, you have to act. You have to save us.'

But he fell back and covered his face. 'You'll have to forgive your old pa. It's because of your mother dying like that. I never could bring myself to take another wife.' He fumbled for his pocket watch, a wedding present from Asa's mother, so worn that the etching of their entwined initials on the silver cover was all but gone.

'That's just an excuse, Father. However sad and lonely you are without Mother, it's no reason to treat the tailor's wife like this.'

'Sad and lonely. That's how it's been, Asa.'

'Just do the right thing, Father, please.'

'The right thing. Ah, now, if only I were your Mr Lambert, how straightforward I would find it, to do the right thing.'

Asa left the room and went to the parlour. Though her hand reached for the key to the drawer containing Didier's letters she didn't have the heart to seek her usual comfort. Instead she climbed the stairs and began faltering preparations for bed. She had expected Madame to be asleep, but as she brushed her hair there was a knock and her companion, in a trailing night-gown, slipped inside and closed the door. 'I have brought you a tisane. You should drink it. You need to calm yourself.'

This display of softness was so unexpected that Asa wept again while Madame stood behind her, studying their two faces in the glass. After a moment she reached out both hands, lifted Asa's hair and dropped it behind her shoulders so that she could rub her temples with her fingertips.

Turning back the sheet, Madame urged Asa to lie down. 'I will sit here beside the pillow and keep you company for a while.'

'You are so kind,' said Asa.

'Sometimes we all need kindness. I have a true example of loving kindness always in my heart. The one I loved, my dear brother, he was a kind man.'

'I wish I had known him.'

'All his life Gabriel cared nothing for himself. We used to argue about it because I thought he could have been a great statesman or revolutionary. Instead he chose to serve the poor.'

All but one candle was snuffed out. Asa was soothed by Madame's gentle voice, the herbal tang of the tea. Madame held Asa's arm by the wrist and elbow and pressed it to her breast so that through the softness of muslin Asa felt the beating of her heart.

'Even when he was a priest,' Madame continued, 'his choices seemed perverse. He chose not the cathedral or the church frequented by nobles, but a village parish, where few people could read or understand his fine sermons. I used to tell him he was crushing his own nature, choosing the most difficult path – that village where he hardly knew what was going on in the world and where his parishioners didn't care so much for his words as for the next meal. But Gabriel laughed at me. I see it always in my mind's eye, that boyish smile of his. He said it didn't matter where he lived or what he did, only that he should serve God and love.'

'Do you have a portrait of him, Madame?'

'I do not.' Pause. 'He would not allow a picture. He had no time.'

'From memory. Perhaps you would sketch him? I should like to see his face.'

'Perhaps. One day.' Madame took a fan from

189

her pocket and flicked it open. 'You will sleep now.' But then, as the air began to stir above Asa's forehead, she heard Madame whisper: 'My God, how that man loves you.'

'Shackleford?'

'He came because he could not keep away. His eyes never leave your face. He is a man in torment. And yet you will not see.'

Asa's eyelids were heavy and as she fell asleep she was conscious of a myriad-coloured thing wafting back and forth, a soft breeze on her cheek and neck, and those impenetrable black eyes.

Chapter Twelve

Next morning Asa rode to Littlehampton to visit Caroline Lambert. Most unusually Madame de Rusigneux said she would stay at Ardleigh and paint. While conscious of the blessed relief of a journey in the sole company of a groom, Asa's thoughts strayed back to Ardleigh Manor and the card table in the parlour at which Madame sat. The previous night, as Asa fell asleep beneath the soft sway of air, she had felt loved like a daughter. And this morning there had been a hint of wistfulness in Madame's eyes as she said: 'You will have much to say to Mademoiselle Lambert. There is not a place therefore for a stranger such as me.'

Asa was greeted with joy in Littlehampton. Caroline's eyes were a greenish grey, as serene as a saint's in an Italian painting. She wore a faded rose-coloured gown and her fingertips were purple with cold. As she served tea (fresh leaves that would be dried and reused when there were no visitors) Mr Lambert reached for the open book on his desk. His hand, on which the veins were as prominent and thick as the bones beneath, was palsied so that he had to rest the volume on his lap to steady it. 'I have been rereading Tom Paine, Thomasina, because I want to understand why everyone is so excited about him all of a sudden. Why the marches through London and the demonstrations against him?'

'Surely it was Burke's *Reflections on the French Revolution* that did all the damage,' said Asa, roused by the prospect of rational discussion. 'Even my sober brother-in-law, John Morton, is joining a political society to counter the revolutionary threat.' The Lamberts' cottage was working its customary magic; the appropriateness of every bit of furniture, each possession; the old teapot with its design of bluebells webbed by hairline cracks in the glaze, the threadbare chintz curtains. Books were covered reverentially in brown paper and the room smelt of ink and the sea and Mr Lambert, who emitted a faint odour of tobacco, though he hadn't smoked for years. An ancient pipe was still upended in a little bowl on the mantel, a reminder, said Lambert, that he had nothing to yearn for.

'I agree that Burke incites fear in people when he talks of the dangers of the mob and the horrors of revolution,' said Caroline. 'Ironic, don't you think, that his own language should be so savage when it is of savagery that he accuses the French?'

'And since the French killed their king, Burke appears to have been vindicated,' said Lambert. 'Of course, there has been far too much bloodshed and more will follow, I fear. Marat and his cohorts are ruthless in their determination to crush dissenting voices. The French have given those of us in England who would like to see changes to our own constitution a hard time. Did Caroline tell you that I received a visit from our local justice, warning me that if I don't disband the Abolition Society I shall be arrested? Well, that is too much. Just because the French revolutionary government is in favour of abolishing slavery, it seems that here in England we must all condone the wretched practice.'

'Will the French really outlaw slavery?'

'They say they will and I believe they must. Very powerful people in the new Convention have pleaded for it; my friend Professor Paulin's son, for example, and Brissot, for whom I've always had great respect, though I fear the pair of them don't see eye to eye on other matters.'

Was it possible that neither father nor daughter noticed the quickening of Asa's breath? 'Have you heard from the professor recently, then?' she asked.

'Indeed I have. Not on the whole good news, I'm afraid. Paulin is at loggerheads with his firebrand son. In his last letter, my old friend wrote that he has become increasingly concerned about the factionalism among those who lead in Paris and fears that the Revolution may fall into the hands of zealots. They have reinstated the Revolutionary

Tribunal because there is famine in the country, the war is failing and they fear counter-revolution. Paulin asked me not to write to him for the time being because anyone receiving letters from England is likely to be under suspicion.'

Guildford's lamplit High Street, the exchange with the clerk in the post office, seeing Madame in the graveyard: at that moment Asa would have given her life not to have sent the letter to Didier. And now? Was the letter resting on the blotter of some interrogator? Had Didier Paulin been clapped in irons because of Asa's moment of weakness, her selfish plea?

'But the Paulins, all of them thus far are well?' she asked, and was conscious of Caroline's faint smile.

'I believe so. Young Didier Paulin has been entrusted with a mission in northern France. His father disapproves of his son's prominence because he thinks the French government is now too centred on Paris, and in any case he is against the war. He dare not say so to Didier, of course: things are so sensitive that a father cannot even risk arguing with his own son. The one encouraging thing is this business of abolition. Young Paulin seems prepared to stand firm, even though many of his friends show less enthusiasm.'

After tea Caroline suggested a walk; her father had work to do and they should leave him in peace. Once clear of the house, though, Caroline murmured that in fact she wanted him to rest. The sun was warm on their shoulders. In the harbour they were soon beyond the fishwives with their flashing knives and squirming infants, and striding along the west cliff. 'I'm sorry that you didn't bring your French companion,' said Caroline. 'We are longing to meet her. She seems to be an exceptional woman.'

'Indeed she is. She has turned out to have such astonishing qualities that I am put to shame. She has a way about her, an understanding so acute that it's as if she sees beneath the skin. She watches me – watches over me, even – but out of affection, I sometimes think, rather than duty.'

'And what has she taught you?'

'Nothing you would wish to learn unless you were to develop a sudden interest in the language of the fan or how to alight from a carriage when wearing a train. But the trouble is, Madame de Rusigneux misses nothing. We are very exposed at Ardleigh. Your lives here in Littlehampton would stand up to any kind of scrutiny but at Ardleigh we have far too many murky corners.'

They had walked half a mile beside the choppy waves before Asa had told the full story of her father's relations with the tailor's wife. Once convinced of the squire's culpability, Caroline's eyes shone with their habitual determination to right an injustice. 'Your father must marry her.'

'He never would. He's deeply conventional at heart and would never marry anyone so lowly, even if he loved her.'

'Then she must at least be given bail and he must protect her.'

'We have no money. If it were a matter of a few pounds I would sell clothes or even mother's ring. But Mrs Dacre will need a lawyer. The bail will be tens if not hundreds of pounds. And a cottage must be rented for her, fuel provided and some kind of allowance.'

'Your sisters?'

'The Warrens are worse off than we are. I've thought of asking John Morton but I suspect he would refuse outright. In the first place, he would hate the scandal. In the second I doubt he would regard Mrs Dacre as being worthy of his charity.'

'Then what will you do?'

'As you say, I must extract her from prison somehow. A lawyer, I'm sure, would do the trick. Dear heavens, perhaps my sisters are right and my only hope is to marry Shackleford.'

They were retracing their steps towards the town. Their skirts flapped as they were rushed forward by the wind. 'You really think he might make an offer?' said Caroline.

'Madame de Rusigneux thinks he is in love with me. He has invited us all to Compton Wyatt. It seems there is to be no escape unless, perhaps, through a miracle. But seriously, Caroline, you know I would never even consider him.'

The silence that followed was very strange. Caroline's pace slowed and she took Asa's arm. 'When I look into the future I am afraid. Father didn't tell you how ill he was after the latest visit from the magistrate. I found him in his chair, unable to move his right arm or foot. For days he lay in his bed and could not eat. He's still not fully recovered, though he hides it very well. We are behind with the rent. Sometimes I think that marriage, so long as the husband was relatively kind and did not make excessive demands, wouldn't be the worst fate in the world.'

'Caroline, what are you saying? You are surely not encouraging me to accept Shackleford?'

'It's true, I've changed... I don't believe you should throw away your chances of marriage for the sake of an ideal or a fantasy, Thomasina. Neither of us should. We have to be practical. Look at the pair of us. We have nothing.'

'Are you telling me I should even give up the idea of France? That's not a fantasy. How can you say so when you are the one who has encouraged me to keep faith? Why would I give up now? Why are you being like this?'

'I am like this, as you say, because I have glimpsed the future and see that it is bleak.'

They returned to the cottage to find Mr Lambert asleep, his head lolling so that he looked far older than his years. Full of sorrow, Asa hugged Caroline and kissed her a tender farewell. During her heavy-hearted ride back to Ardleigh the sky darkened and the vegetation in the lanes whispered as if brushed by invisible footfall. After dismounting at the church she watched her groom lead the horses up the side of the manor along the familiar cobbled track.

On the village green earth scorched by the pyre was covered with fresh growth, grazed by a couple of ill-tempered goats; there was the spot where Madame de Rusigneux had been standing, beyond the smoke, the bedlam-like charivari stilled by the steady gaze of a new French companion. Here was the rickety gate to Key Cottage, which wouldn't close, the overgrown front garden and the door against which the tailor had huddled while the village boys pranced and yelled and beat their drums. Key Cottage had possessed a lock but never a key.

Inside was the stench of decay. The cottage had remained more or less untouched since Mrs Dacre's arrest because the villagers were too superstitious to venture inside. The windows were draped with abandoned cobwebs and soot had dropped down the chimney, accumulating in soft piles on the hearth. Rainwater had seeped through the rafters and collected in slimy pools on the floor. In the other, smaller room was the bed where the pair must have lain night after night listening to the owls in the manor-house woods. A stocking, probably the tailor's, and a few rags, too worthless even for Mrs Dacre to have included in her bundle, were heaped in a corner.

The back door was jammed open. Outside, the yard was even smaller than Asa remembered, with the overhanging beech branch moving gently in the wind. Nettles and bindweed had colonised last year's vegetable patch.

Although the beech was full of new leaf, hanging from the branch was the rope that Mr Dacre had looped about his neck in February; left there, in the hurry of the moment, by the blacksmith, who'd cut the tailor down. And of course it would never have occurred to Squire Ardleigh to have the cottage cleared of such a gruesome memento. The fabric swayed back and forth; four pieces of cloth, pale cambric, black twill, green and yellow spotted cotton, and a thick, light brown wool that looked very familiar. The previous autumn Mrs Dean had prised the squire's favourite waistcoat from his back and instructed the tailor to make him a new

197

one, exactly the same minus the patches, frays and wine stains. The noose was a testimony to the tailor's skill – the even knots, the accurately cut strips of fabric, the precisely measured distance that was required for a man to hang himself.

That evening, after Madame had gone upstairs, Asa unlocked her cache of letters from Didier and took them into the garden. A slant of late sunlight still fell on the far side of the orchard.

1 August 1791

Mignonelette,

It is a month since I wrote and you would be right to reproach me for that. But then, if I know Thomasina, she will have read the papers and she will know why I have been such a poor correspondent. With every breath in my body I opposed the reinstatement of the king. How can we trust him since he tried to run away and throw himself on to the mercy of our enemies? Fifty unarmed people are now dead for daring to stand in the street and protest about this same weak and wretched monarch and his government. I grieve. We are not sufficiently bold, that is the trouble. Everything is still in place, the priests, the king, all the old inequalities. We have not even outlawed slavery, which is so glaringly, incontestably wrong.

We must start afresh. Haven't I been saying that all along? It is impossible to cobble together a new France from the rags of the old.

Perhaps this letter will be intercepted and read. I do not care. I want something to happen. I think of you in your quiet little English house, so close to the sea which divides us, and I grow calmer. I am striving for your sake – to be able to live with you, my girl, in a world where we can work shoulder to shoulder for the good of our children.

Sometimes you seem so far away I cannot see you any more. And then I remember those clear eyes, that purity, that courage. And I know that truly only one future matters to me.

Part Three

Compton Wyatt, May 1793

Chapter One

Compton Wyatt, guilty as sin.

Compton Wyatt; a white, many-windowed mansion completed thirty years earlier by the late Mr Thomas Shackleford, plantation owner, shipping merchant, glass maker and wine trader, high in the valley of a tributary of the Frome between Bath and Bristol, on the site of a twelfth-century castle and later a medieval manor house, all gone save for a ruined chapel which now formed a feature of the circular walk in the gardens.

Two days' drive from Ardleigh in the squire's ill-sprung carriage brought Asa, the Warrens and Madame de Rusigneux, not to mention the coachman and his lad, and a mound of luggage, to a lane bordered on one side by an eight-foot wall then, half a mile or so later, to a pair of gates fit for a palace, with a single-storeyed lodge on either side and, beyond, an avenue of young oaks.

Georgina, who had been hanging out of the window for the last hour, cried: 'There's a lake. I told you there would be. And good God, look at the size of the house, how many rooms would you say – forty, fifty? Oh, and there's a temple on that hillock. Good heavens, I don't believe it; the entire household has come out to welcome us. They must have been waiting for hours.'

And indeed, when the carriage door was flung open, there was Mr Shackleford wearing a sober

203

black coat over yet another dashing waistcoat, this time embroidered with daisies in silver thread, his face filled with pleasure, ready to assist first Georgina then Asa. The rest of the household was ranked on the shallow steps, all in deep mourning: first Shackleford's mother, a plump, sharp-eyed woman; next her daughter-in-law, The Honourable Mrs Susan Shackleford, unsmiling wife of Shackleford's deceased elder brother; and finally a companion, a third or fourth cousin of Mrs Shackleford called Mrs Foster, whose bottom lip worked incessantly against the upper as if to keep her teeth in place. Beyond were rows of footmen and maids poised to leap forward and relieve the carriage of the Warrens' three trunks, Madame's portmanteau and Asa's small travelling chest.

'We *are* honoured,' whispered Georgina. 'Heavens above, Asa, you do realise this is all for you? You might as well be married already.'

Mrs Shackleford the elder placed her white hand on Georgina's arm and led her inside. When Georgina gushed over the sightless bust of a Roman emperor, Mrs Shackleford responded coldly that it was believed to be Caesar, first-century, and her manicured fingers raised themselves half an inch from the lace of Georgina's sleeve to mark her displeasure at her visitor's overenthusiasm. Meanwhile (The Honourable) Mrs Shackleford junior, in the nasal drawl appropriate to a viscount's daughter, enquired after Asa's journey and then fell silent. Behind the ladies, Warren and Shackleford embarked on a discussion about fishing in the Frome.

Compton Wyatt smelt like no other house. Vases

of hothouse lilies adorned alcoves and side tables, sunshine baked the fragrance of polish from shining floors; when the windows were open the scent of cut grass and roses blew in from the garden and the logs burning in the fireplace – even on a mild May afternoon – were of aromatic pine and applewood.

But it was more the absence of bad smells which made the air so pure. The kitchens, in a separate wing, were closed off behind swing doors, and the house, fed as it was from springs high up in the valley, had water closets more efficient even than those at Morton, a couple of marble buffets between the dining room and drawing room in which one might rinse one's hands or fill a glass with ice-cold water, and a bathhouse in the garden.

Later that afternoon they were given a tour by a languid Mrs Shackleford the younger, who had been chosen for a wife, whispered Georgina, because of her father's title rather than her looks. It was said that her family, having got rid of her to the elder Shackleford boy, didn't want her back now she was a widow. Asa at once paid sympathetic attention to the poor woman, whose extreme thinness reminded her of Caroline, though not her pursed lips or evasive eyes. This after all might be Asa's fate – an eternity spent at Compton Wyatt showing visitors its many remarkable features.

They obediently stretched their necks to admire the cupola above the immense polished oak staircases with mirror-image flights of steps and wrought-iron balusters as fine as lace; were paraded from one room to the next until they had completed an entire circuit of the ground floor, gallery, music room, library, drawing room, withdrawing room, dining room, morning room and back to the entrance hall; then toured their various bedchambers, each decorated in the theme of a different country to reflect the late Mr Shackleford's obsession with travel. Asa's room, the second grandest, contained an immense bed draped in Indian figured silk, and wallpaper flocked with exotic flowers. From the window she could gaze upon a perfect landscape; under a blue and white sky were sunlit hills upon which sheep grazed and in the foreground a white rotunda was perched on a mound, while a couple of swans drifted across the lake chaperoning three cygnets.

Dinner, taken at six in a room half the size of Ardleigh in its entirety, consisted of twenty dishes. Georgina filled the gaps in conversation by expressing her awe at every inanimate object from salt spoon to chandelier, while Mrs Shackleford senior dedicated herself to an examination of Asa, whom she had placed to her right. At intervals her beringed hand seized Asa by the wrist as she inclined her bewigged head on its bejewelled neck and spoke confidingly, to show the others that they were engaged in talk of the most private nature. Her eyes, like chocolate-coloured marbles, fixed relentlessly on Asa's face. 'The name Ardleigh is in the Domesday Book, I gather.'

'Yes.'

'And who was your mother?'

'The daughter of a Chichester squire named Dinsford.'

The hand was withdrawn and Mrs Shackleford again took up her knife. 'I've heard the name Dinsford and believe that the family is one of the most prominent in Kent. You must miss your mother very much, my dear.'

'I never knew her.'

'Do you know, I might have guessed? A girl who has never known her mother always has a certain air about her.'

'Although I would dearly love to have met her, my sisters more than filled her place.'

'Certainly they seem to have done very well by you. That's a beautiful gown, my dear. Its simplicity suits you. I wish I could keep up with modern fashion but of course I am an old lady, and in mourning.' Her eyes watered and for a moment she looked forlorn amid her array of priceless porcelain and silver. The hand shot out again. 'Who makes your gowns?'

'I'm afraid I don't know, madam. Georgina brought this one from town.'

'Ah yes, and you have another sister married to a John Morton. Morton Hall is a very modern house, my son tells me. What do you think of our Compton Wyatt in comparison to your sister's house?'

'I'm afraid I'm a poor judge. When I am at Morton I have three nephews to consider, and it's the opportunities those little boys find to tumble down the stairs or slip on the hall floor that concern me.' The old lady looked so disappointed that Asa added: 'But of course there is no comparison. Morton Hall is a quarter the size of Compton Wyatt, and being so new, not nearly as well established.'

'And what of your own home, a manor house, I believe?'

'Ardleigh Manor hardly warrants the title being old and quite small, but it's my home so of course I love the place and should not like to live anywhere else.'

Her arm was pinched playfully by Mrs Shackleford. 'Your loyalty does you credit but most people accustom themselves to more luxurious surroundings in time, given the chance. My dear daughter-in-law, Susan, whose father has houses in Chandos Square and Norfolk, was forever losing herself when she first arrived at Compton Wyatt but she likes it well enough now.'

Poor Susan, at the opposite end of the table, was seated beside Warren, who had been quizzing her about plays she had not seen, music she had not heard and places she had not visited. At the mention of her name she threw her mother-in-law a resentful glance.

'But Susan is the daughter of a viscount and therefore schooled to shine in society. She and my dear son Thomas were the talk of Bristol and beyond when they married. I wish you could have met Thomas, my fine boy.' Mrs Shackleford dabbed her eyes with a diminutive handkerchief.

'Perhaps you'd describe him to me.'

'He was not at all like Harry; dark where Harry is fair and a brilliant head for figures. Sometimes I wonder whether Harry learned anything at all at school.'

Shackleford leaned forward. 'My brother's portrait is above the mantel in the drawing room, as you perhaps noticed, Miss Ardleigh, it being so large.' Asa couldn't help smiling. In the life-sized portrait a young man in mustard-coloured breeches leaned against an oak, a gun tucked under one arm, the other hand holding the leash of a dog. In the background was the angular bulk of Compton Wyatt. Tom Shackleford, according to the painting, had indeed been darker haired than his brother, thinner faced and with a small, shut mouth.

'The fact is,' whispered Mrs Shackleford, 'to be the owner of Compton Wyatt is to be the governor of a small kingdom. Sometimes even I, its chatelaine, find my duties overwhelming.'

Susan Shackleford said suddenly: 'I can't say I find much to do here when I'm not playing the piano.'

'Susan is a gifted musician,' said Mrs Shackleford indifferently. 'She'll play for you later, I'm sure.'

'I can't wait to explore,' Georgina piped up. 'I do hope it will be fine tomorrow so we can take a walk in the gardens.'

'My son has devised an itinerary for you,' said Mrs Shackleford the elder, 'such that you are not to have a moment's leisure. There are to be picnics and tea parties and tomorrow we are all to bathe. And next week, before you go, we are to hold a ball in the long gallery.'

Georgina clasped her hands together. 'For us?'

'I need hardly say that we have not held assemblies here of any kind since my husband and son died so it will be a very minor affair. I am not out of mourning but Harry, an impulsive soul, insists...'

Shackleford glanced apologetically at Asa, who in turn wondered why he was so determined to put her through one ordeal after another.

'Oh, we shall love it,' gasped Georgina. 'How marvellous. A ball. I have not been to a ball for months and months.'

Madame de Rusigneux, dressed in her shadowy blue gown, had been eating markedly less than usual and shaking her head sorrowfully when offered succulent dishes which normally she would have accepted with relish. Her position was made awkward by the fact that at Compton Wyatt she was faced with a nemesis in the form of an English companion, Mrs Foster, who performed the role for all she was worth; earlier, at tea, she had placed herself a few feet behind her mistress's chair so as to limp off at a moment's notice to fetch a shawl or a pin and then shrink out of sight when not required.

It was not long before the full glare of Mrs Shackleford's attention fell upon Madame. 'You are one of those poor French émigrées, I believe? How fascinating. You must tell me all about it.'

Madame gave Mrs Shackleford a brave and dazzling smile. After the meal she offered her frail arm to the much larger English lady and the pair drifted into the drawing room.

'I find myself overwhelmed,' Madame murmured, 'to be so far from home, yet to find so much that is familiar. Is it the proportions of this house, I wonder? Or the beautiful colours of the paint.'

'You had a home like this?'

'Something like it: the Château de Rusigneux. It was much smaller and very old – the central tower which dominated the front of the house dated back to the thirteenth century.'

'And de Rusigneux, your husband?'

'The marquis? There was a terrible fire...'

'Children?'

'Thank God, no children. But I had a brother.'

Next moment they were tête-à-tête on the sofa. Asa, tucked into a window seat near the piano, was surprised by Madame's readiness to confide in Mrs Shackleford. Or perhaps Compton Wyatt represented Madame's proper milieu and her reticence hitherto had been due to a fear of embarrassing her employers by reference to her own much grander roots.

Susan Shackleford proved to be a fine musician; it was the first time, in fact, that Asa had heard Mozart played since Paris, and in that fragrant room, she felt guilty pleasure at being away from Ardleigh, Mrs Dacre and the strain of waiting for news of Didier. Shackleford, after a brief spell with Warren in the dining room, sat beside Georgina, but Asa knew by the set of his shoulder and his frequent glances across the room that he was entirely engrossed in her.

Chapter Two

Next day neither Mrs Shackleford joined the bathing party; the elder claimed she had preparations to make for next week's ball, the younger a slight head-cold. Shackleford left the house early to visit the family glassworks in Bristol accompanied by Warren, who hinted that he too had important business in the city. So the sisters set off into the gardens, together with Madame de Rusigneux (now firmly established as the tragic but unimaginably high-born – though French – figure who completed the trio of widows at Compton Wyatt), a couple of maids and a footman. They were guided down flights of steps through the water garden, the herbaceous garden and the topiary garden, to the lake, where a path ran past the boathouse, undulated through a grove of trees and then at last arrived at the bathhouse, which from a distance looked like a rustic cottage. Inside they were shown a large room furnished with sofas and a roaring fire, before which the ladies might warm themselves after bathing. Beyond were a couple of heavily draped changing rooms from whence the bather padded down a flight of stone steps and entered a winding tunnel leading to a cave with a view of the lake at one end and a deep bathing pool, fed by a spring and lit by braces of candles, at the other.

Georgina dipped her hand in the water and

declared that she had never so much as paddled in anything so cold. 'What about you, madame,' she asked, 'did you take cold-water baths in France or did you prefer a warm spa?'

Madame had approached the very front of the cave overlooking the lake and was holding her face up to the light. Her cheeks were devoid of colour so that in her dark gown and with the sunshine spilling on to her face she might have been a subject for Caravaggio, whose painting of a nubile serving boy had pride of place in the Compton Wyatt gallery between a Rubens and a Gainsborough.

'I cannot bathe today.'

'Madame, you will love it. Think of how refreshing it will be.'

'Please, Mademoiselle Ardleigh, I am quite sure you will not make me.'

'Certainly you are not obliged to bathe,' said Asa. 'Perhaps you would like me to come back with you to the lake.' Together they edged along the tunnel with its damp, uneven floor, up the staircase and out to the lakeside. All the while Madame's feet dragged as if she were afraid of what might happen next.

'I shall be very well here,' Madame said, releasing her grip on Asa's sleeve.

'You are shaking, Madame.'

'There are places where the memories are bad. It was the stone. The cave. No light. And now, if you do not require me, I shall go back to the house and lay the foundations for the copy that Madame Shackleford has asked me to make of her son's portrait, in miniature.'

Madame was soon forgotten in the excitement of the bath. The sisters were used to cold water because as girls their father had encouraged them to sea-bathe at Littlehampton, 'although the sea was positively *boiling* compared to this,' cried Georgina, dabbling her bare foot in the water. She had always been the most daring, and as she flung aside her robe and stepped gallantly down the steps, hair flooding her shoulders, arms crossed on her ample bosom, Asa caught a glimpse of a girl who would risk everything. 'Come on, Asa. Be bold.'

'I haven't as much flesh as you.' Asa laughed and squealed as she dipped her toe then at last threw herself forward into the achingly cold water. 'I dare you, stay another minute,' she shouted, and the sisters thrashed about and splashed each other, shaking the water from their ears. Only as they raced up the steps to the changing room did she think: At Compton Wyatt, even suffering is manufactured.

Nevertheless, she was glad to toast herself before the fire. 'I have no doubt at all that Shackleford will propose to you,' confided Georgina, flexing her toes to the heat. 'I wish Warren would look at me the way I've seen Shackleford look at you.'

'If he does propose I will refuse.'

'You can't mean it.'

'I'm ashamed of being at Compton Wyatt. Where you see a pot of gold, I see only disgrace. How many slaves have been tortured so that you and I might sit in front of the fire in this bath-house? How many women raped and children orphaned? And all so that a few spoilt ladies can

214

stroll down gravel walks, sip tea from priceless cups or yawn through an evening of Mrs Susan Shackleford's music – I saw you last night, Georgina. Mr Lambert says...'

'Mr Lambert is a pauper who has dragged his daughter down with him. Have you any idea how sanctimonious you sound? How many people has Mr Lambert truly helped with his whining talk of kindness to all God's creatures? Whereas I bet you the late Mr Shackleford rescued thousands of Negroes from all kinds of cannibalism and suchlike. Warren has been asking a lot of questions about the Shacklefords on your behalf and he says their plantations are a model of humanity to the point of their slaves being spoilt. Not to mention hundreds of poor children in Bristol who receive an education thanks to Shackleford endowments. Surely even you can applaud all that?'

'Georgina, I will never marry Shackleford. Put it out of your head, once and for all. In any case he definitely won't make an offer when he finds out what's been happening at Ardleigh.'

But Georgina, when told of Mrs Dacre's plight, brushed the subject aside. 'Since there's no proof at all that it's Father's child, why should he take responsibility? Asa, I beg you, don't let Shackleford find out what's happened even if it *is* true. Please, if he makes you an offer, accept.' She began to cry. 'Warren and I are in terrible trouble. We have nowhere left to go. The bailiffs are after us. We daren't show our face in London.' She buried her face in Asa's skirts. 'Warren may be arrested. If we don't get the money to pay for a lawyer he could be imprisoned. He might even be hung or transported.'

'Georgina, even if I married Shackleford I couldn't save your husband from the law.'

'You could. I don't think you realise how influential Shackleford is. I've never seen Warren so hopeful about anything. He's drinking less, have you noticed, and he's been so much kinder... Oh, Asa, don't look outraged. You and Philippa abandoned me and went jaunting off to Paris so what choice did I have? Well, now you must rescue me.'

'What has Warren done exactly?'

Georgina was incoherent – said something to do with exporting goods from Bristol via France so that a ship could then sail on with French papers and under French colours, thereby evading the crippling British restrictions on the number of slaves who could be transported. Unfortunately, when a few dozen slaves perished on the voyage, questions had been asked about dates and timings. She said it could all be sorted out as long as there was a decent lawyer on the case. 'If you marry Shackleford, all will be well. Shackleford could rescue us in a minute. He'd have to, because Warren says the Shackleford family, for all its noble reputation, has been up to all kinds of tricks in its time.'

Chapter Three

A week passed. Each night Asa went to bed not tired enough and rose the next morning exhausted. Inching from room to room, she loitered before a painting or a priceless bit of porcelain, never to study or admire it – as a matter of principle she crushed any tendency to be seduced by objects so dearly bought – but to put off the moment when she must rejoin the ladies. She was surrounded by treasures: a Book of Hours illuminated by a fervent monk lavish with his gold ink and his interlaced designs of flowers and leaves; a leather-bound first edition of Milton's *Paradise Lost;* a deep blue lidded Sèvres vase depicting a maid and her lover reclining on a bank. She often wrote letters, to Philippa, who wanted to know all about Compton Wyatt, and to Caroline Lambert: *Any more news of Mrs Dacre? Is your father better? If I'm needed I will come home.*

Mrs Shackleford senior never stopped talking. When she ran out of things to say she read aloud verses or prayers, and she was in her element when female neighbours came to call, as they frequently did, to look over the new Ardleigh relatives, On these occasions Asa was monosyllabic because she suspected their husbands of investing in slave ships. The trouble was Mrs Shackleford liked Asa's aloofness. Was not Asa the very image of a lady, with her French companion, her ancient name, impeccable deportment and practised whisk of a fan?

There was no escape. If Asa strolled in the gardens she was accompanied by Georgina, who reminded her sister a dozen times a day that all this could be hers. Warren haunted the lake, a borrowed fishing rod balanced beside him. One evening he came back with a thin perch, his only catch. If they happened to be alone – and it occurred to Asa that, recognising her desire for solitude, he was intent on needling her – he would stand far too close. His habitual smell of alcohol was distorted by a dash of perfume and there was a softness about his hands and cheeks which she disliked intensely. 'How beautiful you look, Miss Ardleigh. Fresh as a rose. I can't help thinking your charms are wasted on the few of us gathered at Compton Wyatt. When you're wed I hope to see you in London. You and I could have a rare old time if we could only slip the leash.'

Susan Shackleford was the most self-effacing member of the party. Once, when Georgina and Asa walked up to view the ruined chapel, they disturbed her; she fled past them as if she had been a roosting pigeon, her eyes red with tears, lips white and bitten. Usually she was to be found at the piano in the music room, long fingers floating over the keys, her tripping tunes at odds with her reserve. She didn't seem to mind if Asa slipped into the room to listen: once or twice her lips even twitched in what might have been a smile.

Madame de Rusigneux, meanwhile, had created for herself a niche at a desk in the drawing room, her little brushes spread before her as she made an exquisite copy, in miniature, of the deceased Tom Shackleford so that his mother might hang it on a chain and carry it on her breast. It was understood that some kind of private fee had been arranged, much to Georgina's outrage.

And Shackleford? Asa was alert to his presence in the house because at least he brought variety. If he was home he would shift restlessly from room to room, stare at a painting then walk abruptly away, linger in a doorway listening to Susan's music or sit down to hold a conversation with Madame de Rusigneux or his mother – rarely Asa – only to leap up as if he'd suddenly remembered urgent business. He spent hours in his book room, though he always kept the door half open as though not quite confident enough to close it. More often than not there was someone waiting to speak to him; a servant or tenant, his steward, petitioners, business associates. Asa could not fault his treatment of even the lowliest – each was grasped by the hand and given unswerving attention.

She was, however, critical of his vanity. His dress, though plainer than in Paris, as dictated by fashion and his state of mourning, was opulent. Once a fortnight, it was said, he visited a tailor in Bristol and packages arrived at the house almost daily, requiring Shackleford to be closeted for an hour at a time with his valet. 'I wish he was more like Tom,' cried his mother. 'That boy was such a sportsman and cared nothing at all for the cut of his breeches.'

'I admire a man who pays attention to his appearance,' said Georgina. 'After all, we have to

219

look at each other from noon until night.'

'My late husband had no time for finery. It was one of the reasons he and Harry could never stand to be under the same roof. Harry had no idea of how his father had slaved night and day in his own youth with not a thought for luxury.'

On Sunday the entire party – except Madame de Rusigneux, who was excused on account of the fact that she was not, as Mrs Shackleford put it, *of our faith* – drove to the church on the far side of the eight-foot wall that encircled the grounds, and for an hour contemplated the massive new plaque erected in memory of the late Shacklefords; their heads, side by side, peered out in marble relief, luxuriant wigs, greedy mouths, two pairs of hands clasping sacred books. 'Of course, my husband and I had planned to share a tomb,' whispered Mrs Shackleford tearfully, gripping Asa's arm, 'and so we shall. I have arranged to sleep between my two lost men.'

After their return to Compton Wyatt, Asa stood before a gilt-framed mirror and stared at herself dressed in muslin so lightly tinted green that the colour might have been imagined. Her hair was carelessly pinned, as usual. Reflected behind her was the duck-egg-blue gallery where the ball was to be held, with its white ceiling worked in scrolls and leaves, its row of satin-upholstered chairs with their gold-painted arms, and its long windows overlooking the lake. With a start of horror Asa saw that she fitted. In her misty dress, her head half turned, her features – startled, wide-apart eyes, half-open mouth – very soft in refracted afternoon light and with stray locks of hair fluttering on her cheeks, she belonged in that airy chamber. All that was required was a posy or a small dog on a leash and she might have stepped from a painting by Gainsborough or Thomas Lawrence.

On Monday the entire party drove to Bristol for a picnic on Brandon Hill. Shackleford offered to take Asa in the phaeton but she said she preferred a closed carriage, so Georgina went with him instead. When they arrived in the city they parted company – the Shacklefords and Warrens were to make a call in Queen Square while Asa, escorted by Madame de Rusigneux, had an appointment in Clifton. 'I have friends in the city,' she told Mrs Shackleford, 'whom I met at an abolition meeting in Sussex.' But it was no use being provocative; Mrs Shackleford regarded Asa's radical leanings as the quirk of a youthful, rusticated nature, and she lacked the imagination to connect abolition meetings to her own wealth.

At Miss Hillhouse's little house on Portland Street the ladies drank tea and discussed Wilberforce's latest speech to Parliament, which, they agreed, attacked the very heart of the Bristol slave trade. As an example of barbarity, Wilberforce had cited the case of the captain of a Bristol ship, the *Recovery*, who had ordered a fifteen-year-old slave girl to be killed because she refused to dance for him naked on the deck.

'The trouble is,' said Miss Champion, 'the Revolution in France has made slaving more profitable for our own merchants. The word on the street is that the very sniff of abolition in France or here at home will push prices up.'

'Most of our merchants are completely unscrupulous,' added Miss Hillhouse. 'Take your host, Mr Shackleford. It's well known that his late father encouraged Mr Pitt to offer British protection to French planters in Sainte-Domingue, rather than see a successful slave rebellion.'

'The Shacklefords and their type, I fear, do more damage than anyone else,' said Miss Champion, 'by winning favour through charitable works – look at the model farm that is to be established at Compton Wyatt and the schools that have been endowed in the Shackleford name. They lend slave trading a benign face and the truth about where the money comes from is brushed under the carpet.'

'Although, of course, the current Mr Shackleford had nothing to do with his father's trade until now,' said Asa. 'It has all been imposed on him.'

'Oh, I've heard that kind of argument so often it won't wash with me,' said Miss Hillhouse. 'I'd say your Mr Shackleford was in an ideal position to take a stand against slavery, and would have done so long ago if he'd been truly principled.'

'I do think he would like the situation to be different. It is simply that he's trying to work out where to start,' said Asa, somewhat surprised at her own defence of him.

'As an old acquaintance of our dear Mr Clarkson, Mr Shackleford is aware of exactly what needs to done. What a sensation it would cause, were he to become a committed abolitionist.'

'What do you think, Madame de Rusigneux?

Are there any prospects of abolition happening in France?' asked Miss Champion.

Madame smiled and shook her head mournfully. The conversation moved on to the rumour that some Machiavellian Bristol slave owners had been responsible for spreading word in the French colony of Sainte-Domingue that slaves, thanks to the Revolution, would be freed for three days a week. When this false promise wasn't honoured, unrest increased. 'Most of us care only for ourselves,' said Miss Champion sadly. 'If only people would look at the wider picture. In a civilised world...'

'But what is a civilised world?' asked Asa. 'To a slave trader, it's civilised to tame the "lawless" Negroes and make them do the necessary work of supplying sugar and coffee, which we in turn regard as essential to civilised life. To our government, it is civilised to pass the Dolben Act, which stipulates that only five slaves may be accommodated per three ton of ship.'

'And you, Madame,' persisted Miss Champion, 'what is your definition of civilised?'

Madame interlaced her fingers and raised her chin. 'You tell me,' she said, 'what it means to be human, even? Does anybody know? Believe me, I have seen things in France that would make you turn your faces to the wall. To be human, you might think, is to sit in this room and drink tea and have the grand ideas. But in France, for some, to be human is to lick the moss off a stone because the hunger is unendurable. To be human is to be herded from one prison to the next because you have said or even believed the wrong thing. To be human is to be forced to watch while someone you love is cut down, not because of accident or anger but in cold blood, because he is perceived to hold uncomfortable opinions.'

Silence. The ladies, though abolitionists, had perhaps never experienced such an outburst in their parlour. 'Certainly we understand that change is painful,' said Mrs Hillhouse, 'but those bold men and women who overturned a bankrupt monarchy, who have given authority instead to...'

'You mean, who have given authority to men who have no idea how to use it? To men who play at politics like schoolboys experimenting with ideas, to see which might work? Or to men who are so frightened and so cruel that the only answer they have if you oppose them is to brutalise, imprison or bludgeon you to death?'

'Not every one of the new leaders is like that,' said Asa. 'When I was in Paris, in '88, I met wonderful men who cared nothing for themselves...'

'Who were playing with ideas, in the way that you, Miss Ardleigh, so often do.' The prosaic little room, with its cross-stitch fire-screen, *I work, I serve*, was an unexpected backdrop to Madame's rage. Her blazing eyes were fixed remorselessly on Asa, and she had become a snapping, brittle thing. 'They did not know that they would soon end up hating each other because once they had disposed of their common enemies, the king and the aristocrats, they would find more enemies and even more still, those who would not fall into line. Would you talk freely like this with me, do you think, if you knew that afterwards one of us would contrive to have the other killed, simply because we had disagreed?'

'But that is just one side of the story,' protested Asa. 'As an aristocrat you are bound to think differently to us.'

She had the impression that if they'd been sitting any closer, Madame might have struck her. 'I am a woman, like you. I know what I have seen. I know what has been done in the name of liberty and it is not admirable.'

'The best of those in France are surely like the best of us? Mr Lambert says...'

'Ah, these scholars who treat ideas as if they were children's toys when in fact they are vipers. I'm very happy of course to be in England. I am grateful for the kind hospitality of your family, but I wonder about that hospitality, sometimes, Mademoiselle Ardleigh. It is given at a price, just like everything else; because I am your companion and teacher I may either be ignored or taken up sometimes and shown off as the tragic lady from France. I have become a feature of you, but in reality I mean nothing. So much, I say to myself, for all this talk of equality.'

'Madame, you mean a great deal to us,' murmured Asa, 'you must be aware of how grateful we all are...'

'Oh, grateful. Yes. As I said. Payment for services rendered. No thought of what I truly am. But that is because in England everything is talk. I cannot help but reflect on how much talking is done here, and how different it is when people act rather than merely speak. When one acts in Paris at present, one risks one's life.'

The shutters of Madame's eyelids came down as if to blot out the little parlour, the startled women, the roses in the vase. After a few moments, she calmly picked up her cup and drank the dregs of her cold tea. Someone commented shakily on the likelihood or not of a dry summer.

A quarter of an hour later, Asa and her companion were driven to Great George Street at the side of Brandon Hill. Neither spoke. If anyone was playing games, thought Asa, surely it was Madame de Rusigneux with her little paintbrushes and unpredictable outbursts. But Asa was also grudgingly aware that she would not have been so angry with Madame had her words not hit a nerve. Here she was picnicking on Brandon Hill with slave traders. What sort of a stand was she making here?

The rest of the party, together with another carriage from Compton Wyatt bearing servants and the paraphernalia of a picnic luncheon, were waiting by the gate. After spending such a turbulent hour with Madame, Asa was glad to meet her sister and even Shackleford, who greeted her with all the warmth of one who had not seen her for a month, rather than an hour.

'Such a lovely day for a picnic,' cried Mrs Shackleford, leaning heavily on Asa's arm as they followed a winding track upwards. 'Of course, when we were children this whole area was quite unspoilt.'

'Where did you live before, Mrs Shackleford? Can we see your childhood home from here?' panted Georgina, staggering under the weight of

226

her own petticoats.

Mrs Shackleford knew of a spot where they would have a view of the entire city, but it took several false starts before the servants were at last permitted to unload the picnic, the folding chairs, the wine coolers and napkins. Meanwhile she expected the other ladies to gather at her feet and follow her pointing finger while she mapped out the city below; it must have been apparent to all that she favoured Asa by urging her to sit closer and occasionally touching her hair or shoulder. 'Don't those masts look beautiful, clustered together like that? And there are the towers of our wonderful cathedral, which we passed, you may remember, on the way up the hill. A very shocking event took place there a couple of years back; they burned an effigy of Thomas Paine on the green. We don't think much of him in Bristol, I'm afraid, inciting us all to heaven knows what. But then you are such a radical young lady, Miss Ardleigh, that I expect you agree with every word Paine utters. Beyond is the spire of St Mary Redcliffe, the foremost parish church in Great Britain, where my poor husband and I used to worship when we were first married. He was such a sentimental soul and like many seafarers very superstitious. He used to have models made of our ships – you'll see one, the *Tranquillity*, in a glass case in the book room – and we'd take them to church to have them blessed, so that all who sailed in them might have a safe passage.'

'How comforting for the slaves,' said Asa, 'to know that God was overseeing their journey.'

'Did you own a ship outright?' asked Georgina,

jabbing Asa in the ribs with her elbow.

'Very few people own entire ships,' said Mrs Shackleford, 'but we used to have substantial shares in one or two. My husband loved the sea. Nothing would keep him at home, not even Compton Wyatt. He maintained that wherever his seamen had to go, he would go first. That's why he died, Miss Ardleigh, in the service of others.'

'Father and son both died on board ship,' put in Susan Shackleford suddenly.

'Oh Lord,' said Warren, 'I've been dying to know what of. Not the dreaded scurvy.'

Mrs Shackleford beckoned to Mrs Foster, who had travelled from Compton Wyatt with the other servants and now produced a handkerchief. 'I have been spared the details. Needless to say it was just like my husband to die, as it were, in harness.'

'So what was he doing on board ship in the first place? Where was he bound? Ain't there some kind of mystery attached to it all?' said Warren, who, kitted out in a pale blue coat and the affectation of no less than two waistcoats, one ivory, one yellow, had already quaffed a couple of glasses of wine.

Mrs Shackleford hid her face and murmured: 'My son, my lovely boy.'

Shackleford stood at Asa's shoulder. 'Down there is the port where we have our offices, and high up over there, the glassworks and bottling factory. Can you see the smoke?'

'The times I've sat up here with my dear husband and watched our ships come in or stood

228

above the gorge and seen our brave vessels, at high tide, setting sail for wonderful places that trip off the tongue, such as Calabar and Ashanti. And now it all belongs to Harry, who has so much to learn because he never took an interest when he might have done...' Mrs Shackleford held out her quivering hand to her son.

'You told me I ought to be a clergyman, Mama,' he said mildly.

'But in the event you did not train for anything. I really don't see how we are to manage. Your father and your brother had a feel for business. They never flinched from a hard decision if it was the right decision. Whereas you...'

'*Chère madame*,' murmured Madame de Rusigneux, who had transformed herself, chameleon-like, into an elegant French widow-friend, expertly straddling the divide between deference and equality as she offered Mrs Shackleford a plate of leek tarts. 'You must eat to maintain your strength. These places full of memory, how we torment ourselves...'

'The flies,' muttered Susan, 'I can't stand them.' She got up and walked away.

'What am I to do with her?' wailed Mrs Shackleford when her daughter-in-law was almost out of earshot. 'Someone tell me, do. She's so miserable. I don't know what she wants.'

'She's young to be a widow,' commented Georgina.

'There is never a good age to be a widow, believe me,' said Mrs Shackleford, spreading her black silks. 'One is so vulnerable, so at the whim of others. But madame, sit beside me and tell me

229

how you find Bristol, while Harry fetches you a glass of something. How do we compare with a French city?'

The sun was so hot that Georgina retreated into deeper shade, drawing Warren out of reach of the bottle. Asa muttered something about a desire to explore further and set off uphill in the opposite direction to Susan Shackleford. At the summit she perched on a broken stone wall and took off her hat. When Shackleford appeared, as she had suspected he might, she did not leap up and walk away but looked directly at him.

'It's thought there was once a well up here or possibly a chapel,' he said. 'This area is full of springs.' Shielding his eyes, he stared over the city. 'I have left my mother and Madame de Rusigneux deep in a conversation about the rival merits of French and English cuisine. I find Madame very intriguing, I must say. I can't help thinking there is rather more to her than meets the eye.'

'I hope that's true of most of us, Mr Shackleford.'

'I remember a village called Frenelle in the north-east of France...' He glanced at Asa, who in turn looked angrily away. 'Forgive me. You're unhappy. What troubles you, Miss Ardleigh?'

'I'm grateful for your concern but I doubt you could help.'

'Perhaps you could try me out.'

'All right, then: being at Compton Wyatt troubles me. Bristol troubles me. And Mr Shackleford, you trouble me most of all. You say you want to help. Then could you please tell me, once and for all, what you want from me?'

He drew a deep breath, even closed his eyes for a moment. 'Isn't it obvious? Hasn't it been so from the first time I met you? I tried to tell you that time in the Palais Royal. I have always wanted ... as I've said before, your friendship, at least.'

Of all things she felt affronted by so tentative a suggestion. 'How can I possibly be your friend when I flinch each time my foot sinks into one of your precious Turkish rugs? When you came to Ardleigh you talked of wanting me to understand you. I believe I do, only too well, and in turn I'm quite sure you have no trouble understanding me, Mr Shackleford.'

'My understanding of you, my sense of what you are, has been like a bell striking inside me from the very first day I met you.'

'Goodness. I'm surprised you remember.'

'At Madame de Genlis's salon you were wearing green and white and you were a little nervous, though your chin was up, as it is now. You were ready to take on anyone, except me, of course. But then I behaved like a fool. I allowed myself to be influenced by your brother-in-law, who convinced me from the outset that you were bound to look upon me favourably, given your attachment to Ardleigh.'

With his back to the sun, even his black mourning jacket had an aura of dusty light. When he took her hand and kissed it she was so startled that she allowed him to kiss her fingers again.

She had not been this close to him before or studied the texture of his skin, the apparently smooth lines of cheek and brow that could be transformed when he smiled into most unnerving complexity. 'Will you please listen to me without running away?' he said, and kissed her fingertip yet again, as if for courage. 'I realise that of all the charges you might lay against me, weakness is the most damning. And you'd be right.'

She withdrew her hand and her body a few inches but did not leave.

'When I was eleven years old my father took me to Jamaica for the first and only time. Usually it was Tom who accompanied him. Father said he wouldn't risk us both going on the same voyage for fear of accidents. At the time I felt excluded, believing he favoured Tom more than me, but in the long run his strategy was proved right, of course. We travelled on a passenger vessel, not a slave ship – my father had more sense than to subject me to that – so I arrived in Jamaica dazed by a long sea voyage, the heat, the brilliance of the colour out there. As a plantation owner, my father was a great success. He managed his slaves well, paid for them to have medical attention, never worked them too hard and allowed them time off for holidays and festivals. Most of them were deferential to him and treated me like a little prince. He was a consummate businessman, you see, and knew how to get the best out of people. I was encouraged to talk to whoever I wished and soon I felt proud of being a Shackleford. I admired my father all the more and was jealous of Tom, that he would inherit so much, although Father insisted that I could have a plantation of my own one day.

'But if you take a child to a place like Jamaica it's

hard to shield him from every unpleasantness. Some of my father's friends were less enlightened than he. A rebel slave had been insolent to his master, got into an argument and struck him, almost killing him. As you might imagine, the threat of insurrection is very real so insubordination, especially when violent, is punished severely. I was not supposed to be there, but I had become very confident and went exploring by myself. I came across a silent gathering in a clearing of fifty or so slaves, shackled, and a handful of white men. And in their midst was a naked slave, lacerated by a whipping which must have ended a few minutes previously. His wounds were still frothing blood. They'd dug a hollow and filled it with kindling and laid a grill of metal bars across it. They forced the man to lie down on his wounded back, tied him to the bars and lit the fire beneath. They didn't notice me until I started to scream, and then I was bundled away.'

They sat side by side, hands flat on the warm stones of the wall, looking into the blue sky. Asa thought of another young boy, her clear-eyed nephew at Morton Hall, picking an armful of daffodils for his mother; his plump, eager legs as they gripped the banister on a forbidden slide to the ground floor.

'I dreamed about him for years,' said Shackleford, 'though I tried to run away from my dreams. I couldn't exorcise the image even with drink, even with, forgive me, Miss Ardleigh, women, or travel or gambling. When I was sent to Oxford every word I read was a reproach so I abandoned my studies. However, I did meet Thomas Clarkson, having read his essay on slavery and commerce, and he in turn introduced me to Brissot at a meeting of the Anti-Slavery Society in London. I felt too much of a fraud to join them – I had no income of my own so I was living off my father. My God, how poor spirited this must seem to you. The truth is I was lost, Miss Ardleigh. That man, the tortured man – even now I cannot name him or bring myself to describe his face – inhabits my soul. But I did not protest. I never said a word to my father. Instead I hid.'

Asa was within a breath of walking away. Or of stretching her little finger to touch his, where it lay on the wall inches from her own. Instead she waited.

'When I was in Paris a year later,' he said, 'I met Brissot again. And he in turn had me invited to the salon of Madame de Genlis. She's something of a snob, Brissot told me, and in a very dubious relationship with her so-called employer, the Duc D'Orléans, but you'll meet some interesting people. I arrived quite late and was at once overcome by the old feeling of being an impostor. I shouldn't be amid all those people who talked so eloquently of liberty, I thought. If they knew what I'd witnessed, what I'd been condoning all those years by accepting my father's money...

'But I saw a girl standing by herself at the window. She was very young with nut-brown hair and the brightest eyes I had ever seen. And then, miraculously, your brother-in-law introduced himself and pointed you out as Thomasina Ardleigh, my cousin, and he added, by way of apology, that I mustn't mind you being a bit strange.

You'd been brought up in the country and had all kinds of ideas about abolition and suchlike.

'Miss Ardleigh, from the very first, I saw you as my salvation. You see, I didn't know how to shake off the ties. I still don't. But I thought, with your purity, your verve, with such a woman as my wife, I could finally do something. Of course, I never dreamed then that Tom would die. I imagined that I would be free to remain an outsider.'

Asa recognised his proposal as something akin to the yellow and red butterfly that flickered over buttercups and dandelions; an indirect and tentative offer of marriage with no mention of love.

'The point is you were mistaken,' she said. 'I'm not pure. I wasn't then, when I met you. You may carry the guilt of a dead slave but don't imagine that I am any less culpable. Even my birth had disastrous consequences for my mother – I have felt guilty from the start. Mr Lambert has shown me the worst possible forms of injustice yet I have been as passive as you. Earlier today Madame de Rusigneux accused me of doing nothing and she's quite right. I play at life. Oh yes, I visit prisons and I write letters. But I do nothing truly useful.'

'That's not what I see. I see – have always seen – a woman who might change everything.'

She couldn't help laughing. 'Dear me, Mr Shackleford, you expect a great deal. But I can't help blaming you for bringing me to Compton Wyatt, like a lamb to the slaughter, without discussing any of this with me.'

'I wanted you to know all about me. Then you would understand the full extent of my burden and what you would be taking on.'

'But I haven't seen the worst of it, have I, Mr Shackleford? Your burden, as you call it, also exists thousands of miles away from here. And I really don't see that I can do anything more than you could on your own. What have you done to disentangle yourself from it all thus far?'

'Not much. Written a few letters. Asked questions. Held meetings. It is not straightforward, taking care of all those people. I've scarcely found out where to begin. I've considered selling the plantations in Jamaica but of course there's a good chance they'd fall into worse hands than my own. I can free the slaves but it is a dangerous procedure unless done with infinite care for their welfare and protection. I thought that together, you and I – with your inspiration...'

Asa's head pounded with confusion. At any moment Didier might send for her. But Madame had also thrown down a gauntlet. Asa might sit in parlours sipping tea for years and make not one difference to the life of a single slave, yet as Shackleford's wife anything was possible. At last she said: 'You seem to imply that I might become your wife for the sake of doing good. In my book, the only reason to marry is for love.'

Shackleford did not answer for so long that other sounds seemed too loud; a couple of birds exchanged piercing calls in a nearby oak and far below the city wheezed and rumbled. 'I took it as read that you wouldn't marry me for love,' he said. 'I thought the challenge might attract you, or the potential of what we might do together.'

'I am of course honoured that you think I

might make a difference. Georgina complains that I have too many ideals, Mr Shackleford. Those ideals, I know, can be problematic. But of one thing I'm certain: if I do marry, it will be for love.'

After watching her for a moment longer he smiled and touched her cheek with the back of his index finger. The delicacy of that touch, the yearning in his eyes, left her in no doubt of his feelings for her. Why doesn't he fight for me, if he loves me? she thought. Instead he folded his arms and his head went down.

'You too,' she said softly. 'You, Mr Shackleford, I believe would not contemplate a marriage where there was not love on both sides.'

When he didn't look at her she walked quickly away, thinking really she'd had quite enough emotional encounters for one day; that she would find Georgina, plead a headache and ask to sit with her in the shade. Instead she missed her path and stumbled across Susan Shackleford walking towards her, arms clutched across her chest.

'Forgive me,' said Asa. 'You must find it as hard as I do to be alone.'

The skin on Susan's throat was so white and fine that the veins were clearly visible. She made a huffing noise in her throat.

'I expect you'd rather I found another path. We all need solitude,' Asa added.

'You might think that. Solitude is what happens to me, not what I choose.'

'I'm sorry. That was cruel of me, then, given that you are perhaps missing your husband very much.'

There followed another silence during which a tear seeped from the outer corner of Susan's eye and trickled down her cheek.

'Tell me about your husband. What was he like?' Asa said.

'I suppose you ask because you're bent on marrying the brother.'

'I have no intention of marrying Harry Shackleford.'

'Why not?'

'I don't love him. He and I can't agree on anything.'

Susan's bottom lip, which flaked as a result of all the gnawing it had to endure, quivered. 'I wish you would marry him.'

'Why is that, Susan?'

'He's much better than the other one. And if you and he were to stay at Compton Wyatt, things would be better.'

'Is life at Compton Wyatt so terrible for you, Susan?'

'What do you think?'

'I think you are very unhappy.'

'Do you know how many times I have stood by the edge of that wretched lake and thought, I'll just walk into the water one day. I'll keep walking until I'm gone. Would anyone miss me? I don't think so.'

'Susan.'

'Don't pity me. When my husband died I put my face in my pillow and tried to be sad. I wanted to love him. I thought it was my duty even though he'd never liked me, I could tell. And there was no child.' She marched away, but when Asa followed, she turned suddenly. 'I made it my business to find out what happened. Imagine. A ship becalmed on a tropical sea. A few too many slaves on board because my father-in-law, that pillar of society, couldn't resist bending the rules a little. Not enough water for all those extra bodies. One after another, corpses were tossed overboard. But in the end they were all struck with fever, even the ones who had plenty to drink. Or so the story goes. Of those who set out on that voyage fewer than half survived. But I wonder. Had I been a sailor on that ship, I know what I'd have done with two unwanted, thirsty, selfish passengers.' Her small eyes were animated for once and she was so unused to speaking that her voice cracked. Once again the spectre of marriage to Shackleford hovered before Asa; thousands of days spent in the company of this sad woman.

Voices were calling their names, Georgina's the loudest, and there she was, churning along the path in her pink and white muslin. It was time to go. Shackleford did not offer Asa a lift in the phaeton. That honour went instead to Madame de Rusigneux.

Chapter Four

Madame held hours of dancing lessons in preparation for the ball. At first Asa flinched from contact; the French woman's frail bones seemed sprung with danger. What would she say next?

But Madame's eyes were full of softness and encouragement as she urged Asa to take smaller steps and glance into her partner's eyes. 'It will be Mr Shackleford, first. You know him. At least let him see your face.'

Susan Shackleford crept into the room and, after watching with folded arms, selected a page from a stack of music and placed it on the harpsichord. 'Thank you so much,' called Madame. The gavotte was played with a light, infectious touch and Madame laughed as she squeezed Asa's hand – they were friends again.

The day of the ball dawned the most beautiful of all, with the image in the lake of tree and temple unshaken by breeze or cloud. In the gardens beneath Asa's window flowers were being cut to fill dozens of vases. Next morning the Ardleigh party would return home. At breakfast Asa found, beside her plate, a plump letter in Caroline Lambert's cultivated hand, such a tonic amid the overabundance of the Compton Wyatt table that she took it to a far part of the garden before breaking the seal.

The letter, however, contained the worst possible news.

I will tell you at once, Thomasina, I will write down the words: my father is dead. There has been an inevitability in the course of events that fills me with horror. Of course, he would not cancel the abolition meeting. Half a dozen attended in our parlour. If you had been at home in Ardleigh, you would have been here too. I wish that you had been there. We were betrayed. Two men hammered on the door and said that the meeting must stop. They kicked over furniture and scrabbled up fistfuls of Father's papers. They said that his sermons and essays would be used as evidence against him and that he must go to Chichester for questioning before the magistrate. We pleaded with them. It was late in the afternoon. Father was hungry and tired. The sun was too hot and their old wagon had no shade. They wouldn't let me go with them so I had to run to Mr Shepherd at the farm and beg him to harness up his trap so that we could follow. It was half an hour before we left Littlehampton but we'd gone less than a mile before we caught up with Father lying in nettles at the side of the road, his guards standing about scratching their heads, not knowing how to proceed, as they put it, because he'd simply leaned to one side and died.

I don't remember what I did. We must have laid him in the trap, covered him up and brought him home. The cottage was full of torn paper, but my friends helped to make everything tidy. They would rather not have left me alone but I wanted to spend one last night with him. Given the heat, we can't delay the funeral, Thomasina, even for your return. By the time you receive this, he'll be buried. But, my dear girl, you can perhaps imagine how much I need you.

Typically, in a postscript, Caroline remembered to mention the tailor's wife.

You will wish to know that she will be tried next Thursday, in Chichester. It's widely anticipated that she will hang.

Asa ran back to the house and upstairs to where

241

Georgina was closeted with Warren in her bed-chamber, amid heaps of clothes. The atmosphere was stormy; when Asa asked to speak to her sister alone Warren bowed insolently and left.

'Georgina, I have to leave now. Mr Lambert is dead. I must go to Caroline.'

Georgina, in a grubby pink robe, stared. 'What are you talking about? Of course we can't go now. The ball has been arranged for us. It would be unforgivable to leave today when the Shackle-fords have been so kind.'

'I must go. Mr Shackleford will understand.'

'What about his mother? It's our duty to stay. Mrs Shackleford's guests are expecting to meet you. We can't possibly disappear. And if he's dead, what's the rush? For heaven's sake, Asa, the Lamberts are not even family. Caroline has dozens of friends, I'm sure, who will look after her for one more day.'

'I'm not arguing about it. Stay if you want to but Madame and I will leave now.'

Georgina leaned against the door to prevent her. 'We can't go yet. Shackleford is bound to propose during the ball. Everyone knows he will.'

'He proposed on Brandon Hill and I refused him. I made my feelings absolutely clear so that he wouldn't pursue the issue any more. You must have noticed that since Monday he has scarcely been in the house. So there is no point in staying any longer, ball or no ball. I shall order the carriage and if you and Warren are not ready by mid-day, you'll have to make your own way home.'

Georgina was crying so much that her face was red. 'I can't believe it. You can't mean you turned him down. You must speak to him again and tell him it's a mistake.'

'I won't change my mind.'

'Oh God, you don't understand... You *have* to marry Shackleford because he's agreed to pay for a lawyer to defend Warren. He was most unkind and very unfair about it, and I'm sure he's only doing it because of you.'

'He will keep his promise, whether I marry him or not. And this has nothing to do with Mr Lambert.'

'But it's more complicated than you think. We assumed that Mr Shackleford would know all about the practice of sailing under French colours to avoid the Dolben restrictions. Everyone was doing it before the war. But Shackleford seemed to find it surprising that Warren had been involved and was completely unsympathetic, which is a bit rich given the amount of money his family has made over the years doing far worse things, I don't doubt. There are all kinds of vindictive people after us, customs people and magistrates and horrible men who say we owe them money. Shackleford says he will pay our debts but we must start afresh, build a new life. He even suggested we go to some colony called Sierra Leone, but I told him I couldn't bear to be so far from you and Phil. At any rate, for the time being we've got to disappear or we'll be arrested, so tomorrow we are to travel with you in the carriage as far as Bath, and then separate from you in secret so nobody notices we've disappeared. It's all arranged, but if you leave now the plan won't work.'

'Why would Shackleford make all these cloak-

and-dagger arrangements for you? I think even less of him for that. Why shouldn't Warren pay for what he's done?'

'Oh, Warren didn't mean any harm by it. He didn't even realise it was illegal, it was just a way round Dolben. Mr Shackleford admits that we're family. And after all, he's in the same trade as Warren.'

Georgina's tear-stained face showed such a mix of despair, triumph and defiance that it took every ounce of self-control not to shout at her. 'You are evading the law and Shackleford is helping you. If I agree to help I will be embroiled as well.'

'Don't be so prim, Asa, it doesn't suit you. This way nobody except Shackleford will be any the worse off and he can afford it. All I'm asking is that we leave tomorrow, not today. Please, Asa, I don't know what Warren will do if I have to tell him the plans have changed. You don't know what he's like. He'll be furious, he'll blame me.'

'What is he like, Georgina? Tell me.'

'Nothing. He's not like anything. Don't take everything I say so seriously. We both just love a ball.' Georgina dabbed powder on her face, twisted a curl and swooped about the room to show off her dance steps. 'You know how I've been looking forward to it, and you can't let all Madame de Rusigny's wonderful teaching go to waste.' She gave her old cow-eyed look, and a nod towards the spotted confection arranged on the bed – her gown for the evening. 'It's bound to be my last dance for a very long time. Surely you won't deprive me of it?'

244

Chapter Five

At dinner before the ball they were twenty. Mrs Shackleford surrounded herself with handsome men with whom she alternately flirted and became sorrowful as she talked about her lost son. Asa was seated between a Mr Blanning and a Mr Shatton, who said they were old acquaintances of the late Mr Shackleford from the Society of Merchant Venturers. She obeyed Madame's rules to the letter, dividing her attention equally and making monosyllabic replies to their remarks about how much she must enjoy staying at Compton Wyatt. Shackleford, at the far end of the table, wore a coat of bronze silk, his head alternately inclined to one lady or another, but his thoughts, Asa knew, were always with her. Whenever she happened to glance his way she caught his eye and felt a pang of regret that she was not next to him for this last meal so that she could talk about Mr Lambert, or at least argue with him about what he'd done for Warren.

Afterwards they were ushered to the gallery, where the five sets of glass doors had been thrown wide open so that guests might stroll on the terrace. More and more carriages arrived; thirty families had been invited and, a ball at Compton Wyatt being such a rarity these days, almost all had accepted.

Madame de Rusigneux and Georgina kept a

close watch on Asa, who could scarcely avoid keeping an eye on herself, reflected as she was in countless mirrors; a young woman in pearly pink voile with a dark grey sash (Georgina's only concession to Mr Lambert's death). Her partners, she reflected grimly, would be anti-abolitionists to a man. Meanwhile Shackleford stood beside his mother and set young ladies aquiver with one glance from his amber eyes. Or, thought Asa sourly, perhaps it was his money which enchanted them.

Georgina flung herself into the ball with the desperation of someone for whom this was the end of everything. She laughed too loud and long and glanced anxiously at Warren, who had been drinking steadily since sitting down to dinner. Madame stuck to Asa's side with Mrs Foster-like assiduity but contrived to show by the aloof smile on her lips that this was all something of a game. Her light gown (Georgina's cast-off) was partly obscured by a black shawl, which made her sumptuous hair and gleaming eyes seem more exotic than ever. Time and again she refused to dance: 'I am merely Miss Ardleigh's companion,' she murmured, lowering her eyelids, so that men hovered hopefully and ladies stared at her curiously or whispered behind their fans.

Susan Shackleford hung about in her black dress or stared at the lake. Once or twice Asa caught her eye and they exchanged a smile. The musicians struck up a minuet as Shackleford bowed over Asa's hand. Fuelled by three glasses of wine, she determined to show these slavers that the daughter of a country squire could dance better than they, so she swept on to the floor with a grandeur worthy of Madame de Rusigneux's sternest tuition, deadened the expression in her eyes and set her chin at a haughty angle.

According to Madame's instructions a lady should make three comments during a dance, unless specifically invited to say more. Asa therefore complimented Shackleford on the number of guests. 'They have all come to look at you,' he said, 'and who can blame them?'

The room was very warm and the breeze from the garden agitated a hundred candle flames. Asa had not danced in company for years except for a midsummer assembly in Littlehampton, and discovered that thanks to the wine and Madame's excellent instruction, she was in danger of enjoying herself. For a few moments she forgot Mr Lambert's death, her aversion to Compton Wyatt and that she'd intended to scold Shackleford for helping Warren evade the law. When he put out his hands to escort her down the set she couldn't help smiling up at him. But as soon as the dance was over she curtsied and moved abruptly away. Dear God, the look in his eyes had been enough to make a woman check her reflection and put her hands to her hot cheeks. No wonder the ladies clustered about him and young girls peeked at him yearningly from behind their fans.

Later in the evening Asa found herself dancing with Warren. It was a wonder that he could stay upright, but there he was in a dove-grey velvet coat and a grubby lace cravat, his grip too tight and his steps ponderous. The tilt of his head when he bowed was sardonic, his eyes bleary.

247

'Look,' he said, as they hop-skipped towards their reflection, 'what a handsome pair. Are you enjoying the ball, Miss Ardleigh?'

'I would rather be elsewhere.'

'Oh, I'm sure you would. Or at least with a different partner. I'm well aware what you think of me, Miss Ardleigh.' Then he leaned very close and whispered as if it were a compliment, 'Bitch.'

The dance dictated that Asa, in any case too shocked to respond immediately, should place her hand in his and withdraw it then allow him to pass his arm about her waist and stand hip to hip, but as soon as the dance ended Asa escaped. She flitted from room to room then out into the garden, where she hurried down flights of marble steps to the lake, intending to meditate upon something clean and good and far away from Warren and Compton Wyatt.

Except that there were revellers everywhere. One couple had retreated to the little temple, others disappeared into the bathhouse and emerged in the mouth of the cave, and by the lake a group was admiring the swans, which glided obligingly through the reflected flare of sunset. Asa walked farther, taking a path that wound into the trees. She could smell the lake and even the swans, she imagined, a feather-soft perfume of reeds and water and earth.

'Thomasina Ardleigh.' Warren had got ahead so that he blocked the narrow path like the wolf in *Red Riding Hood*.

'Mr Warren. Forgive me, I'm just on my way back to the house.'

He did not step aside. 'Stay with me a while.

It's cooler out here and the evening is very beautiful. It's not often I have the leisure to stroll in such a setting with my sister-in-law. She doesn't usually give me the chance. She doesn't believe I'm worth the time of day.'

'Mr Warren, you are my sister's husband. Of course I...'

'And what a wife your sister's proved to be. No money. No child. And now I'm doomed to be exiled with her in some godforsaken place and go into trade, which means we shall die of starvation, no doubt. We are supposed to be grateful to Mr Shackleford for saving us from a debtors' prison, but if he chose he could set us up in a smart little establishment with a regular income, which I'd much prefer. Well, thought I, before I go, I'll take a little something from Mr Shackleford. He shan't have it all his own way.'

'Please step aside. We shall be missed.'

'I've seen Shackleford watching you and I rather think he'd kill to be me at this moment,' and he slid his finger down Asa's throat. Too late she tried to spring away as he seized her upper arm. 'How come you and Georgie are sisters, is what I want to know? You appear to be so exquisitely easy to break, I would think, whereas she's a tough old bitch. But I've noticed something else in you that leads me to suggest that if I were to touch you here,' he pinched her breast, 'or here,' he placed his other hand on the small of her back, dragging her so close that his chin rubbed hers, 'you would become very hot and yielding, Miss Ardleigh. Because I do believe you are not quite so pure as we all think. Ah, yes, let us see what happens.'

He ground his mouth against hers so that their teeth clashed and she tasted the alcohol on his breath. For a moment her wits deserted her – this was her brother-in-law, after all, the ineffectual Warren (whom Philippa had once, in a moment of exasperation, described as *pointless*). Surely, in addition to everything else, he wasn't an adulterer. But as she clamped her mouth shut and clawed at his hands part of her said: You deserve this. You have never paid him any attention except to sneer at him.

He was proving surprisingly strong, shuffling her backwards so that her heels caught on her petticoats and she was crushed against a tree. 'How dare you,' she said through his hand, 'how dare you treat my sister like this?' and she kicked and thrashed as he pinioned her neck.

'You want this. I see the way you move. I've watched you since we first met, and do you know what I think? That these soft breasts of yours are not at all virginal. Now don't you struggle, Thomasina Ardleigh, because I'm determined to find out exactly where others have been with you. After all, you're the father's daughter, aren't you? Georgie was telling me about the old man and what he'd been up to...'

When she bit his hand he pushed his fists into her throat and pressed up her chin with his thumbs so she couldn't breathe. 'You give me what I want, Miss Ardleigh, or I shall haul your sister and your father and the Ardleigh name through such a mire you won't be able to hold your heads up.'

She tried to twist out of his grasp, thinking her neck would break and the hardness of his body split her from thigh to throat, but she was abruptly released when he was struck from behind, wrenched away and flung backwards. The ensuing skirmish was accompanied by much scuffling and swearing as Warren attempted to beat off his assailant, then made a lurching effort to escape into the woods. But his legs were seized and he was brought crashing down again, struck heavily in the face then thrust on his way, stumbling and tearing bits of undergrowth from his hair. Meanwhile Asa hovered, panting, torn between the conflicting desire to stay and thank her rescuer or bolt towards the house.

'Thomasina.' Shackleford spoke softly, though he was still breathless and dishevelled, most unlike himself. The ends of his cravat were streaming and his hair tumbled over his face. 'Take a little time. Compose yourself.'

'I shouldn't have been caught out like that. I had no idea that he hated me.'

'You are not to blame for the vile behaviour of other people.'

'My poor sister. Oh dear God, I must get her away from him. She can't know what he's really like.'

'Your sister is a woman of the world. From my conversations with her I would say she knows full well what Warren is.'

'She must be separated from him.'

'Perhaps she should do as she chooses.'

'You would say that, wouldn't you? Let things be, that's your motto. So much simpler.' But then she cursed herself for her ingratitude and the weakness of tears as she scooped up her hair and wound it in a knot, pulled the edges of her bodice together and smoothed her skirts. It hurt to breathe and her throat ached. 'I should like to go inside now, Mr Shackleford.'

When he offered his arm, she accepted, for the sake of appearance, and they walked slowly back to the house. The waters of the lake were dark but the sky was luminous, with just three stars where the sun had set, arranged in an equilateral triangle. Music was still playing in the ballroom.

Asa was too distraught to ask any questions: How had he found her? Shouldn't he be with his guests? What exactly had happened to Warren? Instead she reflected that it would gladden poor Georgina's heart if she could see the pair of them now, arm in arm, walking in the seclusion of the woods.

They had fallen into step and Asa's ill-treated gown made a shushing amid the previous year's leaves. She was sorry when the house came into view, where other guests strolled about on the terraces, because walking beside Shackleford was remarkably straightforward compared to what she must now face; the end of the ball, Georgina, the return to Ardleigh, her father's drunkenness, Caroline's destitution. Not to mention Mrs Dacre.

And one final complication stood at the edge of the terrace, leaning on the white parapet, her figure very slight in its unaccustomed pale dress, her hair lifted from her shoulders by the night breeze. Though Madame de Rusigneux had surely seen them she neither smiled nor waved, only stared at them and then turned away.

To avoid passing through the ballroom, Shackleford led Asa round the side of the house to a little door set into the side of a flight of steps. He lit a taper, took her hand and guided her along a series of narrow passages to an entrance, concealed on the inside by shelves, to his book room. 'My father showed Tom and me this special way into the house when we were boys. He had it built, he said, so that the men could come and go without being constantly under the eye of the women. I fear my old pa was not quite as saintly as Mother depicts him.

'When I was a very small boy we used to live in a high townhouse in Bristol, and we'd drive out here on a Sunday to watch the work in progress. First the ramshackle old house was ripped down – I can remember fragments of glass winking at me from the rubble of a fallen chimney – then the foundations for the new mansion were laid and earthworks begun in the gardens. I used to lose myself among the ancient walls and hedges, and then get lost all over again when the landscape changed and artificial hillocks were created and the lake dug so that I couldn't get my bearings. I was always anxious here. There were so many rooms with nobody in them, just the smell of damp plaster.'

By now he had drawn up a deep leather chair and steered her into it. He knelt at her side, like a suitor. 'You are very pale, still. What can I do for you?'

Her neck throbbed. She leaned her head back and half closed her eyes. 'In a moment I'll go upstairs and wash.' What a peculiarly changeable face he had. In the vestiges of twilight his eyes were darker and shadows had broken the smooth curve of his cheek. 'Thank you for rescuing me, Mr Shackleford, it was very kind, given how much I've argued with you. But what were you doing in the garden?'

'I saw you leave the ballroom and when you didn't come back, I followed, partly because I didn't like the look in Warren's eye when he was dancing with you, partly because I wanted to have one more conversation before you left.'

'What kind of conversation?'

'A foolish one, you might think. An attempt to begin again from first principles.'

'First principles?'

'Some other time, perhaps, when you're rested.'

'What's wrong with now? I like it here. I feel as if I'd like to stay a while.'

He hesitated, laughed, and drew a long breath. 'All right, then, I'll take my chance and say that I believe we began on entirely the wrong footing. From the moment I met you in that Parisian salon, even then, the timing was bad; you were distracted and wanted to absorb yourself in the French, not the English. You look startled, but I remember, Miss Ardleigh. You were bound to think ill of me from the very first and I was wrong to impose myself on you or think you would ever marry me. You, of all people, would not be persuaded by expedience. But I meant what I said on Brandon Hill about friendship and I didn't want us to part without telling you that.'

'Thank you, Mr Shackleford. Given the way my

relatives and I have behaved recently, even I can see that's very generous of you.'

'I had a long speech of self-justification prepared but now is hardly the moment.'

'In any case you have somewhat complicated matters by placing me doubly in your debt. You rescued me from Warren and my sister Georgina from penury. That puts me in the uncomfortable position of having to be grateful to you, Mr Shackleford.'

'I don't want you to be grateful. As you have reminded me often and in no uncertain terms, my wealth is ill gotten. It might as well be spent on Warren if it spares your sister pain, even though you're right and she'd be better off without him. I am resigned to the fact you won't marry me, Miss Ardleigh, but your welfare will always be my first concern.'

'That's very kind of you, Mr Shackleford.' She smiled at him, thinking muzzily that she could not fathom how much his face pleased her. 'Talk to me some more, then,' she murmured, 'say anything and I'll listen.'

'I don't think I have anything more to say. Words fail me. I thought I could hold a conversation with you quite coolly but… Perhaps in the morning, Miss Ardleigh, we'll speak again.'

He took her hand and pressed it to his lips. If only they could really begin again, she thought. If only she had not given herself to Didier and could think clearly about what she felt for Shackleford. Even as her other hand slid into his she closed her eyes, lest she be too distracted by the shape of his head and the lustre of candlelight on his hair. 'Mr

Shackleford, you must have heard what Warren was saying to me in the garden. He's right. I'm not in a position to marry anyone, even if I wanted to. He mentioned that my father ... there's a woman in our village who has been very wronged... And aside from my father there's something else which makes marriage to you impossible. I am not as you think. You should know that in Paris, in the past...'

'I don't care about the past. Do you think anything your father or your sister or especially you have done would stop me loving you?'

His touch was that of a man who for years had longed for the unreachable. She felt so precious to him as he stroked back her hair that she could have wept. She whispered: 'You don't know. If you knew. No man would want me after what I've done.'

'Hush. I love you. That's all, Thomasina.'

Her free hand seemed unable to resist mirroring the movement of his. Under her palm his cheek was a different shape to Didier's, rounded where his was hollow. Warren had been quite right; she was familiar with the feel of a man's skin and craved the firmness of male embrace. Or was it that she had been brutally treated by Warren and felt roughened and ugly and in need of repair? Or perhaps it was simply that the colour of Shackleford's eyes reminded her of good things; her mother's oak nursing chair, a freshly fallen conker and the essence of vanilla. Whatever the cause, she kissed her fingertips and pressed them to his lips. His mouth, which smiled so readily, was not smiling now. To be kissed felt like surrender; it felt like allowing the weight of resistance to roll from her. As she was drawn against him, Compton Wyatt streamed away because this was all it was; this dark, lovely kiss. Afterwards they gazed at each other, and he stroked her hair and neck and kissed her brow.

The music changed in the ballroom, Mozart. There was a brushing of knuckles on the door, a murmured: 'Mr Shackleford, sir, the Macaulays have called for their coach.' Shackleford kissed her forehead and put his fingers to her bruised throat. 'I must show myself to my guests or they'll come looking for me. And I'll fetch some wine because you are so pale you might faint away. I'll be just five minutes.' He picked up her hand to kiss it one last time and replaced it in her lap as if it were made of porcelain. Perhaps he had some premonition because at the door he turned. His smile was to linger in her memory and be resurrected sometimes.

The music in the ballroom was familiar. A minuet. Played … yes, in Paris, at the salon of Madame de Genlis, when the doors were flung open and she first saw Didier. With that surge of memory came a slow awakening of other senses: the smell of Shackleford's book room, the oiled wood of the shelves and panelling, fresh paper, leather. She sat upright, puzzled by a reflected halo of light, and saw that the candle nearest her right hand was illuminating a sheet of glass. At first she could not see past the smear of light, then she realised that what she saw was a display case and that within it was the model of a ship, the length of her forearm, built in light-coloured wood, perfectly to scale even down to the railings on the deck and the windows in the state room; a three-masted frigate with fine thread for rigging and stiffened linen for sails. Asa picked up the candle to take a closer look at a small brass plaque: the *Tranquillity*.

The flame dipped as the truth of the book room dawned on her; flickering light reflected from the gleam of oils in a portrait over the mantel, presumably of the late Mr Shackleford, his hand on a globe and his monstrous wig framing self-satisfied, somewhat brutal features. Deeper in the room she found more etchings of idle white men, bewigged and tricorn-hatted amid darker-skinned natives busy landing canoes on exotic beaches. Her toe caught on a rug composed of the luxuriously furred skin of some hapless animal, and her hand, when she reached out to balance herself, fell on a cabinet enshrining a thick golden chain, ivory carvings of a lion and an elephant, heaps of beads and some kind of ceremonial sword with a jewelled handle.

Beside the desk, where she had often glimpsed Shackleford at work, was a row of massive ledgers bound in red leather, tooled in gold and labelled *Shackleford Plantations, 1760, 1761* and every year to the present. There were piles of shipping logs, gazetteers and scrapbooks, and covering the blotter on the desk an open newspaper: *Felix Farley's Bristol Journal*, with an article circled in pencil concerning a slave convicted of assassinating his overseer.

The music, seeping beneath the door, was another assault; such freshness in an unyielding mausoleum of a house. She glanced back at the

258

chair in which she had been kissed by Shackleford. How could she have allowed it? Gratitude for saving Warren, that must be the excuse, and the demands of her treacherous body, starved of touch.

Stumbling, aching, she left the room, headed along a passage leading to a servants' staircase and slipped from view. Step by step she was shedding Shackleford, the ball and all the seductive places in which he and she had talked together. From her bedchamber she could make out the ghostly shapes of women who still lingered with their escorts by the black waters of the lake. She closed the window, then the shutters, dropping the metal bar into place as if afraid they might suddenly burst open. She carried her candle to the bed, where a small brown paper package lay on the silken quilt.

The address, *Miss Thomasina Ardleigh, of Ardleigh Manor, Sussex, Grande Bretagne,* had been crossed out and the package redirected to Compton Wyatt.

Her hands shook so much she could not at first untie the string. And yet she would not cut it, instead spent minutes on the tight knot. Inside, two items. One, a slip of paper, scribbled in an exquisite French hand. *Viens. J'ai besoin de toi.* The other, a crumpled white parcel, held the insubstantial weight of a square of faded turquoise silk. She took it by the corner, delicately, as if it were a membrane, and it fell open in a shimmer of water-smooth fabric and the faintest hint of perfume.

Didier.

Chapter Six

Asa did not sleep. Because her door had no lock she stacked furniture and packing cases against it, though whether to keep herself in or Shackleford out she could not have said. When he knocked, barely ten minutes after she'd left the library, she retreated to the far side of the room and would not answer. Three times he spoke her name. From downstairs came the clamour of departing guests. Later Shackleford's distant voice bade farewell to yet another visitor. After another half hour or so he knocked on Asa's door again and murmured her name.

In the small hours, when she unlatched the shutters and peeped through, she saw him pacing up and down by the lake and had to clasp her hands behind her back to prevent them from hammering on the window. It was as if the *Tranquillity* had been moored up ready to carry them away. Such, surely, would be her life with Shackleford. Far too tempting to sink into his arms, to seek another long, lovely kiss and be rocked by his infinite wealth. She saw another version of herself, in her pearl-pink dress, floating across the terrace towards him. This other Asa tucked her arm through his and off they set along the shore, back into the woods to spend the hours of the night binding themselves with promises.

Instead, there on the bed, was Didier's letter

and his turquoise silk like a flag unfurled.

At one point Asa ran to the door, moved the furniture and went out into the passage. The guests had all gone and the house was silent. She trod polished oak boards and antique rugs, passing one closed door after another and, at the head of the stairs, the bust of some Greek deity torn from its niche in Athens. A footman swayed with exhaustion in the hall below, supporting himself with one hand on the banister. Asa crept back to her room.

In another hour a maid brought hot water and fastened Asa's gown. Shackleford was waiting at the foot of the stairs and ran up a few steps to greet her but she would not look him in the eye, only gave him a bland smile as she swept past. Madame de Rusigneux and Georgina were at breakfast. Nobody spoke much except to comment on the excellence of the ball and the promise of another fine day. Warren was not present. Asa left a note for Susan propped against a coffee cup.

When they parted on the grandiose steps Asa barely skimmed Shackleford's hand with her own and kept her eyes averted from his face. He spoke low and vehemently: 'Miss Ardleigh, last night you were gone so suddenly. Please believe that I wish you well. If there is anything...'

'Thank you for all you've done. You have been very kind to my sister and me. I'm sorry, I realise that must be all.'

She ran down to the carriage and did not look back as they drove away.

Georgina melted from Asa's life in the hazy dawn

261

of a May morning. One moment she was in the carriage, the next she and Warren – who had travelled sullenly on horseback – transferred to a covered goods wagon. Thanks to the presence of Madame there was no opportunity for private discussion between the sisters. In any case Georgina's determined cheerfulness, the way she fixed her eye on Asa as if to say, Don't you dare, forbade interference. They embraced briefly in the carriage while Madame and Warren kept their distance.

So Madame de Rusigneux and Asa were alone most of the journey home, which was prolonged by the age of the Ardleigh carriage. The interior was so ill sprung and stuffy with the sun baking on the roof and the lanes too dusty for a window to be opened that neither woman had the stomach to read or work. After a particularly lurching descent, Madame went quite green and had to walk in the lane for half an hour. When they set off again she produced a couple of plain fans from her portmanteau to ward off the nausea.

No amount of fanning would cool the turmoil within Asa. How could one body contain such a mix of pain, excitement and dread? On the one hand Didier's note was a clarion call, jolting her wide awake. What had she been thinking of, falling into the arms of a slaver? Had she so forgotten herself that she could waste a moment on Shackleford when waiting for her, across the Channel, was not only Didier but the remains of her bold, idealistic self? On the other hand, Didier's note was equivocal. Where exactly was she supposed to go? And she rebelled at its suddenness; months of silence followed by a peremptory: *J'ai besoin de toi...* But then, given the upheaval in his country, did she really expect a man such as Didier, who had spent the last five years striving at the heart of change, to waste time on soft words? Wasn't it enough that he had called for her?

At regular intervals she dipped her fingers into her bodice and touched Didier's handkerchief or, if Madame slept, pressed it to her face and tried to discern the scent of him. Sometimes her hand strayed to the bruises on her neck beneath her muslin scarf and then her thoughts would swerve to the book room at Compton Wyatt, and Shackleford. She felt the sturdy grip of his hand, the extraordinary sense of homecoming as she allowed her body to fall against his.

Madame scarcely spoke but held herself at a distance, as if she too were sunk into an internal world until, on the second day, they were about ten miles from Ardleigh, in the heart of a forest. Through the greenish light her eyes fixed on Asa. *'Tiens,'* she said, *'Mademoiselle. Je voudrais dire ... c'est fini, je pense.'*

By reverting to French she tapped directly into Asa's obsessive mental examination of Didier's letter. 'To what do you refer, madame?'

'My task is accomplished,' she said in her low, dark voice. 'You have found yourself a husband so all is well and there is no further use for me.' She added, with a hint of impatience: 'Monsieur Shackleford. Did he not propose, during the ball? I saw you walking with him in the garden and I surmised...'

'Ah, no. No.'

'*Mais je croyais que c'était décidé?* I don't believe it. My work is done.'

'You are mistaken, madame. I do not intend to marry Shackleford.'

Madame's small hands were folded in the blue-black mass of her old gown and there was a sheen on her sallow skin. 'But he loves you so. I do wonder at you, mademoiselle.'

'How do you know he loves me?'

Madame studied Asa's face. 'Only a fool would not see,' she said a little coldly. 'He cannot keep his eyes from you and he is a different man when you are present. The rest of us are shadows to him.'

For a moment, Asa contemplated banging on the roof of the carriage and demanding that they turn round at the next gate, but Madame spoke again, in quite a different voice: 'In any case I would ask you to release me because go I must.'

'Go, madame?'

'I am needed in France.'

'*France?* It is surely far too dangerous for you there.'

'Even so I should never have come away. I curse my weakness.'

'You are not weak, madame. Nobody could ever believe such a thing of you.'

'Nonetheless.'

'We have heard that the revolutionary government in France is unforgiving towards émigrés who failed to return by the beginning of last year.'

'I care nothing for my life.' Madame leaned her elbow on the worn cushion and put trembling fingers to her forehead. She seemed so very slight, so full of appalling memory, that Asa regretted having pressed her so far. 'I shall go to Paris to find out where they buried my brother.'

'But you are alive and your brother is dead. Surely he would not have wanted you to risk your life for this? And why now? If you wait, perhaps everything will change and it will be safer.'

'How much longer must I wait? Who knows what will happen next? I failed him by allowing myself to be sent away when I was a witness to his murder. I shall not fail him again.'

'Your devotion puts me to shame, madame.'

'What cause have you to be ashamed? Would you not do the same for one of your sisters?' Madame turned her face to the window. 'I wish you had met my brother. Then you would understand. In looks he was very like me, thin and dark eyed, but unlike me he thought nothing of his own needs. He could have been a saint, if a saint can be full of laughter, as we were when children.' Her smile was the merest compression of the lips. 'In a garden where we used to play there was a great empty urn in which he hid himself once, for half an hour, then popped out when we'd all thought him lost. That was typical of my brother, endlessly patient, playing the fool. He was lured to his death like an innocent...'

'Lured to his death?'

'I brought him to Paris to keep him safe. We were both betrayed.'

'You have said before, madame, that you led him into a trap. You are very harsh on yourself. You must have believed that you were doing the right thing.'

'Gabriel would probably have been quite safe where he was, an insignificant parish priest. What happened was that after Gabriel refused to sign the oath, the authorities sent a so-called constitutional priest, Père Ballard, who *had* signed, to take over Gabriel's humble flock. But because they were loyal to Gabriel, the congregation refused to respond when Ballard said mass. As he processed down the aisle one of the bolder women even followed with a broom to sweep up the contaminated dust from his shoes. She was punished severely – thrown into prison for a fortnight to reflect on her crime.'

'Who arrested her? Surely the Revolutionary Assembly promotes religious tolerance?'

'Is that what you think? The fact is, the woman was punished and Gabriel was afraid that others would suffer because of their loyalty to him. But actually in parishes up and down the country priests like Gabriel have survived by hiding themselves away, biding their time and saying secret masses. The trouble with Gabriel is that he made the mistake of consulting me and I urged him to come to Paris. It was what I was told to do.'

'Who told you?'

'Enough to say ... I was in love.' Madame's glance flickered to Asa. 'I believed the words of my lover. So Gabriel was lured to Paris in order to be destroyed.'

'But why would anyone do that?'

'Gabriel was good and true and unswerving. Paris last summer was a dangerous place to be for a fugitive priest: the king was more or less a prisoner; foreign, royalist armies were gathering at the country's borders; people were still starving; harvests were still failing; the very poor remained very poor. These counter-revolutionary forces were very threatening. What was quite clear to leaders such as Danton, Marat and Robespierre was that if you weren't for the Revolution, you were against it and against France, and therefore must be punished. And an easy target for this new purge was the priests who had refused to sign the patriotic oath.'

'But surely there must have been public outrage.'

'Ah, Mademoiselle Ardleigh, it seems I have failed to teach you that the world does not divide itself cleanly into good and evil. For a start, many people were ignorant about what was happening in those prisons. And others were self-seeking. They feared the priests, or wanted them dead, though they would never say so. The priests were a burden on their consciences, you see, because they did not compromise. When my brother was arrested last August he was one among many.

'I visited Gabriel every day and I was angry with him too. I told him that he was deceiving himself. He and his friends used to plan what their lives would be like when they were exiled. They dreamed of setting up communities where they might bide their time until the madness in France was over. All a nonsense. I'm sure he knew, as I did, that there would be no future of any kind for Gabriel. Each time I went, more priests had been crammed inside the prison. Nobody left.

'Meanwhile, I heard it said that able-bodied

Parisians were refusing to leave the city to fight foreign armies because they were afraid that in their absence the priests would break free, put the king back on his throne and declare the revolution over. I ran from one friend to another, to endless committee rooms, arguing that patriotic souls such as Gabriel were no threat at all.'

'What about the man who had told you to bring Gabriel to Paris?'

'I pleaded with him, of course. I begged him to use his influence to free the priests or send them out of the city. Nobody listened. Worse than that, I now believe that by creating a fuss, I made Gabriel a thorn in their side. And so, when the day came, when Gabriel died, there was no one to prevent it. The man I trusted, my best hope, had left the city.' Madame bit her lip and put the palm of her hand on her forehead, as if smoothing away the painful memory.

'What happened, Madame?'

'I used to take Gabriel soap, which was a rare luxury last summer, and fruit and cheese. The prison itself was foul – you could smell the stench in the streets half a mile away because they had converted a chapel into a prison, and it had no sanitary arrangements at all, although there was a garden. I remember so well how for a little while, when I sat with him in the long grass, when I saw the sky through beech leaves, I could pretend that he and I were young again. I would try to make him eat instead of giving everything away to his friends, and each time I would beg him to sign the oath. Gabriel never got angry with me, he just looked sad, which was worse, and said that he'd made up his mind.

'One day we were again in the garden. Everything seemed much as usual except that there were more guards. Then someone said that the trials of the priests were going to take place that afternoon. I clung to Gabriel, I pleaded with him. I shouted that he *had* to sign the oath. What was it, after all, but a bit of paper, a pledge to support the Revolution? I locked my arms round him and tried to shake him into doing what I wanted. For me, I cried. For me.

'A little door in the corner of the garden, which was usually locked, burst open and a gang of youths crowded in. They wore belts stuffed with pistols and carried swords, knives and pikes. One of them seized the nearest priest – an elderly man with white hair, who had been reading his missal – by the scruff of the neck, forced him to his knees and without a word slashed at his back with a sword. I remember how a spray of blood caught the sun and hit the youth's shirt. The old priest just had time to lift his head and look amazed before they cut his face, forehead to chin. Two more youths leapt on him, laughing and stabbing him with their pikes.

'Everything was still. I never let go of Gabriel's hand. Then the garden was full of bellowing youths who lashed out with blade or pike or pistol-shot, and with priests running to the walls and scrabbling for a hold or flinging themselves to the ground and covering their heads. Sometimes they were caught by guards and cut down. Gabriel and I didn't move. We could not. We just held each other.

'Then a man yelled the order that the prisoners should be lined up and taken inside for trial. I still clung to my brother's hand. We walked past the body of his dearest friend. I begged Gabriel even then to sign. More than almost anything else I regret that my last words to him were not: "I love you" but "Sign." When we reached the door of the church they wrenched me away, though I fought and scratched. I caught sight of my brother only once more through the crowd, so beautiful, the shabby soutane, the back of his head like a young boy's.

'I shouted to him that I would get help. I yelled the names of the famous, influential people I would fetch but the guards had me dragged away.

'I couldn't see, but I heard the question: *"Vous avez juré?"*

'And Gabriel's answer, *"Non."*

'I smelt dirt on the hand of the man who held me. My head was pressed back and all I could see was a white painted ceiling, a doorway.

'After that everything is dark. I was found lying in the street with my face in the cobbles. I knew my brother was dead. I swear I could smell his blood. When I was well enough, I was sent out of the country. As I said, it was not safe for me in Paris, I had seen too much. The killing of those priests was a massacre of innocent people by their fellow countrymen. If the truth about what happened were made known, Marat and his cohorts would fall. I must go back, if only to make one last attempt to bring his killers to justice. I was a witness. And I must ensure that my brother's body is buried well, and not tossed into a ditch.'

Madame's head rolled against the cushions. In a surge of sympathy and apprehension Asa crossed the carriage and embraced her tense body. 'Now I understand. Now I see.' And already, in that moment of passionate connection, Asa felt the first flutter of terrifying intent.

Never had the Ardleigh lanes looked lovelier, the forge and the bakery and the labourers' cottages seemed more homely, their gardens a tangle of honeysuckle and foxglove; never had Asa so relished the glimpses of the Downs as they lurched in and out of view, sometimes sprinkled with sheep, sometimes thickly wooded. At long last the carriage slowed, wheeled round the side of the manor and trundled under the crooked stone arch into the deep shade of the stable-yard. There was of course no sign of the squire, but Mrs Dean hurried out, and a maid.

The house was coolly scented with wisteria. Mrs Dean brought tea and wanted to talk but Asa was monosyllabic so the housekeeper left her alone in the parlour, where she studied the ancient chest in the window, the scarred oak chairs and the skimpy rugs on the flagstones. How small and faded it all was compared to Compton Wyatt, how familiar the ticking of the clock, the tapestry cushion covers worked by her mother, the clatter of dishes in the kitchen.

A pile of letters, unopened, lay within reach. The first, from Philippa, Asa set aside. The clock ticked away a dozen seconds before she picked up the next; an envelope larger than the rest, written in an unknown hand and stamped in

271

London. Inside was another blank envelope.
This note, unlike the last, was dated; 15 May.

Je suis désolée, ma chère. Je meurs sans toi. Ta lettre...
Sans toi la vie ne vaut rien. Mes ennemis m'entourent.
Tu es la seule...

Chapter Seven

Caroline Lambert had grown so thin that when they embraced Asa thought her friend's spine would snap. Her skin had a mushroomy pallor and her eye sockets were dark with sleeplessness and grief. They visited Mr Lambert's grave, marked by a long mound of soil and a wooden cross. Under the hot sun the new-turned earth had already cracked.

She and Caroline stood side by side, gripping each other's hands. 'I tell myself, he would have been pleased to die like that,' said Caroline, 'carried away in a cart to defend his principles. When they came for him he wasn't at all afraid. Amused, rather. I think he relished the prospect of putting his case before a judge.'

'I wish I'd been here.'

'Our friends are collecting money for a headstone. Your sister Philippa has been very generous, so thoughtful. She wrote me a long letter and in the course of it made me a very kind offer. She has asked me to go to Morton Hall as governess to your nephews.'

'Goodness. But you're not a governess. Whatever was she thinking of?'

'In her letter, Philippa – Mrs Morton – said that your family was indebted to my father for the care he had taken of you and that she had such a high regard for both him and me that she would like me to teach her boys until they are old enough for school. By which time baby Kate will be ready for the services of a governess.'

'I hope you refused her at once. Or would you rather I wrote to her?'

'I have not refused her at all.'

Asa waited until they were on their way back to the cottage before she could trust herself to speak again. 'This is selfish of Philippa, to use your loss to her advantage. You are far too clever to be a governess. Besides, John Morton is suspicious of Dissenters. He would never tolerate your views.'

'Philippa is well aware of what her husband thinks. She was very frank and said they had discussed the matter at length and both concluded that they would be fortunate to employ a governess known for her good sense and integrity. Those were her words. The children are much too young to be endangered by my influence, don't you think? And at least it is a roof over my head, Thomasina. Your sister is fond of me and I of her – I could do far worse.'

'I'd rather hoped you might come back with me to Ardleigh. We need to make plans for the future. We've hardly had any time together for months.'

'I accepted Philippa's offer by return of post.'

'Caroline, how could you? We should talk about this. It's not too late. You're grieving ... you don't

273

know what you're doing.'

Caroline was laughing. 'It's not so bad. For goodness' sake, Thomasina, I'm going to work for your sister, Philippa, who is surely no monster. I shall be so well paid I may even be able to save a little, and Philippa has promised me a spacious room of my own.'

'But what about me? How shall I manage without you?'

'I shall only be in Guildford and you will visit often, I hope.'

The cottage was tidier than usual and the shelves in the pantry better stocked thanks to the neighbours' kindness. Mrs Dean had sent cake and a jar of Ardleigh honey. They had tea in the back garden, where Caroline grew herbs, and there were rows of newly sprouted runner beans, each tripod tied at the top with string reused year after year. Asa sat bolt upright while Caroline stretched her legs and closed her eyes to the sun. 'And Mr Shackleford?' she said. 'Did you like him any better or am I to assume that nothing came of the visit?'

'You're right, nothing came of it. But let's not talk about Shackleford. He's of no interest to either of us.'

'Whatever can you mean? Of course I'm interested in Mr Shackleford. Father was too. He always wanted me to read out the parts of your letters that weren't private. He was rather amused by the idea of a match between you and Shackleford; said there was symmetry to it. By the way, he told me to let you know that there had been a certain amount of quiet rejoicing in abolition circles that a man so liberal as your Mr Shackleford had inherited the estate.'

'*Liberal*, is that how he's regarded? I suppose so. But underneath he's no different to the rest of them. He might claim to be uncomfortable – I'd put it no more strongly than that – with the family business, but he is too lazy to make a difference. He never has taken action, and never will.'

'I do believe that you are disturbed by my question,' said Caroline. 'You're not indifferent to him at all. You like him, don't you?'

'Oh, I *like* him well enough. He almost won me over in the end. He's very kind in small ways.'

'Kindness is a good quality.'

'And he loves me. That much is clear.'

'He proposed, then?'

'As good as. Twice, I suppose.'

'But you didn't accept?'

'You know I could never do that.'

'But you were tempted?'

'Tempted? Yes... You're right. One night – after I'd drunk too much wine – I came within a whisker of accepting him. Caroline, everything was right – starlight above a lake, music.' She paused. 'But it was all a veneer. Slaves are part of the fabric of Shackleford's world. He doesn't use excuses or hide the connection; it's what he is. And besides, even there at Compton Wyatt, I couldn't forget...'

'The old reason,' said Caroline, 'is that what it is? Will you never give up?'

How could Asa possibly say, now that Caroline was so firmly in Philippa's camp, that she had heard from Didier, but that having yearned for a message all these years, his summons had cast her into a quagmire of confusion. The previous night, she'd almost had to break the nib of her pen to stop herself writing to Shackleford.

'You're angry with me,' said Caroline, after another silence, 'and I understand why. You think that I've changed sides. Perhaps I have acted too hastily, but I felt relieved when I had written to your sister. My path seemed so clear.'

'Of course I'm not angry. Jealous, I think. Thinking only of myself, probably, because I fear losing you. Isn't that shameful?'

'Not shameful.' Caroline's foot touched Asa's, an affectionate pressure on her toe. 'But let's get to work. I want you to look through some of Father's things.'

In Mr Lambert's study were half-packed tea chests, the worn velvet of the single cushion on his straight-backed chair, his inkstand with three uncut quills and one, ink-stained, lying beside the blotter, that faintest whiff of pipe smoke. 'Take anything you like,' said Caroline. 'What's left will be sold, if possible. I can hardly smuggle subversive literature into Morton Hall.'

Asa chose two books: Barlowe's *Advice to the Privileged Orders* as a reproach to Shackleford, and Montesquieu's *De l'esprit des loix*, in French, a volume much read by Mr Lambert because of the simplicity of its argument for a virtuous republic rather than a despotic monarchy.

Caroline was sifting through a sheaf of papers. 'Look, here's a map of France which might be of interest to you, I think – it's the one Father used during his visit in the 1760s. You might like to keep this as a reminder of your trip to the country before the Revolution. And these little notes are from Beatrice and Didier Paulin, when they were children.' She studied Asa's face gravely. 'Have them if you like. Their address is on the top. Perhaps you'd write and let the professor know that Father has died?'

All these years a letter dated 5 September 1769, written in a child's meticulous hand, had been lying in a drawer in Mr Lambert's study; a letter from Didier Paulin and headed rue Leverrier, Caen.

We were enchanted by your visit, dear M. Lambert, and would wish to see you again one day at our house. My father speaks of you much. Next year, when I go to school, my English will be improved if I study carefully the book you gave me, of John Bunyan. Father says, if I am to be like anyone when I am old, he hopes I am to be like you.

At the bottom a note from little Beatrice, misspelt, blotted, ending with *grosses bises pour cher M. Lambert.*

Asa was crying freely, not so much for Mr Lambert as for the layers of betrayal in which she was embroiled and because those letters, pressed into her hand, were surely an omen. When they hugged she smelt her own tears on her friend's skin, the familiar, musty scent of her old black gown.

Chapter Eight

When Asa arrived back at Ardleigh late the following afternoon, Madame de Rusigneux took her aside and said she would be leaving within a week.

'We will speak about it later, in private,' Asa said.

'Let it be in my room, please. I have something to give you.'

After dinner Madame excused herself from the table early and after a few minutes Asa followed, climbing the panelled staircase with its prints of creatures at bay – fox, stag and pheasant – to the first floor. The passage was narrow and long and at the far end the oak boards were illuminated by a spillage of evening light from Madame's open door. The French woman was seated on the bedside chair as if she'd summoned Asa for an interview. Since dinner, she'd tied her hair back into a tight knot so that her forehead and chin were austerely defined, and she seemed much older. The strap of her portmanteau was undone and on the bed she had laid out her collection of fans, plain and exotic, tattered and intricate, eight in all, spread wide like peacocks' tails.

Her hand hovered above them as if she were casting a spell or blessing. 'I wish that you should have something to remember me by. I gave one of my fans to Mrs Shackleford. You are to choose another.'

Asa pretended to hesitate between the balloon-ing fan and one depicting exotic birds perched among flowers and leaves. 'Madame, I don't want a fan. I want to come with you to France.'

'I can see that you love the balloons the best. Quite right. That is the most precious of all because it depicts an era now gone. Take it. Please.'

'Madame. Listen to me. When you go to France, I want to go too.'

'What you say is mad.'

'If we are together we can look after each other.'

'I don't know what you mean. Why would you want to go to France? It is out of the question. The English are at war with our country. You would have only to step from the ship to be imprisoned as a spy.'

'But I am fluent in French and I need say very little if I came as your companion or maid. I wouldn't give myself away.'

'*Non. Absolument pas.* Do you think I would betray your family by allowing you to come with me?'

'Will you let me explain? Please. I have some-thing to tell you.'

'It will make no difference. Nothing you can say will make me change my mind.'

Asa perched on the window seat and fixed her eyes on the weathercock across the yard, gripping her knees to her chest. Her meeting and sub-sequent love affair with Didier, articulated halt-ingly for the first time, and to a French aristocrat of all people, seemed surprisingly mundane, like the contents of an old trinket box recovered from an attic. Madame rested her head in one hand, as she was prone to do when tired or thoughtful, and made not a sound. Only towards the end of the narrative did she raise her head.

'Until yesterday,' Asa continued, 'when I was with Caroline, I was hesitating. But she has acted decisively in accepting Philippa's offer and her clarity makes me feel like a fool. All these years I have been waiting for Didier. Now I realise that he was trying to protect me and if he has finally called for me, then his need of me must be urgent indeed.'

Madame's back was to the light and she was watching Asa.

'Everything is straightforward now,' said Asa, 'because you are travelling to France too. I have Didier's family address in Caen. I'll go there first. His family will know where to find him. Or I could come with you to Paris.'

'If you have an address in Caen, what is wrong with writing a letter?' asked Madame. 'Find out where this foolish man is, who can't trouble himself to give you an address.'

'And then sit around and wait? No. Madame, in Bristol you accused me of not taking action. Now you are trying to prevent me. His letters are uncompromising. All these years I have been waiting for a sign. Now I have a clarion call. I shall go, if for no other reason than to find out if we still love each other.'

'You should take no notice of what I said in Bristol. I was not myself that day. It was very hot and confined in that drawing room. I should not

280

have spoken as I did.'

'But what you said was true. And look, here are Didier's most recent letters. Can't you see that I must go?'

Madame seemed reluctant to handle anything so private but in the end she took the papers one by one, studied them and spread the handkerchief across her knee. Then, in silence, she stood by the bed, flicked each fan shut, and inserted it first into its case, then the portmanteau. Only when all was tidy did she turn back to Asa. 'I will consider what you have said. You ask much of me, mademoiselle.'

'When will I have your answer?'

'You will have it soon. Very soon.' The smile came like a promise, lighting the backs of her eyes. She gripped Asa's hands and kissed her on both cheeks so that, fleetingly, Asa smelt the grainy scent of Madame's hair and saw up close the disconcerting blackness of her eyes.

Chapter Nine

The following Friday, 7 June, Asa got up at four and kept her father company as he devoured his breakfast kidneys and bacon.

'Father, today Mrs Dacre's case will be heard in Chichester. I intend to be there. Will you come with me?'

No response.

'She will need money, Father, whatever the outcome.'

He got up and headed for the door. She followed him to his study and watched as he unlocked his desk, rummaged for a coin and handed it to her.

'A guinea won't go far. Please come with me. Don't you think you should be there?'

'What good would it do?'

She knew he would not come; he yearned to be ripping along the top of the Downs with chalk dust puffing up from his horse's hooves and the air scented with gorse. When she embraced him his heavy shoulders were unyielding and muscular.

'You are a good girl, Asa.'

She kissed his cheek and forehead. 'I shall be driving Madame and myself to Chichester in the trap. We don't need a coachman. Afterwards we shall stay with Caroline for a week or so, until she is ready to leave for Morton. I'll write to let you know when we're coming home.'

He grunted affectionately and let her go. At the turn of the passage she looked back but he was busy relocking his desk drawer. Mrs Dean, when requested, donated a parcel of food for Mrs Dacre but was sullen as usual at the mention of the tailor's wife. Madame brought down her portmanteau and a maid carried Asa's trunk out to the trap. The stable-yard, where the mare was already harnessed, reeked of manure. Through a gateway Asa glimpsed a border of her mother's roses, in need of dead-heading, and as she lifted the reins the corner of a maid's apron whisked past the open door of the kitchen. A casement on the first floor was flung wide open. The stable-boy whacked the mare's flank and tipped his cap at Asa as they rattled under the arch, along the side of the house and into the lane.

They drove past the forge, which seemed deserted in the morning heat, past the bakehouse, past the narrow bridleway leading to the Downs, at this time of year choked with nettles. Soon they were in woodland, where bracken was waist high, a tunnel of leaf and branch.

Madame said: 'With regard to our plans. Before we reach Chichester, we must be clear.'

'Of course.'

'First, in all matters related to our journey, I must insist on taking the lead. There will be many dangers and if we disagree we may put ourselves in jeopardy. You must not question my decisions. Whatever I ask you to do, however difficult, you must obey. Secondly, we shall be together in Caen but the moment we reach Paris, we will part company. I will leave you at White's Hotel, where you will no doubt find English people to advise you.'

'We won't disagree, madame. I'm sure.'

'You must promise.'

'Yes.'

'Any further questions?'

'When can I let my family know where I am?'

'There are to be no letters until we are in Paris. Surely you don't want to be discovered.'

'It does seem very cruel to them, once they realise we're not with Caroline.'

'Even with a detour to Caen we'll be in Paris within the week. They may not even notice you're missing. Mademoiselle Ardleigh, it seems to me that you are weakening.'

'No.'

'You are still determined?'

'How can you ask?'

In Chichester Asa sold her mother's sapphire engagement ring for nine guineas. Although she gave the goldsmith an imperious nod as she tucked the money into her bodice and watched him drop the ring into a velvet-lined drawer, she was faint with the irrevocable steps she was taking. Despite Madame's hard grip on her elbow she pleaded: 'Please let me have one more look at it.'

The jeweller laughed unpleasantly. 'Now don't you be changing your mind. The deed's done,' and he watched jealously as she slid the ring back on her finger. But already it was just a cold thing of metal and stone; a necessary casualty of the adventure ahead.

Madame said she would guard the trap while Asa went to the court to see Mrs Dacre brought up for sentencing. When the crowd in the gallery saw the prisoner, obviously pregnant, it bayed for her to be hung. Mrs Dacre's eyes scanned the courtroom until she noticed Asa. For a moment there was a flash of hope. But no squire.

Sensation in court: a slickly dressed lawyer stood up to defend Mrs Dacre. In a sonorous London drawl and with great deference he begged leave to address the learned judge, who removed his wig and dabbed at his brow under the strain of being confronted by so sleek an advocate. 'Owing to lack of alternative evidence, the court must accept Mrs Dacre's version of events, namely that she chose to leave the cottage following the charivari because she could not bear the shame she had brought upon her husband. But somewhat unfortunately – she is a simple woman with simple logic, as I'm sure Your Honour, with vast experience in sad cases of this nature, will have surmised – she removed her husband's scissors with a view to raising money, never considering that Dacre would see no alternative but to take his own life following the triple blow of losing not only his good name and his wife, but his only means of making a living into the bargain.'

The crowd was silenced by the lawyer's sophisticated air, but if anything the atmosphere grew more hostile. It wasn't right that someone so lowly should be represented by such a superior advocate; surely this was proof that Mrs Dacre was guilty, at the very least, of overstepping the mark. Suggestive comments were yelled as to the cause of her pregnancy but the judge, who dined annually at Ardleigh and hunted with the squire, barked at the crowd to be quiet. Given Mrs Dacre's callous theft of her husband's scissors, he pronounced, she would be sentenced, despite her condition, to transportation for seven years.

Afterwards Asa bribed a gaoler and was admitted to a cell hardly bigger than a privy. The tailor's wife stood against the wall, her face as pale as Caroline's, her hair a matted mop under her cap. There was no sign of the lawyer.

'I thought you'd come,' she said. 'In at the kill, as your father'd say.'

'I have brought you some money, Mrs Dacre.'

'Did he send me this? Three guineas?'

'It's for the baby.'

285

The tailor's wife stared relentlessly from those oozing eyes.

'And look; some clothes.' Asa showed her a bundle of baby nightgowns sewn by her mother and preserved by Mrs Dean all these years in a chest on the landing, and one of her own plain gowns. 'Sell them or use them, up to you.'

Mrs Dacre didn't even glance at them.

'Where did you find that lawyer, the one who represented you?' asked Asa.

'I thought it was your father's doing. Wasn't it?' Another glimmer of hope.

'It may have been.'

'Not him, then. But who?'

There was only one man with a reach long enough to instruct, with a dash of the pen, such an advocate to descend on Chichester and snatch Mrs Dacre from the jaws of death. But Asa swept aside thoughts of Shackleford.

'I've no idea. A benefactor, of some kind. Mrs Dacre, is there anything else? Will you shake my hand?'

Mrs Dacre folded her arms. Her stare followed Asa as she stepped through the filth on the floor, hammered on the door, turned one last time and, receiving no response, walked away.

It was noon. A light drizzle fell. Madame waited with the hood of her cloak pulled up over her straw hat. Her eyes met Asa's but neither woman spoke. They climbed into the trap, Asa took up the reins, and thus they set out, Miss Ardleigh and her French companion, for Portsmouth.

Part Four

Normandy, June 1793

Chapter One

Portsmouth, 7 June 1793. Five years and one month after Asa's first departure for France. Then she had been nineteen, heart whole, fizzing with anticipation but safe under the wing of prosaic John Morton. This time?

Terrified.

In driving west out of Chichester the fugitives were rushing towards a war. Less than a mile from town they were forced to veer into a field while several hundred militia marched past on exercise, lustrous in close-fitting scarlet tunics and tall peaked hats. Their polished boots struck the soft surface of the road with a uniform thwump and sometimes impudent eyes met Asa's and winked. Stranded in a barley field veiled by drizzle, she had a moment of red-hot panic. Here she was, bound for her elusive French lover while English redcoats prepared themselves for battle and possible death at French hands.

The soldiers went by, the road was clear and Madame's firm hand touched Asa's arm, urging her to whip the mare into a trot. As they journeyed on they saw an immense encampment of tents spread over a dozen fields. Soon the road was crammed with carts and carriages and vendors selling anything from toffee to tarred rope.

The scene of their first disagreement was in Portsmouth itself, in a sun-struck courtyard near the harbour, when Madame announced: 'Now we must sell the horse and trap.'

'Madame, we cannot.'

'But we must.'

'This was not part of the plan, I would never have agreed to it. The horse belongs to my father. I shall send both horse and trap back to Ardleigh.'

'Consider, mademoiselle. We must leave no trace of our departure from England. If the horse arrives at your house, your father will be alarmed and pursue us. Besides, we need the money. Did you not give much of our capital to the tailor's wife?'

'Neither horse nor trap is mine to sell. Don't you realise that Mrs Dacre was sentenced to transportation for the theft of a pair of scissors?'

Madame de Rusigneux merely raised an eyebrow.

'Before we take such a drastic step we should find a boat,' Asa added less vehemently. 'After all, it may not be possible to leave the country and without transport we would be stranded here.'

'We will find a boat,' said Madame.

Thus far Asa had comforted herself with the thought that she could always turn tail, if courage failed, and be safely ensconced in Caroline Lambert's cottage before nightfall. Besides, she was very fond of that little trap with its narrow bench seat and clanking iron wheels, having driven about in it all her life. And quite apart from her own affection for the gentle-natured mare, she quailed when she considered the squire's likely reaction to his horse's disappearance. But her turbulent state, not to mention the pledge she had made Madame to follow her lead, made her the weaker of the two, although she kept her nerve when it came to the sale and struck a hard bargain on the horse so that by nightfall they were nearly twelve guineas better off.

Next they secured a room at an inn called the Pembroke: 'We will be confident and we will be public,' said Madame, 'then no one will ask questions.'

Having eaten supper they set forth to find a boat. Portsmouth harbour was crammed with naval vessels and the town swarmed with military, some presumably detailed to track down suspicious characters intent on travelling incognito to France. In other circumstances Asa might have been comforted by glimpses of the castle, the sea defences, the munitions and the warships. Ardleigh, after all, was only a few miles from the coast and risked being captured by a hostile army within half a day of its landing. Now she viewed these fortifications as barriers.

They headed for a neat, bow-windowed house in Broad Street, home of one Captain Malloy, recommended by some mysterious contact of Madame's in Chichester. Negotiations were conducted while Malloy continued his meal of beef and ale pie and green peas so Asa's last memories of England were inextricably mingled with the smell of gravy. She told him the story she and Madame had concocted, that she had a widowed sister living among the English community in Le Havre who was expecting a child and was in dire need of support, but Malloy gave an indifferent shrug and barely cast his eyes over their papers – acquired by Madame via the same anonymous contact.

'I'll see you landed safely,' he said, spearing the last of his peas. 'There's few can promise you that. I have friends on the other side who will exchange your English money and give you a bed. None of it will come cheap, mind. We leave at five tomorrow morning with the tide.' The price of the Channel crossing made Asa flinch but she judged Malloy sufficiently selfish to take care of his own skin at least, which was a comfort.

'You paid far too much,' hissed Madame as they set off back to the Pembroke. 'We could once have bought a year's dancing lessons from the greatest master in Paris for that amount.' But there was a hint of a smile in her stern eyes and Asa felt a quickening of excitement.

Their room was hot and noisy and they had to share a bed. Madame, whose gown fastened with a simple drawstring, undressed rapidly to her shift and sat cross-legged on the bed, plaiting her hair. 'Sit here, facing me like this,' she instructed. Asa placed herself knee to knee with Madame. 'Now our lessons truly begin. Once in France, as we agreed, you will have to behave as if you are my French maid, a farmer's daughter. If you speak at all, you are to speak like a native. We will claim that your accent is from a region in the south-west and that you are very shy. Under no circumstances must you be discovered to be English. I can assure you, mademoiselle, if you are found out, we will both be in grave danger.'

There followed a barrage of questions in French, simple at first, then more complicated. What is your name? *Julie Moreau*. Who are you? *Mon père est fermier*. What is my name? *Madame Élise Lejeune*. Where do we live? *À Paris*. What was the late Monsieur Lejeune's trade? *Il était fabriqueur des éventails*. Where in Paris did we live? *Rue de Victoire*. From which region of France do you come, Julie? *Les Hautes Pyrenées*.

If Asa's head drooped or her tongue faltered Madame playfully tweaked her cheek or knee. Once she even seized Asa's chin and squeezed it in an attempt to correct a vowel. When Asa yelped with pain Madame tapped her face by way of apology but there was no mistaking the anxiety behind that pinch. About two in the morning, Madame abruptly tucked her feet under the sheet, arranged the coil of her plait as a pillow – the one provided having been pronounced dirty – and fell asleep.

Asa lay there, as still as an effigy. The bed was hard, the floorboards creaked, and drunks on the street made a continual racket. It being mid-summer, the seagulls began their morning cries remorselessly early. Although her arm was warmed by the woman sleeping beside her, Asa had never felt so lonely, and her thoughts strayed to a vision of swans, a walk through the woods, and the lovely ease with which she might have slipped into Shackleford's world.

When light the colour of resin filtered through the shutters, Madame opened her eyes as suddenly as if someone had unclipped the lids. The Pembroke supplied them with breakfast and a yawning youth in possession of a little handcart to carry their luggage. The trio set off through dewy streets towards the harbour, which was wide awake, the masts of great naval ships reaching into the pink sky while the first rays of sunshine were absorbed by the matt-black ranks of cannon.

As the sea mist cleared, another ship loomed into view, greater and older than the rest with a vast hull lying low in the water. The youth set down his cart. 'The *William*,' he said. 'Convict ship. Will be there for weeks yet and then off she will go to the Antipodes, fully laden.'

Their own little boat, the *Lorelei*, was moored amid other fishing smacks, her varnish as thick as treacle and her sails half unfurled. Malloy paused in his work to take each woman by the hand and help them on board. They were to stay in the cabin, he said, until the ship had left harbour; there was little danger of the *Lorelei* being searched but his men were superstitious and preferred that women be kept out of sight. The door to the cabin was left ajar and they sat on narrow benches facing each other in a space reeking of male bodies and fish, subjected to the constant clatter and shaking of the boat as she was made ready for sea.

Someone might yet come in search of them. Asa strained for the sound of hoof-beats in the harbour. When a distant bell chimed five o'clock there was a shout and a hiss of rope as England slipped her anchor and slid away. Madame appeared to

294

take no interest, instead opened her portmanteau, withdrew a strip of red cloth and calmly pinned a row of tucks along its edge.

Chapter Two

Twenty hours after leaving Portsmouth – the *Lorelei*'s voyage having been prolonged owing to a lack of wind – two women were rowed to a rocky beach west of Le Havre, close to the small town of Viller sur Mer. The mistress, the dark-haired, diminutive Madame Elise Lejeune, wore a plain dress with a white scarf crossed over her bosom, and a muslin cap trimmed with lighter blue ribbon. The maid, Julie Moreau, was much fairer and wore a too-small, faded blue gown and crumpled straw bonnet. Each woman had pinned a tricolour cockade, produced by Madame from her portmanteau, to her sash. When the boat ran ashore they stepped into water over their ankles so that their first action on French soil was to wring out the hem of their skirts.

The *Lorelei*'s other cargo, of baskets and barrels, was landed swiftly and whisked away, hand to hand, by the well-practised human chain strung up the crumbling cliffs known as Les Vaches Noires. Within minutes the English sailors had dissolved back into the sea and a brisk, inquisi-tive-eyed Frenchman told the women to follow him up a steep winding path that tunnelled through thick undergrowth. Despite the moonlight they stumbled frequently, but at last came to a thatched cottage beside a small church and were received into its smoky interior by a scraggy, nervous woman, name of Madame Bisset, who closed the door firmly behind them, bolted it top and bottom and signalled that they might sit on either side of a thick-legged kitchen table which had been set for supper.

'Don't get me wrong. I'm used to seeing all kinds of people – it's my job but it don't come cheap.' She mouthed a sum for bed and board which was almost a quarter of their remaining money.

'That's very high,' said Madame.

Madame Bisset got up, shook out her skirts and headed for the door. 'Very well...'

In a few minutes a deal was struck, mutton soup ladled out and wine served – liberally to Madame Bisset, more frugally to her guests. Though Asa was ignored while the other women talked, with every mouthful her courage was restored. She had done it: she was in France. This cottage with its paved floor, its rush-seated oak chairs, its scent of broth and wine, was indubitably French. Every object seemed momentous; the shape of the loaf; the lace runner along the mantel, the particular shade of blue paint on the shutters. Her attention dipped in and out of the conversation but after a while she understood that Madame Bisset was painting an altogether different image of France.

'Obviously it's none of my business,' their hostess said, taking another swig of wine, 'and I don't expect any answers, but I think you're mad coming back to France at this time, when you might have stayed safe in England.'

'It's true we'd heard there was trouble in the Vendée,' said Madame.

'Not just the Vendée, believe me. Brittany is up in arms and there are towns, even here in peaceful Normandy – not Le Havre, of course – that are in revolt against Paris. There has been all kinds of trouble around here, much too close for comfort.' Madame Bisset poured another cup of wine and folded her arms on the table as she fixed her eye on Asa's spoon and watched its progress from bowl to mouth.

'Of course in England we didn't know the truth about what was happening in France,' said Madame, who was eating from glazed earthenware as daintily as she had from Compton Wyatt porcelain.

In the presence of such delicacy, Madame Bisset spoke more moderately. 'I have nothing against the Revolution, you understand, I've never thought much about politics, but now I believe there's to be a levy of three hundred thousand men to go and fight France's so-called enemies, including the English?' She winked knowingly at Asa, the supposed French maid who hadn't spoken a word since setting foot in the cottage. 'Just when those same men ought to be bringing in the harvest. It's because everyone's hungry that they're angry. In Caen, for instance...'

'How far is Caen from here?' asked Asa.

'Goodness,' said Madame Bisset, 'barely a dozen miles. It's normally such a peaceful place. My mother-in-law was from Caen and she was an excellent woman. That broth you're eating is her recipe.'

'What has been happening in Caen?' asked Madame, as if to humour their hostess.

'There was this official called Georges Bayeux – between you and me my husband's family knew him quite well – whose job it was to appoint a jury for the new Criminal Tribunal. The local Jacobin Club didn't like his choices. Well, these days when people disagree it ends in bloodshed, not talk. So next minute Bayeux is torn apart, literally limb from limb, in broad daylight, in St-Sauveur Square. I didn't see it happen, thank God. But the following week when I was in town I saw the bloodstains. The crowd went crazy, apparently, hacked off his arms, then stuck his head on a pike. Nowadays you never know which way people will turn.'

'Do you think it's safe to visit Caen?' said Asa. Madame glanced at her furiously.

'Oh, it's always safe in Caen, by and large, unless your name is Bayeux, obviously,' said Madame Bisset, laughing nervously. 'At least, as safe as anywhere else.'

It was dawn by the time they finally lay down. Madame turned her back, tucked herself in hood and cloak and seemed to fall asleep at once while Asa lay wide awake, looking up at the exposed rafters under the thatch. In her imagination, or perhaps in truth, she could hear the distant rush of the sea, just as she might if she'd been staying with Caroline in Littlehampton.

Having exchanged with Madame Bisset their remaining English money at an extortionate rate and been ejected from the cottage at noon, Asa and Madame had their second disagreement; this one conducted between fields of cows and much fiercer than the last. 'Last night,' said Madame, 'you spoke out of turn.'

'I hardly spoke at all.'

'You must behave like a maid. You should never make comments or ask questions unless invited to do so, especially as your English accent is still detectable.'

'She already knew I was English before I opened my mouth – I could tell. Besides, there was nothing to hide. I needed to know about Caen. We don't want to walk into trouble.'

'Well now, since you were so indiscreet, I do wonder if we shouldn't go straight to Paris. That woman, Bisset, will never keep her mouth shut. She'll tell all her friends about the visitors from England. Caen is a trap.'

'But we must go to Caen. I have to call on the Paulin family.'

'You must learn to keep quiet. We are in France, where every word can be used to incriminate us.'

Asa looked about her at the cattle grazing and the springy turf of the clifftop. 'It is one day's difference. By tomorrow afternoon we will be on the road to Paris. I promise to say nothing out of turn from now on.'

'Do so.' For a moment they faced each other under the hot sun. Madame pointed to the bags, which Asa must carry, and they took the road west for Caen.

After hours of plodding through flat, sun-drenched countryside, they were overtaken by a diligence at Varaville. While their papers were examined by the coachman there was a deathly silence and then, when they were allowed inside, faint smiles of greeting from fellow passengers, though Madame acknowledged no one. She kept herself rigidly apart from Asa, who was sweating in her ill-fitting clothes. No doubt now who was the mistress and who the near-invisible maid. But as the Normandy hedgerows lurched past, Asa's heart beat strong and steady. The softness of doubt, of wanting to change her mind and go home, was gone. Didier had called, she had answered and France had embraced her. In another few hours she might actually be with Beatrice Paulin and then the way forward would be clear. She even thought, in an ecstasy brought on by hunger, tension and sleeplessness, that perhaps she would find Didier in Caen, waiting for her.

Chapter Three

It was as if the streets of Caen had been swept bare by plague. At nearly seven in the evening heat still curdled the air, beat against the sand-coloured walls and carried the stench from the river. A child scurrying along a shady alley was plucked off his feet and whisked inside while his abandoned ball went bouncing into a gutter. Madame, since alighting from the coach, had been oddly passive, or perhaps it was that she was weakened by heat and hunger. Her head was down, her shoulders rolled forward and the frill of her bonnet obscured her face. When Asa hesitated, her companion halted too. 'You are the maid,' she murmured, 'it is for you to find us a bed.'

'I thought you were anxious that my English accent would give us away.'

'Then you must speak without an accent. It is not fitting that I, the mistress, should procure the room.'

By instinct Asa walked south, avoiding the belligerent mound of the castle, until they came to yet another church, the fourth they'd passed in the city, in a little tree-lined square. Sure enough, on the corner of a narrow alley, was a swinging sign; *Auberge*. It took some time before the landlady answered the door, a forbidding affair that creaked as it opened, admitting them to a dank courtyard, and even longer for her to study their papers. She was thin, a little bent in the back and with plaits wound on either side of her head. 'I no longer provide dinner or breakfast, you understand. Food is very short in Caen.'

The money for the room was set on a scratched tabletop beside a crocheted mat. The proprietress's eyes flicked from the coins to Asa and then to Madame, who kept her face averted.

'I have a room,' she said finally, seating herself at the table and dipping her pen, 'but first there are some formalities required these days by the authorities.' Her pen squeaked as she inscribed Asa's replies to a volley of questions. Why were they in Caen, exactly? Where had they come from and where were they going? Why were they travelling unaccompanied?

'We are accompanying each other,' said Asa, 'being mistress and maid.' For this attempt at light-heartedness she received a cold-eyed stare.

They were eventually allocated an unpleasant room on the third floor overlooking the courtyard and furnished with one narrow bed and a washstand. The latrine, up two further dismal flights of stairs, was windowless and therefore pitch black; a hole had been cut in the stone floor and beneath it was a drop to the river.

Madame sat on the edge of the bed, eyes hard with reproach. 'Do not answer back or make jokes. Do you not understand that one hint of suspicion will send that woman running to report us at the town hall and we'll find ourselves in irons?'

'For what?' cried Asa. 'We've done nothing wrong.'

'You're a foreigner with a false passport. When will you realise that this is not a game?'

'Madame, you are very low. We are both hungry.'

'I refuse to leave this room. I am too ill.'

'Then I'll go and find us some supper.'

So Asa went out alone, darting across one street after another as if the town's fear were infectious. First she ran north by the church of St-Pierre, then turned west, deeper into town, through streets of close-built timbered houses until she came to a main thoroughfare, the rue des Bras, where she found a queue of women outside a bread shop. Their eyes, though sharp with curiosity, avoided hers, until eventually someone said: 'You're a stranger, I think.'

'I am. We are passing through. We have been staying in Le Havre with a relative of my mistress.' She had said too much, perhaps, in her accented French, but her answer seemed to satisfy and the queue shuffled forward. Thankfully they were in shade; even late in the day it was still hot. Asa glanced from the unfamiliar paving stones to the honey-coloured wall against which she leaned and thought: *He* would have known all this. I have re-entered Didier's world.

She returned to their lodgings with the bread tucked under her arm, but the stale air within the auberge soon quelled her excitement. There was hardly any light in the stairwell and she had to grope her way from landing to landing. With relief she pushed open the door to their room. Madame de Rusigneux was seated on the bed, exactly as she had been when Asa had last seen her an hour ago.

All night they lay top to tail without speaking. Asa was sure that Madame was awake most of the time but found it impossible to break the silence. When the clock struck three she thought to herself that Didier would have heard that same clock, night after night, when he was a boy. Later, she heard the clop of hooves and the rattle of cart-wheels and remembered lying with Didier in his first-floor room, behind the green and brown screen which smelt of varnish in the heat of the sun. It was as if he were reconstructing himself inside her, cell by cell, so that her desire for Shackleford and the treacherous memories of Compton Wyatt were fading.

She must have slept, for when the clock struck six she was jolted awake.

Madame said: 'I will go to mass. For the sake of my brother.'

'Would you like me to come?'

'That is for you to decide.'

'Then I shall come to church, if you don't mind. I should like to pray too.'

The church was very cool; the yellowish air gritty and smelling of plaster dust. There was an endearing lack of symmetry – each pillar began at a different level on the floor and no arch was quite true – but gradually Asa realised with a surge of dread that there were also signs of recent violence here. The plaster images of saints had been savagely defiled – index fingers snapped off and noses severed – and the wounds were chalky and fresh. The atmosphere was altogether bleak and the responses from the congregation who clustered in the pews farthest away from the altar barely audible. Asa's Protestant ears were offended by the gabbled Latin prayers and her eyes shunned the bloodied figure on the crucifix. Fortunately Madame had chosen the back pew and they were pressed inconspicuously close to a pillar so that no one would notice Asa's unfamiliarity with the proceedings. After a few minutes Madame began to tremble so much that she had to fold her arms across her chest and grip her elbows. She did not queue for communion but sat close to Asa with her head down.

As soon as the priest had said the blessing and scurried away, Madame set off towards a side chapel, tucked behind a pillar, where there was a life-sized statue of the Virgin. Even Asa could not quite resist the charm of a Madonna whose cloak was painted a shade of blue-green lined with gold, and whose features were as ruddy and cheerful as a milkmaid's. Her robust, round-cheeked son grasped her neck with one confident hand and clutched a golden ball in the other.

Kneeling, Madame threw back her head so that her face was exposed to gashes of blue and red light from the window above. Tears trickled from her eyes and hung on her long lashes. Asa knew better than to approach her and offer comfort and she wondered whether she, as a Protestant, was even permitted to pray to the Virgin: Help me find Didier. Don't let my family worry about me. What will Shackleford say when he finds out what I've done?

All of a sudden, Madame thrust her hand backwards, waited until Asa had crept within reach, then fiercely seized her wrist. For a few minutes they remained locked together, then Madame got shakily to her feet. 'I am too ill to go with you to your friends' house,' she said at the church door. 'I need to rest. There is a long journey ahead.'

'I will be back by midday, I promise.'

Madame crossed the square, paused before the door of the auberge to raise her hand in a wave, then disappeared from view.

Chapter Four

The route to the Paulins' house on the rue Leverrier took Asa for the first time under the walls of the castle, a vast stone fortress complete with round towers and moat of the sort which, in England, might have been allowed to fall into ruin. To the north-west, near the university, the streets were lined with trees, and with each step Asa felt more connected to Didier. The old feeling of significance had returned; Madame, the journey to France, this city of Caen, all formed part of her own momentous story. If she turned her head suddenly she might even glimpse him, head held high, papers under his arm, dashing to some engagement.

Number 15, rue Leverrier was a low old house, timbered like many others in the city and set behind railings. She trembled as she unhooked the gate, marched up to a green-painted front door and, before she could lose her nerve, pulled on the bell.

Out came an elderly woman with a hook nose and suspicious eyes. *'Oui?'*

'Mademoiselle Paulin?'

'Elle n'est pas ici.'

'Le professeur?'

'Non plus.'

'Monsieur Paulin, le fils?'

The maid's expression tightened.

'Est-ce que je peux les attendre?'
'Ce n'est pas possible.'
'Alors, si j'écris un petit mot?'
'D'accord.'
'Excusez-moi, madame, mais je n'ai pas de papier.'

The servant sighed gustily but allowed Asa inside, indicated an upright chair, then picked up her skirts and toiled up the stairs, presumably to fetch pen and paper.

Five years. In her dreams, in those heady days of knowing him in Paris, Asa had dared to imagine visiting this house as Didier's bride. The entrance hall was exactly as it should be, beautifully proportioned with delicate brass lamp holders and a red tiled floor; a room of which Caroline Lambert would certainly have approved, its furnishings acquired over centuries rather than bought to impress. For generations it must have smelt of lamp oil, of baking bread and some scented plant. Presumably the boy Didier had whooshed down the curve of that same polished banister, plucked his shoes from the rack and stood on tiptoe to admire his dark curls in the mirror above the marble-topped commode.

Asa got up and peered more closely at the three paintings hanging over the stairs: one a rather fanciful picture of the castle, another a watercolour of a rustic scene complete with church, village and the distant sea, the third a portrait of a young man, hands behind his back, wearing a neat blue coat, plain cravat and with a turquoise handkerchief in his breast pocket.

So here, after all, was Didier, his blue eyes fixed on Asa. In the portrait Didier was perhaps younger than when she'd met him in Paris; his cheeks were more boyish though his skin was that same flawless ivory, his beautiful mouth curved in a well-remembered smile. She crept closer until five years of separation faded away and she was standing in his arms by the window of his apartment, pressed so close that her forehead touched the fine-shaven skin of his cheek.

The stairs creaked; the housekeeper was descending with quill and paper. With shaking hand Asa wrote *Thomasina Ardleigh: Je retournerai bientôt*. But the servant, who read the note, shook her head as if to say another visit would be pointless, then ushered Asa to the door.

Light headed, she rushed back to the city centre. Caen at eleven o'clock in the morning was seething with heat and bustle. Asa bought cherries and cheese from the food market near St-Sauveur, though the cost of each purchase was exorbitant. The cherries were blood red and sweeter than those from the Ardleigh orchard. Juice dripped down her chin as she savoured a few, but what did it matter since she was just a maid? She walked away, still buoyant, until she discovered that she was beneath a scaffold upon which was erected not the customary gibbet but a tall instrument bound with canvas and ropes.

Although hidden, the instrument of execution cast a cold shadow in the square, and the other passers-by were giving it a wide berth. Averting her eyes and taking care not to scan the cobbles for the bloodstains of the doomed Monsieur Bayeux, Asa hurried south towards the auberge. The streets were so crowded now she could barely struggle through and she dared not take a detour for fear of losing her way. When she reached the Place de Liberté it was crammed, but the crowd was silent, huddled in groups and clutching children to their skirts as they listened to a man in shirtsleeves and loose-fitting breeches who was proclaiming excitedly from a mounting block. A leaflet was thrust into Asa's hand and then another.

'Make no mistake,' cried the orator, 'the Convention of Paris is treating the citizens of Caen with contempt. We sent a delegation of nine distinguished commissioners, all trusted friends, to Paris, at great expense. But we hear that they were dealt with disgracefully, refused a hearing and then fobbed off by being sent from one committee to another. Worse still, an entire section of that same Convention – all those who opposed the rule of the mob and the hectoring of the likes of Marat, Danton and Robespierre – is under house arrest.

'Paris is in the grip of dread and turmoil; spies, arrests, public abuse for anyone who does not agree with the Convention... So much for liberty. So much for the freedom to speak our minds. So much for the revolution that makes us equals, one with another, men of Caen with men of Paris.'

The crowd was growing restless. Only a few voices murmured agreement. Nobody applauded.

'What I am asking of you, my fellow citizens,' the orator continued, 'is that you join our insurrection. It's time to make a stand. They have abused our delegation and arrested our Girondin

309

friends, Barbaroux, Brissot, Petion, although they accuse them not of crimes but of differences of opinion. Brissot is denounced because he regrets the death of the king, advised war with Europe and resists the capping of grain prices. But we Normandy farmers don't want to sell our grain too cheaply to Paris. Why should we? What will we get in return?'

The mention of Normandy's grain finally did the trick; the crowd unleashed its rage. Impossible not to be entranced by the speaker's ardent eyes, the emphatic, Didier-like leaning on the first syllable of significant nouns: *Li*berté, *Bar*baroux, *Bri*ssot. The orator now lowered his voice, as if only this particular crowd could be trusted with his confidences: 'The very freedom of Caen is under threat, my friends. Two deputies, Charles Romme and Claude Antoine Prieur, have been sent from Paris to ensure that Calvados pledges obedience.'

'Oh God,' whispered a woman in a blue skirt, standing next to Asa. 'If deputies from Paris are listening to this they'll have us all arrested.' She crossed herself, then clapped her hand to her mouth when she realised what she'd done. But Asa was distracted. Just visible through the crowd and framed by a muslin cap with a deep brim like the one Madame had worn since landing in France was a face she recognised: Beatrice Paulin, surely. She was a little plumper than five years ago, and with her hair more sternly drawn back, but the deep brow and blue gaze were unmistakable. Her arm was linked with that of a younger woman, who had a delicate complexion and tumbling brown hair, and whose eyes were fixed un-swervingly on the speaker's face.

Asa ducked under the arm of a man blocking her way and tried to dodge past another. 'Caen will not be crushed under the heel of the Parisian mob,' the speaker called, raising his voice. 'Caen has sent its own armed men, our Carabots, to fetch Romme and Prieur – who are currently busy dismantling the democratic council in Bayeux – and take them to our own chateau. They will be our hostages until such time as Paris comes to its senses and releases the Girondin deputies.'

The crowd was impenetrable. Asa was told angrily to stay still and keep quiet. 'Meanwhile Caen will raise an army of Carabots and other volunteers to march on Paris and liberate it from the Marats, the Robespierres and the Dantons, so that the great Revolution might be allowed to flourish. *Vive la France. Vive la Liberté. Vivent les Carabots de Caen.*'

A couple of people gave a feeble cheer, others clapped timidly, others still muttered to each other and backed away. At last the crowd was loosening and Asa was able to slip through. There was no sign now of either Beatrice or her companion, though Asa searched one side street after another. In any case, the clock was striking the half-hour; it was high time she returned to Madame.

The room at the auberge was empty. Madame must have gone to buy food for the journey. Hot and weary, Asa flung down her purchases, took off her shoes and lay on the bed. Insurrection …

an army to be raised... One moment the stillness of the Paulins' entrance hall and Didier's smiling eyes, the next talk of violence and rebellion. For the last three nights she had scarcely slept. Her eyelids grew heavy and her mind clouded.

When she woke the clock was striking again: 2.30. Still no Madame. Drowsily Asa turned her head on the pillow then raised herself abruptly on one elbow as she registered that Madame's portmanteau was gone. So was the spare cap that Madame had hung behind the door and the walking shoes placed beside the bed. Only one of Madame's possessions remained. Spread out on the washstand was the fan that Madame had offered Asa at Ardleigh, the design on the silk leaf of a blue urn and birds of paradise perched among slender branches, its guard sticks decorated with gold leaf and lacquer, and then a second layer of silk, like an inner wheel, on which was painted another garden, with a carriage containing a pair of lovers dashing through it, the young woman's hair flying out in the breeze.

Asa told herself to be calm. Madame would be back at any moment. While she waited she prepared herself a little meal and chewed each mouthful carefully. Then she tidied the room, washed her face and brushed her hair. The clock struck half past three. No Madame. For the second time that day Asa had to borrow a pen and paper, this time to leave a message for Madame that she had gone back to the Paulins' house but would return by early evening. Surely it was now too late to set out for Paris today, she thought. Every action she took was precise,

312

convincing herself that this was nothing more than an ordinary step in ordinary circumstances.

It was nearly four by the time she reached the rue Leverrier again. *'Mademoiselle Paulin n'est pas ici,'* said the same servant.

'S'il vous plaît...'

'Je vous répète, elle n'est pas ici.'

'Elle retournera à quelle heure?'

An eloquent Gallic shrug.

'You said she would be back this afternoon.'

'No, mademoiselle, it was you who said that *you* would be back.'

'Please. I need to see her badly. Did you give her my note?'

'As I said, she is not at home.'

'Tell Mademoiselle Paulin I called again. Tell her I glimpsed her in the square this morning and that I tried to speak to her. I'm staying at the Auberge St-Jean. I'll come back this evening. Or perhaps Mademoiselle Paulin would care to call on me.'

She walked away rapidly, taking the most direct route back. Hurry, Asa, what if Madame returns to the auberge and doesn't see the note? But she was delayed again; this time by a troop of armed men, Caen's Carabots, and in their midst a carriage guarded by four soldiers bearing pikes. The procession was accompanied by clusters of townspeople who watched in silence as the carriage rolled up the long slope of the castle mound. 'It must be the commissioners from Paris,' was the rumour, 'Romme and Prieur.'

An elderly man leaned on his stick and muttered: 'I hope to Christ they know what they're doing.'

313

'What do you mean, sir?'

He studied Asa resignedly. 'Let us hope they are well treated, these emissaries from Paris, because what terrible consequences there will be for us if they are harmed.' He brought his face closer to Asa's. 'You're a stranger. I don't recognise you. Where are you from?'

Madame had been right. Caen was a trap. By standing among the crowd Asa was colluding with insurrection and therefore guilty. She ran, certain that Madame would be back now. Soon she was in the familiar square, had gained grumbling admission to the auberge and raced up the stairs.

The room was still empty.

She sat on the bed. It couldn't be true. Madame would not be so cruel. Asa possessed nothing but Madame's fan and her own case, which she turned upside down, scattering its contents across the threadbare quilt: a change of linen, a spare pair of shoes, stockings, an old dress of Madame's with the seams let out – in order to convince as mistress and maid they had swapped clothes – Asa's purse containing just a few thousand sous because Madame held the bulk of their funds, a comb. Thrust between the folds of her shift was the final proof that her companion had gone, Asa's false papers, previously kept by Madame: the passport with Asa's new name and trade, *Julie Moreau, fermière*. And there was a further envelope containing a little more money upon which Madame had written in her firm, flowing hand: *Je vous en pris, retournez chez vous. Elle est trop dangereuse pour vous, La France. Au revoir, mademoiselle.*

Retournez chez vous. Why? How? What had happened at the end of mass to drive Madame away? Was it because of the argument they'd had yesterday morning? Perhaps it had simply been expedient for Madame to use Asa as a travelling companion thus far, and then discard her before Paris. But surely Madame knew Asa better than to expect her to leave France without first finding Didier. Besides, Asa had insufficient money either to reach Paris or return to England. Beatrice Paulin might refuse to speak to her; she might not know Didier's address. What then?

At last, having secured the room for another night and worn out with speculation and anxiety, Asa fell back on the hard mattress but still sleep did not come; her pulse raced, she was too hot, too desperate when she considered her remaining choices. Take the nearest coach to the coast and find a boat to carry her back across the Channel – impossible, surely, for so little money. Write to John Morton or her father, tell them what she'd done and beg for assistance – imagine the fuss, the embarrassment, the distress when as yet they didn't even realise that she'd left the country. The news would be bound to reach Compton Wyatt, reverberate through the lavish rooms and filter down to the lake, where the swans floated so indifferently. Write to Didier's old address in Paris and await a reply. But he might have moved. And what if the letter fell into the wrong hands?

Again and again she scrabbled for an answer. Why had Madame left her alone in France, in the thick of the Revolution?

Chapter Five

Next morning she washed her face, dressed with great care and tidied the room as if she might somehow save herself by organising her shoes and petticoats. She then set forth again for the rue Leverrier and at last struck lucky; a solitary woman was approaching from the opposite direction, dressed in a white cap and grey gown, her muslin under-shift open at the neck and a basket on her arm. Asa pronounced her name, Beatrice, in the English way and ran towards her. 'I am Thomasina Ardleigh. I left a note for you yesterday. Don't you recognise me?'

Beatrice actually held out the palm of her hand as if to keep Asa at bay. She retreated a couple of steps and looked nervously up and down the street. 'Don't come any nearer.'

'What do you mean? I need to speak to you.'

'I can't.'

'Beatrice, *please*. I'm alone. You can't send me away. One minute is all I ask.'

Beatrice turned aside and unlatched the gate.

'I have come so far. Please, Beatrice.'

Again Beatrice looked back and forth along the street. Her head went down and she seemed to be deciding what to do. But at length she seized Asa's arm and pulled her into the shady court-yard. Once inside the house she bundled her across the hall and up the stairs to a parlour on the first floor.

'Stay back so you can't be seen from the street.' The room, at one corner of the house, had two windows and was full of light. Asa had a dazzled impression of books, dappled sunshine and white walls. Memories flickered; Madame de Genlis's salon, the atrium of the Hotel Montmorency and the serene, upturned face of this young woman, Beatrice Paulin.

Beatrice flung down her empty basket. The blood had returned to her neck and cheeks in a blotchy flush. 'What are you doing here in Caen?'

'I needed to see you. Didn't you get my note?'

'Which note?'

'Your maid...'

'Madame Vadier, our housekeeper, is protective of me. Why are you in Caen?'

'I am looking for Didier.'

These words were impossibly brazen. No wonder Beatrice's eyes emptied of expression. 'Are you mad? What do you mean, looking for Didier?'

'He sent for me but he didn't give an address.' Even to her own ears it sounded naive.

'I can't help you. I'll show you out. Don't come here again.'

'Beatrice. For pity's sake.'

'Was it you in the square yesterday? I thought I recognised your face but decided I was foolish to think it was you. I wish I'd been right. Mademoiselle Ardleigh, your being in this house, or even in Caen, places us all in great danger. I can't expect you to care what happens to us but for your own sake I beg you to go.'

'You can trust me. I am your friend.'

'The last thing we need is an English friend.'

Beatrice was the same only in looks. The girl who in Paris had stood shining eyed, holding her brother's confident arm during the salon, and who had moved in her queenly way between father and brother, had changed into a bitter-eyed woman, her expression unyielding and her skin roughened by exposure to the sun. Asa was a little nervous of her.

'Beatrice, please... We were good friends at one time. Help me, if only for the sake of your father's friendship with Mr Lambert. In May I wrote to Didier and this was how he replied. He sent for me. Look.' She took out the notes from Didier and the turquoise handkerchief.

From the kitchen came the familiar clank of a pan lid, exactly as if Mrs Dean were putting on the dinner at Ardleigh. At the sight of the handkerchief Beatrice's breath grew shallow and she retreated, fists clenched. 'We are supposed to report any strangers we see in town to the authorities. This house is already under suspicion. Good God, you have no idea what might happen to us...'

Sunlight spilled on to the painted floor. Asa returned Didier's letters to an inner pocket and straightened her skirts.

Beatrice said more calmly, 'You spoke of Mr Lambert. How is he?'

'Mr Lambert is dead.'

'Father will be sorry to hear that.'

'He was arrested for sedition because he would not keep quiet and he collapsed on the way to prison. In England radicals such as Mr Lambert

318

are being persecuted because their cause has become associated with the Revolution here in France.'

After a pause Beatrice said: 'Mademoiselle Ardleigh, I have been very cruel. This is not like me. It's the times, you see. Stay a while longer. Sit down, please. You seem ill.'

'I don't mean you any harm. Believe me.'

'I can't be of much help, that's the trouble. I haven't seen my brother for nearly a year. We do have news of him occasionally. The last we heard, a few weeks ago, he had been sent on a mission to the south of France, to visit the troops posted at Toulon where your British army is likely to invade.'

'Toulon? Why would he write to me if he knew he was going to be so far away?'

'I don't know. I can't understand it. You say he gave no address.' This time, when Asa held out the letters, Beatrice took them. In the old days her right hand had been touchingly stained with ink, on the third finger, like Asa's own, the mark of a scholar. Now her hands were coarse and the nails had been cut brutally short. 'I can't understand it,' Beatrice said again. 'It is so out of character for him to do anything as reckless as this. And why would he give no address? Of course, I knew Didier had fallen in love with you that time you were in Paris, but I thought...'

'You *knew?*'

'Why, of course. Didier talked about nothing but you for months after you left. But then we all became caught up in the Revolution and I presumed he'd forgotten about you. You never

319

mentioned him in the letters you wrote to me.'

'You must think my behaviour was very wrong.'

'*His* behaviour. *His*. What he did is far worse. I assumed that there was nothing but infatuation on both sides. Now I discover that you've waited for him all this time.'

'We were going to marry...'

'Marry? Surely not. No. He promised you that? When did this happen? You scarcely knew him.'

'You mustn't think we were trying to deceive you.'

'But I was *there* at the salons and the theatre. I can't understand how you managed private conversation, let alone talk of marriage. My brother told me everything at that time, or so I thought. We were very close.' Her eyes had become wary and cold again. 'You met in secret, didn't you? Of course, your hotel was very close... He seduced you. Is that what happened? Oh dear God. I hope not.'

There was a confident knock on the door below followed by light footfall on the stairs, and the next moment the same young woman who had been with Beatrice in the square the previous day burst in. Collapsing into a seat, she tore off her bonnet and began using it as a fan. Her face was damp with perspiration. 'You would not believe what's going on out there. My God, Beatrice, you should come down to the Hôtel de Ville. History is being made before our very eyes.'

'Charlotte, this is a family friend, Thomasina, who is paying me a brief visit. Thomasina, Charlotte Corday.'

'Very pleased to meet you,' exclaimed Charlotte,

leaning forward to press Asa's hand. 'What an unusual name. How long are you staying?'

'She's just arrived in town and doesn't appear to be very well,' said Beatrice sharply. 'You shouldn't pester her, Charlotte.'

Asa was given a critical stare, as if Charlotte was amazed anyone could dream of being weak. 'I'm sorry to hear that. Seriously, though, Beatrice, come into town with me later. Another five deputies are staying in the Hôtel de l'Intendance now, all fled from Paris. The crowds are out, cheering them through the gates. How could such good men be considered a threat? But we are turning the tables on Paris. Have you heard? A committee has been convened.' She waited a moment for Beatrice's response, but none was forthcoming. 'We are going to send a declaration to Paris, and we will make demands they cannot refuse.'

'Hush,' said Beatrice, nodding towards Asa. 'Thomasina doesn't want to hear about all this.'

'Don't worry,' said Asa. 'I'm staying in Caen, after all, and I've listened to the speakers in the square.'

'Good for you,' said Charlotte, glancing triumphantly at Beatrice. 'You're one of us, I can see that. In any case, I don't care what anyone thinks, I'm past caring. What can be wrong with demanding that our deputies should be restored to their places on the National Convention? What is wrong in asking that the Revolutionary Tribunal be abolished? I think you should try writing to that brother of yours one last time, Beatrice. Get him to speak up for us.'

'Hush now, not so loud,' said Beatrice quickly. 'You're forgetting where you are. For God's sake, we don't need any more trouble in this house. We'll definitely be punished.'

'Let them punish us. That'll be proof once and for all that they care nothing for France, if they're prepared to kill their fellow citizens.'

'Look what's already happened to Father,' murmured Beatrice. 'Don't you think he's suffered enough?'

The sunlight had shifted so that it was now burning directly on to Asa's neck. Beatrice's room seemed distressingly similar to the parlour at Ardleigh, full of purpose – books, pens, and newssheets everywhere, and these ardent young women perspiring in their simple cotton gowns. She stood up dizzily and said: 'I should go.'

'Where are you staying?' asked Beatrice. 'Do you know the way back?

'Just a guest house near the Church of St-Jean.'

'Not the auberge on the corner?' cried Charlotte. 'You can't stay there. It's so grim. Beatrice, why do you let her? Listen, we'll all go out. It's quite wrong to be cooped up there when so much is going on in town.'

'Please,' said Asa, 'I'd rather be on my own.'

Beatrice accompanied her downstairs and spoke in a low voice as they reached the door. 'I'm sorry she barged in like that. We've known each other since we were children and she's used to treating this house as if it were her own. The only good thing is she's so full of her own ideas she won't have paid much attention to you. I can scarcely take in what you've told me. I need to think about it – and I'll speak to Father. But I'm sure it would be much better if you went back to England as soon as possible. That would be the best plan. Caen is a dangerous place. Charlotte is not the only one full of rage.'

'I can't go home until I've seen Didier,' said Asa. 'I have to know why he sent that note.'

'Then I'll visit you in a day or two.'

At least Beatrice took Asa's hand and kissed her on either cheek before crossing the shady courtyard and admitting her to the hot street. So, she must survive a few more days alone before Beatrice would see her again. As she returned to the auberge, the streets of the town seemed to have narrowed, the walls of the castle grown higher, so that it was a threatening presence. People kept to the shade except those who couldn't avoid the sun: officials on horseback, the military, wagon drivers, the occupant of a carriage spattered with dirt, his face grey and ill shaven, followed by a mob of youths who banged on the carriage door yelling: *'Vive la Liberté. Vivent les citoyens de Caen. Vivent les Carabots.'*

Asa slipped inside the church opposite the auberge, where the smiling Madonna was cool in her star-spangled cloak. This time Asa knelt as a Catholic would, as Madame had done.

Show me what to do.

From her pocket she withdrew Didier's crumpled handkerchief, exactly the blue of the Madonna's robe only perhaps a little more faded. Turquoise was the colour of Caen, then.

Chapter Six

No word came from Beatrice. Each morning Asa met her landlady lurking in the gloomy lobby by the front door. 'Where is your mistress? I've not seen her for days.'

'She was called away from town. Sickness in the family.'

The landlady thrust out her long-nailed hand and took Asa's money. 'I must say I've never heard of such a thing, a mistress leaving her maid. The room costs the same, whether it's occupied by one or two. And I don't want you hanging around, drawing attention to yourself.'

In the streets Asa was always on the move, in case anyone was looking for a stray English woman thinly disguised as a French maid. But she could never escape the eyes watching: street children begging for a sou; men on horseback patrolling the streets with sheaves of paper tucked under their arms and muskets across their saddles; wild-eyed gangs of youths who raged from square to square searching for a fresh injustice or a new fugitive from Paris needing an escort to the Hôtel de Ville.

More and more deputies who had allied themselves with Brissot came galloping to Caen in fear of their lives. In a bread queue Asa learned that more guards had been set at the gates and grain from outlying farms was being packed into a disused Carmelite monastery lest food should be needed as a bargaining tool to bring hungry Paris to heel. Were it not for mismanagement in Paris, Caen would have plenty, muttered the women. There should be no shortage of grain in Normandy, the dearth was a product of Parisian greed. And there was a call to arms; the town assembly had decreed that a departmental force should be raised to join with troops from other parts of Normandy, march to Paris and wrest the National Convention from the grip of tyrants who were bleeding Normandy dry.

'We must all be prepared to seize our weapons and march forth. This is not a counter-revolution,' cried a fat little orator who seemed unlikely to have wielded a heavy implement in his life, 'quite the opposite. This is about preserving the true spirit of the Revolution. Once the task is accomplished the troops will disband.'

The trouble was, no one volunteered. Day after day Asa walked through the Place de la Liberté to find a few stalwart Carabots marching up and down under the banner *L'execution de la loi, ou la mort* and exhorting childless men aged between seventeen and fifty to join them. 'What an opportunity. To defend one's city against oppression. Who can resist?' yelled the orators. Most men could, apparently.

Asa ceased to listen to all this rhetoric; she was thinking not of politics but of the boy Didier, who must have known these complicated streets intimately. She remembered how in Paris she used to seek him out in every crowd. Yearning for him then had worked its magic: had he not appeared unexpectedly in the Tuileries? Perhaps Didier might appear suddenly in Caen.

And there was another figure hovering at the edge of her vision: Madame. Glancing up, Asa thought she saw a thin hand drawing back the edge of a curtain and dark eyes peering through the latticed window of one of the ancient houses where the lace merchants used to live before the Revolution. Madame tagged behind as Asa toiled up to the Abbaye des Hommes, where Didier had attended school, and trod the gravel paths between its neglected lawns. Then back through town, so exhausted that the cobbles seemed to ripple beneath her feet and the church bells clanging the half-hour went on and on ringing in her ears; oversized St-Etienne built hard up against the abbey, the eerily named Notre Dame de Froide Rue and finally St-Jean. And always the old conundrum: where was Madame now and why had she gone away?

Impossible to resist pushing open the door and taking one more look, in case Madame had returned. Here, in the very back pew as they listened to mass, Madame had muttered the occasional *Amen*, nothing more. No tripping up the aisle to communion, no peeking round the brim of her cap as the priest passed by. And then the darting behind the pillar, the raising of her tragic eyes to a mosaic of colours, the sudden gripping of Asa's arm. There, before the statue of the Madonna, Madame had presumably come up with the simple truth that it was too dangerous for them both if Asa went with her to Paris. Wasn't that explanation enough?

At night Asa lay on her bed, bones aching after so much walking on hot paving stones. Waving Madame's fan back and forth, she listened through the silence between the last voice on the street and the first birds waking, punctuated only by the city clocks striking the quarter. If she imagined herself at home in England it was as if she were watching scenes from a play: her father riding up to the Downs, rumps – his and the horse's – swaying in unison; Philippa and the children in the toast-scented nursery at Morton Hall with Caroline Lambert; Mrs Dacre, feet and hands bound, being transferred from rowing boat to ship then forced down to the hold, where she would lie day after day, gripping her swollen belly and gasping for air. And Shackleford? Did he remember her sometimes when he was in the book room at Compton Wyatt? Was he standing by the leather chair looking down towards the lake, imagining her snug and indifferent at Ardleigh?

As dawn broke, the colours of the fan emerged from the gloom; the blue flowers intertwined to form an intricate border, the minute brush-strokes feathering the wings of the painted birds, a glint of gold leaf like the spangles on the Madonna's cloak. Perhaps Madame had left the fan for Asa thinking that it would be worth the price of a passage home, but who would buy such a trinket in these revolutionary days?

Asa sat up, her heart thundering. In memory the diligence again rumbled into Caen, again she alighted from the dim interior and toiled deeper into the quiet town, Madame at her heels, looking for a place to stay. They had lain awake, unspeaking, top to tail in the hard, narrow bed. And in the morning, those words: 'I will go to mass.'

And now, as she retraced the crossing of the square with Madame, entering the church's dusty interior, which smelt of sand and wax, the first glimpse of those lurching pillars pressed unevenly into Caen's unstable soil by the weight of the lantern tower, the unfamiliar Latin prayers, the recoiling from the body on the crucifix, Asa understood what was wrong. From the back pew of the church where she and Madame had sat throughout mass there had been no sign of the Madonna and Child, pushed out of sight, presumably, to avoid the brigade of slashers and hackers intent on defiling any sign of pre-revolutionary piety. Yet Madame had stepped from the pew, crossed the church, walked unfalteringly round the pillar and cast herself at the foot of the statue, not as if she had fallen upon it by chance, but because she had known all along that it was going to be there.

Chapter Seven

By the fourth night Asa's head throbbed so violently she could not keep it still on the pillow. Gasping with thirst, she willed herself to get up and fetch clean water but was too weak. The following morning, soon after the clock struck nine, there was a brisk knock on the door and

Beatrice appeared in her trim grey gown. She stared at the dirty window, the tangled sheets and the creased petticoat flung on a chair, while Asa swung her feet over the edge of the bed and clutched the loose neck of her shift. 'It's late to be in bed. Are you still unwell?' demanded Beatrice.

'A little.'

'Your eyes look peculiar. You can't stay here. I've spoken to Father and we have decided that you should move into our house for the time being.'

'There's no need for you to go to such trouble.'

'Clearly there's a need. Father says that since Didier is the cause of your presence here, we can't abandon you. I had no idea you were living like this. We have already put the word about that you are a distant relative of ours, down on your luck. If anyone asks we'll say that although you're French you've spent years abroad as a governess, hence the accent. I'll wait downstairs while you dress. Don't bother with a cap. Sometimes people think it's harking back to the old days, for women to wear that sort of cap.'

Too sick to resist and too ashamed to ask for help, Asa thrust her juddering arms into her dress and plaited her unkempt hair. The leather travelling case thumped against her calves as she dragged it downstairs, where the landlady lay in wait.

'I paid you yesterday,' said Asa. 'I'm leaving now.'

'You didn't give me notice. That'll be one more night's rent. If you don't pay your bill I'll have to report you.'

The landlady's eyes glinted in readiness for a fight. After handing over the money Asa would have only a few écus left, but her head was pounding too much for any argument. The walk through Caen's broiling streets seemed interminable; hot air even funnelled through shady rue Froide as they made their way north between close-packed houses and the indifferent morning crowds. Beatrice walked doggedly several paces ahead, neither offering to help Asa with her case nor making any attempt at conversation until they reached the house on rue Leverrier. When the front door was thrown open, she entered without waiting for her guest.

The housekeeper, Madame Vadier, was inside, eyes darting and hostile. She told Asa to follow her and then climbed the stairs beneath the likeness of Didier, with his firm shoulders and brilliant eyes, to a little room at the back of the house where muslin curtains were drawn against the sun so that the air seemed cool and translucent.

'You look very sick to me,' said the housekeeper. 'I suppose you should go to bed. I can't say I'm surprised. Nobody in their right minds would stay at that filthy place. I've not known her air a mattress in fifteen years. Lie down before you fall.'

Asa's bones rattled with fever and the sheets were harsh on her hot skin. She was barely conscious of the scent of lavender as Madame Vadier said: 'On top of everything else she has brought fever to the house. I shouldn't be surprised if we're all struck down, and then what?'

Beatrice appeared at the bedside. 'You must

promise me not to leave the house until I say. Madame Vadier will look after you. I'll decide what to do when you're well. I want people in Caen to forget about you, do you understand?'

At regular intervals the housekeeper brought fresh water and on that first evening she offered to bathe Asa's neck and face, though her hands were decidedly unsympathetic and she muttered: 'As if I haven't got enough to do. What are people thinking of, visiting Caen at this time? I've not had a minute for those chickens. Goodness me, mademoiselle, your skin is burning, how can you possibly be shivering?'

Later that night Asa heard the two women shut themselves in their separate rooms; the house-keeper on the attic floor above. There was no sign of the professor. Asa slept fitfully and woke full of apprehension, imagining that the slightest sound – an owl's hollow hoot, the clatter of a shutter – meant that she had been betrayed and that soldiers had come to arrest this mysterious English visitor. She felt the air move across her brow and thought Madame must be there, fanning her softly and keeping watch. Later she dreamed that she heard knocking on her bedroom door and that it was Shackleford forcing his way through a stack of luggage and upturned chairs.

Dawn came and the distinctive white walls of the Paulin house enclosed her again. How strange to spend day after day under Didier's roof; to hear female footfall on the stairs, the opening and closing of doors and the clamour of chickens. *His* sounds. *His* life. Thus she floated between his world and her own.

After a couple of days Asa was eating morsels of fruit and toasted bread. The next morning she dressed and groped her way downstairs, where Madame Vadier found her in the hall, exhausted. 'When you're well enough I have plenty of work for you. For the time being you can go into the garden, if you like. I don't want you in my kitchen when I'm baking so you can use the doors in the salon – it's due an airing. Wipe your feet when you come back in.'

The salon was in semi-darkness but the house-keeper marched across and folded back the shutters so that light streamed through on to a faded green carpet and comfortably worn fur-nishings, chairs upholstered in pale green damask, yellowed in the seats from too much wear, a card table drawn up to the hearth, and a screen painted with butterflies. Asa stepped from this still space on to a terrace ablaze with sunlight and scented with currants and flowers. At the centre was an empty stone bowl which must once have held a fountain and beyond was a tangle of greenery penetrated by little gravel paths leading to the heart of the garden.

Madame Vadier could not resist following Asa and standing in the shade of a birch. 'My late mistress, Mademoiselle Paulin's mother, loved to work out here. This used to be a wonderful formal garden with statues at each corner and a huge urn at the centre where the mistress grew ferns. You should have seen the garden when she was alive. The professor always brought her plants. Look at those lilies, the white ones. Very rare. You wouldn't see those where you come from.'

'Who looks after the garden now?'

'Who do you think? Everything falls to me. Except for Mademoiselle Beatrice, who helps out when she has time, which she hasn't. And there's a boy but he's lazy and has taken to loitering about in the square claiming to be patriotic. He'll get himself conscripted if he's not careful; he's certainly foolish enough.'

'Madame Vadier, what about the professor? When will he be home? I should like to speak to him.'

'Best not to ask questions. That's what Mademoiselle Beatrice told me to say.'

The housekeeper, whose uneven shoulder blades were too prominent under the thin fabric of her dress, darted back inside. The garden was bordered on three sides by high stone walls sheltering fruit trees and a thriving vegetable garden. In a secluded spot at the side of the house was a washing line, and a smooth lawn for bleaching sheets, just as they had at Ardleigh. But the shrubbery and flower beds were neglected and wild so that the thoughtful faces of mossy statues, half buried in the undergrowth, peered between the leaves of overgrown laurel.

Unlike at Ardleigh on a summer afternoon, here there was no sense of a slumbering pause between morning and night. In the Paulin house absence permeated every moment. Beatrice had left instructions that Asa might borrow books from her father's study but she couldn't bear to set foot inside. The shutters were half closed and the desk scattered with papers, as if its owner might return at any moment and set to work.

In the dining room the oval table was covered with heavy felt, though Madame Vadier showed Asa a linen press stacked with embroidered table-cloths. 'It's years since we've eaten formally,' she said, stroking the top of the pile. 'I ought to be grateful, it was an hour's work to iron one of these cloths and in any event there's no starch to be had these days.' She pointed out a miniature of the late Madame Paulin, who had been dark haired like her children, with a somewhat ferocious stare and an angular face. 'Of course, since this was a professor's house, we had many visitors. At one time there were four servants. But Madame did much of the work herself. She loved to cook – she wasn't proud. And she rarely sat down, was always rushing from one room to the next. No wonder she died young.'

'Her death must have been such a blow to the family.'

'It certainly was. The house was never the same after that. She had so much life in her. The children's friends were always here, running about the garden. She loved to bring them feasts of biscuits and cakes and cheese. The house used to hum when she was alive.'

Madame Vadier looked dotingly about the room. 'In the winter, this is where they'd work. Four heads bowed over their books. Sometimes more. We used to keep the fire burning high for them and make them chocolate. My boy Didier used to take the head of the table, Jean Beyle the foot, the girls in between.'

'Jean Beyle?'

'I thought you'd have heard of him, since you're an old acquaintance of the family. Everyone knew Didier's friend Jean. I remember the arguments. Sometimes the professor would stand by the window and listen, or interrupt with a quotation from one of his philosophers. He never minded the outrageous ideas they had, as long as they could support them with their learning, that's what he used to say.'

'Did Beatrice join in as well?'

'Of course she did. All the girls who came here learned how to argue. They were encouraged to do so. Madame Paulin never said much because she thought she was too ignorant but she had her views all right. That's why Beatrice went to school in the first place; her mother wanted her to learn. Then in the summer out they'd go, into the garden. When they were small it was always hide and seek, wrecking the mistress's flower beds, breaking her precious pots. I can see them now, laughing at me from the trees. When they were older they'd sprawl on the grass with their books.'

At half past two each afternoon, Madame Vadier collected a glass of water from the scullery and went upstairs for her sleep. 'That portrait of Didier, Monsieur Paulin,' Asa said, 'it's very fine.'

'You think so? Estelle did it. Jean's sister.' The housekeeper shot Asa an unreadable glance. 'Personally I don't think much of it. She painted it for Madame Paulin, as she lay dying. Otherwise I don't believe it would still be hanging there.'

'Why not?'

Madame Vadier took a step down and spoke in

a low voice. 'Didier – Monsieur Paulin – took everything he wanted when he was last here. Said we should throw out the rest. It was autumn. You should have seen him, driving up to the door in his smart carriage, and half of Caen rushing up the road to set eyes on our famous young man. Next thing I know he and his father were shouting in the study and when Didier came out he was weeping. I'd not seen him in tears since his mother died. When he kissed me and called me his darling Vadier, like he used to, he said he wouldn't be coming back.'

Madame Vadier continued up the stairs, each step slower than the last, as if her body was already half asleep. As Asa studied the painting, she thought that the housekeeper had been unjustly critical and that the young friend, Estelle Beyle, was unusually gifted for an amateur. True, the laughing eyes and painted smile lacked depth and subtlety but the soft folds of the cravat and in the sleeve of Didier's coat were so meticulously done that Asa felt she might have inserted her fingers into them.

There was no signature, just initials in the bottom right-hand corner in modest grey paint: E. B.

Chapter Eight

A week after Beatrice had plucked Asa from the Auberge St-Jean, she told her to fetch Didier's handkerchief and her false papers and prepare for a walk in the countryside. Beatrice was dressed as usual in a deep-brimmed cotton bonnet and carried a covered basket so laden that even though they shared its weight the handle cut into their palms. At the city gates the guards waved Beatrice through then glanced indifferently at Asa in her crumpled dress and straw hat.

The lane led due west through flat countryside. On the other side of head-high hedges cattle dozed and the wheat was already pale gold, though Beatrice said the summer had been so hot and dry, nobody expected a high yield. On and on they walked, past hamlets of houses poorer even than Key Cottage with patched roofs and broken shutters, the doors lying open so that hens might shelter from the sun.

'I'm grateful to you for not pestering Madame Vadier about Father,' said Beatrice. 'I assume you've guessed – or been told – that he is in prison. He would like to meet you but you still have a choice; if you don't want to visit him, you can turn back.'

'Yes, that is what I suspected – after all, I saw what happened to Mr Lambert in England. Of course I still want to see your father. And I'm used to prisons so I shan't find that disturbing.'

'He told me to warn you that there's always the danger that some official will turn up and arrest a visitor on suspicion of conspiracy or some other trumped-up charge. If anyone found out you were English, we would all suffer.'

'Why would your father risk seeing me, then?'

'He's already in terrible trouble. He's accused of whipping up discontent by speaking out against the policies of the National Convention. That is a capital offence, even though he also says that the idea of Caen taking military action is sheer madness. He's advocating peaceful argument, but either way, it's unlikely he'll survive. If the mood in Caen changes or if those men they have imprisoned in the chateau happen to be released and decide to seek revenge, my father would certainly be sent to the guillotine. His view, therefore, is that he has nothing to lose.'

'What if they find out who I am?'

'Let's hope they don't. Once we're inside the prison there's no need for you to say a word, except to father. But to be honest, I'm worried too. I didn't want to bring you here at all, but my father feels responsible for you because of Didier. That's why he wants to see you.'

The prison, formerly an abbey, was built in local, oatmeal-coloured stone with a lofty chapel on the east side. Within the gates the atmosphere was rather that of suspended normality than of a gaol; men strolled about the cloisters in their shirtsleeves and a few women, grouped in the shade with their sewing, looked curiously at Asa. When a couple broke away to ask Beatrice for news they were polite enough but their exhausted eyes were avid. A red-faced guard with a military bearing accepted a coin as if he were a servant taking a discreet tip and admitted Asa and Beatrice through a side door to a stone passage reeking of rancid meat. At the far end was a flight of worn, shallow stairs leading to a row of cells.

Five years earlier, when the professor had driven with Asa to Madame de Genlis's salon, he had worn a neat wig and a suit of fawn velvet; his complexion had been ruddy and his demeanour smart and proud. Now he was gaunt with a few white hairs sprouting from the sides of his head, and he was dressed in a shirt damp with sweat and stained breeches. His skin had a powdery pallor and he smelt yeasty and stale. After kissing his daughter on either cheek he took Asa's hand in his, and subjected her to a moment of unswerving scrutiny.

Beatrice unpacked an apron from her basket and set to work replacing uneaten food with fresh, folding her father's used linen, changing the sheets on the bed and laying out clean clothes. Help was jealously refused from Asa, who was told to accompany the professor as he took exercise in the passage outside. As they paraded up and down, the old man's hand was a frail pressure on her arm and each step was cautious, as if the ground were moving beneath his feet. Because the doors of the other cells were open they didn't speak except when Paulin exchanged a word with a fellow inmate.

When they were allowed back into the professor's cell Beatrice closed the door, despite the stale, hot air. The women sat on the unsteady bed, the prisoner on the single chair. He poured wine for his visitors, as he might have done had they been in his study in Caen. Despite his age and apparent fragility, Asa quailed before him, recognising that this was the moment when her life would tip forward at last.

'Mademoiselle Ardleigh, my daughter, as she's no doubt told you, brought you here against her better judgement. The truth is I am too old to be afraid and the world has become so unstable that it seems to me one might as well do as one wishes, as far as one can.'

Asa tried to thank him but he held up his hand. 'My difficulty has been in knowing how best to conduct this conversation. I have brought you here for three reasons but I know that your response will be different, depending upon the order in which we discuss them. I shall therefore put my cards on the table as simply as I can. First I need to tell you that two days ago Beatrice brought me this letter which arrived at our house in Caen. You were sick, I understand, and knew nothing about it.'

He nodded at Beatrice, who produced a sheet of closely written paper which she laid on the bed.

'You will doubtless wish to read the letter,' said the professor, 'since it concerns you, and until we have discussed the contents, I have no idea how I might reply to it. In the meantime, I believe you were sent letters and a handkerchief by my son. We couldn't risk you bringing me the letters, in case you were searched, but I'd like to see the handkerchief.'

The letter was written in John Morton's small, competent hand, and was dated 18 June.

Dear Professor Paulin,

May I introduce myself as John Morton of Surrey, England. This will seem to you a surprising and perhaps unfathomable letter, and you must forgive me for imposing on your time. I was given your address by our governess, Miss Caroline Lambert, formerly of Littlehampton, who is the daughter of your late friend, Martin Lambert.

The truth is we are all at sea and know not where to turn. My wife's dear sister, Thomasina Ardleigh, who you may perhaps remember meeting in Paris five years ago, and to whom, as I recall, your family was very kind, is causing us grievous concern. She, together with her paid companion, a French woman, has disappeared without trace. We have no doubt that their sudden departure was planned – there is no question of foul play – though this offers us little relief; the opposite in fact, under the circumstances. Even more disturbingly, we now have reason to believe that they may be in France.

The two women left home in a trap belonging to Thomasina's father, who, becoming concerned about his daughter's prolonged absence, discovered that she'd never arrived at her proposed destination. He then traced the equipage to a village beyond Portsmouth, where it was in the possession of a farmer.

Unfortunately a week had elapsed before we discovered Thomasina gone, and now we have wasted yet more days riding about the country in search of her. She left no note, except to a Mrs Susan Shackleford, at whose house she was lately staying, in which she expressed regret that they would probably not meet again. We have made enquiries about the companion in London and drawn a blank. It would seem hardly conceivable that Thomasina could have been so foolhardy as to venture to France, had it not been firstly for the evidence of Portsmouth and secondly that an even more disturbing possibility has come to light.

As I have said, it grieves me deeply to burden you with the intimate difficulties of strangers, and I appreciate that this letter might appear to you so impenetrable that you will wish to discard it at once, but Miss Lambert, who happens also to be Thomasina's closest friend, has revealed to us – in my view somewhat late in the day – that it's possible Miss Ardleigh may have formed an attachment while in France all those years ago. Miss Lambert suggests that following an unwelcome proposal from a suitor at home, my wife's sister may have decided to pursue her former association. As I write these words, I feel them to be improbable. Thomasina is wayward and opinionated, but surely not so deceitful as to have harboured a connection all this time. However, my wife, who urges me to explore every avenue, insists I explain this to you. Miss Lambert further tells us that she recently gave Thomasina a map of France, and letters headed with your address. Hence this letter.

Sir, if you should see or hear of Thomasina Ardleigh, or could, through any contacts you might have, make enquiries on our behalf, you would earn our undying gratitude. She is a girl of normal height and girth, brown haired. (My wife adds, with an exceptionally good figure, hair waving and thick, and blue-green eyes.) We believe she has taken with her *one pink and one striped gown. The companion is small, slightly built and dark haired, very French in manner and aspect, as I recall only too well. I need hardly tell you that we are all beside ourselves with anxiety and are exhausted from riding up and down to London at the whim of even the smallest suggestion or rumour. Hence this letter, which I am aware in the particular circumstances of your country and ours may not reach you, though we have found connections who have promised to ensure that it does.*

My wife, who is far from well, sends you her kindest regards,

I am, sir, your grateful and obedient servant,
John Morton

'You're weeping,' said Paulin. 'Didn't you expect your family to care?'

'I hoped they wouldn't discover I'd gone until I had found Didier and written home.'

'Surely that was a foolhardy plan. You left England nearly three weeks ago, I believe. How could they not have missed you in all that time?'

'I did not expect to be taken ill.'

'Well, it seems you have created something of a storm.'

'I can't bear to think of my father galloping about the countryside like that. And my poor sister. What shall I do?'

'You or I must write at once to this John Morton, that much is clear. What we shall say will depend on how you feel, once we have talked about Didier. My daughter tells me that my son's letters to you seem genuine, albeit vague and terse. And this handkerchief is indeed the one my wife gave Didier as she lay dying. She hemmed it herself and we would recognise those crooked little stitches anywhere – she disliked sewing intensely, as Beatrice will testify. But I cannot for the life of me imagine why he has contacted you in this fashion. It is not like my son to be obtuse.'

'That's why I came to visit your family in Caen. I have no idea where your son is.'

'Mademoiselle, as I'm sure Beatrice has told you, you have wasted your time. The extent of the estrangement between us is such that Didier, though well aware that I am in prison, has made no attempt to visit me, nor has he written since last autumn. We receive news of my son only second-hand, so all we know is that he has been sent south, to view the fortifications in Toulon.' The professor spoke in the old, measured way, his head held high and his pale blue gaze un-flinching.

'I don't understand, sir. When I knew you both in Paris there was such affection between you.'

'You thought so? Whereas I recall even then that my son had grown impatient with me. He spared us very little of his precious time and we were forever waiting about for him, weren't we, Beatrice?'

Beatrice, intent on darning the elbow of one of her father's shirts, said nothing.

'The truth is that the rift between us grows ever deeper. There are certain issues about which I have spoken and written that particularly irritate my son and his Montagnard friends in Paris. In today's France there are to be no shades of opinion. I happen to believe in freedom of con-

344

science. Inconvenient, I know. I also think it's wise to consult history and philosophy before imposing radical change. That is why I have been condemned.'

'I'm amazed, in the circumstances, that you could bear to see me today,' said Asa.

When the professor gave a sudden shout of laughter his resemblance to Didier was startling; the flash of brilliance in the eye, the way his lower lip became a shallow crescent. 'I confess, when Beatrice told me about you my first thought was, Well, this will be entertaining. It's very dull in here, mademoiselle. The other reason is that I held my friend Monsieur Lambert in great esteem – I'm so sorry to hear of his death – and therefore feel honour bound to look after you. But above all I recognise that my son has ill treated you. If I'd known what he was up to while you were in Paris, I would have knocked him down. He and I have fallen out over many things but I did not think he would stoop so low as to seduce a young English girl.'

'I was equally to blame, sir.'

'I disagree. You were very young and inexperienced, and far from home. But then the tragedy is that I'm not as surprised as I ought to be. The boy knows no boundaries. None of them does. And he cares nothing for his roots.'

'I'm sure that's not so. I remember him speaking fondly of his schooldays in Caen.'

'He did, did he? And yet you must have heard that Caen is on the brink of insurrection, hell-bent on self-destruction. I shake in my shoes when I think of the retribution that may descend on my city. Those men in Paris will stop at nothing to bring us to heel, but I know that my son will not lift a finger to save us, because it would be political suicide for him to do so.'

'Perhaps he's not aware of the true state of affairs? I can't believe he could be so changed that he would not care that you're in prison.'

'It grieves me to speak of my son thus. All my hopes for him have been dashed. Although to be truthful, I have always thought that Beatrice should be the one to rule France, not her brother.' When the professor reached for Beatrice's hand she put down her sewing, kissed his fingertips and allowed Asa a glimpse of her proud eyes. 'My daughter has always been steady and faithful. If she were in Didier's position now, she would not be galloping south to Toulon, but home to Caen. But it is Didier, not Beatrice, who has been promoted so high and so far. My son was never too bothered about how things were done, as long as there was progress and change. At school he was competent but he did not shine. When his best friend, Jean, excelled him in examinations Didier was furious because he thought he should have done better. It was as if Jean had cheated him, whereas in fact Jean had simply worked harder.'

'This is not the Didier I knew,' pleaded Asa. 'I had never met anyone like him. It seemed to me that he had an incisive and brilliant mind, and was entirely on the side of what is right.'

There was a long silence. The professor, it seemed, was not used to being contradicted. 'You knew Didier at his very best. He fitted the Paris

346

of 1788; his hopes, his desires, were exactly in accord with the time. Even now his ambition is undimmed. His new address is in the Place Vendôme, if you please. Ironic, isn't it, that my boy, my so-called champion of the people, should have chosen to live in the former haunt of aristocrats.'

Though Paulin paused, Asa could think of no defence for this.

'And the main purpose of his visit to Caen last autumn – or rather in late summer, right at the beginning of September – was to warn me to keep quiet. He accused me of undermining the progress of the Revolution by championing the cause of the priests who had refused to sign the oath of allegiance. While he was here in Caen, incidentally, many of those same priests were summarily tried and executed in Paris. He told me I failed to see the larger picture. I believe what he meant was that I was damaging his career. It seemed rich to me, as it must to you, that a boy whom I'd educated so that he might have the ability to engage with ideas should tell his own father to be silent. There is no state or institution so terrifying, Mademoiselle Ardleigh, as one that is too browbeaten to challenge the decisions of its own leaders.'

After a pause Asa said, 'And yet, Professor, none of this explains his letters to me.'

'I quite agree. In fact one would think that the last thing Didier might wish for at this point in his career is an entanglement with an English-woman. That's why I was so curious to see you. Beatrice told me he'd proposed marriage when

347

you met in Paris. We are amazed that he did not withdraw that proposal long ago. Being married to an English woman would hardly enhance his chances of political promotion.'

The cell was so cramped that Asa's knees were an inch or so from the professor's and the window was too small to admit more than a breath of air. She longed to escape, not just the enclosed space, but the professor and his daughter, and their relentless criticism of Didier.

'I said there were three reasons why I wished to see you. The first was the letter from England; the second to speak to you about the state of things between me and Didier; which brings me, reluctantly, to the third. It is not my business to know the nature of the understanding between you and my son. It is my business, however, to disclose something to you. I can find no easy way of telling you but hear it you must. We know that Didier, for the last couple of years at least, has been keeping a mistress in Paris.'

'I see that you are shocked,' continued the professor after a pause, 'though you say nothing. You are an intelligent woman, mademoiselle, so the first thing you will want is proof. The point is, we are well acquainted with the woman in question and she has made no secret of her relations with my son. She is a local girl called Estelle Beyle. She and her older brother were close friends of my children. Estelle was infatuated with Didier from a very young age. In fact, in the old days, when he and I could speak of such things, I used to joke with him that he had gone to Paris to escape her. But in the end she followed him. For all I know they may even be married. But then, on the other hand, why would they bother since marriage, like every other institution in our new France, has been deemed expendable?'

Another silence in the little cell, penetrated by a weak call from a bird in the garden. 'Perhaps she has left him,' said Asa, faltering. 'Perhaps she is dead and that is why he sent for me.'

Beatrice said nothing, but the professor leaned forward and rested his hand on Asa's knee. 'You are clutching at straws, mademoiselle. Can you not see that at the very least he has been unfaithful to his promises? All these years you have been waiting for him to send for you and marry you. But you have come to France in pursuit of a chimera, a boy you used to know who has changed beyond recognition. Only one thing, perhaps, is the same; the manner in which he wrote to you, thoughtlessly and probably on a whim. That, at least, is typical of Didier.'

Asa found that she could receive this news quite calmly, could keep her head up and endeavour not to look like a jilted woman. She realised that she had been braced for something of the kind, after all, and remembered how the housekeeper had watched her face as she talked about Estelle Beyle's portrait of Didier.

'What are you suggesting I should do?' she asked quietly. 'I have no friends in France apart from you, and no money.'

Beatrice tucked a cloth over the contents of her basket and tied on her hat. Her father picked up John Morton's letter as if satisfied that the discussion had ended satisfactorily. 'Write to your brother-in-law and tell him where you are and that you are safe. Until he replies, which may take a while given the war, you can stay with Beatrice. We shall also make enquiries of the English community in Le Havre who might offer you better protection than we can until a crossing has been organised.' He got up and extended his chilly hand to Asa. 'We shall not meet again, mademoiselle. May I apologise one last time, on behalf of my son. And wish you a safe journey home to England.'

Chapter Nine

On the wearisome trek back to Caen Beatrice was very quiet and kept herself apart from Asa so that not even their elbows touched. From a distance, the town was a multitude of spires piercing a lustrous sky; in silhouette it might have been mistaken for a prerevolutionary, reverential place.

'Thank you for taking me to see your father,' said Asa.

'I visit him nearly every day. Sometimes, if he's unwell, I am allowed to sleep in his cell.'

'How long since he was arrested?'

'Four months, approximately.'

'You must be exhausted.'

'I do my duty.'

They walked on in silence for several minutes. 'You're suggesting, I think,' said Asa, 'that perhaps I have done the opposite of my duty in coming to France.'

'No, I didn't mean that ... although it is true that you don't seem to be governed by duty and obedience in the way most women are.'

'I thought I was – until I met Didier. It seemed to me, when I fell in love with him, that I had no choice.'

'Certainly I have never felt as strongly for anyone as you have for Didier. I've never been tempted to question what is expected of me. Besides, we were all very serious in the old days. Religion and politics are what interested us and we pretended we didn't care so much about love.'

'And yet this Estelle Beyle certainly loved your brother.'

'Estelle was different.'

'In what way?'

'None of us was ever really allowed to love anyone she loved. Even her brother. She would much rather have kept him to herself. She used to watch us all the time, in case we took a part of him she didn't want to give away.'

'And the brother?'

'You mean, did he mind? Nobody could ever own Jean, not even Estelle. That's why she tried to keep him so close. He had a vocation to the priesthood. Before the Revolution, I used to think I was called to the religious life too, probably because of him.'

'And now? What do you hope for now?' Asa asked gently.

'Now the convents have closed and my family is divided by politics, so what choices are left to me? On the one hand, there is Didier's rapid rise in government, on the other my father's imprisonment. Not only have my father and brother been taken from me, so has my life. Haven't you noticed how quiet the house is? Few people come near us now, for fear of being caught on the wrong side.'

With every step the sunset deepened; the sky ahead grew rosier and the air at long last was a little cooler as an evening breeze wafted in from the sea.

'What about Didier's mistress, Estelle,' said Asa, 'was she religious too?'

'Fanatical. But she had her own religion. It wasn't to do with God but with Didier and the Revolution. If I'm honest I always felt a little lonely when we were together because she came between me and my brother. She was very funny, lively and talented, but she could also be cruel. She knew my weaknesses and sometimes her tongue would lash out and demolish me.'

'And yet Didier loves her.'

'They had a strange relationship. She tormented him and teased him, yet when she wasn't around he missed her. When Estelle's brother went to the seminary, she was needed at home to help look after her younger brothers and sisters and the family business. Didier took to going to the Beyles' house for dinner, or he and Estelle would go walking in the summer evenings. It wouldn't surprise me if she'd persuaded him to marry her by now – it's what she always wanted. Believe me, mademoiselle, you should go back to England. Estelle Beyle has had her clutches on Didier for as long as I can remember. Now that she has him, she won't let go.'

The following day, while Beatrice went to visit her father, Asa began her letter home, but after an hour or so, unable to find appropriate words, she offered to work in the garden for Madame Vadier. Tools were kept in a hut beside the vegetable patch and the housekeeper watched disparagingly as Asa jabbed at the hard soil with a trowel. In the end she tut-tutted with irritation, disappeared into the house and came back with a bucket of currants for Asa to top and tail. 'You can't go wrong with these.'

A blackbird perched on a ramshackle arch and the lilies nodded their wilting heads as Asa sat on a bench under the silver birch and pulled off stalks between the tines of a fork. Estelle Beyle. Didier Paulin. Jean Beyle. Beatrice Paulin. Each name was a currant falling softly into the colander.

Enter Charlotte Corday, who flung herself down in a flounce of cotton petticoats and tossed her untidy hair behind her shoulders. 'I couldn't find anyone in the house so I came out here. Where's Beatrice? Usual place, I suppose.'

Though she didn't offer to help, Charlotte watched the movements of Asa's fork and occasionally picked up a stray currant and dropped it into the wrong container. 'Today there's to be a review of the militia. They're hoping more people will volunteer to march on Paris. Will you come into the town and help me cheer them on?'

'Do you really think many will turn out?'

'Of course they will. We expect thousands to

join once it's clear they mean business. How can anyone hold back when the freedom of France is at stake?'

'Perhaps they don't really know what they are being called to fight for.'

'Of course they do. We have to resist domination from Paris. Marat, Danton and Robespierre are evil men. Did you know they've set up a so-called Committee of Public Safety to make rules designed to crush us all? You wouldn't understand because you are not French' – this was voiced as a reproach – 'You can't know how we feel.'

'I want to understand, though.'

'The point is that I supported the Revolution from the outset. You might think that odd, given that my family were *aristocrats*' – the word spoken in a whisper. 'We had quite a bit to lose, but France was bankrupt and we wanted to save our people from abject poverty. So we did want change, but we wanted change to be peaceful. We had no idea that such monsters were waiting in the wings...'

'But some things are better, surely? At least there are no more peasants starving while the landowners take all the wealth. At least the country is ruled by an elected body...'

'...of lawyers. That's not what we wanted. They know nothing. Look what they've done to our churches and our religious men and women. Everything has changed for the worse.'

Another currant went rolling under a stone. Charlotte darted forward to retrieve it.

'Tell me what it was like in the old days, in

Caen,' said Asa.

'Oh, I didn't live here when I was very small. I was brought up several miles to the south, in quite a large house – my grandfather actually owned a chateau with a moat, though of course we don't admit to that any more. After my mother died I was sent to school here. That's how I know the Paulins. Beatrice and I were both educated at the Abbaye des Dames. I was a boarder, of course, she wasn't. But that's all gone now.'

'What do you mean, gone?'

'Exactly that. Gone. Oh, the building is still there, but after the Revolution they threw out the nuns – even my dear abbess, Madame de Pontecoulant, who was like a mother to me after my own died. They turned the abbey into a warehouse for animal fodder, can you imagine, and now the nuns' quarters are barracks.'

'I'm sorry, Charlotte.'

'We could go there, if you like. I could show you. Please, come out with me. We're wasting so much time. First we'll go to La Place St-Sauveur and watch the troops. It's barely a five-minute walk.'

'I can't go. I have this work to do.'

'Oh, come on. There's so much to see. How can you bear to be stuck here?'

There was no sign of Madame Vadier and the currants were all but done. Charlotte, who appeared to be familiar with every nook of the Paulin house, led Asa through a side gate and into the front courtyard, where chanting could be heard from the crowd assembled a couple of streets away. She was quite right; the people of Caen were out in force, the militia and the Carabots in their white sashes, high hats and polished boots. From a distance at least they gave the impression of discipline, their muskets catching the sun, the soles of their boots resounding against the cobbles as they marched in front of the shrouded guillotine. The townspeople cheered, a brass band played, crêpe sellers drizzled lemon on to hot pancakes and thrust them into children's hands. Calvados, even at mid-morning, flowed, and the air was filled with the scent of fermented apple and fried batter.

Speakers lined up to extol the men of Caen for their bravery and exhort them to cast aside their doubts, even at this late hour. The soldiers shifted under the hot sun as perspiration darkened the backs of their tunics. Asa, remembering the professor's prediction that Caen's rebellion would be crushed, wondered whether the two representatives from Paris interred in the castle a few hundred yards from this spot could hear the bands and the marching. At the end of the parade General Wimpffen, who was to lead the forces out of Caen, stepped forward, accompanied by a drum-roll. The fringes of his epaulettes bouncing on his shoulders, he marched up and down the rows of militia, ordering volunteers to step forward and undertake the historic task of saving their city. At first Asa anticipated the smart stamping of hundreds of feet, but after a long pause only a single, stooped man shuffled out of line, then another, tall, thin and sheepish, and another, until there were seventeen in all.

Charlotte groaned. 'If I were a man nothing

would stop me marching on Paris. What is the matter with them?'

'If this small army from Caen fails,' murmured Asa, 'what then? Won't there be terrible retribution?'

'Possibly, but we're ready for that. We've had enough. Come on, I'm sick of this; I'll take you to the *abbaye*. Then you'll understand.'

It was a long walk under the castle walls and deep into the maze of old streets to the east of town. 'Caen is full of churches,' said Charlotte, clutching Asa's arm and lowering her voice, 'it's a very holy place, and was once very wealthy because of the lace and silk and other textiles that used to be traded here; the lace has all gone, of course, because nobody is allowed to wear it. And there were two abbeys. It's a standing joke in Caen that the abbeys were built on either side of the city because back in the eleventh century the Pope could not bear that William, who became king of England, insisted on marrying his cousin Matilda. As a punishment William had to build not one abbey but two, one for men and one for women, separated by the castle. Yet, as sure as night follows day, those educated in one often end up falling in love with someone from the other.'

'Did you fall in love, Charlotte?'

'Often, but never for long. We were all in love with Didier, needless to say. But he and Beatrice were very close, so it was difficult to get his attention, and then there was Estelle, who managed to attach herself to him even though her family was in trade. I wasn't really part of their set, being a boarder, but sometimes I went to supper at the Paulins' house. I often felt left out because I didn't have a brother. But that also meant I wasn't always in a boy's shadow like Estelle and Beatrice.'

'It doesn't sound to me as if Estelle was in her brother's shadow.'

'Oh, but she was. Or not his shadow exactly. Rather she was intent on fighting for a perfect world in which she could possess both her brother the priest, and her lover, Didier. When she couldn't manage to keep either of them it made her anxious and impossibly moody.'

At the top of the hill loomed the two colonnaded towers of the Abbaye des Dames. Charlotte went boldly to the door and rattled the handle. 'Locked, of course. It never used to be. Have a peek through the keyhole, you might be able to see what it's like inside.

'In the old days I was keeper of an abbey key. The one I held was for the door leading to the convent. It was wrought with a couple of twos, back to front, to form a heart. I was very fond of the weight of it hanging from my waist. The lock was kept very well oiled; I remember how easily the key slid in and the lovely clunk of the latch when I turned it. I would swing open the door and let the nuns through. The abbess always smiled at me.'

'You say that Beatrice used to come to school here too.'

'That's right. And look. Can you see, across the town, that cluster of steeples belonging to the Abbaye des Hommes? Every morning when they

358

left the house, Didier used to walk one way and Beatrice the other, exactly as the Pope had decreed all those centuries ago.'

'Was Didier as religious as you?'

'Perhaps not so much. He and I used to argue because Didier thought that religion should not involve itself in politics. He hated the fact that Louis called himself king by divine right. Jean and I used to argue for the Church. We said faith must always come first. Didier would have none of that.'

Asa remembered how a group of youths had settled like a flight of birds around Didier in the Tuileries gardens. *These are my friends from Caen.* 'What were they like, these other friends of yours? Estelle and Jean?'

'The Beyles? They lived on the rue de Bras, above their shop. It was a huge family. Estelle hated the fact that she didn't go to school because she had to work and look after her brothers and sisters, though she was given private lessons in English so she could use it for the business. Jean Beyle was Didier's close friend. He could have been a curate in any church in Caen but instead he chose a country parish called Mantheuil between here and Bayeux.' Her eyes filled with tears. 'He's not there now. We don't know where he is but we're afraid he's dead. The last time he wrote to us was from a church called St-Joseph...'

They walked slowly down the steep rue Menissier and across the sluggish river, along the tree-lined rue des Carmes, and were soon close to Asa's former lodgings, the Auberge St-Jean.

Asa's feet dragged. She was too hot and the streets were too much a reminder of those first days in Caen after Madame had abandoned her. The truth nudged at her elbow; it was all there, if she dared to look. With her whole being she yearned to escape another visit to the church of St-Jean, but Charlotte had already opened the door and drawn her into its dark interior. Charlotte crossed herself boldly, genuflected and headed for the Madonna and Child.

'She's called Our Lady of Protection,' she whispered. 'Look how lovely she is. She's venerated by everyone in Caen, that's why she's unharmed.'

The infant, perched in the arms of the Madonna, had Normandy eyes; wide set, blue, limpid. What a fool you are, Thomasina Ardleigh, they told her. 'Père Beyle,' she whispered, 'Estelle's brother. You say he was called Jean. Was that his full name?'

'That's it. Jean Beyle. Oh, except that his sister used a pet name to tease him. We all did sometimes: Gabriel. Like the Archangel. Too good to be true.'

Charlotte couldn't keep herself from the Place de Liberté for long so they parted company outside the church. Asa continued alone to the rue de Bras, the street along which she'd scurried when she first arrived in town, in search of bread. It was lined with capacious timbered houses, some, even in these difficult times, with thriving businesses on the ground floor; bolts of fabric lined up for inspection, bonnets, shawls and fichus.

It was the end of the day. Shutters were being

360

locked into place and the great doors leading to the courtyards where carriages used to be kept were pulled half shut. Asa slipped into a shop where plain linen caps were pinned to a red curtain and a girl in narrow skirts was winding ribbon. 'Excuse me,' said Asa.

'Yes, miss?'

'I was wondering if you could tell me – do you know a family called Beyle?'

The girl paused in the act of smoothing the frill of a cap. 'The Beyles who used to live three houses along? You won't find them. They've left town.'

The house in question was distinguished by a blue door. Like others in the street it was several storeys high but had fallen on hard times. A girl wearing a revealing shift was hanging out of an upstairs window and the great door leading from the street was ajar. Asa walked boldly into a courtyard of faded nobility with its worn carvings of cherubs and saints. A washing line had been strung from corner to corner, from which hung stained baby linen, and a woman was perched on a step, nursing a child. 'Yes?'

'I'm looking for a family called Beyle.'

'*Beyle*. They moved out years ago. Went to Austria, I think. They were losing too much money.'

'Do you know much about them?'

'Not really. I remember that as a girl I was allowed to peek into their shop when we brought eggs into town. It seemed like a palace because the paint was all gold and there were all kinds of pictures, goddesses and such, on the walls. And chairs with velvet seats. I used to watch the great ladies arrive in their carriages and sweep inside with their maids scuttling behind.'

'The Beyles were lacemakers, I understand?'

'Good heavens, no. I thought you said you were looking for them? I assumed it was because you knew their trade.'

'I used to know one of the girls. We had lessons together.'

'Well, surely she told you? The Beyles were famous for miles around. A cut above, and didn't they know it. They were *éventaillistes*, fan-makers. Had been for generations.'

Chapter Ten

It was the hottest hour of the day. Madame Vadier, seated at the kitchen table chopping onions, made it clear that Asa was in disgrace for abandoning the currants, but Asa was in too much of a hurry to attempt conciliation. Instead she asked for directions to Mantheuil and ran upstairs to collect her passport. The housekeeper insisted sullenly that she take bread and fruit with her unless she wanted to make herself ill again. This time Asa walked west through the city gates in the direction of the prison where Professor Paulin was being held. After about a mile, however, she cut off north along a narrow lane so seldom used that midges had colonised the space between overgrown hedges. Occasionally, through a gate, she glimpsed the pinnacles of Caen; once, when the horizon dipped, she saw a triangle of sea.

The village of Mantheuil, nearly two hours' walk from the city, had a commonplace church like so many others in Normandy – topped by a short tower and an even shorter, four-sided spire. Asa was hit by a pang of longing for Ardleigh with its luscious lanes, prosperous blacksmith and sleek cows trudging past the manor-house windows twice a day. The timbered cottages of Mantheuil were clustered round a small square with a pump, and children sat listlessly in meagre patches of shade, their bare feet paddling the dust.

Though the church door was open, the interior was far from inviting, given that it had been stripped of all but the pews and the altar. There were no flowers or candles. A statue of a woman, presumably the Madonna, had been slashed across the breast, and the head and neck were missing. But at least the church was cool; a gentle breeze blew through broken panes of glass and the stone floor was unharmed except for the buff from hundreds of years' footfall.

Before this plain little altar Father Beyle had said mass, day after day: dark haired and slight, kind and devoted. So it was along this aisle, according to Madame, that a village woman had taken her broom and swept the dust from beneath the feet of the usurping priest.

After a few minutes Asa emerged into the hot square and gave the children her parcel of bread and currants to share. After that they were eager to answer her questions.

'Who was the landowner here?'

'The one whose house was burned? The marquis? He's gone. Him and his wife and their baby. They say they went all the way across the ocean to America.'

'In which direction is the chateau where the family used to live?'

Grubby hands pointed towards the sea. Asa walked on, past a two-storeyed cottage, timbered but grander than the rest – the priest's house, perhaps, where Père Beyle might have drunk coffee with his sister when she deigned to saunter out from Caen and berate him for not being political enough. The chateau was half a mile from the village, set behind a high wall and a fringe of trees. Built of grey rather than local stone, the castle had three turrets, two on either side of the central porch and one on top. Above the massive front door was a broad, latticed window, and the slate roof was so steep that it was half as high again as the walls.

Asa drew closer until she came to the gate, which was thrown back on its hinges because the chateau was deserted; more than deserted, it was reduced to the bare bones of itself, gutted by fire, the walls blackened and windows smashed so that it was more like a ghost house. When she walked up to the porch and peered inside, Asa could see a stone staircase winding upwards in a spiral, but no floor above. The gardens, which had once been laid out in the formal style, complete with fountain and symmetrical beds, were overgrown. There could be little doubt, from the weeds that grew amid the stone steps

364

and the way the ruin had settled into itself, that the chateau had been abandoned for years.

And no, it wasn't a shock that the sign on the gate read 'Chateau de Rusigneux'; in her heart Asa had known the truth for days. From the burnt or migrated inmates of this place Madame had stolen her name. And it was here that Thomasina Ardleigh, unknowing rival in love to Estelle Beyle, acknowledged beyond a shadow of a doubt that Madame, her former companion, like the fans sold for generations by her resourceful family, existed only thanks to the invention of a flexible and fantastical mind.

Part Five

Paris, July 1793

Chapter One

The Paulins, father and daughter, had borrowed money on the assurance that it would be refunded promptly by John Morton, and had made arrangements for Asa to travel to Le Havre, where she would stay until a means of getting her back to England had been found. She had to wait a few more days, however, because the roads were packed with troops marching towards Lisieux, and Girondin deputies arriving hotfoot from Paris, sweating and terrified, with stories of arrests, imprisonment and interrogation. Since anybody leaving Caen would be searched and questioned by one side or another there was little hope for an English girl travelling on a false passport.

On the afternoon of Sunday, 7 July, Asa drank coffee for the last time with Charlotte and Beatrice in the garden of the rue Leverrier. The fine cups were of white porcelain with gold rims, a wedding present for the late Madame Paulin. Beyond the garden walls the city lapsed into a pre-revolutionary Sunday torpor. Inside, between the low hedges of the parterre, Didier had dreamed of changing the world, egged on by a dark-eyed wisp of a girl intent on owning him and his future.

Afterwards Beatrice followed Asa up to her room, closed the door and stood with her hands behind her back, as though steeling herself to make a speech.

'You're not going to Le Havre, are you?'

Silence.

'You'll go to Paris. You have those letters from Didier and you think he still loves you. Asa, you have to face up to the truth about him.'

Asa sank down on the bed. Beatrice watched her for a moment then sighed and put her hand on the latch.

'I have to go and find Didier,' said Asa, 'I have no choice.' She took Madame's fan from the top of her case and spread it on her lap. 'Take a closer look. It was given to me by that French companion of mine I told you about who abandoned me here in Caen and whose name, or so she claimed, was Madame de Rusigneux.'

Beatrice picked up the open fan and placed it on her palm, tentatively, as if it were a butterfly.

'This companion of mine led me quite a dance in England, pretending to know nothing about me. But I have discovered that her real name was Estelle Beyle and that she must therefore have known everything; especially that Didier and I had fallen in love when I was in Paris. She found a way of getting an introduction to my family and insinuated herself into my house until eventually she was part of my life.'

'Your companion, you say?'

'My companion, teacher, counsellor; all these things.'

The fan trembled on Beatrice's palm. 'Why would she do this?'

'I really don't know. It seems odd for Madame – Estelle – to have gone to such lengths. Perhaps she wanted to find out more about me, or hurt me if she could. Maybe she wanted to punish Didier ... sometimes in the last couple of days, when I realise to what extent she deceived me, I begin to question everything. After all, she was often kind to me ... but then, the next minute, she would be cold. You see – I can't even speak about her without my voice shaking.'

'This is incredible,' said Beatrice. 'That's exactly what she always does; she gets under the skin. All my life I have been haunted by Estelle's jealousy and schemes, and her pursuit of my brother. I thought I was finally free of her.'

'I am worried that your brother is in terrible danger. If Estelle can behave towards me with such cold-blooded calculation, then what will she do to Didier? She thinks he killed her brother. She told me so. When she gave me all the facts about Jean Beyle's death – except his name – she also talked about people of influence, the ones she had relied on to save him. I'm sure she meant Didier.'

'But you don't need to go to Paris. I'll write to Didier and warn him.'

'But it's more than that. I must go, partly for Didier, but mostly for me. My life has been held in check for five years while I waited for Didier. I believed in him, Beatrice. I thought he loved me. I understand that he had a mistress, but re-member he wrote to me. Now I see that there was something desperate in those letters. Perhaps he really did love me. Perhaps he still does. And if he doesn't, if he has deceived me, I want – I *need* – an explanation, from his own lips, so that

I can let go, at last.'

Beatrice put her hand above the bed and let the fan fall with a chatter of ivory guard sticks. 'I remember this fan. Estelle was a genius at making something out of nothing. The original of this painted blue urn used to stand in the middle of our garden. In the autumn, mother and the gardener always turned it on its side and emptied it of soil and dead plants. Once, when we were playing hide and seek, Jean Beyle crept inside it – he was nine or ten, I should think – and when he was found the urn had cracked in two. He was very upset about what he'd done, but Estelle comforted him and said she would resurrect the urn in a fan one day, only it would be more beautiful than ever – hence the birds and the leaves.'

Asa remembered Madame's bent head, the dark hair falling over her shoulder, the tilt of a magnifying glass above a brush so fine it was nearly invisible; she felt a tremor of the old love and the old loathing.

'If you find Didier,' said Beatrice, 'give him a message from me. Tell him please to come home. If Didier were here it might not be so bad for Caen when the men from Paris come to punish us.'

My dearest Philippa,

...Please don't worry about me any longer. I have been staying with the Paulin family and am safe and well. They have been exceptionally kind. My regards to all at Morton Hall and my heartfelt apologies for the trouble I have caused. Give my fondest love to

Georgina and Caroline and, of course, to Father.

In a few days I shall be in Paris, under the protection of Didier Paulin. Oh my dearest sister, I pray that one day you will understand, and even forgive this rash, extraordinary journey of mine...

Your wayward sister,

Asa

Next morning Asa set off in the diligence for Paris, armed with a street map and a letter of introduction from Beatrice to an old friend of the professor, a Madame Maurice, who lived on the rue des Francs Bourgeois and took in lodgers.

The huge carriage, drawn by a quartet of horses, would make the journey in a couple of days. It was composed of two linked compartments, and Asa was allocated a seat at the back which swayed nauseatingly at sharp corners but was at least removed from the pounding of hooves and the badinage of the coachmen. Her companions were a self-satisfied cabinetmaker and his wife, on the way to join an entrepreneurial son who was doing very well, thank you, having learned his father's trade and subsequently set up a furniture company making the new plain chests of drawers, cupboards and chairs so much admired by well-to-do Parisians.

The husband wore a tricolour cockade in his lapel and the wife said (with a meaningful glance at the little cockade in Asa's sash) that were it not unwomanly she would do the same, but she believed a wife's place was at the hearth, except obviously when she was on a well-deserved trip to Paris. Anyway, she wouldn't dream of getting involved in politics. When they discovered that Asa was a monosyllabic farmer's daughter called Julie Moreau, summoned to the capital by her sister who was expecting her first child, they lost all interest. Nevertheless, Asa was sorry when they fell asleep; their self-important conversation at least made her feel safer and distracted her from thoughts of Paris's Revolutionary Tribunal.

The coach was halted perhaps half a dozen times for papers to be inspected and the passengers scrutinised. On the first occasion, when they were told to hop out and wait in the hot sun at a crossroads just beyond Lisieux, Asa's armpits were damp with fear and her cheeks burned, though she forced her hand to remain steady as she removed her bundle of papers from the pocket in her bodice. The official, who had a youthful, scrubbed face, pored over her passport for some time while she smiled blandly and pretended interest in a stray dog. Next time they were stopped Asa was much calmer and stood with folded arms while the forms were given a fleeting glance. After that, she grew more confident, so that by the time she reached Paris she almost believed in the authenticity of her papers.

Occasionally they passed companies of National Guardsmen heading west out of Paris to deal with counter-revolutionary Normandy. Sometimes they were delayed by straggles of refugees and beggars who had no right to be on the road at all, according to Asa's companions. The cabinet-maker and his wife agreed that some people spent their entire lives sponging. The Revolution had provided countless opportunities for those with

374

the wit to use them, so there was absolutely no excuse.

'I've heard that the harvest is likely to fail again,' Asa replied quietly, 'because of this hot weather.'

The cabinetmaker's wife stared. 'We have not noticed any shortages in Bayeux.'

'Perhaps Bayeux has had the foresight to store plenty of grain from last year. In Caen there were long queues and I believe that elsewhere in France, in Paris, for example, there are severe shortages of bread.'

She was subjected to further prolonged scrutiny. 'There is always enough bread for citizens who work hard. It's the ones who wait for their mouths to be filled who claim they are suffering.'

By early evening on the second day they had reached the outskirts of the capital. Asa leaned forward to catch her first glimpse of Parisian shopfronts and alleys and churches, to hear the first Parisian chatter – a heated exchange between a housewife and a vendor of tubs and buckets – until the cabinetmaker's wife clicked her tongue in exasperation, claiming her view through the window was obscured.

Falling back in her seat, Asa gave her companions a dazzling smile. Five years ago, when she had left this city, her heart had been leaden with despair. Again and again she had strained to hear the thud of hoof-beats; each time the Mortons' carriage was halted she was sure Didier had caught up with them at last. When they burst through the gates into open countryside she had thought she would die of anguish. Now she was back it was as if the past had unfurled from her shoulders and drifted away; all this time she had been bound by her yearning for Didier, and then the complication of Shackleford. In Paris she would emerge from the carriage entirely herself, fearful, of course – of what Didier might say and of the dangers of the city – but reinvigorated by this place, to which she had longed to return.

When they were set down in the north-west of the city, however, Asa, projected from the relative calm of the diligence to the hubbub of the capital, shrank back under the gallery of the coach-yard, her confidence displaced by the shock of arrival. There was no John Morton this time to sweep her up in his spanking carriage and arrange an itinerary for her. The cabinetmaker had bundled his wife into the inn, presumably to be met by their grateful son.

Asa set forth, disoriented by tall clusters of buildings blotting out the sky and the unending surge of people on the streets. At first, as she travelled east through the city, everything seemed so reassuringly the same as it had been in 1788 that she began to think the stories of post-revolutionary Paris were overblown. The streets were narrow and thronging as ever, a muddle of mansions and squares, dark alleys and court-yards, and then the massive walls of the church of St-Eustache. But with a renewed surge of apprehension she realised that while superficially the same, there had been a shift which jarred with her memories – no longer was she thrust against a wall while an indifferent nobleman hurtled by in his carriage; now only goods were transported in wagons and carts while people walked or occasionally went by cab. And pedestrians, who in the old days had betrayed their station even by the colour of their gloves or the robustness of their shoes, were dressed in a peculiarly uniform fashion. Gone were the elaborate wigs and towering hats that had imposed such a disdainful posture on wealthy women. Instead hair was worn loose or tucked into plain straw hats or caps with a single frill; skirts were narrow and men wore unfitted trousers and carelessly tied cravats. Everywhere there were flashes of red, white and blue; cockades, sashes, shoe-ribbons.

And this Paris was not as well behaved as the city of the past. Then there had been a brutal drawing of boundaries that consigned the beggar to the church step and a lady to her box at the opera. Now there was a swagger to the step of even the scruffiest youth. Asa sensed this same lack of deference in the hungry eyes of women as she passed through Les Halles, and recognised that when they stood gossiping by an empty vegetable stall, there was not just boredom in their eyes, but rage.

Occasionally from a side street or apartment would come a shout, a scuffle, a hurling of abuse. Sometimes, as Asa passed a church, she noticed that statues on the exterior had been savagely defaced, as they had been in Caen. And despite what the cabinetmaker's wife had said, there was indeed a bread queue with women standing in line as if they'd been there for half a decade.

Asa was wearing Madame's old, dark blue gown, let out at the seams and with a strip of darker fabric inserted above the hem so that the skirt reached to an inch above her ankles. A muslin scarf was crossed on her breast and tied behind her back and her hair was covered by a voluminous Normandy bonnet with a deep, flapping brim. Nobody except the occasional lad gave her a second glance. But as she marched deeper into the city Asa felt herself to be subtly obscured. Either it was the clothes, or the knowledge that their former owner might be close by, but Asa had the sense of seeing the world not as herself, but through Madame's wounded eyes.

Chapter Two

On the following day, Thursday, 11 July, Asa ate a meagre breakfast of hard bread and coffee with her landlady. 'I haven't been in Paris for years,' she told Madame Maurice. 'Where can I find out what's going on?'

Madame Maurice – or Citoyenne Maurice, as she insisted on being called – was the widow of one of Professor Paulin's academic colleagues and would have preferred to talk about the old university days in Caen. 'I still feel a stranger here in Paris. But I suppose you should go to the Palais Royal. That's where most people start. You can buy any number of different newspapers there, from learned to downright crude. What do you want to know exactly?'

'As I think Beatrice Paulin explained in her

letter, I am here to represent my family in paying my respects to someone who has died. And while I'm in Paris I hope to visit Beatrice's brother, Didier, to give him messages from his father and sister. In the meantime I might as well see something of the city.'

Citoyenne Maurice's eyes were disconcertingly incredulous, like those of the cabinetmaker's wife. 'A young lady such as yourself would never have been allowed to travel alone in my day. Well, like I said, the Palais Royal is a good place to start. And most people would want to see where the Bastille used to be, but I should warn you there's scarcely a crumb of mortar left. You might want to put your nose into the Assembly, if you have the energy, though it'll be a crush. I've never attended myself but I'm told it's quite a thing, to hear the debates.'

'Would you like to come with me?'

'Oh no. No. I don't go out if I can help it and there's plenty of work to be done running this place. Sometimes, you know, I wish I was back in Caen. I had such a pretty garden there and so many friends. But I've heard all kinds of stories about Caen and people would ask questions if I left now.'

How extraordinary to be sent to the Palais Royal, of all places, where Asa had refused Shackleford for the first time. She preferred not to think of him, and those unsettling memories of Compton Wyatt; tender, honey-brown eyes, the silence of the woods. Her clear choice was, then and now, not an English estate spread out in a lush valley, but this clamorous city where a

379

cobbler crouched under an awning hammering at an upturned shoe, and where she was pestered by a woman selling tiny lead figures painted in revolutionary colours, their feet sunk in a tray of sand.

And here was the Palais Royal, its gracious arcades bulging as ever with coffee sellers and pastry vendors, with shops selling books and baskets and hats and stockings. Commerce flourished, seemingly, revolution or no, even if the previous owner, the Duc d'Orléans – despite having renamed himself Philippe d'Egalité in a flush of revolutionary fervour – had been clapped in gaol while his long-term mistress, Madame de Genlis, had fled to Switzerland.

Asa bought a newspaper called *Le Père Duchesne* and, seated in the shade, she read every word.

My fine sans-culottes, your enemies are only bold because you stand there with your arms folded; wake up, damn it... Disarm all those bastards who piss ice-water in a heatwave and want no part in the Revolution. The poison of moderation is more dangerous than Austrian weapons... If you slumber only a short while more you can expect to wake up to bloody slavery, fuck it.

And on and on. The Girondins (dubbed *Brissotins* by the journalist) were accused of being traitors who regretted the death of the king and were prepared to side with France's enemies to crush the Revolution. In other words, while France's brave soldiers were fighting foreign armies abroad the Girondins, such as Brissot, who was now safely in prison, thank Christ, had been using every opportunity to turn Parisians against each other and encourage counter-revolution. This is why a Revolutionary Tribunal had been set up; to give swift justice to enemies of the state. And this is why a Committee of Public Safety was needed, to oversee the war effort and save the country from civil unrest. New elections were soon to be held to that august body. Citizen Robespierre was a likely candidate, likewise Citizen Paulin, currently on a patriotic expedition to the south, where he had been firing up the French generals whose task it was to defend Toulon from imminent invasion.

Once the purge of France's enemies was complete the lovely new Constitution, which would bestow freedom on every Frenchman, including the right to vote and have free education for his children, would at last be implemented. Readers who were not required to fight were urged to support the Revolution by watching out for counter-revolutionaries, hoarders of grain and those who bad-mouthed the new order.

When Asa raised her head it seemed to her that the city groaned. In the arcades, caged birds cheeped pitifully. A prostitute, lounging in a doorway, cast a disdainful eye over Asa. The garden of the Palais Royal these days consisted of strips of parched lawn and gravel walks; a cheeky sparrow took a dust bath inches from her feet and dry leaves rustled overhead. A youth yelled from an open window to his friend at another where bedlinen hung limply in the hot air.

On the day Shackleford had proposed, these gardens had been green and fragrant; she had been dismissive of him here, as she had everywhere else. What would the owner of Compton Wyatt have made of the scandal-mongering tone of *Le Père Duchesne?* Asa got up abruptly and walked on past the walls of the Louvre towards the old palace of the Tuileries.

With every step, one way or another, she was drawing closer to Didier. Perhaps he had not yet returned from Toulon. Or perhaps she would actually bump into him at the Convention. It was only a matter of time. She was short of breath and her hands were cold despite the heat of the day. His letters, tucked for safe-keeping into the lining of her case at Citoyenne Maurice's, were such a flimsy hook that she was astonished by her own audacity. Or stupidity, she thought, as she recalled the words of Professor Paulin and his daughter. A queue snaked into the gardens. Apparently the opportunity to sit in the gallery and watch the Convention at work was too exciting to miss, even if you happened to be a woman who had been told by *Le Père Duchesne* that your proper place was in the home, giving succour to the children of France. Sometimes groups emerged, fanning themselves with bonnets or papers and wiping their faces on their sleeves. 'You don't want to go in there,' said one wag on his way out. 'Filthy mood, the lot of them. And no Marat, so hardly worth it.'

Nevertheless, the queue pressed forward, and there were loud protests when someone tried to push in. When Asa reached the door to the old

Manège, the vast riding school previously used by the royal family, she had to show her papers. Her head was high as she removed them from her bodice, but her heart still missed a beat when the official's eye flicked from the page to her face. 'Julie Moreau,' he said with a wink. 'Sweet name. In you go, Julie,' and she was nodded through to a steep staircase.

As she climbed, the air grew hotter until she emerged at last into a cramped gallery furnished with narrow wooden benches and facing a vast hall with seats arranged in tiers, each occupied by a man in a dark coat. At first it seemed to Asa that every person in the hall must have noticed her arrival. Of course, in reality people were coming and going all the time and amid the general clamour a woman called Julie Moreau was insignificant.

Nonetheless, it was many minutes before she felt sufficiently calm to look about her. This, then, was the heart of the Revolution: hundreds of deputies in dark frock coats, most wigless and with their hair cropped in the new, Roman style, others wearing it neatly rolled above the ears and tied in a ribbon at the back. All were waving papers to attract the attention of the chairman or talking to each other sotto voce, or writing memos; doing anything, apparently, but listening to the speaker who was bellowing at the top of his voice. Asa scanned the faces again and again but could not see Didier. Surely she would recognise him, even from behind. She grew calmer when she realised he wasn't there, but her spirits plunged.

Meanwhile in the gallery women with fierce,

intent faces hushed each other so they might hear what was being said and then proceeded to talk loudly about the speaker's appearance. Other spectators sucked oranges, spat out pips or read a newssheet. Many were dressed in what Asa had begun to recognise as the uniform of the so-called sans-culotte – loose breeches and open-necked, collarless shirts with perhaps a cravat at the neck but always the tricolour somewhere. A few carried or wore a red cap, a symbol of the most militant. The hubbub and the heat made it infuriatingly hard to focus on what was being said, until one of the women hissed: 'Shut it. Couthon's going to speak. About bloody time.'

A wheelchair was manoeuvred into the centre of the hall by its occupant, who had a blue rug folded neatly across his legs. He held up his hand and stilled the crowd. 'My friends. I cannot hide the truth from you. The enemies of the Revolution are closing in on us from all sides.'

Silence descended upon the gallery. Beside Asa a man finished devouring a chunk of bread and wiped the crumbs from his mouth. 'An army has left Caen, in Normandy, and is preparing to march on us here, in Paris,' continued Couthon. 'Two days' march, that's all it would take. Not that they'll succeed because they'll be intercepted by our brave men. But it sickens me that our own people are prepared to shed the blood of fellow Frenchmen.'

Shouts of: 'Shame on them. Death to them.'

'The Vendée, as we know, is seething with traitors and insurrectionists and we have just heard from our deputy, Didier Paulin...' *Didier*

384

Paulin. He was here, then. Where? '...that the people of Toulon are actually negotiating with the British – yes, I repeat, our enemy, the British – for supplies of food.' A deathly hush. 'This cannot go on.'

'Oh yes,' cried someone in the gallery, 'and how are you going to stop it?'

Couthon raised his head and gave the heckler a long, slow stare. 'We are taking steps. But it's hard, when our feet are shackled – and my God, citizens, I know how that feels – by the very people who are supposed to be on our side. Yesterday our colleague Danton relinquished his place on the Committee of Public Safety. Yes, there he sits, with his head down. He had served his time, he said, but do you know what I think? I think he's running scared. Well, I say to you, to be a member of that committee you need to have the guts to administer the harshest of medicine. At times like these, there's no such thing as choice or scruple or doubt for those who lead. Those things are the luxuries of the past, of academics in their universities and poets in their salons. We are the men who know there is work to be done. We must roll up our sleeves and labour with our bare hands. Let's win the war against our enemies, not seek a truce. Let's keep a tight grip on the economy so that money is wrenched from those businessmen, the bourgeoisie, who have made themselves the new aristocracy by bleeding our citizens dry. If you think a neighbour of yours is growing too fat, you tell us, citizens. Let's pull together and silence, once and for all, the voices of dissent.'

He paused as if expecting tumultuous applause but there was only a nervous hush. Then came the soft tap of a man's footsteps – a new speaker had entered the arena.

'If I may, Deputy Couthon...'

The voice plucked at Asa's heartstrings – she almost cried out his name.

Couthon grinned. 'Aha. The man himself.'

A few more footsteps and the newcomer came into view, though his back was to Asa: a tall man with a rim of white cravat showing above the high collar of his coat, and dark hair sprung loose from its ribbon. His voice, though light, was penetrating enough to demand attention.

'You mentioned Toulon. What I witnessed there was indeed disturbing. But then the citizens of Toulon are hungry and when a person is hungry, as we all know only too well, they cannot think straight. I pity the citizens of Toulon because they face invasion from the English, and their own supplies of food are being consumed by our French troops. They are my brothers and I came away all the more determined to put things right for them.'

Pulse racing, Asa edged along the row of seats until she could lean her elbows on the rail of the gallery. He wore, exactly as in her memory, a dark blue coat with brass buttons, and light brown breeches. As he spoke he crossed to the very centre of the floor and made a slow, assured rotation so that with each phrase he looked directly at a new section of his audience. When he faced Asa she saw that his cravat was tied precisely under his chin, its ends tucked into his waistcoat. Despite the heat of the day and his close-fitting clothes he contrived to seem cool. He had become very lean and the bones in his face were more prominent. From time to time, exactly as in the old days, he raked his fingers through his hair so that it stood up a little at the front.

He might have been arguing with his father. 'The days of laissez-faire are over. The new France needs firm, principled hands at the tiller. And our first priority? To feed our people. How do we do that? Price controls. It's simple. A child could tell you that it is the price of grain that is crushing the people of Toulon and the loyal citizens of Paris. Friends, citizens, I arrived back in Paris half an hour ago and came straight here because I wanted to support Couthon in his demand for price controls. Brissot and his cohorts were all for allowing the markets to fix their own prices. I'm afraid to say they didn't care if a minority of France grew fat while the rest starved.'

The crowd in the gallery hissed and yelled but Didier smiled, raised his hand and spoke soothingly. 'We have purged ourselves of the Girondins, never fear. The poor of Paris, who after all have brought the Revolution into being by their self-sacrifice and tireless courage, deserve to be fed every bit as much as those in grain-rich regions such as Normandy. Caen, as you all know, is my home town. And the people of Caen, by and large, are good people, or were, until they were corrupted by the Brissotins who have encouraged them to use their stashes of grain as a bargaining tool. Well, they must learn that everyone in France

387

has to stand together. No more hoarding, no more selling at extortionate prices. Our first priority is to feed our people.'

By now the crowd was roaring and stamping their approval. From somewhere came the shout: 'The provinces will revolt – in fact they are already revolting. [Howls of laughter] Look at Brittany, look at the Vendée, and now your Calvados, Paulin. You seem to have been spawned by a bold little place, but it has one foot in the past. Your people are saying that it's unjust that Paris should govern their consciences as well as the contents of their bellies. They say that they want to go back to the old ways.'

'All I hear is that word *unjust* when what we have worked for incessantly is justice,' Didier replied. 'I am a lawyer and I know how easy it is to twist the word *justice*. Is it *just*, for instance, that one town in France, our beloved France, should have stocks of grain while others starve? And is it *just* that Paris, which has already borne the brunt of the Revolution – the turmoil, the pain, the bloodshed – should send thousands of its sons to fight against royalist hordes and at the same time be made to starve for it? It is quite clear to me that everyone has to pay equally for the Revolution. That is justice.'

He was, as ever, utterly compelling. His face was grey with exhaustion and he scarcely had the strength to push back a lock of hair, yet here he was, a blue-eyed son of Caen recognising the needs of starving Paris. 'There is no going back, citizens,' he said softly. 'We must all pull in the same direction. You must trust us.'

The assembly yelled with joy. Asa was on her feet, propelled by the sheer momentum of the crowd. As she watched Didier, the shape of his head, the fall of hair on his brow, the precision with which he moved his hands, a thread tightened between her heart and thighs so that she ached to be kissed, and was lying with him again on crumpled sheets, watching the sleeve of the shirt he'd flung on the screen flutter in a draught from the open window. And she thought, with an uprush of delight: This is what I have been waiting for, this is how it was in Paris. No certainty or thought of convention, just a seizing of the moment by the throat.

Meanwhile the spectators, who had lost interest in the debate, were talking among themselves, vociferously indignant that the provinces should begrudge them cheap bread and, by the way, had anyone been able to afford a bar of soap since the spring?

One woman put her hand on Asa's arm, making her jump. 'Is this your first time? I've not seen you in the gallery before.'

'No. I'm visiting from the provinces.'

'I can tell by your accent. You're not from the Vendée, I trust? No, of course not. But you must be quite overwhelmed. If you like I could point out a couple of people so that when you get back you can say you've seen our famous men in the flesh. That man in the wheelchair is Georges Couthon.'

'And I recognised Didier Paulin.'

'Paulin, yes, he's a good speaker, very quick witted compared to some. But he's often away.

389

They give him the difficult tasks because he's a good negotiator. On the other hand there's Robespierre.' She lowered her voice. 'Between you and me, he's a bit long winded. And that untidy one over there with the big face is Danton. I think he's sulking because he was voted off the Committee yesterday. Marat would normally be here, but he's sick, as I expect you know. Skin disease. He's the best speaker of the lot, a hell-raiser, makes the rafters shake.'

'Do you think he'll be here if I come tomorrow? I'd like to see him in action.'

'I doubt it. I've heard the disease is very bad this time. No wonder. They all work too hard, sometimes twenty hours a day. It's not natural, in my opinion.'

'I suppose they'd say it was necessary?'

'Maybe. But everybody needs to sleep at night and have a good laugh once in a while, don't you think?'

It was time for a break in proceedings. Deputies were bundling out of the door, including Didier, who carried a sheaf of papers under his arm and was deep in conversation. Either the force of Asa's attention was irresistible or he looked up quite by chance, scanning the public gallery, at first casually, then with more deliberation. He seemed not to have noticed her, he was moving on, but then he looked back and this time his eyes met hers.

Such was the intensity of her reaction, the lurch of her heart, that she thought: Perhaps it's true, then. I am still in love with him, despite everything.

He gave a little shake of his head, as if to dismiss something from his mind, then was gone. By the time she had elbowed her way down the stairs and outside there was no sign of him.

Chapter Three

Didier now lodged in a second-floor apartment on the Place Vendôme, barely a quarter of a mile from the Tuileries and therefore convenient both for meetings of the Convention and for the more intimate gatherings of the Jacobin Club, where most of the men who now ruled the country thrashed out their ideas. This, as his father had pointed out, was a much smarter address than his former lodgings on the rue du Vieux Colombier, though it had suffered the same vandalism – or revolutionary fervour – as other grandiose sites in Paris. She remembered the square being dominated by a statue of Louis XIV mounted on his horse, but now there was just an empty plinth.

Asa spent a long time loitering in the shade before she plucked up the courage to approach number 12. After all, if she was right, if Madame had come to Paris looking for Didier, she might be here too. However, it was a high-complexioned, rather aggrieved-looking young woman who opened the door.

'Yes?'

'Is Monsieur Paulin at home?'

'No.'

'May I ask when he'll be back?'

'Couldn't say. You can leave your name, I suppose. People do all the time.'

'Do you think he'll be in later today?'

'I don't know.'

Asa produced a few écus. 'It would be very helpful if you could be more definite.'

The woman looked scornful but more coins produced an answer: 'He's out of town.'

'But I saw him only a couple of hours ago speaking at the Convention.'

'Did you indeed? What are you? Some kind of follower?'

'Please, I just want to know when he'll be home.'

'He's been called out of Paris again,' said the girl sulkily, 'some police matter in the district of Sens. Said he'd be back Saturday night.'

At breakfast the next day Asa said to Citoyenne Maurice: 'I did as you suggested and visited the Palais Royal. And I saw Didier Paulin speak at the Convention. It was extremely frustrating; when I called at his apartment he'd already left and he won't be back until tomorrow. So today I shall try to find the graveyard where my friend is buried. Mademoiselle Paulin gave me a map. Perhaps you'd look at it with me and mark a few places.'

'If it's more than a year old it will be out of date, they've changed so many of the street names. And if you're going out alone again you take care. I'm not sure I like the idea of you wandering about the city on your own. I was telling a neighbour

392

about you and she reminded me that if you get into trouble it will reflect badly on me. Of course, I don't mind you staying, the truth is I need the money, but still...'

'I've told you, Citoyenne Maurice, I only want to pay my respects and pass some messages to Didier Paulin, then I'll be on my way.'

'Well, don't hang about or go down dubious alleys or side streets. It's important to look as if you know where you're going. And don't say too much in that peculiar accent of yours. These are difficult times and nobody likes a stranger.'

'I do know something of the city. I was in Paris five years ago, staying in the Faubourg St-Germain. I shall never forget the weeks I spent there... I met someone...'

Sure enough, at the first sniff of romance, Citoyenne Maurice softened. 'What happened?'

'It came to nothing at the time, I was so young... But I can't help hoping...'

'Well, things are very different now, you'll find. All right, let's mark a route for you. A lot of visitors start at the Temple Palace, to see if they can catch a glimpse of the queen. That's where people would expect you to go.'

'My friend in Caen mentioned a church called St-Joseph.'

'St-Joseph?'

'It was attached to a monastery, I believe.'

'You see, that's what I mean about taking care. It's not a good idea for us to be talking about churches; anyway, most of them have been put to other use. Now I come to think of it, there's only one St-Joseph that I know of – Joseph des Carmes

– and that's a prison these days, so there's no point going there. Pity. In the old days I'd have said it was worth a visit. I remember attending mass once and seeing a Bernini Virgin. Not that I mean the old days were better – don't get me wrong – not at all. Just different.'

'Even so, perhaps you could mark it for me on the map?'

Citoyenne Maurice turned the map around and hovered over it with a pen. At last she inserted two crosses, one for the Temple Prison, one for the former church of St-Joseph.

'Citoyenne Maurice, are you sure that's the one? Is that St-Joseph des Carmes?'

'Why, certainly. It's off the Vaugirard.'

A return to first principles is how Shackleford might have described Asa's expedition that day. In 1788, Asa, Philippa and John Morton had begun their exploration of Paris by viewing the royal family's residence at Versailles. Whereas Morton had manoeuvred himself into a royal levee, the sisters had had to wait for a visit to the opera before they glimpsed the queen in her jewelled satin skirts, her hair puffed and padded and curled under a headdress the size of a boat and adorned with waving ostrich plumes. What a tragedy, Asa had thought, that France's destiny rested upon the flimsy mind of such a pampered doll.

Now, once again, Asa set forth to visit the queen, but this time, like the fairy-tale princess she had always wanted to be, Marie Antoinette was locked in a tower. The Temple Palace was a historic building of some importance and grace despite its small windows, steep roofs and little steeples. But in a far corner, narrow and imposing, and twice as high as the rest of the building, was a sinister structure with four turrets, like a miniature Tower of London. Beneath its steep walls a crowd had assembled.

Like everyone else, Asa stared upwards. No pale face appeared at the window. Everything inside the tower seemed to be quiet, though someone whispered that only last week, the queen's last living son had been taken from her and imprisoned elsewhere in the building, so that sometimes you could hear him crying for his mother.

'Why would they do that? It seems too cruel.'

The woman stank of raw onion. 'Because the filthy slut insisted on treating him like a little king. At table he had to sit at the head and be served first. What sort of a mother would stuff a child's head with that kind of nonsense?'

Asa felt she was being watched by certain members of the crowd – in this company, even the whiteness of her Normandy bonnet drew attention. Close by, a man threw back his head and yelled up at the empty window: 'Show us your face, you fucking whore. We all know what you've been up to, fucking your own son.'

'That too,' said Asa's neighbour, leaning closer. 'Haven't you heard? Sharing a bed, sucking his little prick. That's what she did.'

'You know what,' said a young girl, 'they say the poor lad can hardly walk any more because of what she's done to him. Look at this.' She smiled so sweetly that Asa, disarmed, took the card from her. It was a print of the queen in a sexual embrace with one of her ladies, mouth to mouth, grasping each other's bodies.

'Foreign bitch,' someone screamed, and the crowd took up the chant, pressing forward and landing gobs of spittle on the wall.

Asa turned away. Surely Didier must be aware of these crude jibes; the evil that had been unleashed in his city? This was not what they had dreamed of in Madame de Genlis's salon.

It was noon and the sun was high and scorching. She began the long trek south across the river under the great towers of Notre Dame (renamed the Temple of Reason) on to the rue de la Harpe, crossing the end of the rue des Cordeliers to the Vaugirard, the longest, straightest road in Paris. Try not to look so nervous, Asa kept telling herself. You only have to survive until tomorrow. But when a cart rattled by, too close, she leapt back. It turned the corner so aggressively a wheel jolted off the road, provoking a stream of curses from the driver.

Leading north from the Vaugirard was the rue Madame, which in turn led to the rue du Vieux Colombier, where Didier used to live. Asa knew that if she turned left at the top of the Cherche-Midi she'd reach the Hôtel Montmorency. And between these streets, adjacent to Vieux Colombier, Madame Maurice had placed the cross indicating the church of St-Joseph des Carmes.

Asa stood with her back to the wall, shaded by a tree that had extended its branches far over the street. There, on the opposite side, was the shabby green door that used to be Didier's, through which she had passed with such excitement and fear and amazement at herself. Up the stone steps she had followed him, to the room where they had drunk strong, tepid coffee, served in a blue and white jug. There was the window where she had stood sometimes, in a preliminary to their lovemaking, pretending that she cared what was happening in the street or beyond the garden wall. And in this very spot she had stood after the hailstorm, a sodden note clenched in her hand, staring up at his window and willing him to return.

In those days Asa had known nothing of the garden opposite except that it belonged to a religious establishment. She might even have caught the occasional scent of herbs. Had Didier and Madame been living in this apartment last autumn, when the massacre occurred? Had Estelle Beyle left through that blue door, carrying a covered basket just like Beatrice's, filled with food and clean clothes for her brother? If so Didier might actually have been able to glimpse his old friend Jean Beyle and his sister sitting in the prison garden.

Asa walked the length and breadth of the monastery walls, along the rue du Cherche-Midi to the Montmorency, which was no longer a smart hotel but a tired-looking set of apartments with grimy windows and weeds growing from the paving stones on the steps. Through those double doors, now tight shut, she had burst forth to explore Paris or to flee the Mortons so that she might reach Didier. Here, a few paces farther on, was the entrance to the courtyard where she had waited after the storm, longing for Didier to come. Today the smell of human waste was pervasive and, like the rest of the city, the courtyard panted for moisture. And there, on that corner opposite the Montmorency, Asa had glimpsed Shackleford as she raced out of the hotel to visit Didier. Ever afterwards, the taste of lemonade had reminded her of how she had sat with him in the lobby; he yearning for a kind word, she yearning to be gone.

She retraced her steps back to the monastery wall and south again, until she was outside the heavy door to the convent itself.

She knocked, a panel in the door slid back, and the sweating face of a warder appeared.

'Excuse me. Might I have a quick look inside?'

'Whatever do you mean? This place is a prison. Do you want to visit someone? What's his name?'

'Not exactly visit. Someone I knew was once here. Please, I just want to take a peek.'

His eyes were a bleary, Didier-blue, boring into hers and tracing the lines of her body under Madame's dark dress. She clinked the coins in her pocket. 'It's just the garden I want to see. Won't you let me have a look at the garden?'

'For Christ's sake, I spend my whole life these days doing guided tours as if this was a bloody museum.'

But in the end he opened the door, revealing a red cap stuffed into his breast pocket and keys on a ring at his waist. Glancing at the small heap of coins in Asa's palm, he nodded.

The garden was overgrown and, unlike in Professor Paulin's prison in Caen, nobody was strolling about. Lawns were indistinguishable from former beds, except where a patch had been cleared so that vegetables might be planted, although in the heat of summer nothing much would grow. Occasionally an oasis of green had survived in the shade, a suddenly verdant patch of daisies or nettles. Behind Asa rose the convent buildings, perforated by tiny windows. A voice shouted out: 'Give us a smile, darling.' She waved up and smiled though her lips ached with the effort, then walked on until she came to the back of the little church and by its side a locked gate against which another warder leaned.

Were there marks here of last September's massacre? From Madame's description on the journey home from Compton Wyatt there should at least be stains on the paving stones, a crushing of shrubs. To the right was the wall that bordered the rue du Vieux Colombier. Near the centre of the garden was a massive tree with gracefully extended branches beneath which the grass grew thick and mossy. Perhaps this was where Estelle and Jean Beyle used to sit, sharing their bread. And in the far corner, behind the stone hut, or oratory, that Asa used to see from Didier's window, was the bolted door through which those youths must have burst, eyes blind with bloodlust.

Asa felt sick. She could not stand much more of this overlay of a violent narrative on what had seemed so perfect a landscape. As she left she asked the warden, 'If someone were to die here, a prisoner ... where would they be buried?'

'In the cemetery, like everyone else.'

'Which cemetery would they take the body to?'

'If you've got a few hours to spare you could try

the one right at the end of the Vaugirard. It's a long walk, mind.'

Asa toiled in the blazing heat, past Les Invalides, where the arsenals had been invaded at the start of the Revolution, supplying the mob with thousands of muskets with which they'd laid siege to the Bastille. Here the intention was apparently to repair rather than demolish – labourers were busy working on the great domed church. Asa walked on between the austere Ecole Militaire and the Champs de Mars, the vast military parade ground she had once viewed from a carriage with the newly wedded Mortons.

And on, through the increasingly poor and desolate fringes of the city, heading towards open country on the far side of the Seine, until at last she reached the wall of a graveyard from which rose the gut-wrenching stench of human decay. The cemetery was full of newly dug plots and fallen stones, with women moving about, tending a grave or arranging wilting posies of flowers.

A couple of guards lolled in the shade of the wall, presumably to enforce the stipulation that it was forbidden to hold the wrong kind of funeral. 'Is there a list somewhere or a plan of where people are buried?' Asa asked.

The men were surly and indifferent. 'You'll just have to look, my dear, like everyone else.'

Asa pressed her scarf to her nose and began a search for Beyle's name, but she soon realised it was hopeless. Although some of the newly dug graves had stones or plaques, many were unmarked. Sometimes a much broader heap of soil signalled a mass burial. In the end Asa chose any grave, put her hand to the soil and uttered the name Jean Gabriel Beyle.

'A letter was delivered while you were out,' said Citoyenne Maurice, who was noticeably stiffer in her bearing, 'from England via Caen. Citoyenne Ardleigh, Professor Paulin is an old and trusted friend, but you do realise that every letter these days is liable to be opened and its contents used as evidence? We are all under suspicion, so I would beg you, please, no more correspondence, particularly from England.'

The letter was from Caroline Lambert.

Morton Hall
Monday, 1 July 1793

Dear Thomasina,
I am writing on behalf of your family as well as myself. Your sisters are at my shoulder. We received your letter this morning. While on the one hand we are more than relieved to hear from you, on the other, words can hardly describe your sisters' consternation now that we know for sure not only that are you in France but that you have gone to Didier Paulin. Needless to say Mrs Morton blames her husband for not being more vigilant while she was ill in Paris. She feels that shame has descended on the family but she cares nothing for that, she says, if only she could be certain you are safe. Your father insists he will swallow his pride and that all will be forgiven and forgotten whether you marry a French revolutionary or not.
Thomasina, I wonder if you understand how much

you are cherished by your family, and how dearly they all wish you well. I am instructed to inform you that you may return in <u>any</u> circumstances, if you so wish, and in <u>any</u> condition. Nobody will reproach you. Your father rides between Morton Hall, Littlehampton, Portsmouth and Ardleigh as if he might discover that you have been hiding all along behind a hedge or in a ditch. Your sisters spend hour upon hour speculating upon what you are doing – you will be concerned to know that Mrs Morton is again with child, and therefore unwell. And lately, the burden on our household seemed to have been increased by the arrival of Mr Shackleford and his sister-in-law. However, Mrs Susan Shackleford, a reserved woman, I thought at first, but with whom I have since spent a considerable portion of my spare time, unlocked the piano in the music room, and by her extraordinary aptitude has saved us all. Even the children have been calmed by Mozart.

The reason for their visit is that they have disturbing news regarding Madame de Rusigneux, whom you did not mention in your own letter from Caen but with whom we know you left England. Mr Shackleford made enquiries in London of Mrs Silburn and others who recommended her to your sisters, and it now seems that very little was known of her, and that quite exceptionally among the émigré community in London, she has no connections. Worse, Mr Shackleford tell us that the town, Frenelle, where your companion said she used to live, does not exist, at least in southern France, and Mrs Susan Shackleford, who has made a close study of your companion's paintings, has cast doubt on her claims to be a lady artist. She says they are rather the mechanistic works of a professional copyist and adds that no lady of her acquaintance is quite unable to play the piano. As a consequence of these speculations we have deepened our enquiries – I shall not burden you with the details – and as a result have little doubt that Madame de Rusigneux is a fraud and you must therefore be extremely wary of her. I'm sorry I didn't meet her. I like to think I might have noticed.

Mr Shackleford and I walk in the garden with the children. He is at all times calm and kind, a source of great strength and encouragement. The origins of his family fortune notwithstanding, it seems to me that you were blessed in suitors indeed that you could reject such a one as Shackleford, who speaks of you warmly and always takes your part. Apparently he met Paulin while in Paris and thinks highly of him, and he tells me that Paulin has now been promoted within the National Convention. Of course, I always suspected that your lover was Didier Paulin – your letters were full of him while in Paris – and I do not to this day know why you withheld his name from me, unless it was for my father's sake. Perhaps I have been cold in discussing certain matters, preferring to read about passion in books rather than probe its existence in my own heart or yours.

I have strayed a little from the point. The point is we miss you. We think now only of your happiness. We wish you were home, but above all we want you to be safe. If you can be content married to Didier Paulin, then so be it. We will rejoice for you. But if you cannot, and you want to come home, you have only to say the word and we will find the means to bring you.

I am as ever, Thomasina, and always, your loving friend,

Caroline

Chapter Four

It was clear, subsequent to the inauspicious arrival of the letter from England, that Asa was no longer welcome in the house on rue des Francs Bourgeois. Her bed was left unmade and as she ate her spartan breakfast the landlady barely spoke. So, on the morning of Saturday, 13 July, while she awaited Didier's return, Asa was forced to go walking again, this time heading through restless crowds to the site of the Bastille and then to the church of St-Eustache, which she had visited with John Morton. The former had disappeared entirely – every last crumb of rubble seized to build a new bridge or as a souvenir – and there was no access to the latter, the church having been put to municipal use.

Throughout that interminable day, Asa viewed Paris through the prism of Caroline's letter. Far away in England was the safety of Morton Hall with its fountain modelled hopefully on Versailles, its draughty top floor sparsely furnished for the long-suffering maids and Mrs Susan Shackleford, unaccountably transferred from Compton Wyatt to the new piano stool in the music room, her notes trickling like a balm. All that activity coupled with all that waiting for news. Philippa, pregnant again, when the birth of baby Kate had almost killed her. And Shackleford, who *speaks of you warmly and always takes your part*. No danger that he would trouble Asa with further requests for her hand. How he must despise her subterfuge, now that it was clear to him that she had been preoccupied by Didier all along, even while kissing him after the ball.

And despite all those people in England loving Asa, longing for news, here she was in Paris, rootless in a city that had no use for her, which in fact repelled her with its locked churches and wary-eyed women, generating in her a fear of being still. She could scarcely bear the thought of turning up at her lodgings and encountering the hostile Citoyenne Maurice, of being forced to wait for Didier until another day, the shame of knocking again and being told he was absent. Yet what refuge did she have but him? In any case, she had waited for so long to see him once more, had so longed for him, she could not possibly give up now. The Didier of her memory had been usurped by the Didier described by his father and sister. Yet it seemed to Asa that both Didiers had flashed before her in the Convention. Of course she must confront him, and find out which was the real one.

Late in the afternoon at the Place Vendôme, even at the end of the summer's day, the air was full of soot. Deputy Paulin, said the maid, was still not home.

'You told me he would be back this afternoon.'

'And so he will be, I presume, though I don't see what business it is of yours.'

Asa was of course not invited to wait inside but this time remained in the square, pinioned by the superstition that if she missed Didier again he might disappear for ever. Although she kept to the shade, she rarely took her eyes from the door of number 15. In the early evening a burly official in a red cap approached, and advised her not to hang about or people would get the wrong idea. Sure enough, a bunch of youths lurched over to offer her money if she'd go to the rue Cambon with them, where they knew of a cosy room.

By the time the sun began lowering itself behind the rooftops, Asa was weak with tension. What if he didn't come? Of all those who had passed through the square, she was sure that none had entered the door to number 15 and yet, soon after the clocks struck eight, she noticed movement across the second-floor window and the casement was thrown open. Maybe the servant was making preparations for Didier's return, or maybe, it now struck Asa, there was a back way into the apartments. In a rush, she crossed the square and again knocked on the door.

The same servant answered, this time wearing a clean cap and apron and with her manners notably improved. 'Monsieur Paulin is at home but is about to eat. He says he isn't expecting visitors. Who shall I say is calling?'

'My name is Thomasina Ardleigh.'

It was several minutes before footsteps were again heard on the stairs; this time a man's tread. Asa's neck ached as she strained for a glimpse of him. Then she saw a pair of naked feet descending, and there was Didier, standing in front of her, eyes shining in the dusk. She heard herself speak his name. For a moment he was still, then shook his head, as he had in the Convention when he had seemed to catch sight of her.

From somewhere above came the sound of the maid closing a door. The shock in Didier's eyes softened to incredulity. Asa's heartbeat slowed. He came no closer but stretched out his hand and indicated that she should follow him. In silence they walked up two flights of stairs, she watching the tendons on the back of his heels, the tautness of his calf against the dark cloth of his breeches. In her mind was an incantation of his name: Didier. Didier. This is Didier. When they came to his apartment he gestured that she should enter first; she passed so close that her skirts brushed his leg. In the small vestibule she glimpsed through an open door a bed covered in a plain white quilt with a scalloped edge.

At last he spoke, very softly. *'Viens.'*

Here she was, alone with him once more, in his salon above the Place Vendôme, overlooking the blind arcades where she had waited all afternoon. He watched her through half-closed eyes, as if wondering whether she was a trick of the light. 'This is indeed Thomasina Ardleigh, is it not? Thomasina.' It was his pronunciation of her name, the stress on the second syllable, which brought her fully into his presence. *'C'est toi?'*

'Yes.' In her mind a blue and white jug, his knowing hands, his shirt hanging over a screen, the monastery garden, his aged father in a prison cell...

He gave a shout of amazed laughter. 'Never had I expected... You astonish me. I thought I'd never see you again.'

'Here I am.'

'Indeed you are.' He was even more beautiful than in her memory; the gentian eyes, the prominence of brow and chin and the dipping curve of his lower lip. Again he gave a little shake of the head. 'Do you know, I thought I saw you the other day? You weren't in the Manège? I could have sworn I caught a glimpse of your face. But then I came to my senses and thought no, it couldn't be. After you'd gone that summer, I saw you everywhere, in the gardens and boulevards. I used to follow girls thinking they were you.'

'In England, I did the same. I would see a young man with dark hair and be convinced that you had come to find me.'

'My God, I can't believe you're here. Look at us, we're both shaking. Stay there, don't move. I'm afraid that if I take my eyes from you for one second you'll disappear like you did the last time...' On a table by the window a place had been set for dinner, with a basket of bread covered by a cloth. He got up and poured some wine, held her hand to steady it and gave her the glass. Their fingers, his warm, hers cold, touched for an instant so that the blood hammered under her skin. The potential for further touch, even for an embrace, hung between them.

'Drink,' he said. 'You know, I've been away from the city for weeks and might easily have missed you. What on earth brings you here?'

'Please may I sit down?' He had not kissed her. And if he had, what would her response have been? She thought, panic stricken, I must be clear. I must be sure of my own feelings.

'What am I thinking?' Didier slapped the palm of his hand to his forehead and brought a couple of chairs to the centre of the room so they could sit knee to knee. The evening darkened a notch and details of the room faded; the desk covered with papers, a glass cabinet of books, furniture upholstered in creamy fabric. She was aware of the scent of fresh bread and that she was very hungry. Leaning forward, Didier propped his chin on his hand and studied her. 'It is so very good to see you. Where is the rest of your party?'

'I came to Paris with a French travelling companion.'

'Do you mean your husband? Are you married?'

'Of course not.' She registered that there had been no dismay behind his question, only curiosity. 'As I told you in my letter, my family employed a companion to prepare me for marriage – to Mr Shackleford. After I'd posted my letter to you, when it was too late, I was very afraid that I might have harmed you or your family. But then you sent for me...'

'I sent for you?'

'You did.' Even as she uttered the words she knew that she had long since ceased to believe them and that she and Didier weren't quite alone: Madame's little shadow had slipped into the room, found a dark corner and folded its arms. 'As there was no address on either of your letters I first visited your father in Caen.'

'My *father?*'

'My friend Mr Lambert told me where he lived. And of course Beatrice used to write to me too.'

'Christ, you mean you actually visited my father

409

in prison?' His gaze never left her face as he took the glass from her, its rim still warm from her lips, and drank from the same place, as if they were lovers still. 'It's ... *extraordinary* to see you again. I can't get over the way you have just appeared here in Paris. So much the same and yet so changed...'

The edges of her consciousness blurred. She was lapped by the past. Her hand, which had held the glass, dropped on to her thigh.

There was a sudden clatter in the kitchen; Didier's arm jolted so that a drop of wine splashed on to his shirt and he sprang to his feet. 'What must you think of me? Look at me. I'm not wearing any shoes. Excuse me a moment.' She heard him call to his servant, a murmured exchange, the closing of a door and the sound of feet on the staircase. Asa crossed to the little table, lifted the cloth and helped herself to some bread, the softest and whitest she had eaten since leaving England. Beneath the window the maid walked across the square, tossing her head and straightening her shoulders.

When he came back Didier had put on shoes and stockings, even a clean shirt. He sat opposite her at the table, clasped her hands, and looked at her earnestly. 'Now, please tell me, you say I sent for you?'

Asa took out first the handkerchief, then the two letters which by now had been read so many times there was a danger they might fall apart. At first Didier treated them tentatively, much as Beatrice had done. This was why I loved him, she thought; the fierceness of his concentration, the knowledge that one minute of his attention was worth an hour of anybody else's.

'Where did you get these?'

'You of all people will know the answer to that question. At first I was sure that you had sent them to me in reply to my own. Now I'm afraid that wasn't the case. My companion, by the way, the one I told you about, called herself Madame de Rusigneux and she arrived at my home in February. We thought she was a marquise but I have since discovered her name was Estelle Beyle and that she was a fan-maker's daughter from Caen.'

'Estelle Beyle. What are you saying? Don't tell me Estelle came to your house.'

'She was my paid companion.'

'Oh God.' He put his head in his hands. 'God. That woman. This is my fault. Thomasina, what have I done? It never occurred to me that if I sent her to England she would cause trouble for you. Where is she now?'

'I don't know. She abandoned me in Caen. I think she felt a little sorry for me after all, because she left very suddenly. There was just a note, telling me to go home.'

'Well, we must find her. The very last thing I need is for Estelle to turn up here.'

Didier's dismissal of his former lover, his indifference, which should have thrilled Asa, in fact gave her no pleasure at all. The sense of displacement that had often been present since her arrival in France had settled again, a dull ache in her belly. What was she doing here, in an elegant room above the Vendôme, with a man she barely recognised? 'I think she'd originally in-

411

tended that I should come to Paris,' she said. 'When I realised who she was, I came to warn you. I'm sure she wants to hurt you.'

'Thomasina, you came to Paris, all this way, for my sake? But why on earth didn't you write to me first?'

'I told you. I thought you'd sent for me.' The words now sounded unbearably naive.

Didier held his mother's handkerchief to his lips. 'Oh, my dear Thomasina, I believe that these are in fact about the only notes I ever wrote to Estelle. Surely you can see they weren't for you? Look how rushed they are. I probably left them for her on the table when she'd gone storming off after one of our arguments. And obviously I gave her the silk handkerchief as a token.' He leaned back in his chair and linked his hands behind his head. 'I'll be straight with you – you have to know. She was my mistress for a while.'

Asa straightened her back and took another sip of wine. 'So your father said.'

'Ah, yes, he would. I wish he'd let me tell you... I know what you must have thought. But you're wrong, it wasn't that I'd forgotten about you... Thomasina, it had been more than three years.'

'You wrote to me that we would be married. I waited all that time.'

He kissed her hand and studied the palm. 'My dearest girl. You were nineteen when we met. It had been years. I had not dreamed you would have waited for me. And I received no letter about this Shackleford and your sister's plans. Estelle was available. No, more than that, she came knocking at my door. We'd known each other for years and she made it too easy.'

'Then what did it all mean, when I was here with you in Paris? *Tell me* what it meant.' Asa saw herself standing with Caroline on the shore at Littlehampton watching wave after wave, enthralled by the image of herself; a daring young woman with a mysterious French lover. Had all that passionate longing been merely the fantasy of a lonely girl?

'Thomasina. It meant that we were young and we fell in love. There was so much happening. I knew even when you were here in Paris that I should not have permitted myself to love you, but that was my head speaking. It could not govern my heart.'

'Did you ever love me?'

'Of course I loved you. You were my beautiful English love.' His head dropped, then he turned to gaze out of the window. 'It's astonishing that you're here. I hardly know what to think. If only I wasn't so tired, but I'd just got back from Toulon when I was called out of Paris again. There's endless trouble these days. This couldn't have happened at a worse time.'

Worse time for whom? Asa wondered. But his self-absorption emboldened her.

'Estelle told me she wanted to come back to France so that she could bury her brother. She seemed to think there was some doubt about what had happened to his body.'

'I know nothing about that.'

'I think she blames you for Jean – Gabriel's – death. She said she wants to punish those responsible. It seems to me that there are no limits to what she may do. That is why I came.'

He smiled and shook his head. 'No other woman in the world would have done so much for me.'

A gentle breeze blew across the square and ruffled the muslin at Asa's breast. Drawing the papers together, Didier pushed them back across the table, sprang to his feet and lit candles on his desk. Then he took out a clean sheet of paper and dipped his pen. 'I will send men out to find Estelle. It won't be difficult. We'll arrest her, then I'll talk to her. You have made a great sacrifice for me – my goodness, it's astonishing you should have taken such a risk coming to Paris. But as my father should have pointed out, I'm very well protected.'

'I also have a message from your sister,' said Asa, determined now to break through his air of having matters entirely under his control. 'She thinks you should go back to Caen. If you did, she says people would be reassured that not everyone in Paris is an enemy.'

'Is that what she thinks? Well, when I have a moment, I shall go. How's that?' The flash of his old, brilliant smile.

'Your sister is still grieving for Father Jean Beyle. So is her friend Charlotte.'

'I grieve for him too. He was very dear to me.'

'Yesterday I visited the rue Vieux Colombier and stood under the wall of St-Joseph des Carmes. I could see the window of your old room.'

He blotted the page and drew out another sheet. 'Actually I care very little either for Estelle or her brother at this moment. It's you I'm concerned about. Christ, Thomasina... The more I think about it, the more I realise we must get you out of Paris. It is not safe for strangers here, especially the English. And given my role in the police...'

'Perhaps if you do have such an influential role it will be easier for you to be rid of me.'

'You sound hurt, Thomasina. You mustn't be. The last thing I want is to be rid of you, as you put it. But we must act, do you understand, for your own sake? We need to work out how best to get you home without attracting attention. I still can't fathom how you managed to arrive in Paris without running into trouble.'

'I travelled under a different name.'

'A false name? Don't tell me you have forged papers? *Christ.* Oh, don't look at me like that, I can't bear it. You weren't to know. But the situation in Paris is very delicate. Next week I stand for election.'

Asa got to her feet so suddenly that the glass tumbled over, spilling its contents on to the white cloth and the edge of one of the letters. 'You don't have to worry about me; I expect nothing from you. And actually I'm grateful to Madame Estelle, because who knows how long I might have gone on thinking you still loved me, had she not lured me back. My God, Didier, hadn't I said time and again that you had only to whisper my name and I would have come? But it seems you gave me up long ago, and all these years, while I was still waiting for your letters... Now I realise that what bothers you most of all is that my presence here might damage your career. Is that what happened to your friend Jean Beyle? Did he get in your way too? I want the truth, Didier. What have I been loving all these years?'

'Hush, hush.' He took hold of her arm and brought her forehead against his shoulder. She let her face rest on the coolness of his shirt, inhaling the essence of Didier while he stroked her hair. 'Thomasina.' He drew her closer and kissed her hair. 'Do you remember, when we were together in Paris, we used to dream of such a wonderful future? Sometimes I do wish I'd scooped you up then, and taken you to Caen, where we could have lived our lives as a provincial lawyer and his wife. But how would that have been?'

'You would never have been satisfied. You were far too restless and eager to do the right thing.'

'The right thing. Yes, that's what I wanted.'

'Then why has it proved so difficult, Didier? You and I used to dream of ending slavery. We talked of freedom. But now even your own father is in chains.'

He laughed. 'Hardly chains. He is being kept out of harm's way for his own protection. Lord knows what calamity the people of Caen are drawing down upon themselves. But yes, it's all coming back to me, how you used to be. That was one of the things I loved so much; you also believed in doing the right thing. But can you possibly understand, I wonder, how hard it is for me?' When he raised her chin and gazed down at her, the blueness of his eyes ought to have been spellbinding. 'Do you know what I'd like to do, more than anything in the world at this moment? Be with you. Spend time with you and learn you all over again. I look at you and remember how it was. When you left I was grief stricken, I promise you. It seemed to me that everything was perfect while you were here, and that it never would be again.'

It was as if, for the first time that night, he really saw Asa. His arms settled about her, remembering her shape, and his eyes had shed their determination and were instead filled with desire. With his fingertips he touched the side of her forehead. 'Oh, I remember you. The scent of you. The freshness of your skin, here, in this hollow. I hadn't realised, I had forgotten what I once had.' And that was the moment, standing in his arms where she had for so long wanted to be, that Asa knew for certain she didn't love Didier – not because he'd changed, but because he hadn't. She saw now that same eager young man, who could be caressing her breast one minute, the next dashing forth to a meeting that would wrench France on to a new course, his whole being attending to each extraordinary moment, but not assimilating, not caring for one experience once it had been transplanted by another. And so that race went on within Didier, to find the perfect moment, and Asa knew that when she disentangled herself, when he remembered where he was and with whom, and saw the heap of papers on his desk, she would be consigned ruthlessly to the shadows once more.

She put her hand on his wrist. 'Didier, does it have to be like this? Jean Beyle was your friend. He seems to have been a good man. Why did he have to die?'

'A good man. A saint, in fact, and didn't everyone say so? But I saw a rather different side to Beyle. You forget, I knew Jean Beyle from when we were children, and he had a will of iron. He was far more ambitious than I; it was simply concealed by all that prayer. Jean, I'm afraid, was always destined to be a victim. In fact, I often think he *wanted* to die so that he could make his point. He was the type who would never look to left or right once he'd made up his mind.'

'Surely people don't choose to be killed. They make a choice, and are killed for it.'

'You're wrong. In Jean's case, he chose. I should know because it was I who gave him a chance to save his life. Listen to me. Of course I wanted to spare him – he was my friend as well as Estelle's brother – so I arranged a meeting with a colleague of mine who was high up in what was then called the Legislative Assembly. He promised to have Jean released and sent to a safe place, if only he would sign the oath. So I visited the prison yet again and took Jean the appropriate papers – I even had a witness with me – but still he refused to sign. I shouted at him: "Do you realise how cruel you are being? I'm doing this for Estelle. Why can't you put her first, above a piece of paper?"'

Didier rubbed his forehead with the side of his fist and gave Asa a pleading look, as if he must convince her, of all people. 'Beyle always pretended to be so mild, but he knew exactly how powerful he was. The trouble was that he was trapped in the past, refused to see that in the new France we must all pull in the same direction, that the Revolution is fragile and must be led with clarity and strength of purpose.'

'But *you* used to argue with everyone all the time. It seems to me that the only crime Beyle and your father committed was to disagree with you.'

'They were *wrong.*' She stared at him and he added, more quietly: 'On the day Beyle was killed I was out of the city, in Caen, as a matter of fact, visiting my family. Estelle blamed me, of course. She thought I had deliberately arranged to be away. But even had I been in Paris there was nothing more I could have done. Paris was seething. Civil war might have flared up at any moment and then the counter-revolutionaries would have joined forces with foreign powers. The killing of those priests and prostitutes was like a purge, an example.'

'So you did know it would happen. Estelle was right.'

From outside came the sound of running feet. Didier roused himself. 'But we must forget all that now and get you out. And no, Thomasina, it's not for my sake that I'm doing this, but yours. Times are very bad in Paris. I want you to be safe.'

'I have no money except the amount your father borrowed for me.'

A woman was shouting in the square and someone was ringing a handbell. 'I'll send him the money, don't worry about that. But you mustn't go back to Caen; it's not safe at present. I'm going to have you taken to Calais. It'll be a day or two before the papers are ready. Where are you...?'

More bells rang, a cacophony of clangs from bell-towers near and far. People were rushing into the square, throwing open windows, collecting in doorways. Didier urged Asa to stand out of sight and called down: 'What is it? What has happened?'

Word was passed from mouth to mouth until a man in a red cap raised his head and bellowed: 'It is Marat. Our great Marat. Our country's saviour. He's been murdered.'

Didier leaned out farther. 'What do you mean? When? How do you know?'

The crowd surged on, carrying with it the man in the red cap, who yelled back at Didier: 'At home. He was at home. A woman done it.'

When Didier again faced Asa he seemed to have forgotten who she was. 'Christ, if it's true, if Marat *is* dead, everything will change.'

He crammed papers into a case and left the room to fetch his coat. More and more people were streaming into the square.

'We must go,' said Didier when he came back. 'I'll have to convene a meeting and get my men on to the streets. We must keep the city calm. At times like this anything can happen. They will be looking for scapegoats. You...' He stared at her, the horror of the situation dawning. 'You are a foreigner. You especially will be at risk. *Move*, Thomasina. We must get you out of this city.' He returned to his desk, sat down, pondered, then again sprang up and seized her hand. 'Listen, for both our sakes you must do as I say. Go back to your lodgings. Do *not* talk to anyone. Stay indoors until I send for you.'

'Nobody out there will care about me.'

'It's a precaution. We don't know what's happened or whether Marat really is dead. But if he is, there'll be a shift. Everyone will be watching everyone else.' He was urging her towards the door.

'I'll walk home.'

'No.' He led her along a passage to a flight of narrow stairs. 'I'll see you into a cab but you must go straight back to your lodgings. And stay put, do you understand? I need to get you out of the city fast, before anyone finds out that you and I are connected. You're English, for God's sake.'

He found a cab, paid the man, thrust his arms into his jacket, and disappeared through the crowd. The street was jammed with people alerted by the tocsin, which was taken up by one bell-tower after another. They were grabbing each other, demanding to know what was happening. One woman screamed: 'They should kill the lot of them. Anyone who knew this woman, everyone from her district.'

Eventually, despite Didier's instructions, Asa was forced to clamber out of the cab and make her way on foot.

By now the sky was dark. Faces, illuminated by flickering lanterns, were masks of hollows and shadow with gleaming, frightened eyes. Asa had set off in the wrong direction and fell back in a doorway while a mob of men roared past, carrying torches and chanting: *Marat, Marat.* She smelt burning wax, the stink of unwashed clothes, and saw the roughness of their hands, their relentless energy as they bayed for retribution. Women

421

formed a knot behind them, keening and clawing at the fabric covering their breasts.

Nobody noticed when Asa turned her head to the wall. The pain that shot through her was sharp and pure so that the tears came easily, quenching the last spark of the glorious love affair, in which she and Didier, the beautiful and the righteous, had strode forth scattering love and a desire to reform on all they encountered. When she moved on, still sobbing, someone passed her a jar of wine and she took a swig before handing it back. Afterwards she raised her head, wiped her eyes and set off again, fully awake now to all that she had lost.

Chapter Five

Four years after the fall of the Bastille the citizens of Paris again took to the streets. It was the day following the murder of Marat – former doctor, radical journalist, member of the Insurrectionary Committee and of late a leading voice in the National Convention.

Despite the chaos, Citoyenne Maurice was relatively unperturbed. She was even a little more friendly towards Asa in her eagerness to show her knowledge of the city and its ways. 'It's always happening these days. You can never bank on peace and quiet. One minute we are full of love, holding festivals in the Champs de Mars, the next we are murdering each other or denouncing a neighbour because she's joked that the red cap doesn't suit her husband's complexion.'

'If Marat was so great,' Asa said, 'why was he the object of such hatred? Certainly in Caen I heard people speak of him as the country's worst enemy.'

'It doesn't matter whether he was great or not. Marat's was the voice people listened to here. Whoever killed him has played straight into the hands of his friends, the Montagnards, who'll say it's no use being reasonable because the Girondins and their associates have resorted to treachery and violence by murdering an innocent man. Now the Montagnards will have a cast-iron excuse to cut their enemies down for good.'

'But who exactly *is* the enemy now? I thought the Girondins had already been banished.'

'The finger might be pointed at any of us. That's why we should go straight out and join the mourners. We don't want anyone to think we're being unpatriotic.'

'If you don't mind, Citoyenne Maurice, I believe it might be better for me to stay inside.'

'What do you mean? You've been running all over the place these past few days.'

'I was told that as a stranger I should stay indoors.'

'No, we must show our faces like every other loyal citizen.'

Outside they joined the rush of people heading towards the river. The frenzy of the previous night had been replaced by sobriety, women clutching posies or billets-doux to their fallen hero, Marat. Leaflets printed with unlikely images of his hollow-eyed face and extolling his virtues as a republican martyr were thrust into Asa's hands. Marat's embalmed body was to lie in state in the Church of the Cordeliers near the Luxembourg; the crowds were heading there so that they might queue up and file past his body.

Meanwhile, extraordinary rumours about how Marat had been killed were flying from group to group. 'You'll never believe what I heard. The poor, sick man was murdered in his own home, in his *bath*. Damnation, is nothing sacred these days?'

'You'll never believe who the killer was,' said another voice. 'A *girl*. Not a Parisian, thank Christ, but a country wench who'd come all the way to Paris hell-bent on killing our saviour Marat. I've always said the provinces can't be trusted.'

'Is she still at large? Have they captured her?'

'Have no fear. She was sitting by his bath when they found him, cool as anything while she watched him, in his death throes, thrashing about in his own blood.'

As they neared the river, more news filtered back: the killer had a name. 'Cordon, or some such. Charlotte Cordon or Corday... From Normandy. She's hardly more than a girl, but she wasn't operating alone, obviously. We all know she must have been put up to the job. Some even say she's a man in disguise. There's probably a whole gang of brigands hiding out somewhere in Paris.'

'Who will they kill next, I wonder?'

'I'll be locking my door at night, that's for sure.'

'Marat was a politician. Surely they won't be

after people like us?'

'Don't you believe it. Weren't you at the Convention when Marat was speaking the other day? You were cheering him on. Well then, they'll be after you. I've heard they've recruited children to carry out their dirty work.'

'What was that name again? You don't mean Charlotte *Corday?*' Asa asked incredulously. 'From which part of Normandy?'

'Place called Caen. Have you heard of it? Hot-bed of traitors, apparently. The population staged an uprising that took place the very same minute that Marat was killed in his bath. So don't tell me that this Corday wasn't part of a conspiracy to destroy our new republic. They should bring back the wheel and smash her to pieces, in my opinion; the guillotine is too good for her.'

Citoyenne Maurice was determined to join the queue that would eventually wend its way past Marat's corpse – there was always a danger that her neighbours would file an unfavourable report if she neglected this duty – so at the river they parted company and Asa set off towards the Tuileries. On the way she picked up yet another news-sheet. She must have heard the name wrong, she kept thinking. It couldn't possibly be the Corday she knew. How could Charlotte Corday have got herself from Caen to Paris and murdered Marat in so short a time? Only last week they had been sipping coffee together in the Paulin garden. Charlotte was ardent, angry and perhaps not very clever. But a murderer?

Chapter Six

When Asa returned to her lodgings late that afternoon, Citoyenne Maurice was frigid in her manner and ushered her into a little back room where the dresser was stacked with an assortment of pre-revolutionary china. 'Citoyenne Ardleigh, you travelled from Caen, yes?'

'I visited Caen before I came here.'

'This Charlotte Corday, who they say killed Marat, is from Caen. Did you know her?'

'A little.'

'Dear God. Please don't tell me that my friend Professor Paulin knew her too.'

'She was a family friend.'

'Dear God.' Citoyenne Maurice closed the curtains and the door. 'What have I done, letting you into this house? We are finished.'

'Madame – Citoyenne – nobody except you knows who I am or where I'm from.'

'You must go. But not at once, that would draw suspicion. You must behave absolutely normally.'

'Madame, I hardly knew Charlotte at all. I had no idea what she was planning to do.'

'That doesn't matter. They'll think you're guilty. I want you out. You must leave in a couple of days, when all the fuss has died down.'

'Madame, on my life, I swear that I had nothing to do with Marat's death. But I promise you, I'll leave as soon as I can. In fact arrangements are already being made – Didier Paulin is seeing to it, and you know he's well respected. I should be out of the city by tonight or tomorrow at the latest. You mustn't worry.'

'Of course I'm worried. Well, I suppose you'd better go on sleeping here, it would look very odd if I turfed you out, but I don't want you hiding here during the day. You're to come and go as usual. And if anyone asks, whatever you do, don't say you've just come from Caen.'

The next day, when there was still no word from Didier, Asa left a message with Citoyenne Maurice that she would be in the Palais Royal, where she sat in her customary place, reading a newssheet, anonymous, she hoped, among the crowds. There was no doubting now that it was Beatrice's friend, Charlotte Corday, who had committed this extraordinary act, and the papers reported in lurid detail the steps she had taken.

Having arrived in Paris by diligence, just as Asa had, Corday had found lodgings in the rue de la Victoire in the north of the city. On the morning of 13 July, while Asa was visiting the site of the Bastille, Charlotte had set off on a shopping trip here, to the Palais Royal, where she'd bought a hat with green trimmings, a newspaper and a kitchen knife. Such was her desire to strike a public blow that her original intention had been to kill Marat in full view of the National Convention, but because he was ill she'd taken a cab to his house instead and asked to see him. She was told he was too ill to receive visitors.

Later in the day she called again, insisting that

she had information for Marat's eyes only. Marat was so tormented by his skin disease that he currently spent most of his time in the bath, up to his neck in some kind of emollient solution, so it was there that he received Citoyenne Corday. She held out a list of names of those she claimed were citizens of Caen and traitors to the cause of the Revolution. When her victim reached for the paper she took out her brand-new kitchen knife and lunged, striking, by chance or design, the one place in his breast where bone would not impede entrance.

All the papers agreed that Charlotte Corday had simply been a puppet in a wider plot to destroy the Revolution. On the very same day that she had struck Marat, forces from Caen had fired against brave troops from Paris. Fortunately, there had been a wholesale retreat and the insurrection seemed to be over, at least for the time being, but didn't all this smack of a high-level conspiracy? Paris must be infested with Corday's co-conspirators, waiting to pounce on the innocent sons and daughters of the Revolution.

Asa read the account again and again until she no longer felt incredulity but a sense that this was what Charlotte had been bound to do. On the hilltop outside the Abbaye des Dames, enthusing about holding the key to the nuns' door, Charlotte had been enraptured by the memory of her own significance. The detail of the green-trimmed hat, bought on the morning of the murder, was the most telling of all. Charlotte must have regarded her trip to Paris as worthy of celebration, a treat. In her mind, killing Marat was to be the glorious finale to her stay in Paris and an end to the impotence and bewilderment she'd endured in Caen since the first exciting days of the Revolution.

The trouble was that, far from ridding the country of Marat, she had made him more significant in his murdered state than he had ever been in life, just as Madame Maurice had predicted. In the Palais Royal people crowded along the arcades to view the notorious shop where the hat had been bought so that soon the milliner was forced to put up the shutters and disappear from view, in case it should occur to anyone to accuse him of conspiracy to murder. Charlotte Corday's preposterous intervention had tipped the balance of power still further towards the Montagnards, and now there would be a clampdown. Everyone must be wary of strangers, said the newssheets. Arrivals from the provinces were to be searched rigorously and anyone who bought an item that might be used as a weapon was to be regarded with suspicion.

Women were particularly anathema. It was quite clear to journalists and politicians and the louts who stood about jeering at groups of women on their way to market that the whole female breed had got well beyond themselves in thinking that they could intervene in national affairs. Charlotte Corday had proved beyond a shadow of a doubt that if a woman was given too much leeway she would become deranged. Rules must now be enforced in order to restore the virtuous French female to her proper place: the hearth. No more forming clubs. No more demanding that she should have a voice in the Convention. Her place was at home, breastfeeding babies.

In fact, said the Jacobin press, enemies of the state were springing up like weeds, determined to plunge the fledgling republic into chaos and bloodshed – Girondins, royalists, hoarders, thieves, foreigners, women who talked too much. And here was Asa, recently arrived from Caen, a foreigner with false papers and without ties in the city except for Didier. What would Charlotte Corday, currently under interrogation, say about her associates in Caen? What if she mentioned Beatrice Paulin? Surely the entire family would be at risk, and anyone connected to it.

At first Asa determined to keep away from Didier in case she put him in further danger. But after another day spent pacing the gardens, dashing back to her lodgings – still no message – she weakened and visited his apartment late in the evening. He was not at home so she left a note with the maid. *You of all people will know that I need to get out of the city. You told me I must wait to hear from you, but you should be aware that the situation has become urgent. Soon I will be forced to leave my lodgings.*

At one point she planned a route to the city gates and began walking north. Perhaps she could just keep going, be picked up by some passing coach and transported to the coast. At the very least she would take a look at the kind of checks that were in place. At the corner of rue Charlot she was stopped in her tracks. For some time a couple had been ahead of her, a small child prancing between them, his short arms raised so that he could be swung off his feet by his parents. The family had

430

paused to admire a pyramid of oranges on a fruit stall when a cart rumbled up and three men in uniform leapt out and demanded to see their papers. The woman, clutching the child in her arms, was shoved aside and the oranges went tumbling into the gutter as the man was escorted away, head wrenched back for a last glance at his wife and child.

Another time Asa walked to the inn-yard where she had been set down by the diligence from Caen, only to find it surrounded by men in blue jackets wielding pistols. When a coach arrived its passengers were ushered out and lined up against the wall to have their papers scrutinised and their clothes searched. Asa retreated.

At least for the couple of days that Marat's embalmed body was on display in the church of Cordeliers the atmosphere in the city was peacefully reverential. Asa, who had taken to hiding herself within crowds, glimpsed relics even more macabre than the corpse itself; his fateful bath held aloft by four women, and his bloody shirt, employed, it was said, in a vain effort to staunch his wounds, displayed like a flag on the end of a pike.

But on 17 July, the day of Corday's execution, the crowd whipped itself into a frenzy of righteous anger. The eyes of young men were spiked with rage and their bodies tough and unyielding as they thrust their way to the front of the crowd. Dressed in the loose trousers of the sans-culottes they held leering conversations about how they'd like to be given the task of establishing Charlotte Corday's gender for good and all. Asa was crushed among them so that she could see the hairs on their naked chests, their broken teeth and fingernails, smell the garlic and wine on their breath. Corday had been taken first to the Conciergerie, where she was to be tried and found guilty, then carried across the Pont Neuf to commence the long procession along the rue Honoré to the Place de la Revolution and the guillotine.

As the day progressed and it became clear that Corday would die by evening, the trip to watch her passing turned into a family outing. Asa was elbowed out of the way by men carrying children on their shoulders, and women with bundles of food. Relics of Marat were peddled from one hand to another – screws of paper containing a few hairs or a purported scrap of his clothing. As far as the eye could see the streets were crammed with people waiting to witness the passing of the scarlet woman, the witch. 'Although it's said she has the face of an angel,' someone said. 'Now that I'd like to see.'

Asa was held fast by the memory of Charlotte's companionship in Caen, a time when others had abandoned her – Charlotte with her ardent eyes, cotton frock and soft hair. If possible, Asa decided, she would catch Charlotte's eye and show her that she had at least one friend in the crowd. But when news was passed back that the tumbrel was on its way, there was no possibility of even a fleeting glimpse of Corday. The view was obscured by guards who held their pikes horizontal to form a barrier so that the mob would not surge forward, drag the murderess from her cart and rip her to pieces. There was a shout of amazement as people in prime positions registered that this aberration of nature was indeed just a fresh-faced young woman.

Once the cart had gone by the crowd fell in behind it, the late afternoon sun slanting golden on their heads, while some young girls pranced and skipped so that their light skirts billowed out as if it were a feast day. In a strange way Charlotte might actually be pleased to see all this festivity, thought Asa. Perhaps in her mind she was witnessing a new dawn for Paris, because after all she, Charlotte Corday, had excised the scourge, Marat.

Often Asa lost sight of even the guards, but suddenly, through a random rearrangement of the crowd, Charlotte's face swayed into view. Utterly familiar, she was as rosy as ever in a plain cap, though wearing a shapeless red gown to show that she was a murderess. She was sitting bolt upright, eyes shining, knees braced against the edge of the tumbrel, her hands tied behind her back. For an absurd moment Asa was jealous of Charlotte: to perform an extreme act, however ill judged, and then to die, that at least was a conclusion, a statement.

They came at last to the Place de la Revolution behind the Tuileries gardens, where the scaffold upon which the king and dozens of others had been guillotined was constructed broad and high so that the crowd could surround it on all four sides. Asa, pressed far back, could see only a faceless puppet, but the crowd must have sensed something of Charlotte's ardour and strangeness because the jeers and oaths gradually ceased.

What was she thinking as she waited patiently for her hands to be retied? Did she believe it was all a game and that soon she would be back among the Normandy apple orchards or strolling through the Paulins' garden? Her step was buoyant when she approached the guillotine, as though she were about to take communion under the loving eyes of the Madonna in the church of St-Jean. There was a youthful pliancy to her limbs as she first knelt then lay face down on the wooden board and positioned her neck under the blade, lifting her chin as if settling into a pillow. The last thing on earth she would see was the bloodied basket into which her own head would fall.

The crowd was silent as the blade caught the sun and began its unstoppable descent. Asa looked away, partly because she could not bear Charlotte's insouciance, partly because she realised that she, in turn, was being watched. Perhaps fifty yards away, deep in the crowd, almost concealed but unmistakably there, her entire attention fixed not on Charlotte Corday but on Asa, was a small, dark-haired woman dressed in a pale pink gown that had once been Asa's own. The tricolour ribbon formed a sash at Madame's waist and she wore over her tumbling hair the little red cap she had sewn during the voyage from England.

Those huge, hypnotic eyes were exactly as when Asa had first seen them after the charivari. In an instant Asa had thrust herself into the crowd amid people screaming with joy, hurling their caps into the air and hugging each other. Madame ducked away, but Asa was relentless in her pursuit. The difference in their height, as always, put Madame at an advantage; she was small whereas Asa, being taller, found it less easy to worm her way through.

'*Estelle Beyle.*' Madame went still, as if she'd been shot in the back. Finally Asa caught up with her. 'I want to talk to you.'

'Not here.'

'I'm not letting you out of my sight.'

'Then come with me or you'll get us both arrested.'

Madame had grown so impossibly thin that her fingers on Asa's arm were skeletal. Having lost so much flesh, her face had an almost animal quality, the eyes as globed and blank as a nocturnal creature's. Holding fast to Asa, she led her through the crowd. Sometimes they were jostled and sworn at, always, after a glance at Madame's face, they were allowed through.

Her lodgings turned out to be ten minutes from Didier's apartment, on a narrow street with a cemetery on one side and a row of high buildings on the other. The cloying stench of putrefaction forced Asa to cover her mouth and nose. They crossed a gloomy courtyard, entered a tunnel-like entrance hall and climbed flight after flight of stairs that smelt of damp and urine until they reached the sixth floor. Madame occupied one tiny garret room that was stiflingly hot. She closed the door then turned on Asa: 'Stupid woman. What are you doing here in Paris?'

The tension between them, confined to so small a space, raked the air raw. The tools of Madame's trade were laid out on a rickety table under a window barely a couple of feet square, just as she had colonised corners of the parlour at Ardleigh or Morton Hall, and the air was pungent with the smell of watercolour mixed with corruption from the cemetery below. Her little box of paints was open beside a jar of discoloured water; she had been painting a fire-screen in shades of crimson and blue against a white background, depicting flowers and floating wreaths and a flag in liberty colours. Poor Madame – Estelle – who had been described in Caroline's letter as nothing more than a professional copyist. Other blank panels were stacked against the wall, presumably awaiting her attention. Apart from the table, the room was furnished with a narrow bed, a chair upon which a few clothes were piled and, inevitably, the portmanteau.

'I have nothing to offer you by way of nourishment, not even water.' Madame's voice was as always low and controlled. 'I left you in Caen to keep you safe. Why did you not return home?'

'I made connections and when I found out who you were I came to warn Didier. And to find out the truth for myself. How could I creep back to England, knowing what you'd done to me?'

Madame smiled. 'Ah, you are angry. My tepid English friend.'

'Did you find your brother's grave, madame? I went to the cemetery in the Vaugirard and half expected to see you there. I have been looking out for you everywhere I go.'

'I don't believe he was taken to the Vaugirard. Some say all the bodies were carried there by cart and tipped into the cemetery, but I know there were too many and that there would have been an outcry if people had seen such heaps of corpses.'

'What do you think happened to him, then?'

'I have heard rumours that those gardens at Les Carmes, where he died, are haunted. It's said that after the massacre the guards were embarrassed because they had to dispose of so many bodies in one day, and that instead of removing them all to the Vaugirard, some were tossed into a well in the garden itself – as many as would fit. And then they filled in the well with soil and covered it with shrubs. One day I shall break in there, and I shall find him.'

'Madame you cannot ... it was so long ago...'

Madame jerked her head towards the grimy windowpane. 'That little cemetery down there is where the dead king's body and head were thrown. These days the pit where they fling the corpses is left wide open – there's no time to cover it up. If you were to lean out of the window you'd see one corner of it, crawling with flies, and the smell would make you vomit. But at least *his* family know where he is. I like to look at the cemetery. I like to think of his bald head and naked, pampered body that used to be taut and keen in the saddle, greedy to hunt and kill, just like your father is. It will be Charlotte Corday's turn next.'

'You sound contemptuous. I thought you'd be proud of Charlotte Corday. From what I learned at the Paulins' house, I had understood that she was your friend.'

'Charlotte. She was always full of self-importance at being some kind of unpaid secretary to the abbess, but in fact it was only because her family was minor nobility that the nuns took any notice of her. What annoyed Charlotte most, when the Revolution came, was that she no longer had anyone's attention. Well, she got the attention of everyone in the end so I hope she's satisfied.'

It felt familiar to be in a room with Madame. To be there under the eaves, looking up at chinks of light shining through the roof tiles, to hear the rustle of some creature in the skirting. Madame was so precise with her long lashes and her curling hair, the tautness of her body that had been made love to time and again by Didier; yet so much not herself, so obsessed and so broken that Asa had a compulsion to put out her hand and touch her arm.

Madame cleared the chair and sat with her back to the window so that a shaft of light fell on her black hair, tinting it auburn. With a flick of her hand she indicated that Asa should sit on the bed. Afterwards the hand was held suspended for an instant longer than necessary, the gesture calculated and indeed refined to draw attention to itself and perhaps to the distinct tremor in her fingers.

'In fact, I knew you were in Paris because I saw you go to Didier's apartment. I was watching. I expect he told you his story about trying to save my brother.'

'I do understand what you must have suffered. But it had nothing to do with me.'

A strangely wistful glance. 'Of course I know

438

that's true. Poor Mademoiselle Ardleigh.' Madame picked up a minuscule paintbrush in her brittle hand. 'I gave you a chance. I could not believe it when I saw you'd come to Paris.'

'What did you expect me to do? I had no friends, no money...'

'I left you the fan. What have you done with it? You haven't lost it?'

'It's at my lodgings.'

'You have no idea, do you, of the worth of that fan?' She spat out the words. 'It is a cabriolet, one of the most rare and beautiful of its kind, like the wheel of a carriage. I don't expect you've really looked at it and seen that it is composed of a fan within a fan. Even you, who are supposed to be so clever, have missed the detail. It was an old fan, torn at the top, so I replaced the original silk with my own design. That fan would have bought you a passage to anywhere.'

'Or had me arrested. Surely it is of no value now. Who carries a fan these days?'

Madame cast Asa a burning glance. 'So you're telling me that I gave my life to a thing of no value? I crouched over my desk painting these fans for the great ladies who came to our shop. I watched them hold my creations to their faces and peer at themselves in the mirror, and like you they never saw the fan that I had made, only their own greedy eyes peeking over the edge of it. When the Revolution came I thought that Didier and I would change all that. I thought we would make a world where the fan-maker would be valued more than the useless woman who bought the fan. My family was packing to leave but I

439

stayed in the old house on my own, waiting for Didier to send for me. I was part of the Revolution, even in Caen. We were young and we wanted a new world so we drove the marquis from his castle and the fat, spoilt nuns from their abbey. And all the time, I thought Didier was in Paris paving the way for our life together. As it turned out he'd fallen in love with an English girl.'

'I didn't know about you. Had I known...'

'...you would have done exactly the same. When I came to Paris that summer with my friends I was so full of joy that sometimes I thought my bones would catch fire. On the journey we were short of money so we ate stale bread and drank the roughest wine. Sometimes we walked behind the carriage to give the horses a rest. It was warm at night and you could hear the crickets in the hedgerows. For the first time in my life I saw fireflies. I was travelling to Didier and I knew everything was going to change. What could be better than that? That was the best time of all, the journey from Caen to Paris, to see Didier. We arranged to meet him at the entrance to the Tuileries. I thought he would be as excited as I was but he gave me only a little kiss on either cheek, then he turned away, and I knew something had happened.'

'But it wasn't my fault.'

'He was my Didier and he had fallen in love with you. That is the one thing I did understand – how could I not? I remember ... you... I remember when we met you in the gardens and afterwards he broke away from our group and dashed off, out of sight – you see, I forget nothing of those few minutes, your pink cheeks and your shining eyes, the way you moistened your lips with your tongue and glanced at your sister to see if she noticed what you were feeling. Didier returned to my side flushed and full of laughter, but he pretended that you were nothing but a passing acquaintance. I hung on to his arm and looked back at you and said: "You can tell me. I think it's exciting, Didier, that you have met someone new." "Don't you mind?" he said. "I thought you'd mind." "How could I? All that matters to me is that you are happy." He was only too willing to take me at my word and pour out every detail of your love affair. We were delayed in Paris by the hailstorm and I sat with him in his room, far into the night after you'd gone, and listened to him talking about you.'

'I had no idea that you even existed,' Asa protested. 'Anyway, you got Didier back in the end. His father told me.'

'I got him back, as you say, but he wasn't the same. After he'd met you he thought that the French should be rational, like the English. He thought he could bring down the king and change France through *reason*. I had no patience with him or his endless debates. I broke free of him and went with the other women, and when at night I took him back into my arms he loved to smell Paris on my skin and see the dirt of the streets under my fingernails. I marched on the Bastille, I marched on Versailles, and I brought the monarchy to its knees. When he saw me with my bare throat and my bare arms, my eyes full of the things that I had done, he used to shake with passion. He shuddered when I touched him with my hand – the hand that had held the harness of the horse that had dragged the royal family's carriage back to Paris.'

'So you had him. You won. Why did you come looking for me in England?'

Madame set down the paintbrush and folded her hands as she always used to, perfectly still, the very picture of acquiescence. 'After they had killed my brother, I was so sick that I couldn't raise my head. I don't remember anything. Didier arranged it all because he wanted to be rid of me. I was scarcely able to think for myself, but when I arrived in England I remembered two names. One was Ardleigh, Thomasina, his English mistress. The other was Shackleford, her cousin and Didier's former English correspondent. In London I struck lucky and found a woman who got me an introduction to your sister. When I first saw you arguing with those youths by the tailor's cottage I decided: at least she will be a challenge, it will be amusing to bring her down. Then, when you caught sight of me, I was worried that you had recognised me from that time in the Tuileries, but no, of course not, that day you only had eyes for Didier. And yes, I thought it would be the perfect revenge, to bring you to Paris and tell the authorities that Didier had an English mistress who had smuggled herself across the sea. But then I went to church in Caen – I couldn't help myself, I had to go back one last time – and it was my undoing because I remembered how my brother had loved that Madonna when he was a little boy, and used to make me take him to visit her, and I was ashamed.'

After a pause, Asa said: 'Is it at an end now, madame?'

Madame brought her face very close to Asa's, her eyes shining with tears. 'I blamed you because I thought Didier didn't love me enough to save my brother. But it wasn't you. It was Didier. You should not have come to Paris. You should have stayed in Caen.'

'What have you done, madame? Tell me. Please.'

But Madame had lain down on the bed with her head in the crook of her elbow, her face covered by her black hair. 'I have given him one more chance.'

Asa knelt beside her and touched her head. Madame's scalp was hard under her fingertips. Her eyes closed and she gave a sigh, like a child preparing itself for sleep. Her hair shifted under Asa's hand and fell back in a thick wave.

Chapter Seven

The walk back to the rue des Francs Bourgeois seemed interminable. Every raised voice or passing cart jarred Asa's nerves. She had been foolish to spend so long with Madame; it was late to be out on streets, which had been colonised by youths roaring Marat's name, or Corday's, or simply *Liberté*. When at last she reached the house and knocked on the door there was no answer.

She tried again. A neighbour stood in a doorway, watching.

'Do you know if Citoyenne Maurice is at home?' asked Asa, and knocked again.

Madame Maurice opened the door a crack. At the sight of Asa she picked up her case from inside the passage and hurled it into the street. 'Get away from here. I told you. I begged you...'

'Citoyenne, please, there's no need to be afraid. Let me in.' The torpor of the street was interrupted by the clop of hooves and the rattle of a carriage. Madame Maurice backed into the house and slammed the door. The carriage stopped and a couple of men climbed out.

'Thomasina Ardleigh. Are you she?'

At last Didier's men were here. In a flash Asa saw herself being whisked through the city, on her way home. She picked up her case. 'I am.'

'Step this way, *citoyenne*. Let me take your bag.'

She mounted the step and peered inside the carriage, which was very dark, small and plain, with narrow bench seats and a blacked-out window. 'I presume you have come on behalf of Monsieur ... Citoyen Paulin,' she said, turning to one of the men, the heavier of the two, who'd grasped her elbow.

'That's it. In you get.'

'Please show me your papers.'

'Just a tick. We need to get moving. Here, allow me.' He wrenched the case from her hand and threw it inside.

'Did Didier send me a note?'

'Just get in and then I'll find it. Hurry up now.'

Casements were being thrown open in the

444

houses on either side of the street, ears pressed to the cracks in doors. A silent crowd had materialised at the corner. Someone shouted: 'We don't know who she is. We've seen her hanging about on her own and we don't think it's right.'

The men, who wore a uniform of sorts – plain caps and tattered coats in shades of blue – were nudging her into the carriage, which stank of sweat. Her mind was racing. 'Let me see Didier's letter.'

Too late, she was inside, and the door was locked. One of the men had propped his backside on the bench opposite, spread his legs wide apart and was grinning.

The carriage lurched forward. 'Where are we going?'

'Now now, *citoyenne*, it's not for you to ask questions. It's for you to come along with us all quiet and gentle.'

She threw herself at the door and rattled the lock. Her companion didn't move, simply folded his arms and leaned back.

'Where are you taking me?'

'You'll find out, my love. Now just stop clawing at that lock or I'll have to bind your hands.'

'Show me your papers.'

'All right. If you'll sit still and be quiet I'll read them to you.' He reached into his jacket. 'This is what you'll be wanting to see, I do believe – the warrant for your arrest.'

'Arrest? What am I charged with? I've done nothing.'

'Very well. Let's take a look, shall we? I'll read the charges out to you. What it says is that you are charged with being an English woman disguised as one Julie Moreau, and therefore a suspected spy. Further, you are associated with the murderess, Corday, having recently arrived from Caen by diligence, travelling under a false passport, and are therefore suspected as being an accessory to murder. Will that do?'

'But I had nothing to do with Charlotte Corday...'

'Look, don't blame me, I'm just doing my job. Now, no more struggling, miss, sit quiet.'

The drive took barely a quarter of an hour. Through a slit of window Asa saw that people steered well clear of this carriage and on the whole were quiet, kept their heads down and looked cowed as it passed by. The streets were settling into evening; goods were brought inside, doors locked, shutters closed. Asa's mind had gone blank and her ears were ringing. She was aware of being prodded out of the carriage and supported as she almost fell to the ground, of a change of temperature and a smell she recognised – enclosure, neglected human flesh. She was nudged up a flight of stairs and into a little room that was almost completely dark and furnished only with a mattress.

Asa took two panicked steps from one side of her cell to the other, slamming her hands into the damp wall, beating her forehead on the stone. Her own voice cried out over and over: 'I've done nothing. You can't touch me. I'm English. Please let me go home. I don't belong here.'

In a wave of sheer terror, she smashed her fists into the wall until they bled. Her throat ached and her hair was wet with her own tears. A distant voice begged her to be calm: Asa, think of Caroline Lambert and how dismayed she would be at this loss of control, think of Mrs Dacre, who behaved with far more dignity under similar circumstances. But how to be calm, how not to crouch and howl, when she had seen Corday's journey to the guillotine, when she had been aware since arriving in Paris of the thousands of prisoners rattling their bars and the cemeteries in which mass graves had been filled with quicklime to hide the headless bodies of countless people like herself, who had been alive yesterday, last week, last month, and believed themselves to be innocent of any crime?

Perhaps Didier would come. Surely Didier must have been unaware of the danger she was in or he would not have let this happen. He'd probably been sent out of the city again. Or perhaps he had reasoned that there could be no point in acknowledging her, if she was accused of conspiring with Charlotte Corday. Much better to disassociate himself, to save his own skin, and that of his father and sister in Caen. Then Asa thought of an even more terrible prospect: if Madame had betrayed Asa to the authorities, she had probably named Didier too.

You fool, Asa. To pitch yourself against Madame and the Revolution; to be so vain as to think you could change anything.

In the minutes of calm, Asa thought of the yard at Ardleigh, Mrs Dean at the pump, her father stepping up to the mounting block and riding off under the crooked arch over the entrance to the stable-yard. Of Caroline Lambert in the nursery at Morton Hall, her long arms embracing the little boys, her heart grieving for her dear father, and those lovely hours she and Asa had spent together in the cottage parlour at Littlehampton. Of the bewildered Mortons reliving again and again those weeks in Paris when Asa had seemed so buoyant and safe under their care. Of the Warrens disappearing into the morning mist. Of Shackleford's eyes, which betrayed his love every time he caught sight of her; eyes the colour of tender, familiar things, fresh-made tea, an autumn leaf, amber.

Her own words haunted her, that dismissive letter home. When they heard about what had happened now, what would they say?

Gradually, with the dawn, Asa became conscious of her surroundings. Above the dirty mattress was a square of window, too high to reach. Gradually she grew calmer. You still have choices, Asa, she thought. You can do this well or badly. Be courageous. Remember Mr Lambert. At least make it difficult for them by showing that you are not afraid of justice.

A few hours later the door to Asa's cell was unlocked – in a moment of wild hope she thought Didier had come – but it was only two women, prisoners, judging by their dull eyes and motley clothes, bringing her a gift of bread.

'You must keep up your strength, dear. Try to stop crying. We heard you in the night. You never know, it might all come right. Later they'll let us go down to the courtyard for a breath of air.

That'll do you good.' So there *was* to be a later, a morning and perhaps an afternoon. 'Tell, us, lovey, what are they accusing you of?'

'Of being English, using a false name, of being in Caen where I met Charlotte Corday.'

They frowned, shook their heads and had no further words of reassurance. One, who ran a grocery business, was accused of hoarding honey; the other had made a couple of gowns for Madame Roland, who'd recently been arrested for her Girondin sympathies and for the fact that her husband, formerly a minister, had fallen out of favour. 'Although Madame Roland, I might add,' the dressmaker said with a rueful smile, 'certainly had ideas of her own which irked the powers that be no end.' Her voice was soft and sibilant and when she moved Asa smelt the faintest whiff of perfume.

Later, in the courtyard, they briefly exchanged the reek and chill of ancient stone for the sweet air of summer. However, as they passed a doorway, the foul smells of the prison reached out to them. Asa was supported on either side by her new friends. 'They say La Force is haunted,' said the dressmaker. 'Not surprising, given it's one of the most notorious prisons in Paris.'

'No wonder you cried out in the night,' whispered the grocer woman. 'So many terrible things have happened in this prison.'

'I never thought I'd see the inside of a place like this,' said the dressmaker. 'Part of me wants to laugh at what my mother would have said if she could see me now. She brought me up so carefully. And here I am in what used to be the dumping ground for prostitutes.'

'You meet all sorts in here,' said her companion. 'Ladies, whores, anything in between. Women like us – we're in between.'

'Look up at the sky. See how blue it is. Above all, don't look down,' advised the dressmaker, who was plump and pretty, with beautiful teeth and wide eyes. 'There are bloodstains on the pavement.'

'Why? What happened?'

'Have you heard of the massacres that occurred last September?' said the grocer. 'La Petite Force was a target, of course. The mob killed five priests in the main prison, behind the gates over there; then they turned on the women's prison. Ironic that the poor prostitutes they slaughtered would have been locked up for a couple of months and then released under the old regime.'

'Nothing like that will happen to us,' said the dressmaker, holding tight to Asa's hand. 'That was in the days before the Revolutionary Tribunal. Everything is more civilised now.'

'The trouble was that the queen's friend, Princesse Lamballe, was also a prisoner in La Petite Force. People say they held her down and hacked her head from her body, right here in the courtyard. Others talk of rape and lynching. Depends who you speak to,' said the grocer woman.

'That's all nonsense. They simply stuck her head on a pike, carried it to the Temple and thrust it up to the queen's window. Wasn't that cruel enough?'

The grocer woman looked offended. 'Call it nonsense if you like. That's what I heard,' and she moved away to join another group.

The dressmaker and Asa leaned against a wall with their feet in shade and their heads in the sunshine. 'I have a son,' said the dressmaker, who told Asa her name was Lucie. 'Christophe. He's three years old. Do you have a child?'

'I'm not married.'

'My husband serves with the National Guard. He's fighting on the border. I've written to him, of course. I'm praying he'll be back in time to put in a word for me. The trouble is there's no plan or timetable here. Nobody can predict what will happen next.'

'Where is your son?'

'My mother's taken him out of the city. I haven't seen him for a fortnight. When they came for me we were sitting together on the floor, building a tower of cotton reels.'

'I'm so sorry. At least I have no child to grieve for.'

'Every woman you see in this prison could tell you a similar tragedy. In here I've found that what you hope for can be narrowed to something very small. At first all I could think of was getting out. Now I just hope there will be enough time to see my boy again. My mother wrote that she would try to raise the money for the journey by next week.'

Meanwhile the other women stood about in listless groups or sat hunched, their heads buried in their arms. Asa felt the terrible weakness of her own flesh as she and Lucie set off again, parading round the yard. Women edged away from her and she heard the whispered name: *Corday*.

In Lucie's company, in the daylight, it wasn't so difficult being a prisoner after all. But in the evening, when she was locked up in her cell, Asa began shaking again and couldn't eat. The gaoler's wife brought her a cup of water mixed with wine and patted her shoulder. 'You're a good girl, I can see that, won't give me no trouble. Nobody will come for you today. You're quite safe. Just rest.'

Asa's travelling case had been brought to the cell. Although her money and papers had been removed, a shift, a plain petticoat and a skirt remained. And tucked into the lining, perhaps because nobody thought that it had any value, indeed might be considered seditious, was Madame's fan. Asa spread her petticoat on the dirty pallet and lay down.

Even in that dirty light, when she flicked open the fan she could make out the shape of the birds and the occasional glint of gold on a guard stick. This was, as Madame had said, a fan within a fan and it was quite clear that the artist who had painted the dashing carriage amid a riot of summer flowers was different to the one who had made meticulous but somewhat stiff representations of an urn and exotic birds.

The air in the cell stirred softly. A change had occurred in the last few hours. For the first time since arriving in Paris, Asa felt a sense of connection.

Chapter Eight

The next afternoon Asa's name was called and she was told that she was to be questioned prior to trial.

'But I need a lawyer.'

'It's quite all right,' said the gaoler's wife, twitching the creases out of Asa's skirts as if she were a little girl and urging her towards the door, 'don't you go getting agitated. You won't have to face the entire tribunal in the first instance. There'll just be a committee of interrogation.'

'I'm English. What if I don't understand what's going on?'

'Stay calm, that's the trick. If all goes well you may find yourself walking free within half an hour or so. Some people strike lucky. The very worst that can happen is that you'll be snug in your cell again by this evening because they've decided not to release you just yet. I'll keep a bit of supper back in case.'

'But what shall I say?'

'Be honest but say as little as possible, that's the advice I give all my ladies. They will want a confession and they will want names. Admit to what you can, protect those you must. You'll do well. We've all been saying you talk French like a native. All you need to do is put on that nice little cap and off we go.'

Asa was led downstairs and across the courtyard, where the other women fell back to let her through. Lucie, who was standing by the wall where they had talked yesterday, raised her hand and waved, a gesture of comradeship. The guards unlocked a set of gates and marched Asa along yet another dark passage to a half-open door, behind which was a medium-sized room with barred windows. Sunlight pooled in a chequerboard pattern on the floor and at one end was a table covered by a blue cloth. There was a reassuring smell of polish and ink; clean, familiar smells.

She was ushered to a chair facing a couple of men seated on the other side of the table. More people were ranged on benches. And then Asa was on her feet again, with a yelp of recognition because, yes, there in the corner facing her, leaning casually against the wall, arms folded as if he'd just happened to drop by, was Didier. In the moment that she caught sight of him he glanced up at her, then away. Oh God. Thank God. The relief was too much, it threatened to engulf her. Surely this was all just a formality, if Didier was here? In a minute she'd be in a cab, pleading with him that he should intervene on Lucie's behalf too.

But now that she looked at him again she noticed that he was pale, with red-rimmed eyes. In a rush of anxiety she thought: What is he doing here? Has he come voluntarily, or is he a prisoner too? What has he told them?

'Is your name Thomasina Ardleigh?' asked the chairman, who had been watching her with soulful brown eyes.

She turned to Didier but his gaze was fixed on the back of the chairman's head.

'That's not usually too difficult a question to answer,' observed the chairman.

'The name on my papers is Julie Moreau.'

He nodded patiently. 'Julie Moreau. Yes, we have indeed studied your papers, but we'll come to them later. All we want now is confirmation of your name.' His cravat was tied rakishly and he and his colleague wore identical brown hats like inverted half-moons with feathers. 'Answer,' he barked.

'Yes. My name is Thomasina Ardleigh.'

'Prisoner Ardleigh, it is said that you are an English woman who arrived in France disguised as a French servant, using the name Julie Moreau. You then visited Caen, where you held conversations with Charlotte Corday, and conspired in the plot to murder our great statesman, Marat. Are you innocent or guilty?'

She heard Didier sigh as if to say, this is all very dull. If only she'd had time to discuss with him what she was supposed to say. How long before he intervened?

'I am innocent of everything except of being English,' she said.

'You did not forge your papers and your identity, then?'

'Not forge, exactly. It's true I used a different name. It was not easy to cross the Channel because of the war. I thought that if I used my own name I would be arrested the instant I arrived in France.'

'So you admit to using a false name and false

papers.' The chairman drummed his meaty fingers. 'This is a busy tribunal. If we could get to the truth the first time round, prisoner, it would save us all a great deal of time. So, you had yourself smuggled into France – we won't trouble ourselves with the details of that little achievement just now – and next you visited Caen. Why?'

'To see a friend.'

'Named?'

If only Didier would speak. How much did they know about her connection with him?

'I would rather not say.'

'There's no point in hiding from us. We have plenty of agents in Caen. Since the murder of Marat there has been a great deal of interest in that town, as you can imagine. We'll have the information in no time.'

'I have nothing to hide. But I don't wish to implicate anyone else by naming them at this stage.' She tried to catch Didier's eye but still he would not look at her.

'Did you have any conversations with Charlotte Corday?'

'Yes. I knew Charlotte Corday. I happened to meet her. Caen is not a huge place.'

The chairman settled back in his chair and folded his hands on his belly. 'Now why don't you tell us more about the time you spent in Caen? We'd all like to hear about it.' He grinned at his colleagues and glanced up at Didier. The clerk to Asa's left leaned forward, pen poised. Didier was looking at the floor and there was a sheen of sweat on his forehead.

'As I said, I stayed with a friend there. I had

intended to come to Paris earlier but I was ill and ran out of money, so my stay was prolonged. I happened to meet Charlotte Corday from time to time, in fact I drank coffee with her and went for a walk, but what we talked about was mostly the past and I knew nothing of her plans. In any case, do you really think she would have shared them with an English woman?'

'We know that you arrived in Paris in a diligence two days before Corday. We have witnesses who shared a compartment with you and they tell us that you said very little, except to complain about the way things were in France.'

'I did nothing of the kind.'

'You said that people were hungry. *I've heard that the harvest is likely to fail again*, were your exact words, I believe. You talked about bread shortages. That suggests criticism of our National Convention. Our witnesses said you were hostile to the idea that the Revolution might have caused people to prosper.'

'I hardly exchanged a word with those people...'

'Yet they remember you extremely well. They thought it very odd that you were travelling alone, and they noticed that nobody came to meet you when the diligence arrived in the city. Do you still deny that you were a co-conspirator with Corday?'

'Of course I do.'

'Very well. We have another witness who might nudge your memory a little. Could Citoyenne Annette Maurice step forward?'

'Nobody told me you would be producing witnesses,' cried Asa. 'I'm not prepared.' She cast a frantic glance at Didier, who was watching Madame Maurice. The pair exchanged the briefest of nods – of course, she was a family friend and Didier would remember her from Caen.

'Why do you need any preparation if you're going to tell the truth?' demanded the chairman. 'You will have an opportunity to question this witness later. Citoyenne Maurice, thank you so much for taking the time to come here. We won't detain you for long. Here is your tenant, Prisoner Ardleigh. How did she come to be lodged in your house?'

'She brought a letter of recommendation from Professor Paulin's daughter – an acquaintance of my late husband, in Caen.'

'The court has that letter. Here it is, let's take a closer look,' said the interrogator. 'It's signed *Beatrice Paulin.*'

'Beatrice is just a friend. She had nothing to do with any of this,' Asa cried out. It seemed certain now that Didier must be accused too, yet he stood against the wall, near the door, as if he could walk through it if he chose.

'As I've said, your time will come, Prisoner Ardleigh. Now, *citoyenne*, apart from using a false name and showing you forged papers, is there anything else the prisoner did during her stay with you that aroused your suspicions?'

Madame Maurice, dressed in a clean blue gown and visibly trembling, fixed her small eyes on the face of the second interrogator, who was smiling at her kindly. Her hands were clenched together and there were dark patches under her arms. 'She showed me a map and asked me to

458

mark certain places on it: the Temple Prison, the Bastille, another prison called St-Joseph – Les Carmes.'

'Anything else?'

'She would not come with me to see Marat's body. She seemed very agitated and walked away. Yet when it came to Corday's execution, she was out all day.'

'That's all we wanted to know. Now, prisoner, it's your turn.'

Part of Asa's mind had disconnected itself in protest at the absurdity of these proceedings. How was she supposed to manage if she didn't know the rules? When would Didier speak up for her? It was all happening too fast.

'Citoyenne Maurice, about the letter of recommendation. I admit that we did not tell you I was English.'

Madame Maurice's eyes were snapping with resentment. 'I would not have taken you in if I'd known from the start you were lying to me.'

'I wanted to protect you. Don't you see? Look what's happened to me, now that everyone knows I'm English.'

'I'm surprised at Beatrice Paulin, that she would deceive me. I can only assume you forced her to write such a letter.'

'I apologise. And I'm truly sorry that I've put you to so much trouble. But don't you see, Beatrice had to conceal the fact that I am English?'

'I don't see why,' drawled the chairman. 'As far as I recall, it is not a crime to be a foreigner in Paris. It is a crime, however, to pervert the course of justice.'

Didier, if possible, was paler still and his brow was furrowed with concentration. What has he told them? Who is he trying to save? thought Asa.

'Very well, Citoyenne Maurice,' said the interrogator, 'you are free to go. And now perhaps you'd like to explain, Prisoner Ardleigh, what you were doing wandering about Paris with a map, if not to conspire with Corday against Marat.'

The heat was treacle-thick so that the chairman's words seemed to swirl and boom. Take your time, Asa. Find out how much they already know about your relationship with Didier. 'I came to visit a friend,' she said.

'Is this friend French or English?'

'French.'

'How did you know this French friend?'

'I was in Paris in 1788. I met him here.'

'So the friend is male. Prisoner, your country is at war with ours. If what you say is true, haven't you been foolhardy in the extreme to travel to France in secret, in pursuit of a male you met five years ago? This is not how we in France would expect a virtuous girl to behave. I almost think my colleague and I should find you guilty of stupidity or immorality, more likely both.'

Obliging chuckles around the room.

'Put like that, it does sound very foolish,' said Asa, 'but then I had no reason to fear France. I love France. When I was a child I used to stare across the sea and wish to be in France. I rejoiced when the Revolution came. In England, I am a member of an Abolition Society. The aims of the Revolution reflect my own ideals perfectly.'

'There are presumably other people in England

who sympathise with the Revolution but who do not disguise themselves as a French farmer's daughter and who do not travel in a diligence from Caen a couple of days before Charlotte Corday. You have given no plausible explanation as to why you took such a risk in the first place.'

Pause. 'I thought it was for love.'

'You *thought*, prisoner?'

'How can one tell, after five years?'

'And you will not give us the name of your lover.' Silence. 'Perhaps we can offer you a little assistance. Look about you. Who do you see?'

To her left was the secretary, who seemed to have abandoned the task of making a record and was picking dirt from his fingernails. To her right a pair of guards slouched by the door. Behind her the other observers were muttering to each other. And by the door, smiling faintly as if amused but a little frustrated by the proceedings, Didier.

'In a moment,' said the chairman, 'we shall ask Deputy Paulin a few questions. In the meantime, now that you know that we are aware of your connection with him, let's just clear up a few things. Prisoner Ardleigh, did you go to Caen in order to visit this man's family?'

Didier nodded at her.

'Yes.'

'And is this the man for whom you risked a journey to Paris?'

'Yes.'

'You see Deputy Paulin, as one would expect from someone in his position, has been completely frank with us, and told us all about what you were both doing on the night Marat was murdered.'

'Then he knows I am innocent. Could we not have established that long ago?'

'*He knows you are innocent.* Does he indeed? Deputy Paulin, if I might trouble you to step forward? As I promised you earlier, this won't take very long.'

When Didier approached the table he did so with an air of disinterested professionalism. Asa had never seen him at work, but it must have been clear to everyone that this was familiar territory to him as he stood with feet apart, grasping his elbows, listening attentively to each question.

'Deputy Paulin, do you know this woman?'

'She is Thomasina Ardleigh of England.' His voice was calm and clipped.

'When did you first meet?'

'Here, in Paris, five years ago.'

'And what was the nature of your relationship?'

'We were lovers.' There was muttering in the benches beside her and the chairman's brow lifted.

'What happened as a result of your relationship?'

'Nothing happened. We were separated because the prisoner had to go back to England. For a time we wrote to each other. Then, when our two countries declared war, I put a stop to the correspondence.'

'Why, exactly?'

'As there was no prospect of our meeting, it seemed to me that there was a conflict of loyalties if the correspondence continued.'

'So when did you meet her again?'

'A week or so ago. On 11 July, I glimpsed her at

462

the Convention. Then two days later she came to my apartment.'

'The purpose of her visit?'

'To see me.'

'Tell me again when you last met.'

'As I've said, five years ago. July 1788.'

'And you say you last wrote to her about two years ago.'

'About that.'

'She must have given some reason for arriving so suddenly in Paris?'

'She said she had received letters from me begging her to come.'

'Had you sent any such letters?'

He gazed straight ahead. 'I had not. But...'

'So, let's be clear. You had not written to Prisoner Ardleigh inviting her to come to Paris.'

Asa realised, as she stared at Didier, that his version of the story was already well known; the interchange between him and the interrogator was so measured they must have rehearsed it beforehand.

'You're not asking him the right questions,' she interrupted. 'You're making him twist the truth. They were *his* letters, in *his* hand, that was the point.'

'In good time, prisoner, you may ask your own questions. For now, please be quiet. Deputy Paulin, where were you on the evening of Marat's murder?'

'In my apartment with Citoyenne Ardleigh.'

'And during the course of that day, and the day before?'

'I had business out of the city.'

463

'You cannot vouch for Prisoner Ardleigh during that time?'

'No.'

'Did she tell you where she'd been that day?'

'She said she'd been exploring the city – as I would expect of a visitor to Paris. She'd not been here for five years so she was curious.' For the first time Didier smiled at Asa.

'Did she tell you her route through the city?'

'Not precisely.'

'What does that mean? You of all people will know, Deputy Paulin, that such vague answers simply will not do.'

'She said she went to our old haunts, the district of St-Germain.'

'Anywhere else?'

'I don't know.'

'And when she was in Caen? Do you know what activities she'd been engaged in, while the town was in a state of civil unrest?'

'I do not.'

'You know that she stayed with your sister.'

'Because she says so, and because of my sister's letter to Citoyenne Maurice. My sister was also in Paris five years ago, so she and Citoyenne Ardleigh had become friends.'

'The prisoner Ardleigh declares that she knew nothing of Charlotte Corday's plans. The reason she gives for travelling under a false name and with false papers is that she wanted to find you. Can you suggest why she would not come to you openly?'

'As she said, she is English...'

'You are concerned with police matters in Paris,

464

Paulin. Perhaps you can answer this question: Is it a crime to be English?'

'Our two countries are at war.'

'I repeat, is it a crime to be English?'

'No.'

'As you aware, Paulin, on the day before the murder of Marat, Prisoner Ardleigh went walking close to his house. This map, found at her lodgings, is marked with crosses, some of them supplied by her landlady, Maurice. The prisoner had asked to be shown certain locations in the city. It is known, therefore, that she walked first to the Temple Prison, then across the river to the Luxembourg, thereby passing along the end of the rue des Cordeliers where, as we all know, Marat lived and was subsequently assassinated.'

Didier was breathing more rapidly. He wiped a dribble of sweat from the side of his face.

'Didier,' said Asa, 'tell them why I wanted to visit St-Joseph's and the street where you used to live.'

Didier stared at the interrogator but did not speak.

'I believe you received a note from the prisoner, Deputy Paulin, a couple of nights after Marat's death. Is this it? I'll read part of it aloud. *You of all people will know that I need to get out of the city.* Can you explain the note?'

'I must admit I was very surprised when I received it. It was quite unlike her, to be so irrational.'

'Didier, you told me yourself...'

'It is indeed your turn for questions, prisoner. Is there anything else you want to say to Deputy

465

Paulin before we allow him to return to his work?

'I sent him the note because I was waiting to hear from him. He'd promised to help me.'

'Is this true?'

'Certainly I thought she should go home.'

'Didier, tell them I didn't know anything about Charlotte's plans. Nor did Beatrice. Tell them why I came to France.'

Didier shook his head, smiled at the interrogator, took a deep breath and raised his shoulders as if to say: This is really beyond me, I don't understand it. The chairman said softly: 'Much better if you don't tell the witness what to say, prisoner. Much better to ask a simple question and let him answer.'

'Didier. Tell the court how I came by those letters from you.'

She sensed that the bond between the interrogator and Didier was under strain. It wasn't clear now how sympathetic he was to Didier. 'Answer the question, Paulin.'

'I can't say for certain how the prisoner got hold of them. I had certainly written them – not to her but to another woman.'

'So let's take a look at these letters, shall we?' The interrogator withdrew them from his folder. 'Any fool could see these are not recent. Look at the age of the paper. So on the basis of these letters, which bear no address and are unsigned, you are expecting us to believe, Prisoner Ardleigh, that you returned to France to seek out Citoyen Paulin. Please credit us with a little intelligence.'

Asa stared at Didier. 'I wanted to see him, of course I did. I thought he still loved me.'

'Did you indeed? You seem to have let our prisoner down, Paulin.' General laughter.

'Now what else did you wish to ask, prisoner?'

'Didier, I told you the reason I went walking in Paris – it was because I wanted to see for myself where a certain priest had been killed. That is why I went to Joseph des Carmes.'

A deathly hush. In that moment, Asa understood, the revelation like a drumbeat in her stomach, that she had committed the heinous crime of exposing one of the darker secrets of the Revolution's past, and had therefore perhaps sealed her fate.

'Is this true, Paulin?'

'It is.'

'Here is the map,' said the interrogator, pointing with his manicured fingernail. 'Here is Marat's house. Here is Les Carmes. Ten minutes apart. To reach Les Carmes she must have walked past the end of Marat's street. The prisoner was marking out the territory for Corday.'

Didier laughed. 'Oh, come, come. That is pure speculation.'

'Anything else to ask Citoyen Paulin?' the interrogator enquired of Asa.

'I can't think. I must be given time. This is all so absurd. Didier, just tell them, please, how I was tricked into coming to France.'

'Tricked, now, is it? I think we've been over that point quite often enough. Thank you so much for your time, Deputy Paulin.'

'Didier.' He was already at the door; his back was turned so that she could see only his neatly tied hair and trim shoulders. *'Didier.'*

They took Asa by the shoulders, forced her into a chair and waited until she was quiet. She strained to hear his retreating footsteps and the distant closing of a door. 'Now we have established that Deputy Paulin was the object of your affection – your devotion gives you credit, prisoner, given that it seems you and he had been parted for five years – we simply have to clear up the small matter of your acquaintance with Corday.'

'I have told you...'

'Were you or were you not in the vicinity of Marat's home on the morning of 12 July?'

'Not intentionally. Please tell Didier Paulin to come back. I want to ask him some more questions.'

'Deputy Paulin is a very busy man, prisoner. We have detained him long enough, don't you think, given that he was clearly bewildered by your sudden arrival in Paris. The truth is that you have told us a pack of lies. How could it possibly be coincidence that you arrived in Paris at the same time as Corday? Under interrogation she...'

'I'm sure she made no mention of my name. She certainly won't have known that I was in Paris.'

'How can you be sure?'

Asa, recognising the trap, spoke more calmly. 'She didn't know my plans.'

'You said Corday *certainly* wasn't aware that you were in Paris.' The interrogator leaned forward, a gleam in his eye. 'That sounded very clear.'

'She, like almost everyone else I knew in Caen, thought that I was on my way to Le Havre when

468

I left the city.'

'Why would they think such a thing?'

'It was where I was supposed to go. There's an English community there. It was thought I would be safe with them, but I changed my mind.'

'You changed your mind? Your plans seem to have been very fluid. You changed your mind, and instead you came to Paris two days ahead of Charlotte Corday.'

'That's not what I meant.'

'You seem very confident about contradicting us, Prisoner Ardleigh. Perhaps, when you are transferred to the Conciergerie, you will be less sure of yourself. If I might be allowed to continue with my earlier comment?' He raised a brow, as if Asa had a choice. His companion laughed again. 'Under interrogation Corday refused to identify any of her co-conspirators. Perhaps you can help us out. We will try naming a few people with whom we think you might have been in collusion. What do you know of Barbaroux?'

'I heard his name mentioned while I was in Caen. That's all.'

'Brissot?'

'The same. Even in England I had heard of Brissot and his role in the Revolution. You see, I favour the abolition...'

'Brissot, as you know, was a sworn enemy of Marat. But we'll let that pass. You could not be bothered to pay your respects to Marat. Why was that?'

'I was there in the streets like everyone else.'

'Yet you turned out for Corday's execution.'

'I'd met her in Caen. So yes, I did go to the

469

execution. I wanted to show her that she was not quite alone in Paris at the end, though I never had the chance, of course, the crowd was too large...'

'At last. There we are. Thank you so much for your confession. Let me repeat it back to you. *I'd met her in Caen... I wanted to show her that she was not quite alone in Paris.* I think we have more than enough. You clearly do not comprehend, prisoner, that after what has happened, even to claim sympathy with Corday is treason. Tomorrow you'll be transferred to the Conciergerie for sentencing.'

'I don't understand. I was told that this was just a preliminary to trial. I haven't had a trial. I don't have a lawyer...'

'Prisoner, you had a lawyer. Didier Paulin, I would have said, is one of the greatest legal minds in our country.'

'But he was your witness.'

'That's enough. Take her away.'

'I've made no confession. Please, ask Didier to come back... Please.'

The chairs were scraped across the floor. Asa was seized and led away.

Chapter Nine

The gaoler's wife supplied Asa with a sheet of paper on which to write a letter home but it took hours to compose, given that she could not afford to waste space, had great difficulty in steadying her pen and struggled to find the right words. Terror was a physical condition, like fever. At one point she stopped writing altogether, gripped her warm neck with her cold fingers and closed her eyes.

I don't regret what I have done for my own sake so much as for yours. Forgive me the suffering I have caused. I am so sorry. But though of course I wish there had been a different ending, I cannot help but feel a sense of rightness in what has happened to me. I came back to France and found it much changed, not as I'd hoped, and yet that old word, liberty, still is not sour on my tongue. There must be a way. And you know – Oh God, I wish I'd told you – there was a man I loved. He was the reason, yet I think I knew, from the moment I set out, that he might be false, or at least be proved different to what I'd hoped. Forgive me, please. I fell in love. But I am still your Asa. And I have been very wrong, and rash and thoughtless, then and now. It must seem to you that I didn't consider you but instead abused the freedom of mind and body that you gave me. I beg you to see it differently – I have come to grief, but truly I have felt alive.

Her last note, written cross-wise after a further hour of deliberation, was a postscript regarding the Shacklefords.

Give Susan my love. Wish her well. I'm sorry I couldn't have known her better. And Mr Shackleford, likewise. I regard him as very dear, please tell him.

When it was done she held the letter in her lap, as if her own words might somehow save her. It was one thing to convey a portrait of resignation for the comfort of her family, quite another, once alone in the dark, not to feel searing, gut-wrenching outrage. Why hadn't Didier spoken up for her? Why had he not thrown up his hands and cried: Thomasina is innocent. Instead, when the door had closed behind him, it was as if Madame had snapped shut her capacious portmanteau for the last time.

Perhaps there was still hope. Perhaps even now Didier was rallying his arguments or visiting influential friends on her behalf. But hope, she decided, was a tricky bedfellow. She understood that she had been a sore inconvenience to him and suspected that already, back in his apartment, he would be engaged in a thorough washing of hands.

The next day Asa was transferred to the Conciergerie. During the short ride in a closed carriage she glimpsed only dull spurts of colour – dark grey cobbles, an occluded sky, the dirty jackets of the coachmen. Occasionally some passer-by would thump the side of the carriage.

The journey was shared with Lucie, the dressmaker, who occasionally touched her hand for consolation, although her eyes were closed, perhaps in prayer. Asa would much rather have been alone. To endure her own fate was bad enough; to witness the suffering of another innocent woman intolerable.

But this was all that was left of the world, and these last sensations would have to be savoured – a wheel bouncing on a stone and the smell of horses; the familiar, leathery reek that made Asa ache with longing for the stable-yard at Ardleigh. At one point Lucie opened her eyes and they managed to exchange a smile. Easier to appear calm in the carriage, much less so when they were bundled up narrow steps and into the Conciergerie, where they were pushed through one crowded space to the next until they came to a cell occupied by half a dozen other women.

Asa could barely remember her name. 'Asa. Julie. Thomasina. I was interrogated about my name until I can't remember who I am.'

Nobody was much interested, although one or two wanted to know whether it was true that she was the English woman who'd been part of the plot to kill Marat. Don't dare give in here, she told herself. You show them how an English woman, an abolitionist with revolutionary sympathies, can behave. So she sat very still with her back to the wall and her hands folded, as Madame might have done. The other women wandered about in the passageways or elbowed their way outside to a courtyard, where they stood in tired groups or queued to wash undergarments at a little fountain.

When they gathered once more in their cell it was like a travesty of a tea party; an assembly of women in dirty gowns with weary faces and dull hair. Some told crude jokes, reminisced or recounted the story over and over of how they had been unjustly denounced; others were numb. A woman hunched in a corner was yelping from the pain in her abdomen. When Asa sat beside her and offered to rub her back she began to talk about the old days before she and her husband, a successful timber merchant, had been discredited by a long-term debtor turned government agent. She was a delicate soul with round eyes and a swollen belly, bewildered by the violent change of fortune that had brought her within a few days from a dainty turquoise drawing room to a stinking cell in the Conciergerie.

Once the door was locked for the night Asa and Lucie undressed to their shifts and made a nest of their skirts. The other women were restless as they settled to sleep, clearing their throats, cursing, exuding the appalling stench of cooped-up lives. Asa knew that beyond these four walls were countless other such chambers. The scent of Lucie's hair was the only counterweight to the sound of a woman vomiting into a pail, to the ooze of reeking sludge, to the knowledge that this was probably the last night of all.

'So, it doesn't look as if I shall see my little boy again,' Lucie whispered. 'The gaoler's wife back at the other place told me she thought I didn't have much chance. But it seems so unfair – just because Madame Roland is a Girondin. I made two dresses for her. That's all.'

'Your husband will be back soon. They'll listen to him, if he's in the militia. Is he a good man?'

'Not so bad. A bit jealous; a bit full of himself Not really cut out to be a soldier but he's keen to do the right thing. He'll be horrified that I've been arrested, not because he'll think it's unjust but because someone in our family should have disgraced themselves by stepping out of line.'

Lucie fell silent for a moment and there was just the eerie mutter of women half asleep in the incalculable dark. Asa's thoughts clawed for a way out; again and again she dragged them back into line. There was no hope. She was condemned on two incontrovertible counts: she had alluded to a forbidden topic, the massacre of priests, and above all she had expressed sympathy for Corday.

'What would you do if they said you had one more day left and they would allow you to spend it exactly where and how you wanted?' whispered Lucie. 'It's easy for me. I'd just want to be with Christophe. I would have an ordinary day, nothing special. I'd lift him out of his bed in the morning, and kiss his little neck and smooth the tangles from his hair. I'd feed him his bread and milk and perhaps walk with him in the sunshine, tuck him up in the afternoon and watch him sleep. And then I'd want them to take me quickly, while I was still smiling, so that's how he'd remember me, not in tears, like I was when they came for me.'

'I think I'd also choose a sunny day, in spring,' Asa replied. 'I'd walk by the sea with my friend Caroline and we'd pause to watch the waves. And I'd really pay attention to each one. I'd follow the line of a breaker, lose myself in a bit of froth until every last bubble was gone or it had disappeared under the next wave. And then we'd go back to Caroline's cottage. The fire would be lit, and we would sprawl in our chairs with our skirts pulled up to our knees, and we'd hear the fall of a log and the rustle of a page and we wouldn't say a word. And in the evening I'd go home and eat dinner with my father and we'd argue because I would be wanting him to attend to something on the estate and he'd make an excuse about having neither the money nor the time, and then I'd stomp up to my bedroom, and press my forehead to the windowpane, and wish for a different life.'

'There is no man, then, apart from your father?'

When no reply was forthcoming, Lucie sighed, tucked her head into Asa's lap, and seemed to fall asleep.

A lantern flickered on the far side of the cell, but darkness encroached, like the wing of a great bat. A woman was screaming and others yelled out for her to be quiet.

Asa drew a long breath of foul air and thought again of that parlour in Littlehampton, and of Mr Lambert resting his head in his old hand and talking about eternity. All I know for sure, thought Asa, is that darkness will come swiftly. Or perhaps, on the other side, there will be light. And all the dead people – Corday, Mr Lambert, even my mother – will be waiting. She tried to concentrate on small things: the tapestry cushion on her parlour chair with its design of coral-coloured roses and the mis-stitch in one of the petals, a violet in the hedgerow above Ardleigh wagging on its hair-

476

like stem; the creak of a board as her father climbed the stairs to bed, a worn leather chair, empty, and a Mozart minuet.

She prayed that the last journey would be quick and dignified, and that her tongue would not unlatch and beg for mercy.

Chapter Ten

With the daylight came a deceptive degree of normality. It couldn't be true that any of these women washing their faces at the crowded fountain would be dead by nightfall. Lucie managed to dress impeccably in a copper-coloured gown and a snowy-white scarf. Her hair was loose and glossy and as she moved there was still a whiff of fragrance. When her name was called, in the first batch of the day, she and Asa embraced as if they had been lifelong friends, and then Lucie was led away.

So, a couple of hours left, at most. Asa sought out a wardress she had noticed the previous night; elderly, with crumpled skin and an air of competence that might have suited a cook or gardener. 'I want you to do something for me, *citoyenne*,' she said. Her voice was soft and reasonable, scarcely a sign of dread. 'Take this fan and preserve it for me. It was given to me by a friend and is very precious. I should hate to see it destroyed or broken.'

'I don't take bribes.'

'It's not a bribe. It's a gift. It may not be worth much money any more, but it is beautiful, don't you think? It's called a cabriolet fan, and is very rare. The leaf is pure gold.'

'Take care, prisoner, I report all exchanges such as the one you're attempting to the tribunal and this conversation, were it known, would be enough to sign your death warrant.'

'There is nothing anyone can do for me. I am bound to die. They have associated me with Charlotte Corday.'

'Then what do you want? Nobody would give me such a thing for no reason.' Yet she was clearly entranced by the colours, and no wonder. In this place, where colour meant every shade of grey, Madame's soft turquoises, blues and golds bloomed.

'What I want is time, for the dressmaker Lucie, who's just been called to trial today.'

'Who do you think I am? Isn't time what everyone wants? You'll be asking for the key next.' Her hard gaze roamed across the fan and her finger stretched out and caressed the glinting enamel.

'All she wants is time to see her son.'

'Out of the question.'

'I'm sorry you can't help. But I still want you to have the fan.' Asa flicked it shut, pressed it into the woman's hand and moved away.

'I suppose I could have a word. I might be able to put off her execution for a day or so.'

'It must be a week, at least.'

The wardress stared at Asa. 'You say you are the friend of Charlotte Corday.'

'I knew her.'

'And what is your connection with this dressmaker woman?'

'Just that. A connection.'

'Well, I must say, I admire your nerve. Get along with you. I'm making no promises.'

At midday Asa's name was called and she was marched away through files of prisoners. Besieged by panic, her consciousness split in two and she had an exalted vision of herself stepping from the hired carriage, slipping her hand on to John Morton's arm, treading a marble floor to enter a room filled with sparkling light. And in a parallel world, here was another Thomasina Ardleigh, thrust into a courtroom which echoed like a cavern, with a momentous Gothic ceiling. She caught sight of a copper skirt whisking through a far door. What had been the verdict on the dressmaker?

The grandeur of the hall was diminished by makeshift tiers of seating backed by wooden panels upon which spectators were ranked as if at a theatre. Nobody took much interest in this new prisoner and the room was noisy with muttered conversation. The gallery was a blur of assorted reds and blues, grubby white caps, dark hats, gossiping mouths.

Of the five judges, the most senior was round faced and ponderous with huge hands. A jury of twelve men lounged on benches. Asa was told to sit facing the dais but said she preferred to stand; if she gripped the chair-back they would not see that her knees were shaking. By now she felt calm, exactly as she had when she used to bathe in cold water with Georgina; there was always a moment between anticipation and the final plunge when the body was absolutely committed and the mind was clear.

'Prisoner Ardleigh, you are an English woman charged with travelling under a false passport and in disguise, and of conspiring with Charlotte Corday to murder Marat. How do you plead?'

'I am innocent of...' Her voice was frail in the massive room. She was altogether too insignificant for this moment.

'Do you admit that you were smuggled into France under a false passport?'

'I had no...'

'You said that you spent the day prior to Marat's assassination walking up and down his street, in order to get the lie of the land.'

'That's *not* what I said. It's true I walked past the end of his street. By chance.'

'Under interrogation you admitted that you had remained in Paris following Marat's assassination, for the sake of Charlotte Corday. Do you now deny that?'

'That's not what I...'

'Citizens of the jury, here, briefly, are the facts: Prisoner Ardleigh admits to having arrived in France illicitly, to having met Corday while in Caen and to travelling to Paris in advance of Corday by two days. She admits to visiting her former lover, Deputy Didier Paulin, in his apartment in order to discuss politics with him and thereby discover more about Marat's likely movements. Can you therefore doubt that she is a spy, sent from England in order to conspire...?'

'What you are hearing is a distortion of the facts,' Asa cried. 'It's true I met both Corday and my former lover Didier. But it's a matter of pure coincidence that it happened to be shortly before Corday decided to kill Marat.'

'Ah, but prisoner, at the very least you admit to meeting Corday. It's quite clear that you made no attempt to dissuade her from her wicked intent.'

'How could I when she didn't confide in me?'

'Perhaps you were her inspiration, you an English woman...'

'We walked about Caen, that's all. We discussed her childhood.'

'Look at it from our point of view,' said the judge, perhaps a little irritated with himself for engaging in argument with her, 'and ask yourself how we can possibly be expected to believe so many coincidences. To continue; next thing we know, having met Corday, you come to Paris two days ahead of her. What I say to the jury is: can you doubt that this woman used her relationship with Deputy Paulin in order to track the movements of our beloved Marat? We have wasted enough time on this English woman. Gentlemen of the jury, do you find her...'

The jury was already conferring. An elderly, thin-lipped man, having muttered a word or two to his companions, threw back his head and yawned luxuriantly. Asa stared at the bobbing feather in the judge's hat.

'With respect, citizen,' came a cool voice from behind Asa, 'you have not listened to Prisoner Ardleigh's defence.'

It took a while for this crisp intervention to register in the more distant corners of the gallery, but eventually the courtroom fell silent. The judge removed his hat and mopped his brow:

481

'Deputy Paulin, I believe you were given every opportunity to speak yesterday. Do you have anything further to say?'

'I do.' Didier's tone was wry, as if he were a little amused by the proceedings. Asa did not turn her head. 'For the sake of France and the reputation of our great nation, I demand that this woman be given a fair trial. Yesterday, when I was brought to her interrogation, I'd had no time to assemble my evidence. I said, therefore, only what was necessary. Now I have to tell you that you are basing your case against Thomasina Ardleigh on entirely false assumptions.'

The audience in the gallery leaned forward as Didier walked briskly to Asa's side. Gone was yesterday's lacklustre delivery, the avoidance of her eye. Today he was dressed in a neat dark blue coat and a laundered cravat tied with jaunty finesse and he actually reached for her hand, pressed it in both of his and gave her a loving glance. None of this was lost on the spectators, who clapped and cheered.

'Yesterday I understand you gave unequivocal evidence against this woman, Citoyen Paulin.'

'I beg to differ. The evidence I gave was little more than the information that I had entertained the prisoner to supper in my rooms.' The crowd moaned with salacious pleasure. 'I was not asked crucial questions about Thomasina Ardleigh's reasons for coming to France.'

'Yet you could have volunteered an explanation, I believe, citizen, you needn't have waited to be asked.'

'Yesterday's interrogation concerned itself with

one question only: the prisoner's connection to Corday. The evidence I shall give you today will show that the prisoner was not concerned with Corday at all. To accuse her of conspiring in Marat's death will be utterly absurd in the light of what I have to say. It would be like accusing a vole of slaughter simply because it had passed through the same forest as a ravening wolf. Yesterday, we were not even told who had denounced Prisoner Ardleigh. There were two possibilities, I realised. The first was her landlady, Citoyenne Maurice, who had every reason to be frightened of harbouring a mysterious visitor from Caen. The second, I would suggest, is a woman called Estelle Beyle, whom I saw a few moments ago in this courtroom and who is, I confess, a former mistress of mine, and therefore the prisoner's rival in love.'

The courtroom was now deathly quiet.

'I will argue that in order to entrap her rival, Thomasina Ardleigh, Estelle Beyle concocted a fabrication so clever and intricate that we have all been seduced by it. I will further argue that the only crime of which the prisoner is guilty is that of misfortune: she happened to be in Caen a few days before Marat's death, and to become loosely acquainted with Corday. That is all.'

'Ah, but in my experience,' said the judge, linking his fingers and twirling his thumbs, 'there are no such things, in our modern France, as coincidence or misfortune. If a citizen is virtuous, she has nothing to fear. People come to grief solely because they have done wrong.'

'Well, perhaps the prisoner is guilty of being a

little too ardent, too rash. Though you can't expect me to agree with that, since every action she took was for my sake.' Didier flashed a self-deprecating smile at the gallery. 'But surely, in the name of the Revolution we must halt these proceedings. We cannot have a woman condemned simply for being ardent.'

The judge folded his arms, resigned, while the spectators in the galleries roared their approval and leaned forward in delighted anticipation. Where was this woman, Estelle Beyle? Didier stood in a posture he must have employed in court a thousand times, right hand gripping a sheaf of papers, left pressed into the small of his back. 'Let me show you proper evidence. Far from Thomasina Ardleigh being involved in some devilish English plot – and by the way, my friends, do we really think the English capable of anything so subtle as to send a young woman across the Channel in the hope of inspiring a total stranger from Caen to commit murder?' Hoots of laughter from the spectators. '–Or coming of her own volition to conspire with Charlotte Corday, she was lured here by the very woman, Estelle Beyle, who now accuses her. Here are two letters and my mother's scarf, which I gave to Estelle years ago as love tokens. I wish to God I hadn't because Estelle kept them safe, not out of love for me – oh no – but so that she might use them against me, if necessary. And behold, the moment came when she could indeed harm me. She pretended that I had sent the letters to England, to Thomasina Ardleigh, as a sign that I needed her. Such is Thomasina's loyalty and devotion,' Didier's voice broke and his head lowered for a moment, 'that, without asking any questions, she risked everything, and came.

'But how did Estelle Beyle perform such a sleight of hand, you might ask. You see I, fearing for her sanity – she had become very ill following the death of a beloved brother – had sent her to England to keep her safe from herself. Yes, it made her an émigrée, but I thought our country would be better off without her. I was a fool to believe that if she was away from France she might come to her senses. Little did I realise that she would seek out her rival, Thomasina Ardleigh, with whom I'd fallen in love,' a clearing of the throat, 'during the summer of 1788, by working her way into the good opinion of Mademoiselle Ardleigh's family.'

'Deputy Paulin,' the judge exclaimed, 'you are merely replacing one narrative with another. How is the jury to know that you are not offering a fabrication for the sake of the prisoner, your mistress – or should I say, one of your mistresses?'

'I'm sure the jury is already ahead of me. They will know that just as we believe Charlotte Corday could not possibly have been working alone in Paris, Estelle Beyle could not have pursued her plan all by herself in England. And such, indeed, is the case. Thomasina Ardleigh's sister, who lives in London, is married to one Geoffrey Warren, a most undesirable type, a frequenter of gaming rooms and drinking dens. In his cups he was more than happy to share Ardleigh family secrets so that Estelle could insinuate herself and even be employed as a companion to Thomasina Ardleigh. Ironic, you might think, that a woman who claims to be a faithful devotee of this new France of ours should disguise herself as a servant to an English girl from an old family.

'The first package, purportedly from me, containing a letter and this handkerchief, she probably delivered herself, having used an old envelope and copied my handwriting. The second she had forwarded from London. I know this because I have a statement here from this same Geoffrey Warren, in which he admits to being blackmailed by Estelle Beyle, who was then calling herself Madame de Rusigneux.

'The identity of this Geoffrey Warren will interest you, citizens, since he is a notorious fraudster and crook, wanted both here and in England for his attempts to abuse British and French laws on the trading of slaves, thereby depriving both governments of vital revenue. Estelle Beyle must have been aware of this information, possibly even by rifling through my papers while she lived with me in Paris, and she used it to blackmail Warren.

'Here is his affidavit. And here are further testimonies; of a post boy who can swear to Warren's sending the letter from London on the night before it arrived at Ardleigh, and of others, among them respectable matrons, who knew Estelle Beyle as Madame de Rusigneux. Is this the kind of woman – one who would lie and cheat and consort with criminals – upon whose denunciation our great revolutionary tribunal would wish to rely?

'*Citoyens*, I regret to say that this entire trial is a

sham, and that my former mistress, Estelle, has deliberately accused an innocent woman. Out of love for me, the prisoner,' he shot Asa an affectionate glance, 'dared to enter France at a time when our countries are at war, because she thought I had sent for her. That is all. I swear that I am telling the truth. If necessary, I would swear it on my life.'

There was a long silence. The chairman leaned back and engaged his colleagues in a mumbled conference. Asa closed her eyes as the floor threatened to tip up and collide with her face.

'Deputy Paulin, you have shown great courage,' said the chairman. 'We might also add that your public life perhaps does you far more credit than your private. But for the time being it is up to the jury to decide on innocence or guilt, and it is a matter of who you believe, *citoyens:* Estelle Beyle, whose denunciation led to the prisoner being arrested for collaborating with Charlotte Corday, or Didier Paulin, who says that the prisoner's association with Corday was nothing more than a chance encounter. If you believe the former, you must find the prisoner guilty; if you believe Paulin, she is innocent, at least of involvement in the plot to kill Marat.'

The chair-back cut into Asa's palm and the surface of the judges' table buckled and swayed. The gallery was quiet as the jury conferred quickly, then someone cried out: 'We find the prisoner innocent.'

The crowd erupted. There were smiles, shouts, the waving of caps and fanning of faces, then a resettling for the next case. No sign of Madame, just that collection of hot faces, some already turned away to look at the door through which the next prisoner would soon enter, no dark-haired little woman in a pink dress, only a disconcerting flash of a new colour, green.

Didier took Asa by the hand. As he led her away his arm came round her waist to support her and she was conscious of how smart he must seem beside her own wan figure. People seized her hand, cheered then fell back to let her pass.

'What happened to the woman who was tried before me?' she whispered. 'Lucie. The dress-maker who was wearing a copper gown. Was she also found innocent?'

Didier was distracted by a young man who pounced on him and slapped his shoulder. They embraced, laughing. 'My God,' said Didier, 'that was a near thing.'

'The dressmaker,' Asa repeated.

'You're free. We won. We beat them. Don't worry about anyone else.'

'I want to know. What happened to her?'

'She could not have been innocent. She was a Girondin, intimate with Roland.'

'She was just a dressmaker. She made Madame Roland a couple of gowns.' There was a peculiar freedom, Asa found, in having faced death. She braced herself against the crowd that was pressing her forward. 'I have to know what happened to her. She was innocent, Didier. You cannot let her go to the guillotine.'

'What's the matter with you? There's no time. We have to get away.' He put his mouth close to her ear. 'You were cleared of only one charge –

conspiracy with Corday. Don't you realise that if they were to look again at all the lies you've told since arriving in France you would likely be arrested all over again.'

'I'm not moving until I know.'

Her eyes felt hot and hard. Didier said: 'I risked my life for you.'

She slid down against a stone pillar and perched on its base. He stared at her, then cursed and disappeared. As she waited, Asa imagined an alternative self, convicted of being an enemy of the Revolution and led to an empty room where they would hack off first her hair, then the cloth covering her neck, to free it for the guillotine's blade...

Didier seized hold of her arm.

'She was found guilty. Are you satisfied?'

'Is that all you know?'

'She's not to be executed immediately. There's been some kind of remission. One of the wardresses suspects she maybe pregnant. They'll wait a couple of weeks to know for sure. It's an old trick.'

He was shifting her towards the open door but her teeth were chattering violently and her knees refused to support her. 'Yesterday in La Petite Force I thought I would never see you again. I thought you were on their side.'

'You should have had more faith in me.' Yet another cluster of young men fell upon them, squeezed Didier's hand and flung their arms about his neck. Asa swayed against his arm. 'To leave you was unbearable for me,' he said as they walked on, 'but my instinct was to bide my time rather than protest too much at that moment. I needed to gather my evidence.'

'I was afraid you'd given up.' Her thoughts refused to knit together. She was walking free, with Didier. From time to time a tremor ran through her body, first fire then ice. What had changed since yesterday? Ah yes, Warren; testimonies from England.

They climbed the stone staircase and burst forth into the noisy heat of Paris. 'What are we to do now?' she said.

He brought his face very close to hers and kept tight hold of her elbow. 'You are to listen to every word I say. Here is the cab, thank God. The driver has very clear instructions. He is one of my men and he has been told not to let you go. Do you understand? Don't even think of getting out. Remember that there were many things they didn't ask about your trip from England and my family's friendship with Corday. If they did, if they thought about how closely connected I was to her, I'd be done for. You and I must have nothing more to do with each other.'

'Aren't you coming with me, then?'

'I was within a whisker of being dragged down with you. They might have killed us both. I have to get back to work and pretend that all this meant nothing to me.'

'Where am I going? Tell me what's happening.'

But already he'd slammed the door and muttered an instruction to the driver. Asa found herself in yet another enclosed space, this time a cab with shabby blue cushions. She could do nothing but watch as Didier walked rapidly away.

The cab edged across a crowded bridge but was soon at a standstill. The stink of the Seine seeped under the door and the flimsy vehicle rocked each time someone barged past. She saw a fat woman with a clutch of children huddled in her skirts, a lank-haired youth with a shaggy broom on his shoulder, an old man with hollow cheeks carrying a heavy sack.

'Where am I going?' she said aloud. 'I don't know where I'm going.' She heard the driver yell at the crowd to get out of the way. Someone hammered on the door; the face of a young boy was pressed to the glass, nose distorted, lips pushed back as he made an obscene kissing gesture.

The carriage jolted forward and picked up speed. Asa was still shaking violently. She had nothing, not a sou, no clothes or papers. Ahead was the church of St-Jacques. She should get out, disappear into the crowd. Then what? They were on the Honoré. Perhaps she was going to Didier's apartment; she shuddered at the thought of the hostile serving girl, the pristine white bed – but no, they had turned into a dark street behind Les Halles.

Hoof-beats. Another much larger carriage was bearing down on them. Oh God, let it be over quickly, if they are coming for me, let it be now. The cab had stopped. She closed her eyes and hunched down into the seat, her arm across her face. The door opened, there was a moment's hush and a voice spoke her name. When she looked up she glimpsed a green coat, ivory silken breeches; him.

He held out his hand, seized her wrist, and half

carried her from the cab into the waiting carriage. At once he hammered on the ceiling and they lurched forward so suddenly that she was thrust back. For a few seconds they sped onwards, then ground to a halt behind a cart bearing a dozen live pigs. Asa's teeth were chattering; she was unable to comprehend that this was really him, leaning forward to lift a plaid blanket from a wicker hamper, sitting beside her, tucking it about her waist and feet. Next he removed a flask and, with stiffly decorous movements, placed his arm about her shoulders, held her chin steady and urged her to drink. Her teeth clattered on metal. Wine spilled. He returned to his own side of the carriage and peered from the window. They were moving again, but so slowly Asa thought they must be under water. She couldn't speak, could only stare at him.

He was dressed with a reckless disregard for the fashions of revolutionary Paris; the waistcoat in particular was one of his most dazzling – an embroidered meadow of dainty flowers on bronze silk – and his fair hair was pulled back into a black ribbon, though the customary strand had broken loose and was hanging over his forehead and cheek. She caught the scent of citrus, and polished leather. His face, though, was much altered; his eyes bloodshot and a harder brown, his cheeks sunken.

They had reached Porte St-Denis. Shackleford leaned out and thrust a sheaf of papers at an official, who scrutinised them briefly, glanced into the carriage and waved them on. Now they were moving more freely, and sunlight streamed on to Asa's hand as the overhanging buildings spread out into market garden and open fields. Her eyes never left his face.

'You must sleep,' he said at last, 'you have nothing more to fear. Sleep if you can.' Even his voice was a balm; she had forgotten its slight hesitancy, its exact depth.

After another few minutes he added: 'Give it time. In time, you will find that the memories soften. It will be easier. Soon we'll be in England. Caroline is to meet us. We'll take you to your sisters.'

He put his head back against the cushions, and for a moment watched the fields, which were yellow with drought. 'It had to be me,' he said, 'nobody else could come. I was the one with connections. But you mustn't worry – it won't be for more than a couple of days. You'll soon be with Caroline.'

When she still said nothing he shook his head and sighed. 'It *had* to be me. I was the best person. I had no ties. You mustn't think that you are indebted to me in the least.'

At last she was able to speak.

'I've been trying to work out how you did it.'

'We did it between us. I was merely the messenger.'

'You bribed the information from Warren with ease, I'm sure. But how on earth did you get Didier to speak up for me? I thought I was done for yesterday ... he hardly seemed to care.'

'He did well by you today.'

'Were you there, Shackleford, at my trial?'

'Until the verdict.'

493

'But how did you know what was happening to me? How did you know I would need you? I wrote to my family from Caen and told them that I was all right. You knew I was going to Didier.'

'If all had been well, I would not have imposed myself But we thought it best I should come, when we asked questions about Madame de Rusigneux and found that nobody had a clear idea of who she was or where she'd come from.'

'Tell me what you said to Didier. I need to know.'

'I can see why you love him. I always knew you loved him. At a different time it would have been possible ... marriage, a life with him. When you get home, you won't forget him, but it will be easier or, rather, different. You will find yourself able to live and talk and work, despite the pain. Believe me.'

'I don't care for Didier any more – at least, I don't love him. I'm ashamed to say that one of the things that bothered me most about dying was that he might think I died for him. It was a dream, Shackleford. It wasn't real any more. So you need not worry about my feelings. Tell me what you did, to make him speak for me.'

He didn't look at her but tapped the back of his hand against his mouth. He was so very much himself, but not himself, the brilliance of his clothes, the strain in his honey eyes.

'The odd letter. From Clarkson. Linking Paulin with Brissot in the old days, when they were corresponding about abolition. I brought a whole sheaf of documents from England as insurance, in case of trouble. I pointed out to Paulin that he might not want to be associated with Brissot, who is now unfortunately also in the Conciergerie.'

'That was very kind of Clarkson.'

'He wrote nothing but the truth.'

'And what if Didier hadn't stood up for me?' She shook so much that Shackleford again crossed the carriage, hooked her under his arm and helped her to drink. This time, when he tried to withdraw, she held on to his wrist. 'What if Didier had refused to stand up for me? What then?'

'It's immaterial. He did.'

'You would have spoken up for me yourself, wouldn't you? But Harry, you're English. You must have been involved in all kinds of bribery and blackmail to get yourself across the Channel. You own half the West Country. The tribunal would have hated you and had you arrested.'

France, beyond the carriage, was rushing by, strange and dangerous. She saw only Shackleford's face.

Epilogue

September 1793

What could be lovelier than Compton Wyatt, mid-afternoon, early September?

'Just like a painting,' said Mrs Shackleford's visitors as they bowled up the drive in their carriages. And indeed the lake, reflecting the blue sky, the ambers and greens and honey shades of the woods, was mirror-still, so that when the family of swans drifted by, two adults, one cygnet, they left in their wake long ripples which smoothed away until minutes later there was the merest splash of water on pebble at the shore. The reeds were brown and brittle, their tips hanging at acute angles. The adult swans and the little temple on the knoll were brilliant white in the sunshine, the bathhouse in the form of a cottage snug in the spillage of light.

Mrs Shackleford was holding court in the drawing room, fanning herself with Madame de Rusigneux's gift; perhaps rather to show it off than out of necessity, because the room was rather cool. She wore black since she was still in mourning for her husband and elder son. Occasionally, amid the wafer-thin bread and butter and the wedges of moist Dundee cake, she shed a tear. Her callers were patient and polite, full of commiseration as they muttered agreement that her youngest boy, Harry, was indeed behaving with extraordinary ingratitude, some would say fecklessness. Their eyes, however, missed nothing. That ormolu vase, if Mrs Shackleford happened to put it in the auction, would be perfect for the mantelshelf of the blue drawing room in Queen's Square. And perhaps the Caravaggio in the gallery, being so lurid and unfashionable, would go for a song.

'But console yourself, Mrs Shackleford,' they murmured, 'we're sure you'll be comfortable in the new crescent in Clifton. After all, you'll be inundated with callers. We shan't leave you alone.'

Susan Shackleford was playing the piano; a minuet by Lully. Since the music-room windows were open, visitors who wandered out on to the terrace – ostensibly to admire the view, actually to wonder whether the new owner, whoever it might be, would prove rather more generous in inviting them to balls and dinners – were treated to sprightly trills and crescendos. Though Susan took no notice of the callers, her playing was a little distracted as she thought of the packing case, recently arrived and stored in an empty stable, in which her piano would be transported from Compton Wyatt to the new-bought house in Chelsea. Her head these days was full of plans. Where, precisely, had this idea for a school come from? It was unimaginable that the Hon. Mrs Shackleford should be reduced to teaching in a school. But a high-class instructor of the piano; that might do, if accompanied by opportunities to perform to parties of appreciative adults.

Between them, she had been assured by Miss Lambert, they would manage admirably. Susan would teach piano and Miss Lambert everything else. And in the evenings, Susan would play and Miss Lambert, a worthy audience, would listen. Or maybe they would venture out together to

London parties and discover what was going on, because it seemed, given the events of the past three months, that rather a lot might be.

Upstairs in the Chinese guest bedroom, having pleaded Philippa's delicate state to excuse themselves from tea in the drawing room, the two older Ardleigh sisters were in the midst of an argument. Philippa lay on the bed, hand on stomach, though in truth she was feeling much more robust these days, being past the third month of pregnancy, while Georgina was applying a frill to the neck of a chemise. 'Fifteen hundred a year,' she moaned. 'I'd like to see you and John Morton manage on so little.'

'Under the circumstances Mr Shackleford has been more than generous. I can't imagine how much money he has already paid out to extricate you from your debts.'

'It's short sighted of him to give us such a small allowance. If we had more, Warren could invest in something worthwhile. If only he had been with me here at Compton Wyatt to argue our case, but he claims that Mr Shackleford doesn't like him, despite the fact that my Warren risked his neck for Asa.'

'What about Sierra Leone? I thought Shackleford suggested you try your luck there.'

'It wouldn't suit us. Africa's too hot. Nobody to talk to. And somebody has to be in England for your next confinement.'

'You hate babies, Georgina. Don't stay here on my account. I'll manage, though I must admit with Asa gone and Caroline Lambert in London I do feel a little bereft.'

Georgina, most uncharacteristically, threw down her sewing and hugged her sister so violently that Philippa was at risk of suffocation. 'You mustn't be afraid. I'll be there, I promise.'

'Of course I'm not afraid,' said Philippa. Georgina returned to her work but from time to time she glanced at the curve of her sister's stomach and her swollen ankles, perhaps remembering the day, nearly a quarter of a century ago, when they had been told to go outside and work on the little vegetable plots they'd planted with their mama. Hours later Mrs Dean had come for them as they huddled together, hand in hand in the now chilly garden, and led them inside to where their father sat at the end of the dining table, deep in a bottle of port. Upstairs, beside the still figure on the bed, they were shown a hot little scrawl of flesh, their new sister Thomasina, howling in her cradle.

In the book room, behind a locked door, the latest Mrs Shackleford was rereading a letter.

Rue Leverrier
Caen, 21 August 1793

Dear Thomasina,

I was relieved to hear of your successful return to England and must congratulate you on your recent marriage. The precipitate method with which you conduct your affairs leaves me breathless. Rest assured that the money you sent us, with such generous interest, has been safely returned. The additional gift, for Father, was unnecessary but welcome.

I have little news except that in Caen we are suffering the effects of yet another poor harvest. The two deputies from Paris have been released and our other visitors, who brought so much trouble upon our heads as they fled Paris, moved on to Rennes. But this dearth of news, though it makes for a dull letter, is in fact all we ask. Here, on the far edge of France, we hope to have escaped retribution for our sad little rebellion, but we cannot be sure. My worst fear is that if Father were to be freed – and I expect it at any moment – he would be made an official of our new council. He has been on the side of right, you see, in being so staunchly opposed to the insurrection, but I think he is too frail to withstand such responsibility. And in any case, who knows which way the wind will blow in the future?

My brother, should you retain an interest in his welfare, has been sent to the north. On reflection I'm glad he has not come home after all. As I've said, the last thing we want is attention.

You asked if I'd heard anything of Estelle. The truth is I have now lost not only J.B. and C.C. but also Estelle, the last friend of my childhood. I happened to meet the priest, Ballard, now incumbent at Mantheuil, when I was visiting Father. He told me that he'd heard Estelle had been arrested, and is currently in a prison called La Saltpetrière. He is not a man given to hyperbole, but he used the words shackled, and insane. I wrote to her, but have received no reply. Ballard says that Estelle was found early one morning, in the garden of the prison known as Les Carmes. You will be aware of its significance. She was lying face down under a tree, her fists full of soil. When ordered to get up, she refused. The priest said, with more wit than I had previously credited him with, that grief is not yet a capital offence, and that *therefore the authorities had no choice but to lock her up and declare her mad. He added that perhaps this would surely put an end, once and for all, to Estelle Beyle's most unwomanly and counter-revolutionary tendency to take matters into her own hands.*

You will perhaps infer from this letter that my heart is heavy. I am writing in our garden, where I sit in the shade and remember how it was when we were young.

My last request is that you pray for us here in France, as I shall pray for you there in England.

I embrace you,
Beatrice

At Asa's side her new husband, amid a sea of papers, was planning a journey. Since they were so newly married his work was interspersed with kisses on her cheek and shoulder and neck. Just as well because those kisses sweetened the fact that nothing was straightforward. Easy enough to say, as the carriage had hurtled away from Paris towards Calais: 'I'll sell everything. We'll farm. We'll live simply. We'll give money raised from the estate to establish the Shackleford slaves as freemen...' But how to ensure that all of Compton Wyatt's dependants, those employed in England and those enslaved in Jamaica, would not suffer by falling into less humane hands?

Much easier, they were discovering, for a slave-owner to buy slaves than to free them. And since the vast Shackleford wealth was dependent partly on renting out land to other planters, the process of extrication would be slow indeed. Fortunately, in John Morton, Shackleford had a competent associate who would manage the sale of Compton

Wyatt. And in Asa, Shackleford had found a woman keen to travel with him on any journey, the farther and more challenging the better.

Judging by the sound of voices in the hall and the distant clatter of hooves, Mrs Shackleford's visitors were departing. Asa put aside the letter and went to kneel on the leather chair by the window. 'I thought of this chair often when I was in France... Sometimes I felt sick with longing to be here.'

'I'm not fond of that chair myself. In fact, I wouldn't mind if I never set eyes on anything in this room again.'

'Even me?'

'Ah, you.' He buried his hand in her hair.

'Why did you bother to come for me, Shackleford? I was so cruel to you that night after the ball. I'm still amazed you would bother to come all the way to Paris for my sake.'

'I've told you, it was an outing, as Georgina put it. My only fear was that you would think I was in the way. That was the only risk, as far as I was concerned.'

She held his face between her hands and kissed his lips and forehead. Behind him, the cynical, painted eyes of his father receded into the gloom. Outside, a party of two women – one carrying an infant – and a trio of small boys ran down to the lake.

Caroline Lambert and a nursemaid had taken their charges to sail a model boat. The request from Shackleford had been clear. The boys could play with the boat to their hearts' content, they could be educated as to the function of each sail, and its various other components, including the design of the hold and its iniquitous purpose, but then they must push it far out into the lake and ensure it disappeared.

The boys lay on their stomachs among the reeds while Caroline, with baby Kate propped on one hip, crouched down and armed them with sticks so they might prod at the hull until it was clear of the reeds and the shallow waters by the lakeside. Since there was no sign of the swans, the good ship *Tranquillity* found no rival. A puff of evening wind ushered her farther on her journey.

The boys squealed and shielded their eyes as the ship entered a pool of fierce orange light. And then, to their even greater delight, she lost confidence and began to take in water, proving to be fatally ill constructed when it came to lakeworthiness. First the prow tipped forward then she floundered sideways. The water was so shallow that her hull still protruded until Caroline and the oldest boys had to remove their shoes and stockings and paddle far out, hand in hand, to give the ship one final shove into oblivion.

Acknowledgements

With thanks to Fred Groom, John Woods and Helena Attlee for their advice on research and Charonne Boulton for sharing an icy expedition to Paris. I am indebted to Kirsty Dunseath for her meticulous editorial support and, as ever, to Mark Lucas.